LST

D.J. Connell was born in New Zealand and has lived and worked in various countries, first as a writer for a newspaper then for a non-profit organisation and later in advertising. The humour of *Julian Corkle is a Filthy Liar* reflects the writer's background of growing up in a large, noisy family. D.J. Connell is a British national.

Praise for *Julian Corkle is a Filthy Liar*:

'Laugh-out-loud funny and genuinely touching. A magical journey. *Julian Corkle* is a big fat masterpiece.' EOIN COLFER

'A tour de farce which goes straight for the jocular vein!'
KATHY LETTE

'One of the funniest rites of passage novels in a long time . . . a great summer read.' *Time Out*

'A genuinely funny book with a great big heart. I fell in love with Julian Corkle.' JENNY ECLAIR

'Warm, funny and deeply engaging. You'll love this one.'
Waterstone's Books Quarterly

'D.J. Connell has unleashed a set of characters bigger than Tasmania. Julian may be a filthy liar, but he is also a corker.'
Australian Women's Weekly

'A coming-of-age story with extra laughs, lashings of quirkiness and a very memorable hero.' *New Zealand Herald on Sunday*

Also by D.J. Connell

Sherry Cracker Gets Normal

D.J. CONNELL

Julian Corkle is a Filthy Liar

blue door

Blue Door
An imprint of HarperCollins*Publishers*
77–85 Fulham Palace Road
Hammersmith, London W6 8JB
www.harpercollins.co.uk

This paperback edition 2011
1

First published in Great Britain
by Blue Door 2010

A catalogue record for this book
is available from the British Library

This novel is entirely a work of fiction. The names, characters and incidents
portrayed in it are the work of the author's imagination. Any resemblance to
actual persons, living or dead, events or localities is entirely coincidental.

ISBN 978-0-00-733215-1

Typeset in Minion by Palimpsest Book Production Limited,
Falkirk, Stirlingshire

Printed and bound in Great Britain by
Clays Ltd, St Ives plc

Mixed Sources
Product group from well-managed
forests and other controlled sources
www.fsc.org   Cert no. SW-COC-001806
© 1996 Forest Stewardship Council

FSC is a non-profit international organisation established to promote the
responsible management of the world's forests. Products carrying the FSC
label are independently certified to assure consumers that they come
from forests that are managed to meet the social, economic and
ecological needs of present or future generations.

Find out more about HarperCollins and the environment at
www.harpercollins.co.uk/green

To my mother Marion, who first got me interested in funny business, and to my sister Jocelyn, who's never stopped laughing at me.

ACKNOWLEDGEMENTS

I humbly thank my publisher Patrick Janson-Smith and my agent Sophie Hicks for their wonderful support. To Christoph Kim, my appreciation and gratitude. Sincere thanks to Michael Lyons and my writing mates Jennifer Anne Donnelly and Laura Angela Bagnetto. A tip of the hat to Tomoaki Murakami, Martin Breiter, Terry Malone and Brian O'Donnell. Warm thanks to Julie Davies. To my family and those friends who never lost faith in me – you know who you are – thank you.

Dag: 1. Australian for the dung that collects on a sheep's backside. 2. An unfashionable, unappealing person. 3. A fool.

'Look at that dag with the mullet cut!'

1

Ulverston

Colleen Corkle knew her son had star quality from the moment he appeared. She was straining forward on the delivery bed when his head popped out. The baby's eyelids flicked open, and in the instant before the nurse scooped him up, his eyes locked on hers. Colleen recognised the spark in the murky depths of the new irises and smiled. As the baby was whisked away, he started wailing.

'Listen to those lungs!' The doctor finished examining the newborn and handed him back to the nurse. 'Another Sinatra!'

The baby continued to wail as he was carried to a room down the corridor where the nurse wiped him clean and dressed him in a muslin gown.

'For goodness' sake, shut that baby up!' A nursing sister poked her head in the doorway. She was frowning. 'We've got a woman in labour next door.'

The nurse hurriedly wrapped a blanket around the baby and carried him back to the birthing room. Colleen was still on the delivery bed being cleaned up. She was exhausted but the hormones surging through her system made her smile when she heard the baby's cries. He was thrust into her arms.

'Will you be breastfeeding?' The nurse had to shout to be heard.

'No, there'll be none of that. Formula like the others.'

'Right then, I'll get his bottle.'

The nurse scurried out of the room. Colleen held the baby up and looked into his eyes again. The spark was still there. Something hot and liquid stirred behind her ribs. She pressed her lips to his forehead and drew in the new animal smell of him. With expert hands, she placed him face down on her chest and began rubbing his back. He kept crying.

'That's my boy.' Colleen giggled. 'You show them.'

The nurse reappeared with a bottle of formula and the baby was flipped over into the fold of his mother's arm. Colleen tested the warmth of the liquid on her wrist and then thrust the teat into the open mouth. The baby's lips moved against the rubber and encircled the tip. They tugged tentatively. The cries stopped abruptly and he began to feed.

The nurse wiped her forehead with the back of her hand and let out a sigh. 'Thank goodness he's a strong sucker.'

Jim was at the sports desk of *The Bugle* when the nurse called to say he was the father of a healthy baby boy. In 1965, a new father's place was not at the side of his wife. His place was down at the King's Arms. Jim made an announcement and was patted on the back by his colleagues. He arranged to meet them later at the pub and knocked off work early.

He was standing at the bar studying the *Punter's Gazette* when a small, elderly woman eased herself on to a barstool beside him. He hadn't seen her in the King's Arms before. She was dressed in a floral frock and multicoloured hand-knitted cardigan. The knitted hat on her head resembled a tea cosy. Jim was idly looking for spout and handle holes when the woman spoke.

'If you buy me a drink, I'll tell you something interesting.'

The woman's voice made him smile. She had an Irish accent. He wondered if she was from County Cork, like his parents.

'My pleasure. I've just had some good news.'

'Ah, that'd be your baby.'

Jim had just told the barman about the new arrival. He looked over at Midge and winked. The barman shrugged and claimed the *Gazette*.

'What's your poison, *madame*?' Jim said it the French way to make the woman laugh.

Her expression didn't change. 'Oh, I could take a whiskey, yes I could.' She turned to the barman. 'I'll be having an Irish drop. None of that bilge water from the Tay of Dundee.'

Midge reached above the dispensers and took down a bottle of the Spirit of Cork. He shook two nips into a small glass and placed it gently on a Tickworth Ale coaster in front of the woman.

'To your health, sir, and to that of your son.' She lifted the glass to Jim, then pushed her head back and let the whiskey run down her throat. She banged it down empty and wiped her lips with the back of a hand. 'Nothing like a rare drop of Irish sunshine.'

'Anotherie?' Jim was feeling generous. He turned and nodded to Midge who refilled the woman's glass. 'So, how do you know I have a son?' He hadn't told the barman it was a boy.

'You now have two sons and, by the look of you, there's also a girl.'

Jim felt a prickly sensation along the band of his Y-fronts. An electric current ran from the elastic up his spine and did a circuit around his shoulder blades.

'Do I know you?'

'Depends what you mean by knowing. There's things I know that I can tell. I know your son's not what you expected.

3

You'll try to change him but you can't. This will give you heartache.'

'He's only an hour old and he's already giving me grief. Ha, ha.' This was Jim's way of changing the subject, making a joke and rounding it off with a forced laugh.

She either didn't understand or chose to ignore him. 'You'll think he's against you but he's not. The boy's different, that's all.'

Jim shifted in his seat. The woman made him uncomfortable. She looked directly into his eyes without blinking. He'd only known one other person to do this: Father Donahue. The priest had been the most feared presence in the school dormitory. The boys had called him Father Doneafew. The thought of the crusty old priest made Jim shiver. Father Donahue had kept his fingernails perfectly manicured.

'You've got to learn to forgive. You don't forgive for what happened in the past. This is a bitterness that eats at you.'

'Beg pardon?'

'Try to accept your son. For your sake and for his.' The woman got off her stool, gave him an abrupt nod and left the bar.

Jim stood completely still. The electrical feeling in his spine had spread to the outer edges of his body. He felt as if the membrane separating him from the rest of the world was dissolving. He knew he would be slapped on the back before Trevor Bland's hand fell between his shoulder blades. The force of the gesture made him feel solid again. Bland was a typesetter at *The Bugle* and Jim's oldest friend.

'Congratulations, Corkle. I'll have a Tickworth on the new baby girl, thanks, mate.'

'It's a boy, Trev.'

Colleen was placed in an empty six-bed room in the maternity ward. She'd slept a few hours and was feeling wonderful when the nurse carried in the baby and placed him in her arms. He'd been fed and was quiet. She counted his fingers and toes and was peeking inside his nappies through a leg hole when another new mother was wheeled in. The woman had given birth to her fourth daughter. This was not a good gender ratio for a Tasmanian woman of the sixties. A husband needed sons for cricket and other purposes. Colleen now had two boys and a girl. Pushing aside her pride, she tried to console her new neighbour.

'Don't worry, love, you'll have a boy next time.'

'There'll be no next time. We can't afford another mistake. I'm having the tubes done on Tuesday.' The woman flattened her lips and crossed her arms over her chest.

'Oh? I'm sure it's for the best. Would you like to hold Julian?' In Colleen's universe giving the woman her baby boy to hold was good juju. It was also very satisfying. Two boys to one girl was an excellent ratio. She slipped out of bed and held him out to her.

The woman didn't unfold her arms.

'That's a mistake for a start. Julian sounds like Julie.' The woman nodded for emphasis. Her face was still mottled from the birthing process. She looked tired and unhappy. 'You'll regret it.'

'The name has religious significance.'

'We're not religious.' The woman unfolded her arms and took the baby from Colleen. 'He's a heavy little thing.'

'He's a healthy boy. Boys are more robust than girls. You should hear his lungs.'

'His lungs disrupted my Debbie's crowning. They couldn't get him to pipe down. The sister was at her wits' end.'

'Frank Sinatra has fantastic lungs.' Colleen crossed her arms.

'Sinatra's more of a crooner than a screamer.'

'That's just voice training. Julian's got the right lungs. Lungs and personality. My boy's got star quality.'

'What a shame.' The woman pointed to the baby's mouth.

Colleen's eyebrows shot skyward. 'What a shame, what?'

'He's got a cupid's bow.'

'He's a good-looking baby.'

'Brigitte Bardot has a cupid's bow but it's a curse on a boy.' The woman sucked air between her teeth. 'Odd really. The father's not French?'

'My husband's one hundred per cent Australian, a real man's man. This is my second son. Two healthy boys.' Colleen pointed to the baby's top lip. 'That'll come right once he's off the bottle.'

'I doubt it.'

'He's really taken to the bottle. He's a very strong sucker. All the nurses say so.'

'I suppose that's one good thing.'

'Let me take him off your hands. Boys are heavy.' Colleen reached out for the baby.

'He's quite pretty.' The woman hesitated. 'Like a little girl, really.'

'That face is made for the small screen.'

The woman looked doubtful. 'Possibly, but you'll be forking out a fortune on voice training.'

'Here, pass him over to me.' Colleen yanked the baby out of her arms. 'You need to rest up for your big operation on Tuesday.'

The woman gave a start.

'I'm heading down to the TV room. *The Dick Dingle Hour* is on soon.' Colleen eyed her opponent over the baby's head. 'May as well give the boy his first taste of culture.'

2

I was born in Ulverston, a small town on Tasmania's north coast. I know all about my arrival at Blue Gum Central Hospital from my mother. She even told me how I was conceived. I could've done without that information but there's no way to censor Mum. She's always known what's best for me. Ours is one of those exclusive mother-son relationships. We even look alike. Mum says we're Black Irish which means we're more attractive than the rest of the family. We have thick dark hair and green eyes. Dad and my siblings are the other kind of Irish: gingery with freckles. It's not a good look.

It was Mum who bought me my first *Celebrity Glitter* magazine. It's important to keep up, she says, star quality is not enough in the dog-eat-dog world of show business. Mum should know. She was the Tasmanian finalist in the Golden Microphone Contest and would've gone on to the nationals if disaster hadn't struck. She still has the newspaper clipping in the back of her recipe book. Her hair is big and wide and she's holding a bunch of dahlias next to a microphone. She looks beautiful – like Elizabeth Taylor, only thinner.

Mum calls me the Songbird of the South and says I'll win trophies one day. If it's not the Golden Microphone then it'll be the Tassie Wallaby which is the highest entertainment award on Tasmanian television. Dick Dingle has won the Wallaby twice. He's our local television icon and does a lot to promote Tasmanian youth. Mum says he will be promoting me one day. She says I've got small-screenability.

'One day we're going to see your big face on the cover of *Celebrity Glitter* magazine, Julian. You're my own little star. Twinkle, twinkle.' The magazine in her hands had Liberace's face on the cover.

'Is my face big, Mum?'

My father does not share my mother's ambitions for me. I became aware of this at the age of four when I overheard a conversation from under our house in Kangaroo Crescent. We lived in a buff-coloured brick bungalow on a rectangular quarter-acre. The house sat on raised foundations which were hidden from view by a white weatherboard trim that skirted the bottom of the bricks. A trapdoor at the back provided crawling access to the area under the house. It was designed for plumbers and electricians but used exclusively by children.

It was my neighbour Raymond's idea to crawl under there. He was two years older than me and should've known better. He should've known not to leave our clothes beside the trapdoor for my brother John to find. John had immediately alerted my father to our whereabouts. Raymond and I were directly under the dinette. I could hear the transistor and muffled voices. Someone switched off the radio and the voices of my mother and father became audible.

'Jim, for goodness' sake, they're just little boys.'

'Little boys? Colleen, they are *naked* underneath this house, probably under our very feet.'

I heard the shuffling of Dad's leather-soled shoes on the linoleum above me.

8

'I know exactly where this sort of thing leads and I don't want a Catholic priest in the family. No thank you very much.'

'Jim, he's four years old.'

'Exactly. We've got to put a stop to this right now. If it's not a priest then we'll have a hairdresser on our hands. Or a male nurse.'

'A hairdresser would be handy.'

'You know what I'm talking about.'

'Hairdressing.'

'No, your brother Norman. I don't want his type fluffing up the cushions on my settee.'

'Don't be awful.'

'The man's as straight as a dog's hind leg.'

'Norman's got a thriving salon in Melbourne. He's not interested in our cushions.'

'It would only start with the cushions. Next thing you know he'd be teaching our boys to play leapfrog.'

'What's wrong with leapfrog?'

'There's a lot wrong with it if you do it without trousers.'

'Give it a rest.'

'Not until I sort that Julian out.'

I heard the door slam and then my mother's footsteps cross the lino. My father's voice boomed out near the trapdoor.

'Julian. Come out immediately.'

My father was a stout man but perfectly capable of squeezing under the house and dragging me out. Raymond and I scrambled to the trapdoor where Dad was waiting with our clothes. He handed them to us and stood with his arms rigid at his sides and his head turned away while we dressed. When we were done, he grabbed me by the elbow and pulled me toward him. The shorts I'd just put on were yanked down and I was smacked several times on the bum with his bare hand. Raymond didn't get touched.

I pointed to my neighbour. 'What about Raymond?'

Raymond's lips parted in horror.

'Shut up!' Dad didn't look at Raymond. His face was red and glistening with sweat.

'But he's older.' I jabbed a finger angrily at Raymond who backed away.

'Shut up!' Dad reached out and smacked me again. 'Never let me catch you with a naked boy again or there'll be trouble.'

He smacked me several more times. I nodded yes with each smack. I promised I would never ever let him catch me again as long as I lived.

I managed to keep my promise until I was eight.

Dad had built us a fort in the backyard out of some old timber and corrugated iron he'd been given by Trevor Bland. This was completely out of character and something he never attempted again. My father generally didn't invest time in projects that weren't directly connected to his personal comfort. He wasn't the type of father to take his kids fishing or help us with homework. He did things like give us bottles of raspberry drink while we waited in the car outside the pub. This was one gesture I appreciated. Some kids weren't given drinks. We'd poke out red tongues and wave our soft drinks at them while they died of thirst in their Holden station wagons.

It was a war game that got me into trouble. The boys next door were the Allies and we were supposed to be the Germans. I told my brother John I didn't want any part of it. I'd only heard bad things about Germans. They were swine.

'I want to be a nurse.'

'You can't be a nurse, stupid.' John sneered at me. 'Nurses are girls.' He laughed out loud and began dancing around me, chanting. 'Julian's a woolly woofter. Julian's a woolly woofter.'

The other boys sniggered.

'I'm a nurse. I'll do bandages in the hospital.' I pointed to the fort. The boys turned to admire Dad's construction. It was the only one in the street. Everyone loved our fort. It gave us the edge.

'We need bandages if we're shot.' It was little Johnny Hawkins from next door. There were five Johns on our street. It was a very popular name in Ulverston.

Eyes turned to my brother. He was the oldest.

'OK, you can do bandages in the fort, but you're a doctor.' John was as proud of the fort as the next Corkle.

'I'm a nurse.' I shouted this over my shoulder.

My first patient was my brother. He came inside grimacing and dragging his leg. 'Za Brits shot me srew za knee.'

I pointed to the pretty makeshift bed I'd created out of the couch cushions. These were laid out in a line under the sheets I'd hung in a decorative way from the ceiling. It was great to have a fort but having a fort with flair made all the difference.

I put some vinegar on a piece of cotton wool and rubbed around the area where there was supposed to be a wound. John groaned like a wounded soldier. I used the hard plastic snout of the vacuum cleaner to examine the wound. John had his eyes closed and was moaning.

'I have to get the bullet out.' Taking a stick I'd found under the plum tree, I drove it in hard under the kneecap.

'Fuck!' John had screamed the F word. 'You fucking bastard.'

'It's just a flesh wound.' I jumped out of the fort and stood on the grass below. I called up to John who was rocking on his back, cradling his knee to his chest. 'If you hit me I'll tell Mum you said the F word, twice.'

My next patient was little Johnny Hawkins. He came in doubled over saying he'd been shot in the stomach. I made him lie on his back.

'Take your shirt off. It's covered in blood.' Johnny was no stranger to this game. We often played together in his garage. I undid the zip of his shorts and had just pulled them off when I heard someone outside. I knew it was my brother. He wanted to get me back for the knee job.

'Piss off, you German bastard. I'm not finished with this John.'

The door flew open and my father stuck his head and shoulders into the fort. He looked at Johnny's naked body, then at me, then at Johnny again. Johnny's underpants were in my hand.

'I'm a nurse, Dad.'

My father reached in and grabbed me by the collar, dragging me outside where I was smacked in front of the other boys. He then marched me to the bedroom I shared with John and told me to stay there until dinnertime. I watched from the window as he cleared out the fort and then went at it with an axe and hammer. It took him an hour to reduce it to a pile of splintered timber. I was crying as he loaded everything on to a trailer and drove away.

A couple of days later I saw Mum rummaging in the cupboard where she kept the cleaning things. She then did a room-to-room search, looking under beds and furniture. She was flushed when she came back to the kitchen.

'Are you all right, Mum?'

'I must be going mad. I can't find the extension to the vacuum cleaner. The little plastic end bit. I've looked everywhere.'

John took the loss of the fort hard and refused to talk to me for a full month. This was fine by me because I was busy preparing for the end of year pantomime at St Kevin's. Mum was thrilled. I was to play Joseph which was a much bigger speaking role than baby Jesus who only got to gurgle. My sister Carmel was recruited to work the pulleys and change the backdrops. Several boys had wanted this job but they were no match for my sister who at the age of nine could already run faster and punch harder than anyone I knew.

My stage debut would have been a triumph if Brother O'Hare had not torn the veil off my head at the last minute. It was Mum's navy blue chiffon scarf and looked fantastic with the pale blue caftan I'd been given to wear. O'Hare had wanted a bareheaded Joseph but this made no sense when the Three Kings had fancy headgear. He'd stopped me in the wings, insisting that a nativity scene was no place for a lady's scarf. My cue came and went as I was trying to argue my point. By the time we noticed, Mary and the donkey had been waiting on stage for a full minute. She might have stayed there longer if a familiar male voice had not boomed out over the audience.

'Move that ass!' Dad thought he was a funny man.

The laughter spurred Brother O'Hare into action. I was thrust from behind and propelled across the stage, running with my head down as I struggled to get my footing. I heard the laughter even before I hit the donkey head-on and broke it in two. Mary toppled off and fell to the side with a squawk and a *thud*. The audience roared. The hindquarters of the donkey turned and lunged at me. It was Robbie Skint and, despite the handicap of his donkey leggings, he lunged very fast. The audience roared again as he tackled me and clasped his hands around my neck.

I was gasping for air and twisting my head to free myself when my eyes fell on Carmel. She was standing in the back holding a rope above her head. With a smile she let it go. The backdrop of the stable scene unfurled at high speed and hit Robbie's head with a *bonk*.

3

At the start of the new school year, I was given a seat next to Paula Stromboli. I was the only boy in the class who had no desire to sit next to old Smelly Pants. She was very bold for a girl of eight. I'd heard all about her and didn't want to go anywhere near her cotton tops.

Brother O'Hare had written a line from a psalm on the blackboard: 'Hear my cry, O God, listen to my prayer.' Our job was to copy it into our exercise books with as much precision as possible. Erasers were not allowed. The task was one of concentration. I'd done a brilliant job and was up to the 'prayer' bit when Paula grasped my knee and squeezed. My leg shot up and banged the bottom of the desk, causing my hand to leap forward with the pencil. I finished the word but it now read, 'Hear my cry, O God, listen to my player.' I looked at it for a while. There was no way to repair the damage without an eraser. The clock was ticking. I wedged a small V before 'player' and wrote the word 'record' above it. At least it now made sense.

'You think you're funny, don't you, Corker.' O'Hare had gripped my shoulder and was digging his fingers into the flesh.

The other children were looking at me.

'It's Corkle, sir. I was just trying to—'

'—be the class clown. Corker, you'll stay here during lunchtime and write out the entire psalm.'

Paula squeezed my knee again as Brother O'Hare turned back to the blackboard. I twisted in my seat, ready to drive a pencil into her thigh, but stopped with my hand in mid-air. She had lifted her dress and pulled down her knickers. I was staring at a bare pink mound. I looked up at Paula's face. She was smiling, oblivious to the frightening non-event in her underpants. It was bad enough watching men and women kiss on television but to have the Stromboli mound at my elbow was more than I could stand. I turned to the front and put up my hand, waving it about until I got the brother's attention.

'Yes, Corker.'

The class laughed.

'It's Corkle, sir.'

'Yes, Corker.'

The class laughed again.

'Brother O'Hare, can I swap seats with Ralph Waters?'

'No you cannot.' He turned back to the blackboard and resumed writing.

'Excuse me, Brother O'Hare.'

'What now, Corker?'

The class laughed again.

'Can I swap seats with Robbie Skint?'

'No. Now be quiet!'

'Could I just stand then?'

Brother O'Hare marched up to my desk and pulled me out of my chair. 'You want to stand? Then stand still now.'

He yanked out my hand and hit the palm six times with his wooden ruler. I sat back down cradling what felt like a throbbing baseball mitt at the end of my left arm.

*　　*　　*

15

Ralph Waters approached me at playtime. I would've run off but I was scraping the hundreds and thousands off a fairy cake and didn't see him coming. Ralph was one of the toughest kids of my year. He was skinny and sinewy. His blond hair was cut extremely short with barber's clippers and his nails were chewed to crumbs. Ralph spent the breaks playing with plastic soldiers under the white-painted tyres that some genius had half buried in the playground as a stepping-stone game. No one ever stepped on them because they were placed too far apart for primary-school children. The older kids never went near them because they were in the primary section of the school.

'I know what you were doing. Thanks for that, Corky.'

I didn't bother correcting Ralph. He was one of the few people I'd allow to mispronounce my name.

'Uh-huh.'

'Did you see her keyhole?'

Ralph was standing there smiling, waiting for me to confirm the sighting of Paula Stromboli's thing. He'd never spoken to me before. I knew I had to prove something or I was going to be in trouble. Ralph was one of those who singled out boys and ridiculed them for being poofters. This was a regular sport at St Kevin's. Gary Jings was a poofter and everyone knew it. He had a girl's shiny pink pencil case and drew swirly things in art class. He even folded the hems of his shorts up like fancy trouser cuffs. Gary Jings paid for these crimes at lunchtime when he sat on his own near the caretaker's shed pretending to read while kids circled and yelled things like 'bum-kisser'.

I didn't call Gary names. I watched others ridicule him and felt sick inside. It was fear and frustration. I felt drawn to and disgusted by Gary Jings. He should've known better than to display his poofterism. There were several boys who did it at St Kevin's but we kept our activities to ourselves. There was a

16

place for that sort of thing and that place was the nature reserve behind the bike sheds.

It wasn't right the way Gary always bore the abuse. He sat passively with his knees pressed together, occasionally looking up with a dull smile and a faint spark of hope in his eyes. This only infuriated thugs like Ralph who would then administer a Chinese burn or half-Nelson. It was awful to watch the torture of Gary Jings. He never tried to run away. He just went limp and took it. He should've denied being a poofter and hidden his pencil case but he didn't. The one thing I didn't want to be in life was a Gary Jings.

Ralph narrowed his eyes. I had to prove I was as much a man as him. I looked down at the fairy cake and the hundreds and thousands that were stuck to my fingers. When I looked up, I met Ralph's eyes with a piercing stare.

'Yeah.'

Ralph smiled. It was a man-of-the-world smile. We understood each other. I was the sort of boy who regularly looked inside girls' underpants. Ralph liked me and it felt good. I tightened the grip on my fairy cake.

'Why did you ask old O'Hairs if you could stand up?'

The fairy cake collapsed in my hand, sending crumbs flying over the front of my shorts.

'You know.'

'Nah.'

'I was just, ah, just trying to stir up old Hairsie.'

'He was so mad. Did he hurt you?'

This was a stupid question. Ralph was only too familiar with O'Hare's ruler. Being hit over the hand with a slab of wood was incredibly painful. It was a white pain that made your ears go silent with blood pressure.

'Nah.'

'Yeah, O'Hairs is too weak. He's a big fairy. Brother O'Fairy. Ha, ha.' Ralph bent his wrists like Kenneth Williams and paraded around in front of me. 'You think he's seen Stromboli's keyhole?'

The idea of Brother O'Hare poking around inside Paula Stromboli's underpants made me want to laugh out loud in Ralph's face. I controlled myself. Ralph didn't know a thing.

'Yeah I bet he has.'

'She's a slut.'

I wasn't going to argue with Ralph but I didn't think Paula Stromboli was a slut. If anything, she was like me, an entertainer looking for an audience. She'd apologised after the bell went for playtime. She hadn't meant to get me into trouble. 'I was just trying to give you a look.' I hadn't refused when Paula offered to lend me her *Cherish* LP. I was a big fan of David Cassidy. He wore very tight trousers and had silky hair that stayed swished back even during vigorous dance moves.

My big day was coming up but like every year Carmel was going to cheat me out of the attention that was rightfully mine. I was a year younger than her but had the misfortune of being born on the day after her birthday. This gave my special day a definite second-best status. Carmel called her birthday the main event. Mine was the repeat performance.

On the morning of her tenth birthday, Carmel got a doll called Nancy. It was made of pony-coloured plastic and had movable limbs and long white synthetic hair. Nancy came with a vinyl make-up kit and an irresistible set of tiny pink hair curlers. I loved curlers and spent hours playing with the set my mother had received from her brother Norman. He'd also given her a portable hairdryer with a floral plastic cap. On the days when Mum had two hours to spare I was allowed to roller and set her hair.

Carmel finished unwrapping the doll with impatience. When she saw what was inside, she said 'Ugh' and put it to one side. I swallowed a mouthful of breakfast cereal and reached for the box.

'Hands off, fat boy.'

'I just want to touch her hair. It's so long and shiny.'

'That's enough, Julian!' My father was giving me his don't-you-start look.

I felt tears building. Carmel poked her tongue out and made a chopper with her hand, a warning not to cross the invisible line between the doll and me. She moved on to the next present. It was a Nancy 'Evening Fantasy' outfit in a clear plastic tray. She let out another 'Ugh' and tossed it next to the doll. The urge to touch the little pink curlers was almost unbearable. Carmel sighed and felt the other presents through their wrappers. I knew she was looking for a cricket ball and I knew she wasn't going to find one. At least her frustration was some sort of consolation.

Carmel left her other presents unopened on the dinette divan and went back to her rice puffs. As Daddy's girl, Carmel was entitled to be ungrateful. My father gave her an indulgent smile, pushed his chair back and stood up.

It was now or never. It would be my birthday in less than twenty-four hours. I had to convince my parents to buy me something practical, a present I could actually use. I tugged Dad's sleeve.

'Dad, can I have a Nancy?'

'No you cannot! Nancy dolls are for girls! You're a boy and boys want Dinky toys.'

My father's response was too fierce and too loud. Carmel snorted into her cereal, sending a shower of rice puffs and milk over the Aussiemica tabletop.

'Not me. I want a Nancy.' The tears had started and my voice was shrill. I didn't want junk. I wanted a doll.

'You're not getting one and that's final.'

Dad shoved his empty chair against the table and made a move for the door. I leaped off the divan and flattened myself on the floor face down. I started to kick and punch the lino, wailing.

'Shut up, Julian.' It was too much for my father. He hated displays, especially from boys.

'It's not fair. Carmel gets everything.'

I reached out and grabbed Dad around an ankle. He straightened his leg and tried to shake me off. I held tight, crying into his trouser leg.

'For God's sake, get off and stop being a cry baby.' He swiped me over the head with the *Punter's Gazette* and shuffled toward the door, dragging his leg with me attached.

'I want a Nancy, Dad. Please, please, please.' The words came out in shrieks between sobs.

Mum bent down and pulled me off. My father hurled himself out of the house and slammed the door behind him. I was still kicking and flailing my arms as Mum pulled me against her chest. I felt her turn her head toward Carmel.

'Carmel, go wash your face.'

'I'm not dirty, Mum. It's my birthday.' There was laughter in her voice. She'd been enjoying the main event.

'Get out of this dinette right now, madam!'

'It's not fair. It's *my* birthday!' Carmel stormed out leaving Mum and me alone.

Mum whispered in my ear. 'Julian, there'll be a nice surprise for you tomorrow. But you'll have to be a good boy and wait till dinnertime.'

My tears stopped abruptly. 'What?'

'Wait and see. It's not going to be a stinky Dinky.'

* * *

20

I woke the next morning to a box of Shelby's chocolates on the end of the bed. Yes, it was my birthday! In our house, a double-layer box of soft centres and a roast-chicken dinner were standard birthday issue. Presents were a different matter. Their quality depended on who chose them and the mood they were in when choosing. If it was Mum, we tended to get one thing of value among junk she bought to please my father. If Dad bought them, we'd get stuff that was completely useless. I had a Meccano set, a rugby ball and several Dinky toys in the bottom of my wardrobe. I knew by now Carmel would have thrown Nancy on top of the manicure set and necklace-making kit she'd hidden at the bottom of hers.

I knew exactly what went on inside everyone's wardrobes. I monitored them on a regular basis, particularly my mother's. She was the only one in the house with flair and quality fabric. I spent hours going through her drawers and trying things on. This could only be done when Dad wasn't home. He didn't think boys should like nice things and hit the roof if he saw me as much as finger the fabric of a dress my mother was wearing. I tried to explain that fashion designers earned a fortune but Dad didn't want to know.

Carmel's wardrobe was dangerous territory for another reason. I only ventured into her room when she was a good kilometre from the premises. It wasn't worth getting caught. She could punch extremely hard and thoroughly enjoyed practising her Cassius Clay Royale. John and I were forbidden to thump her back, especially below the belly button. This mysterious zone was for making babies. Carmel was only too aware that the same protection did not extend to our testicles.

As soon as I opened the magnet collection, I knew Dad had chosen the presents. His self-satisfied smile told me everything I needed to know. He sat there every bit the happy sadist as I opened the *Boy's Own Annual*, the cricket ball and the kit-set model of a German tank. Crap, crap, crap. The only thing I could use was the cricket ball. It would come in handy as a bargaining chip with Carmel. I said thank you through my teeth and turned to leave for school.

'Hey, Stan McCabe, you're not taking your cricket ball?' Dad wore the crooked smile of an insane sports fanatic.

'I wouldn't want anyone to pinch it. Far too valuable.' I spoke through a locked jaw.

When I got home from school, my mother was shoving bread and mixed herbs into the rear end of a defrosted chicken.

'Where is it?'

'What about hello?'

'Hello, darling Mummy, where is it, please?'

Mum pointed to a package on the table.

My heart was thudding as I ripped it open. Inside was a cardboard box with a clear plastic cover. It was a doll and, according to the box, he was called Billy the Back-up Singer. I removed the cover and touched the miniature golden microphone wired to his hand. Billy was wearing a white shirt and black vinyl trousers. I would wait until I was alone before checking inside the vinyl.

'He's perfect, Mum.'

I put my arms around her waist and held her tight. She bent down to receive a kiss but I licked her cheek instead. I liked licking my mother. She tasted both chemical and floral.

'Ugh, Julian. That's disgusting.'

Mum giggled and wiped her face with the back of a crumby hand. She leaned against the sink and watched me remove Billy from his box. I put the doll up to my nose and breathed in the new plastic smell of his copper-brown synthetic hair. It was cut in a David Cassidy, just long enough to style with tiny doll curlers. Billy came with a change of clothes: a tiny pair of beach shorts and sunglasses. This was an odd outfit for a singer but I didn't care. I'd make him something new to wear, a snazzy Liberace number for the spotlight. In my hands, Billy wouldn't stay a back-up singer for long.

'You know what to do, Julian.' Mum laughed and ruffled my hair. 'Go hide him in your wardrobe before your father gets home.'

4

'Julian, have you seen the *Companion*?' My mother was making her way down the hall toward me. She sounded irritated.

I was lying on my bed in my underpants and singlet reading a feature on Christiaan Barnard, the doctor who'd transplanted a heart into a grocer's chest in 1967. The magazine had a photo of Louis Washkansky before he received the donor heart. He was smiling with a tube up his nose.

I knew the word 'donor' meant dead person and was fascinated. The heart would've been cold, like one of the defrosted chickens my mother stuffed on birthdays. I put my hand over my heart to make sure it was still beating. There was nothing happening. Panic knocked at the back of my throat as I moved my hand to the left side of my chest. My mother snatched the magazine from my hands and left the room.

Mum and I both enjoyed the *Australian Ladies' Companion*. It didn't have the glamour of *Celebrity Glitter* but it did keep us plugged into the Australian entertainment scene and even featured Tasmanian celebrities. Dick Dingle occasionally made it into the *Companion* for his work as patron of the state's Little Aussie Rising Star awards. Mum told me to keep my eye on Dick Dingle. He was an impresario for talented young Tasmanians like me. The Little Aussie Rising Star was a stepping stone to the

Golden Microphone which was an even bigger stepping stone to national television stardom.

Christiaan Barnard was a star even though poor old Washkansky had almost immediately died. The failed heart transplant intrigued me. I closed my eyes and tried to picture what was going on inside my skin. We were currently studying the human body at school. Brother Duffy had started at the top with the brain and was working his way down toward the interesting area. We'd got to the kidneys, which I knew were attached to the important bits. Duffy had more or less admitted this when he said the kidneys were responsible for producing urine. I understood what that meant and was looking forward to the next lesson.

I already knew how babies were born thanks to Ralph Waters. He'd led us into the Ladies' toilet behind the Whipper Snapper fish-and-chip shop and pointed into the bowl where something brown and enormous was bobbing about in the water. It was three times the size of anything I'd ever produced.

'The lady who dropped this A-bomb has had a baby.' Ralph had raised one eyebrow and spoken with authority. 'See the size of her floater. She's stretched to buggery from giving birth.'

I hadn't considered how babies got out from inside their mothers. If they used the same exit as number twos, they had to come out filthy. That meant I'd come out filthy. I asked Ralph the obvious question.

'Don't babies smell when they come out?'

'Nah, they're inside a kind of bag.'

'Doesn't it hurt the baby then?' I knew nothing about the dimensions of ladies' bum holes. Female bum anatomy had absolutely no appeal to me. This was not information I needed to share with the likes of Ralph Waters.

'If it's a lady's first baby, the baby's head gets squashed to the size of a lemon.' Ralph cast an eye over our heads.

'And if it's the third baby?'

'Normal shape and size.' I let out a lungful of air. Ralph had two older siblings like me.

My brother was fixing a puncture on his bicycle when I got home. I stood for a moment examining him from behind. His head was definitely pointier than Carmel's. He was trying to put the tyre back on his wheel by wedging two of my mother's dinner spoons under the rim. A spoon fell out and clattered on to the concrete of the driveway. John cursed. As he turned to retrieve it, he noticed me. His mouth pulled downward in a sneer. John only had to look at me to get upset. There was something about the way I was put together that disgusted him. I suspected it was the same thing Ralph Waters felt about Gary Jings.

'What are you looking at, poof?'

'Nothing.'

'Piss off then. Go and try on some of Mum's pantyhose or something.'

There was no use explaining John's condition. It would just alarm him. I went inside to examine my mother's bottom.

The heart transplant article haunted me. I thought about it constantly. My version of the operation went something like this: I've had a major heart attack on Hollywood Boulevard. Christiaan Barnard is busy so they call in a trainee called Herb to do the job. Herb disconnects my heart before a donor can be found. He keeps the blood pumping through my body with a machine powered by a lawnmower engine, but time is running out. Still no donor can be found. Herb substitutes my heart with a defrosted chicken. The chicken refuses to pump. I regain consciousness with a Tender Choice broiler in my chest, still wet and cold from the defrosting process. Herb attaches electrodes to the chicken and turns on the juice. It jumps but flops back lifeless next to my lungs.

Dad regularly drank with a man called Herb. It was common knowledge that Herb didn't wear socks. He simply blackened his ankles with shoe polish. This habit had been discovered when Herb crossed his legs and swiped the beige trousers of one of his neighbours. The owner of the trouser leg had then traced the origins of the black smudge back to Herb's ankle. No one said anything about this habit, at least not to Herb's face. They just gave him plenty of legroom in the public bar.

It was Herb's socks that gave me the idea for the fishnets. I tried to tell my father this but he didn't want to listen. He was too busy shouting at my mother about her brother Norman. I had performed the Olivia Newton-John show to cheer Mum up. Dad wasn't even supposed to come home. It was race night at the pub. I was singing along to '*I Honestly Love You*' into the handle of a hairbrush when he burst into the lounge and found me dressed in one of my mother's frocks. It was when he noticed my legs that he started shouting. They were criss-crossed with ballpoint pen in the fashion of fishnet stockings.

I felt my heart again. It was still ticking, ticking like a time bomb. I could feel tiny ripples of pain each time a tick happened. I went to consult the house physician.

'Mum, I think I'm going to have a heart attack.'

'Really, Julian.' Mum was peeling potatoes over the sink and didn't turn round.

'It's got a funny tick. I think I'd better not do any phys. ed. tomorrow. Can you write a note?'

'Physical Education is probably the best thing for a dicky heart.'

'My situation is very delicate.' My situation was that I hated sports.

'All the more reason to build up your stamina.'

'Ralph Waters says he's going to smash my teeth in if I set

27

foot on the rugby field. That sort of thing could ruin a stage and screen career. I'll need a good set of teeth if I'm going to be a star.' Ralph had done no such thing. He'd kept a respectful distance since the Stromboli incident but Mum didn't need to know this.

'Go find a pen and paper.'

5

My family generally didn't do holidays. We didn't own a caravan
or tent and Dad didn't want to rent a beach house. That would've
been throwing good money away. My father liked to point out
that there were plenty of decent beaches around Ulverston. He
called our stretch of coastline the Tasmanian Riviera. If
Ulverston's sand was good enough for him when he was a kid,
it was good enough for us. We could like it or lump it. Dad's
idea of summer fun was to get us throwing a cricket ball to
each other while he drank beer and shouted from the back step.
This was fine for Carmel and John who had an obscene attach-
ment to balls but it was hell for me. Cricket balls made me
carsick.

Summer holidays were difficult because they meant Dad was
home during the day and this meant pressure to go outside
and play. I was getting depressed about the post-Christmas
period when he suddenly announced we were going to stay in
a real holiday house on the east coast. Trevor Bland's brother
had a cabin and said we could use it for two weeks. We only had
to pay for electricity. Mum was thrilled and began baking immediately. Even Dad got into the spirit of things. I overheard him
telling Mum we should start getting used to candlelight.

The beach settlement had five cabins and a small shop that

sold frozen and tinned food. Fresh milk and bread arrived every other day. Our cabin was a two-room wooden shack under gum trees. My parents put up camp stretchers in the main room and we took the bunks in the other room.

The beach was miles from the nearest town and didn't have a sewage system. Our cabin had a septic tank for the kitchen waste and the run-off from the outside shower. The toilet wasn't connected to the tank. It was a hole in the ground over which sat a small corrugated iron shed that could be moved when things reached maximum capacity. Inside was a makeshift bench seat with a hole to put your bum through. The stink of the shed would've been unbearable if the hole hadn't provided such an interesting view of what was going on in the family.

Dad had recently stopped trying to make Carmel play with dolls and started encouraging her interest in cricket. The sports desk at *The Bugle* was seeing more articles on women's cricket. Dad still relegated these to an obscure corner of the sports pages but he'd realised that it was now almost respectable for a woman to play the game. He'd bought Carmel a bat and a new set of wickets for Christmas. John and Carmel pulled this equipment out of the Holden Kingswood not long after we arrived and headed down to the beach. While they were off making fools of themselves, I made friends with the kids from the next cabin, Donna and Dean Speck.

I'd noticed their Holden Statesman as we arrived and wondered whether they might be my kind of people. The car was brand new and fitted with snazzy hubcaps. The Speck kids exhibited the same kind of style as their car. They wore new beach outfits and spoke with a posh Hobart accent. Dean did all the talking. He was a strange boy, loud and aggressive, but I decided to overlook these faults when he said his father worked on radio. Mr Speck had been reporting on the sheep trials in

Ulverston that morning. Any fool knew that radio was tele-vision without pictures. Mr Speck was more or less a star, just the sort of contact I'd need in the future. The Specks were building a hut out of tea-tree sticks when I leaned over the wire fence. I loved building forts and asked if I could help. Dean shook his head in a final sort of way and suggested a more interesting game called Disease. I was flattered.

'You'll love it. It's really exciting.' Dean said this with confi-dence as he picked up the long, wooden pole his mother used to prop up her washing line.

I followed him to the back of their cabin and watched as he poked it into the hole of their toilet.

'Now run for your life or you'll catch the disease!' Dean had a violent smile on his face when he spun around, waving the damp end of the pole in the air.

Donna must've played the game before. She immediately disappeared inside the Speck cabin and slammed the door. I turned and ran as Dean charged at me, holding the pole in front of him like a jousting lance. I didn't want anything to do with a game called Disease and headed straight for our cabin and the safety of my mother. As I rounded the corner of the fence, I slipped on the sandy soil and fell hard on my chest. I was face down struggling for breath when I felt the wet end of the pole poked under my chin. Dean was laughing.

'Now you've got the disease. Ha, ha.'

I decided to avoid the Speck kids after that. There had to be a cleaner way to get on television. I washed my neck with the hose and went off to see how Carmel's bowling arm was devel-oping. It was the same arm she used for punching.

Mum had been talking to other mothers and discovered that the beach was located close to a scenic national park with a waterfall. One morning Dad told us the family was going to see some real Tassie bush. By the way he spoke, I knew it was the last thing he wanted to do. Neither was he happy about having an extra passenger in the car. John had invited his new best friend to come along. Dean Speck and John had a lot in common. They loved throwing balls and both got sadistic pleasure out of calling me names. Their name of preference was 'poof'. I didn't like them making a Gary Jings of me and made a point of keeping my distance. This was difficult in the back seat of a Holden Kingswood but at least I had Carmel as a buffer. I also had Mum in the front seat if push came to shove.

It was already hot when we arrived at the nature reserve. Dad parked under a tree and walked off to urinate behind some man ferns. It was a three-kilometre hike to the waterfall. I decided to retain all fluids until we reached our goal. Brother Duffy had described what dehydration did to the Australian soldiers in North Africa. I didn't want old sneakers for kidneys.

I kept a wary eye on the boys as they prepared for the hike. John obviously looked up to Dean. He let him carry the cricket bat while he lugged the wickets. They ran on ahead with Carmel while I kept pace with Mum, Dad and the plastic picnic bin, silently agreeing with Dad as he griped about every step. It was the most physical activity I'd ever seen him do. My father was a sports maniac but only when other people played the game. I felt my heart at regular intervals to make sure it was still ticking.

At the base of the falls, we laid out the picnic on a wooden table and then ate while brushing flies off our egg sandwiches. When Carmel pulled out a cricket ball after lunch, I decided to do some exploring. I didn't want to be roped into a ball game with a thug like Dean.

The track to the top of the falls was well marked and Mum

said I was allowed to venture off on my own. I followed it for ten minutes until I reached the large pool above the waterfall. The picnic table was somewhere beneath the treetops below. The thrill of absolute power guided my hands to my fly. I was the source of the Ganges, the spring of Lourdes, the piddling bronze boy of Belgium. I urinated into the river with pride and calculated how long it would take to flow past my parents. I imagined my father scooping a plastic picnic cup into the stream and taking a drink.

As I descended, I could hear a strange noise filtering through the bush. It sounded like the high-pitched wail of an injured animal. I imagined a wombat being torn apart by a Tasmanian devil and hurried down the track to the picnic area.

My mother was standing next to the picnic table hunched over Dean. She was pressing a damp cloth to his forehead with a worried look. Dean's face was red and wet with tears. He was crying openly like a girl. Dad was packing up the picnic bin with his lips in a hard line. John was looking at his friend in an embarrassed, disappointed way. Only Carmel was smiling. Her eyes were on Dean but her hands were busy with the cricket ball. She was tossing it expertly from one hand to the other.

I was the first to be diagnosed with hepatitis A. Carmel followed within a week and a few days later Dad came down with the disease. We were told not to leave our house in Ulverston for four weeks. Dad wasn't allowed to go to work or the pub and was forbidden to drink alcohol. He spent his days feeling sorry for himself in front of the television, swiping flies with the *Punter's Gazette*. The disease wasn't pleasant but it did have one very shiny silver lining. We were forbidden to engage in any physical activity. Television was out with Dad hogging the set so Carmel and I took up board games and poker. These we pretended to play while kicking each other under the table.

Mum and John miraculously didn't get the disease. They were told to be very careful and to wash their hands with special soap after handling us. John held his nose and flattened himself against the wall whenever he met me in the hall. He even got a room on his own after Carmel and I were shunted in together. This was a temporary arrangement but a vast improvement on life with John. Carmel punched hard but at least she made me laugh. She also had imagination. Her eyes lit up when I suggested forming a singing duo.

'You'd make an excellent back-up singer.' Carmel had a keen eye for natural talent. 'We could be the next Carpenters. We just need the charm of Val Doonican with the staying power of Andy Williams.'

I felt a glow of pride in the defrosted-chicken department of my chest. Carmel knew what she was talking about. She'd seen me perform often enough. Mum and I had been working on my voice since I was old enough to say Dick Dingle. I performed for my mother whenever she got something mysterious called her period. These unhappy periods occurred quite regularly and entailed tears and hot-water bottles. My job was to sing into the handle of a hairbrush and dance until she smiled and remembered where the family block of Shelby's fruit and nut was hidden.

'What about Frank Sinatra?' I didn't like the Carpenters and wasn't particularly fond of Val or Andy. They appeared on Sunday-night TV music specials. I always felt slightly carsick before the start of the school week and associated these singers with a feeling of doom.

Carmel smiled. 'Once every five years you say something intelligent.'

The chicken stirred again behind my ribs. This meant I'd said at least two intelligent things in my life.

'Sinatra's where the money is. You're Dean Martin and I'm Ol' Blue Eyes.' Carmel examined her eyes in the mirror over the mantelpiece. She blew a kiss to herself.

'No, I'm Sinatra.' My voice had the whine that preceded tears and a tantrum.

'OK, OK, we're both Sinatra. I'm Frank and you're Nancy.'

Carmel put together a routine of Frank Sinatra songs from Mum's Sinatra records. My job was to do the harmonising vocals for every song except for a 'You Make Me Feel so Young' medley. For this number, I was allowed to sing the Nancy part unaided.

'You have to sing it even higher and warble the end bits because it's a girl's part.'

'But you sing Frank's part in your normal voice.'

'Yes, but my voice has a naturally deep timbre.'

I couldn't argue with her on that point. People sometimes mistook Carmel for Dad when she answered the phone.

Carmel arranged an evening performance for the family in the lounge. My stomach was fluttery as we dragged the Aussiemica table in from the dinette and draped a red candlewick bedspread over it. Carmel placed three chairs in front of this stage but took one away after John refused to join. He said he had no intention of being showered with disease.

Mum and Dad were quiet for the first four songs, politely clapping at the end of each number and occasionally nodding. It wasn't until the Frank and Nancy duet that we got the re-action Carmel had anticipated. Dad smiled for the first time in two weeks when I broke into Nancy. He was clapping wildly next to Mum by the time Carmel and I did our final harmony.

At the end of the show Mum handed us each a bar of Shelby's. She ruffled my hair and whispered 'Twinkle, twinkle' in my ear before going into the kitchen to cut a cream sponge cake she'd baked for the occasion. Dad was still smiling when he came up to me. He pounded me on the shoulder in a manly but friendly way.

'I needed that. The laugh's done me the world of good.'

'It wasn't supposed to be funny, Dad.'

'I was laughing with you. Did you think I was laughing at you?'

'Yeah, I did.'

'You think I'm the type of father who laughs at his children?'

'Yeah.'

'I was humouring you. It's a form of encouragement. You'll understand when you get older.'

'I doubt it.'

'Don't worry. In a couple of years you'll lose that whinny.' He walked away laughing to himself.

6

The illness was ideal for receiving special treatment and avoiding sports, but it was bad news for Mum and Dad's relationship. They'd always been a mismatched couple and never had the lovey-dovey sort of arrangement I saw on family TV shows. Mum and Dad didn't exchange compliments or show open affection to each other. It was more businesslike than that. The arrangement became even less amicable after the beach trip. This lack of warmth transformed into hostility during Dad's illness. While it had never been acceptable to show affection with children in the room, it was now fine to go at it hammer and tongs in front of us.

As the weeks dragged on, Dad got progressively more miserable and touchy. Even Carmel avoided the lounge where he'd taken up residence. My father spent his days not drinking and glowering at daytime television, which was dominated by cooking shows, farming programmes and reruns of old films. Even Dick Dingle produced boring daytime programmes. It was one of these, a Dingle documentary on the scouts of Tasmania, that finally stirred my father into action. He called John into the dinette and took out his chequebook. John waved the cheque at me to make sure I'd seen the sort of power relationship he had with our father before leaving on his bicycle.

That evening, a van arrived with a load of timber and

chicken wire. Dad sat on the back step to avoid passing on his disease and called instructions to the man driving the van. The next-door neighbour started his lawnmower just as Dad began speaking. The bedroom I currently shared with Carmel was located at the back of the house and provided a view of the van and the back step. We watched from the window.

'Just leave it under the plum tree, mate.' Dad had to shout over the noise of the mower.

'What's that, mate?'

'Under the plum tree, mate. Plum.' Dad drew a plum in the air with two fingers but it may as well have been a heart or an upside-down bum.

'Another bum treat? What the hell are you on about, mate?'

The man in the van had no way of knowing Dad was ill. Bum treat sounded poofy. To the driver, Dad was implying something unAustralian.

'Under the fucking plum tree, you idiot.'

The mower stopped and Dad's words hung over the neighbourhood. I imagined families frozen in front of their barbecues, sausages going silent on the grill. The F word had power. A thrill went through me. It was the first time I'd heard it from my father. I had to make the most of it.

'You want to watch your mouth, mate. I'm not paid to be abused by some queer bastard who's too lazy to get off his back step.'

Dad stood up and walked over to the van with long, deliberate strides. By the crimson of his neck I could tell that he was sizzling with anger. He poked his head in the van window and shoved it up close to the driver.

'I'm not queer, mate. I've got hepatitis A. You can catch it from saliva spray. A microscopic speck is enough. Makes you as crook as a dog.'

The driver rolled up his window as soon as Dad had pulled his head away. He waited until my father had retreated to the step before hastily unloading the timber and wire. As he drove off, his wheels spun in the grass and left two long brown furrows under the plum tree.

Dad called the chicken coop a boys' project and expected me to pitch in and help with its construction. He said it would teach us about building things, responsibility, life and death. I reminded Mum about my hepatitis and my father was warned not to let me lift a nail let alone a hammer. It took Dad and John three days to build. John was then sent on a mission to the local poultry farm, returning with ten chicks in an aerated shoebox on his bike carrier. The chicks were past the fluffy stage and had the beginnings of combs and feathers. Dad put them in the coop with some porridge. They pecked madly at the meal, spraying grey missiles in all directions. I ventured out to watch them feed. They were busy, funny things that took my mind off the miserable state of affairs inside the house.

We got the all-clear to rejoin the human race just as school started. The chickens began laying eggs a month later. A few months after that, Dad began introducing new chicks and culling the older girls. He bought himself a large metal chopper and placed a sawn-off tree trunk in the backyard.

I was supposed to take part in the slaughter but Dad ordered me to the back step when I refused to catch a chicken. I told myself that it wasn't a big thing; chickens got killed every day. Carmel said they regularly got killed crossing the road. Dad put on a barbecue apron and sharpened the chopper. He wiped down the wooden stump and pulled the hose out to the back-yard. John took his place next to him with a stupid grin.

Dad had prepared us for the slaughter by solemnly declaring that killing animals for food was natural to mankind.

'We're omnivores. That's why we have molars and canine teeth. In nature, it's survival of the fittest. It's either them or us.'

I watched him run his finger along the chopper's edge and began to sweat. 'Them or us' was a stupid idea. The chickens had no intention of pecking us to death.

My stomach tightened as Dad reached into the coop and grabbed a bird by the legs, carrying it to the stump upside down with its wings flapping. He asked John to hold the legs while he stretched out the neck. Bringing the chopper down fast, he sent the head flying off the stump at high speed. The chicken's legs slipped out of John's grasp as it gave its last jerks of life. Blood sprayed in an arc from the chicken's neck, showering John and Dad with a line of bright red dots.

My stomach heaved. I ran to the bathroom and splashed cold water over my face until the carsick feeling eased. When my legs felt solid again I went to the kitchen to see Mum. She was boiling water to remove the chicken's feathers.

'Mum, I can't eat that chicken. It was murder.'

'I'm making a roast-chicken dinner, your favourite.'

'I can't eat it for religious reasons.'

'OK, honey. Carmel can have the drumsticks and wings and John can have the juicy white meat from the breast. I'll just have those two little flesh oysters from the hollows of its back. They're probably Elizabeth Taylor's favourite bits. Your father can have the skin and the pickings on the carcass. There, that's settled then.'

They were welcome to it. I'd had a religious transformation. It was wrong to eat a murdered chicken. The only chickens I would eat from now on were those from a supermarket. Happy, bloodless things that came in sealed plastic wrappers.

Religion was a non-negotiable subject in our house. We were Sunday Catholics. We didn't bother practising much of what the priest preached but we went to Our Lady of Miracles every Sunday like the other good Catholics of Ulverston. On the subject of church, Mum and Dad were in agreement. It didn't matter how crappy things were in real life: once a week we had to pretend to be a normal family.

'Dad, I can't go to church today. I've had a religious transformation. I had a visitation. Like an archangel, only bigger and shinier.'

Dad was putting on his tie in front of the hall mirror. He looked at my reflection and tightened his lips. I pushed on.

'I was sucked up into the clouds where I met a man sitting on a large Brazil nut.'

My father raised his eyebrows in the mirror.

'He looked like Mr Patel from the fruit and vegetable shop but he had long hair.'

Dad frowned and tucked the tail of his tie into his shirt.

'I'm being called by a higher voice,' he said. 'I should follow the voice, wherever it leads me, even if I have to walk through the valley of death and all that.'

Dad turned from the mirror and gave me one of his looks. 'I heard a higher voice on the radio this morning. It was Joan Sutherland. Put on your Sunday jumper and get in the car. I'm in no mood for one of your stories.'

Church services at Our Lady of Miracles were a complete waste of time. The priest should have looked good in his glittery frock but managed to completely ruin the effect with a tragic haircut and old-fashioned horn-rimmed glasses. Father McMahon wasn't just a frump. He had absolutely no talent for working a crowd. It wouldn't have taken much to liven up his sermons: a few 'A funny thing happened to me on the way to the church this morning' starters, some audience participation, novelty giveaways. But when Father McMahon talked, people

41

picked lint off their cardigans and dug holes into pews with car keys. The priest lacked showmanship. My mother and I called this quality 'pizzazz' and divided the world into those who had it and those who didn't. Mum and I fell into the first category while Dad and John occupied the second. Carmel was impossible to categorise. Mum said I had so much pizzazz I glowed. This was an exaggeration but I knew what she meant.

A shiny ecclesiastical gown would not have been wasted on me but the priesthood held no appeal. The Catholic Church had too many nutty rules and not enough handsome role models. Father McMahon managed to be even less attractive than the Pope, which was saying something. The best way to get through the hour of what he managed to stretch into half a day was to squint my eyes at the other churchgoers and imagine them without clothes. I'd actually seen my mother naked once when I'd surprised her coming out of the shower and taken in a few crucial points. Ladies had the Stromboli mound, only it was covered by a thatch of what I now knew to be pubic hair. Carmel had explained the mechanics of this anatomical oddity. 'It's like Velcro. It helps keep your underpants up.'

I'd done more research and come a long way since the Ralph Waters field trip. I knew for a fact that women had something called the lady hole, hidden away below the Velcro line. Where John got the point on his head, however, was still a mystery.

My father had done nothing to help my research. I'd shared a bathroom and towels with him for over a decade but had never seen him naked, not a pubic hair, not once. I'd seen him with his shirt off a handful of times but no Velcro. The mystery of the adult male had been cleared up by Greg Bean, a boy with Down Syndrome who visited the Ulverston Municipal Baths every Saturday in summer. Greg had the body of a teenager but the smiley temperament of a six-year-old. He had absolutely no concept of modesty and walked around inside the changing shed without clothes, singing, while his brother Denny tried to get him to step into his bathers.

The only times I considered God was when I wanted something expensive or when I was touching myself. If it was the latter case then I preferred to think that God didn't exist. It made no sense that a higher intelligence would've provided such excellent equipment then forbidden me to use it. Masturbation was a key theme at St Kevin's. We constantly heard about the perils of it from the Christian Brothers who ran our school. I might've taken notice if the message had come from another source, but I had no confidence in these particular men of the cloth. For the most part, they were a miserable bunch of failures. They'd given up the worldly joys but didn't have what it took to become priests. Brother Punt was the school's anti-wanking fanatic. He gave the religion class twice a week.

'Masturbation is dangerous, boys. It's a very difficult habit to break.'

Brother Punt turned his palms upward and spread his hands in front of him with a sweeping gesture. I'd seen a magician on television do the same thing to prove he had nothing to hide. Thomas Owen put up his hand. He was the tallest boy in the class and had permanently chapped lips.

'What about in the bath, sir? I mean how do we wash ourselves *down there*?' Thomas pointed to the hot zone below the belt of his trousers.

That question would've been a joke from anyone else in the class but Thomas didn't have a ha-ha sense of humour. His mother came from somewhere in Germany.

'Good question, Owen. I have two keywords for washing

yourself. Be fast and be sure. Soap your flannel into a lather and clean your privates with a brisk rubbing motion.'

'I tried that, sir, but I'm having problems.'

We all knew what kind of problems Thomas was talking about. These were not problems as far as I was concerned.

'Be brisk, Owen. Do not linger.'

Poor Owen. His problem wasn't masturbation. His problem was that he thought it was a crime. I knew he had it wrong. If there was a God and he didn't want us to touch ourselves, he would've given us something useless like the joyless mound of a girl. Thomas was making a Gary Jings of himself. He wasn't supposed to attract attention to himself. His job was to get on with business and keep quiet about it. Someone had to come to his rescue.

'Do you think Jesus had a problem with . . . you know?' I looked Brother Punt in the eye and shrugged knowingly. My question seemed to throw him off balance.

'What sort of question is that?' The brother's hands clamped the edge of the desk.

'Well, I mean, did they have flannels in those days? When Jesus Christ took a bath and all, do you think he—?'

'No! Jesus was the son of God.'

The brother was firm on this point. He lifted a hand and brought it down hard on to the desk. Thomas Owen jumped and let out a squeak.

'But he had a man's body.'

This I knew for a fact. I'd admired it every Sunday in its shiny plaster form on the wall of Our Lady of Miracles. I imagined Jesus had quite a Thermos flask inside the old tea towel wrapped around his loins. I'd spent many services redesigning the sculpture in my head, with and without the loincloth. My Jesus was clean-shaven with sexy little sideburns. He had a yellow brocade

44

scarf slung around the hips, just low enough to reveal a hint of pubic hair. My scarf wasn't tucked between the legs like Our Lady's tea towel. In my version, the long tassels dangled cheekily in front of the groin. My design was a definite improvement on the original. It certainly would've encouraged more people to attend church and look up to Jesus.

'He wouldn't have done anything impure with his body.' Brother Punt was leaning forward over his desk in a threatening manner.

'But maybe he touched himself by mistake sometimes.'

'He wouldn't have.' The brother's word was final. The look on his face made that clear.

'But he might have, you know, bumped against something accidentally. Maybe a chair or a goat.'

'Shut up!'.

I wasn't sure if it was the mention of the chair or the goat that inflamed Brother Punt, but he moved toward me with the speed of a great white shark. I knew these particular sharks moved very fast because I'd just read an article in the *Australian Ladies' Companion* about a man who'd lost a leg at Bondi Beach. I'd read it through to the end because it featured a photo of the surf lifesavers who had pulled the victim from the waves. The lifesavers wore tiny nylon bathers and little multicoloured caps that did up under the chin. The story inspired me to add surf lifesaver to my list of possible careers. But I wasn't going to be one of the lifesavers who actually went in the water. I was going to provide cold drinks and suntan lotion, and speak to television cameras.

The teacher grabbed me under the armpit and dragged me to his desk. Reaching into the drawer, he pulled out a long, thick, leather instrument of torture. Punt had his own peculiar style with the strap. He brought the base down hard on to the palm, leaving the length of leather to slap at high speed across the delicate inner part of the wrist and forearm. I imagined it wasn't too different from having nails driven into the wrists then being hung from a wooden cross. The brother's technique made the veins stand out and left huge red welts on the skin.

The only good thing about being strapped was the attention it drew. Strap marks were the stigmata at my Catholic school. They were the mark of a star and sent popularity ratings sky high. At playtime I had an audience and even got a pat on the back from Ralph Waters.

7

Popularity had a strange effect on me. The more I had, the more I wanted. The Christian Brothers called me a show-off but they didn't understand the value of good entertainment. My classmates did and so did my mother. This was a good base but if I was going to take my pizzazz to the next level, I needed to develop a look. That look was a lot thinner. I found the ideal solution to weight loss in an advertisement in the back of *The Bugle*. Ten days later, a plain brown-paper package was sitting on the table when I got home from school.

'What's this, then?' My mother tapped it with her fingernail.

'Private and personal.'

I picked it up and took it into the bathroom. I could feel my heartbeat in the back of my throat as I locked the door. The package had cost me all my pocket-money savings. It was worth it. I needed to start making preparations now if I was going to win the Little Aussie Talent Quest. I had four years to prepare myself. Mum said that the talent quest was a stepping stone to the Golden Microphone and advised me to keep my eye on the prize. It didn't matter how I applied my pizzazz, she said. The important thing was to make full use of my star quality and one day I'd end up on television.

As an incentive, Mum had taped a photo and caption from

the *Companion* to the door of the fridge. It showed a smiling teenage girl from Geelong, Tania, holding the Golden Microphone trophy. Her cheeks were bright pink and her teeth had braces. Mum said I would be a Tania one day. It was just a matter of doing the right thing in the right place at the right time. She called it the Golden Microphone Moment and warned me not to squander my talent as she'd done. Marrying my father just after the Tasmanian finals had been the biggest mistake of her life, she said. She never made it to the nationals.

I opened the package. It contained an instruction sheet.

- Remove all items of clothing including undergarments.
- Wash your body thoroughly to remove skin toxins.
- Towel your body dry.
- Slip the SlimQuik Body Skin on underneath your regular clothes.
- The body-hugging SlimQuik Body Skin is worn against the skin and is not visible under clothes.

I took off my school uniform. The SlimQuik was made of stiff pink plastic that crackled and was designed like a Charlie Chaplin bathing suit with short legs and a sleeveless top. I climbed into it and pop-closed the row of domes running down the chest. It was too big. I'd ordered an adult medium to be on the safe side but it was hanging off me. I put my school uniform back on and looked at myself in the mirror. Apart from the suit bottoms hanging out of my shorts, no one would ever know. I rolled the legs up, stuck the instruction sheet in my pocket and opened the door. My mother watched me from the back step as I put the empty packaging in the rubbish tin.

'You going to tell me what's going on?'

'It's scientific, Mum, for the good of mankind and all that.

You'll see in ten days.' That's how long it would take me to lose five kilograms.

I gently nudged Mum on my way back inside. The suit crackled as we bumped.

'Snap, crackle, pop!' She laughed and ruffled my hair.

I ignored her and headed back to my bedroom without moving my arms. A new *Celebrity Glitter* had arrived and I had research to do. The magazine had an exposé on Elizabeth Taylor's secret second marriage to Richard Burton, a good move in my opinion. Burton was a generous man. He'd given Liz all her best necklaces and didn't seem to mind her plumpness.

My own body was supposed to have projections and hollows like the bodies of other boys who were now elongating and sprouting. But puberty was not so kind to me. I was increasing in density and getting softer and rounder. My father did nothing for my confidence. I was foolish enough to walk past him one day without a shirt. He'd looked at my chest and laughed. 'Look at those bottle tops! Ha, ha.'

This was rich coming from him. The pair he had on his chest talked to each other when he climbed the three steps to the back door. I knew where the bottle tops on my chest came from and I resented him for it. His other physical deformity I didn't want was body hair. I desperately wanted pubic hair but I feared what adolescence might do to my back. Dad's hairs marched their way north from his bum crevice like a hungry army, fanning out at the top of his back and sweeping over his shoulders. From there they worked their way south again, over his chest and down past his stomach. Carmel said if we rubbed him along our nylon carpet we'd generate enough static to attach him to the back of the couch.

My body density would've been unbearable if I'd suffered it alone but it was reassuring to suffer it along with Elizabeth

49

Taylor. The *Celebrity Glitter* article was particularly unkind. It referred to Liz as a bejewelled porker. I decided to write to her personally through her fan club.

Dear Liz,

Don't worry about being a little on the big side. You're the world's best ambassador for big people because you've still got a beautiful face and anyway, you could be a lot bigger. So don't worry. You're a big star, big and shiny like a real star in the sky.

I just wanted to tell you that.

By the way, is the Cartier diamond heavy? Sixty-nine seems a lot of carats even for a big diamond like the Cartier. Those carats must be heavy. That's what I think anyway.

Liz, you and I have a lot in common. I'm sure we'll be good friends after I move to America. I just have to win the Golden Microphone or equivalent trophy. Mum says it's a sure thing. I first have to win the Little Aussie Talent Quest but I can't enter this until I'm fifteen. So you will have to be patient. In the meantime, why don't you visit Ulverston? You can stay at our house. Our couch is a four-seater so it should be big enough.

Love from YOUR BIGGEST FAN,

Julian Corkle

The Songbird of the South

There, that would make her feel better. I licked the envelope flap several times and pushed it flat. It curled up again. The sticky tape was in the dinette where Mum was entertaining our neighbour, Roslyn Scone. Roslyn was a sharp woman with a pinched face and limp blond hair that sat on her head like wet seaweed. She could have done something to remedy her looks but Roslyn wasn't the type to invest money in something important. She was proudly describing her husband's new Ford Escort when I entered the dinette. The Royal Albert tea set was out and a cake plate with three chocolate Tiffany biscuits was sitting in the middle of the table. I loved Tiffanies almost as much as I loved Shelby's chocolate. My idea of happiness was sharing a packet of Tiffanies with Mum while I did her hair and she talked about my career. This we could do only when Dad and John were off the premises.

I sat down next to Roslyn with a crackle. She didn't look in my direction or even acknowledge me. Roslyn didn't like me and it was all Carmel's fault. The papers and television had been making a lot of noise about a Scottish stripping sensation touring Australia called Gladys McGinty. Gladys had enormous breasts that sat on her chest like two Russian icebreakers. The media referred to her as Gladys Maximus and got a lot of mileage out of jokes about her massive tartan bagpipes. According to Carmel, our neighbour Roslyn had a sunken treasure chest with grains of sand for breasts. One day I was sitting with my sister behind the hedge when she called out, 'Roslyn Minimus, the scrawny tart and bag!' Carmel had run off and left me to my fate. I was cowering behind the hedge, smiling foolishly, when Roslyn found me. She hadn't forgiven me.

'Mum, can I have a Tiffany?' I took a biscuit as I asked.

'Just one, Julian, then go outside and play.'

'I need some sticky tape.'

'You know where it is.'

I got off my chair and found the tape in the drawer. I sealed the envelope and returned to the table, crackling as I sat down. It was getting hot inside the suit. I could feel sweat tickling

51

down the backs of my knees. I reached out and took another Tiffany as swiftly as possible. The suit crackled again. Roslyn looked at me suspiciously.

'What's that rustling sound? The boy's got something in his trousers.'

The sweat was now running down my legs. Roslyn made me nervous but I couldn't leave while there was still a Tiffany up for grabs. If I let the biscuit slip through my fingers, it would haunt me all afternoon.

'Everything inside my trousers is normal, Mum.'

'Colleen, young boys are pleasure-seekers. He's got something alien down there.' Roslyn folded her arms over her two grains of sand. She wanted war.

I wanted the Tiffany. I decided to offer her an olive branch. 'Mrs Scone, I bet you're an expert on carats. Women love them. The bigger the better and all that.'

'I beg your pardon?' Roslyn gave me a horrified look. She obviously didn't read the right magazines.

'Carats. You know, the big ones. You've got to have them if you're a glamour puss. Film stars can't get enough of them.'

Roslyn made a high-pitched whistling sound as she sucked air past her dentures.

Mum rattled her Royal Albert teacup in its saucer. 'That's enough, Julian! Get outside.'

I grabbed the last Tiffany and slipped off my chair with a crackle. I heard Roslyn whistle-gasp as I made for the door. Outside, I squatted down and waddled like a duck until I was directly below the open dinette window.

'You want to watch that boy, Colleen.'

'For goodness' sake! He's wearing a sweat suit to lose weight.'

Mum's statement was followed by the clatter of plates. She was clearing the table and being rough on the Royal Albert.

This was out of character for Mum. The tea set was the nicest thing we owned and only made the voyage from the lounge mantelpiece to the table when there were guests to entertain or impress. She'd bought the porcelain with her Golden Microphone prize money.

'Boys shouldn't wear sweat suits.'

'Roslyn! Julian is a good kid and I don't appreciate you implying otherwise. He's got a lot of talent and will go places one day.' More china rattled.

'I wasn't finished with that cup of tea.'

'I think you were.'

'Well, I know when I'm not wanted!'

'At least you know that.'

A chair scraped. The door slammed. I watched Roslyn's rigid back as she marched down our driveway. She turned at the gate and saw me crouched under the window. I thought of Carmel and gave her the fingers.

The family was going out to the King's Arms and had dressed up for the occasion. I was wearing my new maroon stretch trousers and gingham check shirt. Mum had on her knee-length apricot skirt and cream twin set. I'd spent hours curling and setting her hair and she looked just like Bobbie Gentry. The dinner was Mum's idea. We were going out to celebrate John's sixteenth birthday in a grown-up way at the hotel's new Sunday Family Buffet. Dad didn't like family outings but had been won over by the pub's all-you-can-eat deal.

I'd never been to a buffet and wanted to make the most of it. The three Tiffany biscuits I'd eaten in the afternoon had been digested hours ago. I was starving and keen to get going. Dad must've felt the same way because he was the first in the car. I followed John and Carmel into the back seat with a crackle. Carmel made a face and slid away from me. John gave me a disgusted look and wound down his window. I leaned over to talk to Dad.

'Can we really eat as much as we like?'

'What?' Dad was occupied with counting the one- and two-dollar notes in his wallet.

'Can I really eat until I'm full, without stopping and all that?'

'Yeah.'

'Can I fill my plate and go back again for seconds? And are the desserts and drinks included?'

'Yeah.'

'What if all the food's gone when we get there?'

'It won't be. We'll be there at opening time. That's the Corkle way.'

'But a rugby team might turn up. Or a herd of sheep farmers.'

'Ulverston's got fish-and-chip shops for that sort of thing.'

'Do you think they'll have chips?'

'Probably, they're cheap to make.'

'That's all right then.' If I could eat as much as I like, and if the buffet had chips and dessert, then everything would be fine.

Dad was right. We were the first family to arrive and had to wait ten minutes for the staff to finish laying out the buffet. Trestle tables had been set up in the lounge bar under a banner: 'Caterers' Choice Brand. Mouth-watering cuisine made from home-style recipes'. It was like something out of *Celebrity Glitter*. The stainless steel and porcelain shone under the fluorescent lights and the food steamed inside the bains-marie. There were fancy dishes like beef curry and macaroni and cheese along-side normal Tasmanian food like chips and sausage rolls. Mum led us to a table as Dad paid. He followed us over scowling.

'Sharks! We should've come yesterday when John was fifteen. I had to pay full price.'

John smiled smugly. He was now officially almost an adult.

I got off my chair and stood beside Mum, waiting for the signal. She nodded and I made my move. I'd surveyed the tables and knew exactly where I was going. Avoiding the tasteless stuff like vegetables and salads, I loaded my plate with sausage rolls and chips. I went back and filled another with desserts in case the sheep farmers arrived while I was stuck on mains. We all took more food than we needed.

I worked my way through the first plate of savouries and then went back for another of crumbed chicken pieces and spaghetti. By the third round I was feeling gassy and hot. The SlimQuik was tight inside my clothes. Carmel heard domes pop as I got up a fourth time. She pinched her nose and made a waving motion with her other hand. 'Ugh, not in the public sphere.'

I filled the fourth plate with beef curry and rice. It was a ridiculous choice. I didn't like beef curry any more than I liked Irish stew. I ate it anyway.

Little rivers of sweat were running from under my arms when I started in on the apple sponge and chocolate cake. By now the suit had ripped open underneath my clothes. I didn't care. I just had to make enough room for a chocolate éclair and a helping of pavlova and then I'd be done.

I swallowed the last spoonful of pavlova and put the bowl on top of the stack of empty plates in front of me. I felt bloated and carsick. Complete calm was the only cure. I just wanted it all to end and to go home.

The family was still eating when a man came up to the table and spoke to Dad. 'I'd like to have a word with you, sir, away from the other paying customers.'

Dad got up and followed him. When he returned, his face was an angry red grimace. He didn't sit down.

'What's the matter, Jim?' Mum was brushing crumbs off the tablecloth in front of me.

'We're going. Some family discount they have here! That idiot just asked me to pay full price for Julian.'

Dad's eyes fell on me. I tried to sink lower in my chair but the interior of the sweat suit was slick with sweat. The suit and my clothes remained upright on the chair while I slipped down inside them. The suit made a squeaking sound as my skin rubbed against the plastic. Carmel aimed an elbow at my ribs but hit my shoulder.

'He said Julian ate four plates of mains. I told him to shove his buffet up his bum. Come on, let's get out of here.'

'But, Dad, I haven't had dessert yet and it's *my* birthday.' John's voice was a sickening whine.

Dad shook his head. We were leaving. John shot me a dangerous look. I knew by the look that I'd get hell later but I was in too much discomfort to care. I burped and tasted pavlova and beef curry in the back of my mouth.

As soon as we got home, I rushed into the bathroom and locked the door. I tore off all my clothes and removed the SlimQuik. It had ripped from the crotch to halfway up the back but I didn't care. It felt wonderful to be free of it. I pulled out the bathroom scales and stood on them naked, holding my breath. I'd been wearing the damned suit for an entire day and deserved some weight loss as compensation. The scales indicated I was two and a half kilograms heavier. I got off, wound back the little arm a few notches and then got back on. There, I was just under my regular weight.

8

It was one thing to have love handles bulging over the top of my shorts but it was quite another to overhear my father referring to me as a podge. *Podge*? I stopped in my tracks. I'd been on my way to the fridge to get cheese for a sandwich.

'That little podge eats like a horse and watches too much TV. It's not natural for a boy of his age. He should be outside playing not watching Dick Dingle on the box.'

Dad was sitting in front of the box talking to Mum as she ran a duster over the porcelain. He couldn't see me in the dinette because his eyes were fixed on the All Blacks who were getting pounded into mincemeat by the South Africans. The New Zealand rugby tour of apartheid South Africa had stirred up a hornet's nest on the pages of *The Bugle*. Dad didn't want to miss a minute of it.

'When was the last time you did any physical exercise?' Mum's hand had stopped moving. Her duster was hovering over the Royal Albert teapot.

'I'm not eleven years old.'

'No, you and that Trevor Bland act more like five-year-olds.' Mum let the duster fall and put her hands on her hips. 'Not all boys were made for sports. Julian has other talents. He's sensitive and original.'

'I've heard that before about you-know-who.'

'Leave Norm out of this.' She leaned over and waved a hand in front of Dad's face, forcing him to look at her. 'You know what you are, James Corkle? A big, fat, bigoted, beer-swilling sports dag.'

'Sports dag? You can't call me a sports dag.'

I should've left the dinette right then but I was riveted by the scene that had just unfolded before me. As Dad stood to confront my mother, he noticed me out of the corner of his eye. I heard him yell as I scurried for the back door. When he caught up with me I was near the plum tree. His face was red and his eyes were blazing. I knew he wanted to wallop me but he didn't have a justifiable crime, especially with Mum watching from the back step.

His eyes narrowed and a smile appeared. The next thing I knew, he'd put Carmel's cricket bat in my hand. It wasn't fair but no court of law in Tasmania was going to convict a father of cruelty for making his son play cricket. Mum gave a sympathetic shrug and went back inside.

I was made to stand with my back to the tree and told to hit hard and high. Dad rubbed the ball on his trouser leg, put it to his lips, blew on it, and then bowled it in my direction. The next thing I knew I was on my back gasping for air. The cricket ball had hit me in the middle of the chest and thrown me on my back.

'Did you just close your eyes?' Dad was standing over me.

'Yes.' Honesty was the best policy when it came to my father.

'You idiot.'

'I mean no.' I changed my mind. Honesty was definitely not the best policy. Flattery was. 'You throw just like Stan McCabe.'

'I can't believe your stupidity. I could've killed you.' Dad cared. He really did.

'I mean I did close them.'

'Your mother would have had a fit. Why in God's name did you close your frigging eyes?'

'The ball was blurry.' For some insane reason, there was the truth again.

Dad's head tilted to the side. He was paying attention. It encouraged me.

'You, too, Dad. When you stand over there by the fence, your edges go all fluffy like Doris Day on TV.'

This description had an immediate impact. I was grabbed by the shoulder and marched into the kitchen where my mother was peeling potatoes. She looked at me and frowned. 'What's happened?'

'Colleen, the boy's afflicted. His eyes are buggered. I'll have to see old Dent.'

Dr Dent was one of my father's co-drinkers. They met nearly every night down at the King's Arms with Trevor Bland to hash over meaningless topics like cricket and football. Dent was Dad's idea of good medicine. The doctor had a speech problem which prevented him from asking too many questions or giving much medical advice. His small, unpopular practice was located above the Whipper Snapper fish-and-chip shop in the centre of town.

My mother held up three fingers. 'How many fingers, Julian?'

'Two.'

'There's nothing wrong with his eyes. Apart from their gorgeous green colour.'

This was my mother being funny. She smiled at me. I almost smiled back but stopped myself. I'd always wanted glasses and couldn't allow humour to jeopardise this opportunity.

Yves Saint Laurent wore glasses and he was an actual French fashion designer from France. Everyone recognised Yves by his thick dark glasses. They were his signature, and all the big stars had a signature. Elizabeth Taylor had the Cartier diamond. Gladys had her icebreakers and Liberace, who had made another dazzling tour of Australia, had his candelabra.

Dent must've been a real doctor at one stage because he had a brass plaque on his door. The grubby waiting room was furnished with three vinyl chairs and an Aussiemica table. The ashtray on the table was full. There was no receptionist and obviously no cleaner.

'G-g-g-g'day, Jim.'

Dent held out his hand to my father. He was a short man with an oily scalp encircled by a strip of grey hair. I immediately thought of Louis Pasteur. Pasteur's discovery of bacteria and its destruction by boiling was one of Brother Duffy's favourite subjects. Dent's lab coat had grime around the button-holes and along the pocket edges. It was asking to be boiled.

'G-g-g-g'day, Dent.' My father copied his friend's stutter and then laughed at himself.

Dent didn't seem to mind. He listened to Dad with a vacant smile before going ahead with the examination. After putting me through the eye chart, he brought over a huge pair of black test frames and told me to put them on. The eye circles were like cogs and had numbered notches around the edges. Dad spluttered with laughter.

'Don't I know you? You're Brains from *Thunderbirds*. No, hang on, you're Mr Magoo.'

It was awful to be teased by my father because I was forbidden to retaliate. I could've come up with some extremely funny names for him, like Phar Lap or Lassie, but name-calling was a one-way street with Dad.

The frames had grooves on the sides for inserting test lenses.

Dent selected two lenses with his nicotine-stained fingers and slipped them into the grooves.

'H-h-h-how's that?'

'Still blurry.'

He added more lenses.

'B-b-b-better or w-w-w-worse?'

It wasn't only better; it was brilliant. The lower letters on the eye chart had clearly defined edges. A thrill went through me. It was like finding a ten-dollar note on the footpath.

'B-b-b-better.' I should've turned around before I tried any funny business. The Magoo glasses would've provided an excellent view of my father striding across the room towards me. The smack across the back of my head made the lenses rattle inside the frames.

'That's enough.'

'But you talked like—'

'I said that's enough!'

Dent put a hand up. 'J-J-J-James, your boy's sh-sh-sh-short-sighted. H-h-h-he probably can't r-r-r-read the blackboard at sc-sc-sc-school.'

The doctor wrote out a lens prescription and arranged to meet Dad at the pub later. We drove in silence to the optometrist. Dad must've been thinking about what Dent had said and was unusually kind when we reached the shop. He told me I could choose any pair of frames I wanted. It was like being told I could have the best callipers money could buy. I trawled the racks several times, finally narrowing the choice down to two models. My heart said yes to a pair of blue frames with gold rivets on the sides. These were the signature candelabra of fashion frames. Another part of me, the part that read *Celebrity Glitter*, said yes to simple black plastic frames, not unlike the signature spectacles of Yves Saint Laurent. I showed Dad the two options.

He raised his eyebrows and jabbed a finger at the blue frames. 'Put those back on the ladies' rack, right this minute!'

Mum said I needed a signature tune to go with my trademark frames. I sang her Frank Sinatra's 'My Way' as we drove to the optometrist to pick up the glasses, stretching out the last 'waaaaay' until my voice disappeared for lack of air. We were both excited about my new style accessories. Mum agreed they'd give my face a certain something. I told her that certain something was '*Je ne sais quoi*'. That's what all the stars had, according to *Celebrity Glitter*.

The woman behind the counter was chewing something when we entered the shop and seemed irritated by our arrival. She located my glasses on a shelf under the counter and jerked them out of their case. As she handed them to Mum I realised with horror I'd made a big mistake. They were not Yves Saint Laurent. The frames were too circular and chunky for Yves. The lenses were thick and convex. The overall effect was like a party novelty, the sort of thing that went with a plastic nose and moustache.

'Mum, my eyes have cleared up. I think we should get our money back.'

'What? Now you'd prefer a white stick or Labrador?' She laughed and elbowed me.

I didn't smile back. The situation was critical. I couldn't accept novelty glasses. I wanted to be a celebrity, not a clown.

'I didn't want to tell you this, Mum, but last Sunday I looked at the statue of Mary in Our Lady of Miracles. She was crying real tears. Then suddenly I could see everything perfectly. Even those little hairs inside Father McMahon's nose.'

My mother shuddered. 'Why don't you just try them on, Julian.'

The woman behind the counter sniffed with impatience. She wasn't interested in Christian miracles. She was as hard as they came, probably Protestant. I was going to tell my mother as much as soon as we got our money back and left the premises.

Mum slipped the glasses over my nose and tucked the arms behind my ears. I blinked and gasped in surprise. A rack of Albert Tatlock frames came into view. So did a poster behind the woman. It wasn't a scene of Japanese maple leaves but an aerial photo of the Disney castle in Bavaria. Turning, I looked out of the shop window and saw a small dog lift its leg against a tyre. A woman walked past pulling a wailing child by the arm. It was magic. I could see everything in detail. I looked back at the saleswoman and noticed a wiry mole on her neck. On the bench behind her was a half-eaten sandwich. In the mirror, I could see someone in a shamrock-green T-shirt wearing big black glasses. It was me and I looked like Nana Mouskouri. My heart sank.

'So, do they make a difference?' My mother had her hands extended in front of her. She did this when she was going to adjust my shirt or give my hair a ruffle. Her head was tilted to one side.

'Not one bit.' I tapped the lens with a fingernail. 'Total waste of money.'

The saleswoman snapped the glasses' case closed and handed it to my mother with the prescription. 'We don't do returns on prescription glasses. A lot of work's gone into grinding those lenses.' She pointed to me. 'Very necessary with the sort of eyes your boy's got.'

My mother's head jerked back to upright position. 'There's nothing wrong with my son's eyes.'

It was a ridiculous response but my mother did this when I was under threat. It was one of the things I liked most about her. Mum's hand landed between my shoulder blades and I was propelled out into the real world, a world that suddenly had shapes and textures. I left the glasses on as we drove home. They made me feel disoriented and dizzy, but the thrill of being able to see was worth the carsickness. I could read names on letterboxes and see merchandise in shop windows.

'You know who those glasses remind me of?' Mum knew I was disappointed.

'I hate myself and want to die.'

'Roy Orbison.'

'That cheers me up.'

'Sammy Davis Jr has black frames, too, and he's part of the Rat Pack.'

'He's the smallest member.'

'Don't forget Rolf Harris.'

'You're not cheering me up.'

'Norman had glasses when he was your age.'

Mum pulled up at traffic lights next to the Whipper Snapper fish-and-chip shop. I was looking at people waiting in cars when my heart skipped a beat. Elizabeth Taylor was sitting in the passenger seat of an orange Chrysler Valiant! There was even something sparkly around her neck. It had to be the Cartier. I waved. She waved back. The lights changed and my mother put her foot down. I was about to tell Mum when I saw David Niven heading toward us in an old Vauxhall. I took the glasses off and rubbed my eyes.

A letter from the United States of America was waiting for me when I got home.

Dear Fan and Friend,

We're delighted by your interest in the official Liz Taylor International Fan Club. You're one of thousands of fans around the world following Liz's sparkling career.

Full membership in the official Liz Taylor fan club is just ten American dollars per year. For this nominal fee you receive a fan-club badge and certificate. Naturally, you also get our quarterly Liz Taylor fanzine, *Liz, Camera, Action!*

We look forward to hearing from you soon.

Don't forget to include your money order for club membership.

Yours truly,

Barbara Bushel

President of the official Liz Taylor International Fan Club

The envelope contained a studio photo of a young Liz Taylor with her arm around a dog's neck. There was also a quote from one of her movies: "'It's a very odd feeling – to be someone's God." Liz Taylor as Kathie Merrick in *The Courage of Lassie*.'

9

Mum and Dad were having money problems. Dad said his problem was having to support a moaning wife and three thankless children. Mum said the problem was his having to support his drinking and horse-racing habits. She went out one day and got herself a job on the production line at the Tassie Textiles factory. We were each given a set of keys to the back door and warned not to let strange men or brush salesmen into the house.

Mum's timing was unhelpful for my career aspirations. I'd just decided to take up tap-dancing after watching Gene Kelly with an umbrella and required her encouragement on the old heel-toe routine. Her abrupt decision left me high and dry. In one fell swoop I'd lost both my impresario and audience.

I struggled to adjust to this sudden loss. Mum had always been there for me after school. She was my cheerleader and I was her beauty consultant. The focus of our relationship shifted once she started work. She was tired after a day at the factory and wasn't as switched into my pizzazz or the Golden Microphone. I had to work like hell to make her laugh or get a 'Twinkle' out of her and, even worse, I lost my only beauty client. I knew better than to touch Mum in front of Dad. Whenever I got her alone, I did my best to fluff and style but this didn't give me the same satisfaction.

One day, in a moment of desperation, I bribed Carmel with a family block of Shelby's to sit for me. I hadn't even put all the curlers in her hair when she finished the chocolate and shook them all out. I let her go without a squeak of protest. She was now an active member of the girls' cricket and hockey teams. She and her friends had budding breasts and thick arms. They openly smoked cigarettes and rode their bicycles everywhere in third gear. Boys were frightened of them.

A couple of dismal months had to drag by before I could appreciate the benefits of not having parents around. Under the new arrangement, no one knew what time I came home and no one told me what to do when I got there. While I enjoyed this new freedom and the extra television-viewing it permitted, I still craved an audience.

I'd started taking French at school. It was one of the elective culture lessons set aside for the last hour of every Friday. The choices were limited: debating, charity work, Bible study, crochet or French. When I discovered that boys were excluded from the crochet class, I chose French. It was not only the language of Brigitte Bardot but it also did something nice to the back of my throat. The lesson was taught by a big friendly woman with the unlikely name of Mrs French. Most of the vocabulary we learned was related to food and restaurants: my kind of language.

Jimmy Budge had also chosen French. He lived around the corner from us in a notorious bungalow in Wallaby Place. People stopped at the Budge hedge and shook their heads. Jimmy's father was a quiet-spoken widower but a sore point with the mothers of the neighbourhood because he bred and raced pigeons. His birds flew over our houses as a massive cloud to land on his front lawn in a grey flutter of feathers. People didn't like the pigeons. There was talk of disease and droppings.

My father said Mr Budge's hacking cough was pigeon-fancier's lung and warned me not to get too friendly with his birds. I liked Mr Budge. He was a vast improvement on Dad. He was a friendly man and never told kids off.

Jimmy was probably the best-looking boy in our school. His sandy-blond hair was faultless and flopped perfectly over his eyes, which were slightly different colours. He told me that one eye was green with envy because the other was blue. 'That's what my father says. He's got the same genetic defect. Bung eyes and lungs run in the family.' I started walking home with him after school on Fridays.

On the third Friday, I stopped in front of our gate and invited him into the garage. 'You want to see my amphitheatre?'

I had a feeling about Jimmy Budge. It was the way his eyes had shone when he repeated '*La cuisine de la France*' for Mrs French.

I'd created the amphitheatre behind the firewood in the garage. From the outside it looked like a normal stack of wood but inside it was a private chamber with bedding and other personal comforts. It was where I kept my valuables and ate contraband.

The only way to get inside this secret chamber was to climb up the exposed timber framework of the garage wall and jump. I did this and disappeared from Jimmy's view. He scrambled up the wall after me and watched as I stripped off my clothes. I was twirling my underpants in my hand when he jumped into the amphitheatre, peeling off his clothes with the efficiency of a German tourist.

I'd learned all about the German enthusiasm for nudity while staying at the Bland holiday cabin. From a sand hill, I'd observed a couple of tourists prepare for sunbathing by removing all their clothing except for their socks and sandals.

*   *   *

My father should've been happy that Mum had a job but he was more disagreeable than ever. Mum said he lacked pizzazz. He certainly had no interest in music or show business. The only celebrities he appreciated were famous thugs who played sports. At least since the Dent diagnosis he'd stopped harassing me about ball games. My Nana Mouskouris confirmed for him that I wasn't quite right and he now avoided eye contact. This was fine by me. He'd diverted his attention to John who'd come up with the insane idea of becoming a doctor and started doing homework every evening after school. John thought this choice of career made him superior and Dad seemed to agree.

They could keep each other as far as I was concerned. I had better things to do. Jimmy had put in a word with the distributor of *The Bugle* and I'd started delivering newspapers with him in the mornings. Within a couple of months I'd lost weight and looked almost normal when I held in my stomach. I had to get up at five in the morning but the job gave me freedom and power. For the first time in my life I had real coinage in my pocket and no longer had to play Dad like a fiddle to get a dollar. I could buy what I liked and be as thankless as I pleased.

Some of these earnings I invested in a joint project with Jimmy: a fort based in the overgrown conifer hedge of an abandoned house. Only we didn't call it a fort. We were too mature for that. It was a club. Using Dad's chicken chopper, we'd hollowed out the hedge to create a spacious inner sanctum. This we furnished with a boat tarpaulin we'd found at the dump and some old cushions my mother was throwing away. We'd then created a ceiling with black polythene and hung some sheets from Jimmy's house to create a Lawrence of Arabia effect. Our club was both private and secret. The only way to access it was by crawling underneath prickly conifer branches. We made sure no one saw us enter or leave.

The club became a busy nude and leisure centre after I recruited two boys from school, David Perk and Grant Humber. I'd figured these two out on the sports field. Like me, they regularly forgot their sports clothes and spent the phys. ed. hour in punishment, doing laps of the cricket pitch with a weighted medicine ball. Brother Punt was too stupid to realise that some of us preferred this activity to the real punishment of regular sports. It certainly beat kicking a leather bladder around a football field with a bunch of thugs on our backs.

As club founders, Jimmy and I got to make the rules. The first thing we did was appoint ourselves to executive posts and give the club a name: the JCJB Club. The next rule was another of my ideas. An entertainment hour was established and club members were obliged to either participate or listen. I got to sing Frank Sinatra and Jimmy did Sammy Davis Jr. Grant Humber could whistle but the only thing David Perk could do was make fart noises by pressing a palm into his armpit and pumping his elbow up and down. A smoking-only policy was also established. I suggested we smoke French brands. Jimmy seconded my motion and we learned to smoke the hard way, choking on filterless Gauloises.

I was inside the club, dividing a packet into four piles, when I heard David Perk arrive.

'Corkle, let me in.'

A large, spiky tree branch functioned as the door to the club. It was easy to move from within but almost impossible from outside. This made the club impenetrable to intruders. One intruder I was particularly keen on repelling was John. I didn't want his sort making reports to Dad.

'Who goes there, fiend or foliage?'

'Corkle, you know exactly who goes here. It's me.'

'You know the rule. Say the code.'

'I forgot it.' He was starting to whine.

'No code, no entry. That's the rule.'

'Pore kwah?'

'That was last week's.'

'Pore kwah pah?'

'That was also from last week.'

'It's not fair, you change the code all the time. How can I remember French?'

I knew by now he'd be hopping from foot to foot with frustration. I'd let him hop a little longer. Perk was our least-appealing club member. He had a sneaky, unconvincing personality and had been cursed with the reddish curly hair and large dollopy freckles that were part and parcel of life as a gingernut. What Perkie lacked was *panache*. This was almost the same as pizzazz but with the added quality of French sex appeal. Jimmy and I used panache to rate boys at school. On the sexual panache scale I was nine and a half and Jimmy was nine. David Perk was somewhere between zero and one.

'French confuses the enemy.'

'What enemy, you wanker? You're just trying to be posh.'

'Grow up, Perk.'

'*Qu'est-ce que c'est?*' Jimmy had arrived and was waiting for the branch to be moved. He was the only one who remembered the passwords. Jimmy Budge understood the French Way. He read *Celebrity Glitter* and even looked like Alain Delon in *Girl on a Motorcycle* when he pouted.

I pulled back the branch and let them in. Perk came in scowling but Jimmy crawled up to me and kissed me on the lips. Jimmy couldn't get enough of my panache and I didn't blame him.

71

10

All the JCJB Club members were thirteen years old except for David Perk who had been held back a year and just turned fourteen. It was an exciting time to belong to a boys' club, especially one with a nudity theme. Fascinating things were happening to our bodies. We monitored each other with enthusiasm, noting growth spurts and key developments.

Our activities were conducted in utmost secrecy according to the golden rule: 'What goes on in the club, stays in the club.' I found this rule surprisingly easy to obey. My parents never asked what I did after school or noticed that I didn't bring friends home. They were too wrapped up in their own misery. My mother shuttled between Tassie Textiles and home and was always tired. The only real quality time we spent together any more was *The Dick Dingle Hour* when Mum joined me on the couch to eat her dinner off a tray. If I worked hard enough at it during the commercials, I could get her talking about me.

It was during a commercial break that Mum mentioned the changes taking place in my body: the down on my upper lip and unpredictable voice. There was something else, too, she said.

'You're glowing these days.'

'But I glowed before.'

'Yes but now you glow in a different way. What's going on with you?'

'Just warming up for the Tassie Wallaby. I'll need all the glow I can get.' I knew what was going on with me. It was Jimmy but this was not something my mother needed to know.

Mum's eyes lingered on me for a moment. Her hand reached out and swept the hair off my forehead as if to see me better. It was too much, her look. I turned back to the TV.

With a sigh, she got up and went to the dinette, closing the door behind her. I knew she was going to call Norman. She did this at least once a week, always in the evening and always before my father came home.

Dad shuttled between the newspaper office and the pub and only came home to eat, sleep and watch sports programmes. He'd become even more uncomfortable in the role of husband and father and was incapable of maintaining a consistent standard in either job slot. His efforts came in rare bursts of activity followed by long periods of disillusionment and apathy.

One night I was woken by a series of loud thumps that made the bed rattle against the wall. The thumps sounded dangerous, like an earthquake or a volcano blowing its top. I left a sleeping John to his fate and ran into the hall. Mum was running toward the lounge in her nightdress. We stopped at the doorway.

The floor was covered in rubble. The lounge suite and my mother's ornaments were white with plaster dust and bits of mortar. My father was standing with his back to us with a sledgehammer in his hand. He'd knocked a hole in the wall between the lounge and the sunroom. This small room had begun life as a veranda and been glassed in by the previous owner. It was the storage room for things that were never used like the barbecue and the beach umbrella.

'What on earth are you doing, Jim?' Mum laid a protective

arm over my shoulders. I leaned into her to make the most of it.

Unaware of our presence, Dad took another swing with the sledgehammer, knocking chunks of wall flying in all directions.

Mum raised a hand to her mouth like a megaphone and shouted, 'Oy! Dumbo!'

Dad turned, removing a pair of sound-absorbing ear muffs that he'd obviously borrowed from someone. The muffs were clean and professional-looking. All Dad's tools and equipment were old or rusty.

'What's all this?'

'I'm converting the sunroom into a bedroom. The boys need separate rooms.'

I stood up straight. I was getting my own room! Dad did care.

'John needs his own space for study.' He flashed a small-toothed smile. It was his stupid lop-sided *après*-pub smile. Dad could be uncharacteristically generous and optimistic when he was pissed.

'My Royal Albert is covered in dust.' Mum pointed to the tea set on the mantelpiece.

Dad was leaning on the sledgehammer, still grinning. 'Colleen Corkle, there are two frozen chickens in the deep freeze. Won the chook raffle tonight.'

Dad was a winner. The two chickens made up for the hole in the wall and the dust on the tea set. They gave their relationship hope.

'Why the hole?'

'That's the new doorway to Julian's room. I'm going to block the side by the dinette.'

It was true. I *was* getting my own room. Dad should've won the chook raffle more often. We definitely needed a colour television.

'How long is this going to take?'

'It'll be all done in a week. Mark my words.'

It took over a month and a concerted effort on the parts of John and myself. It was the only time we'd ever worked as a team. We were both relieved when Dad finally put down his paintbrush and told us to wash it and put the tools away.

I finally had my own space. No more dirty football boots and no more of my brother's foul personality. John never hit me; my mother made sure of that. But enduring his constant jibes and sullen moods was worse than taking a punch from Carmel.

My new room was going to be spotless and decorated in grand fashion. The first thing I needed was curtains. The sunroom's large picture windows were nice but privacy was essential. Mum said she could get polyester off-cuts from work and run me up curtains on her Bingo sewing machine. I suggested I pay half and we buy real fabric from the Blue Gum Plaza department store. I wanted proper drapes with a bedspread to match. My decorating efforts at the club had sparked an interest in interior decor. If my stage and screen ambitions didn't pan out, interior designer was an excellent back-up career.

The fabric department was one of the most inspiring places in Ulverston. It was stacked with bolts of multicoloured material and managed by a well-groomed man in tailored clothes. Every woman worth her Bingo bought her dressmaking supplies from Des. He had shiny white satin for confirmation frocks and large bridal gown patterns for last-minute weddings. Local women treated Des like a god in his fabric department and then walked out and gossiped about him behind his back. Most agreed he was one of *those*. This annoyed my mother who liked to point out that Des was married. The more malicious gossips would then remind Mum that Des didn't have children.

I observed the goings-on with a wary eye and didn't add fabric floor manager to my list of back-up career possibilities.

I'd seen Des a few times and knew for a fact that he was one of those. He wore colourful shirts and a gold signet ring on his marriage finger. I recognised a kindred spirit when Mum took me to select the fabric for my bedroom.

'How can I be of service today, Colleen? I see you've got a new man in your life.'

Mum laughed as he kissed her French style on either cheek and told her she looked as beautiful as ever. I'd done her hair before leaving home and matched her handbag and shoes. Des was wearing a silky kingfisher-blue shirt that was open at the collar. I noticed the glint of a medallion. Mum put a hand on my head and ruffled my hair.

'Julian's choosing fabric for his curtains and bedspread.'

'What kind of theme do you want for your *chambre de lit*?' Des looked directly into my eyes, something adults tended to avoid doing. 'Are you a space traveller, a cowboy or a dandy, young man?'

I'd never had a grown-up ask my opinion before, especially not the French Way. Adults generally told me off or told me what to do.

'I'd like something . . .' I looked at Mum and then at Des. They were actually waiting to hear what I had to say. '. . . something silky. You know, something that fluffs out in the wind.' I moved my arms in a billowy way. There, I'd said it.

Des smiled. 'Wonderful. You're a gentleman like myself. We have some lovely jersey silks over here.'

He pointed to a shelf with bolts of soft David Bowie leotard material. I'd recently discovered David Bowie and decided he was the most beautiful man in the world. The jersey silk had a silvery gloss on one side. Mum coughed.

'Julian, let's not get your father started.'

'But, Mum, it's just right. David Bowie's a big fan of this stuff and he's famous. He's got a feature in *Celebrity Glitter*.' I knew she was right, of course. My father would have a fit.

Des must've seen a bit of this in his fabric department.

'I see your son's got an artistic temperament.' He said this without a hint of sarcasm and gave my mother a conspiratorial nod. 'Let's avoid fabrics with a more obvious *éclat*. For a bedspread, I personally love the jacquard. It has a motif but is very understated. We have it in a range of colours. Here, young man, run your hand over this.'

Des held it out for me to touch. It was soft and luxurious. I pointed to the fuchsia and looked at my mother. She shook her head.

'Why not go for blue? It appeals to the masculine eye even in this lovely aqua shade.' Des was pointing to a bright turquoise blue. 'Now, if you team this with, say, a brocade curtain in royal blue, you've got an interior design that says male but male *à la mode*.' He made a *grrr* sound like a tiger. I thought of Jimmy Budge and wished he was with me. He would've loved Des.

The brocade was going to billow out like Hollywood curtains. Any fool could see that. And it was shiny around the little dragon designs. An idiot like Dad would look at it and see navy blue. Men *à la mode* would notice the shiny dragon highlights and fluid texture of the material. My chest was warm and tight as we left the department store. Mum saw me smiling.

'Twinkle, twinkle.' She started the car engine then reached out to squeeze my knee. 'Happy?'

'Yes, Mum, it's perfect.'

'Des is quite special.'

'He's very nice, Mum.' This was an understatement. The man was a saint.

'I don't know what I would've done without him when I got married. It all had to be arranged so fast and I was in no state to do anything. All I could think about was the Golden Microphone. I was so disappointed. Des and Norm took over. Des took care of the wedding dress while Norman made all the reception arrangements.'

'Des knows Norman?' This was news to me.

Mum didn't hear me. She was studying the road ahead with a tight unhappy expression.

Norman was one of several subjects that were off-limits in our house. Dad only ever mentioned him with a snigger or scowl and Mum went vague and defensive whenever his name was brought up. Sex education was another touchy area. My parents left this business to the school and the school left it to my imagination. Any research on the matter had to be done quietly and on my own time.

I knew the testicles were important. I'd tried to tell Carmel that a thousand times. I'd just learned they were capable of producing enough sperm to populate six towns every minute. It was there in black and white in the medical book I'd consulted in the Ulverston Municipal Library. The testicles churned out fifty thousand sperm every sixty seconds. If I used each of these for the purpose proposed by the Catholic Church, I could more than replace the population of Ulverston every ten seconds. I moved in my seat to give my big boys more room.

To get into the adult section of the library, I'd had to pass the small sharp woman with glasses on the information desk. She'd been about to stop me when someone in the children's section let out a loud fart and a group of kids started laughing. The librarian shot out of her seat and marched over to the source of the noise. I slipped into the adult section and went directly to the S shelf where I selected a book entitled *Sexual Organs at a Glance*. I sat discreetly at a corner table, trying to look as serious and adult as possible, then got down to some serious research. Just the day before, I'd had my first ejaculation. The book explained that I'd lost between eighty million to three hundred million sperm. My first impulse was to mourn such a loss but the sheer scale of the massacre made me feel important.

Someone coughed behind me.

'What are you reading?'

I turned and discovered a skinny boy of about sixteen looking over my shoulder. I couldn't tell whether he was one of the staff or a library user. He had oily hair and pimples and wore a checked shirt with the buttons done up all the way to the collar. His hands were in the pockets of his beige cone-stud stretch trousers.

'I'm doing a science project for school.'

'Science? Isn't that human reproduction?' He leaned over me and tapped a finger on the diagram of sperm.

'We're doing a project on the penis.'

'What school do you go to?'

'Pendergast School for Boys.' I chose a private Anglican school to be safe.

'That'd be right. It's a boarding school, isn't it?'

'Yeah, my parents live on a big cattle station north of Adelaide. That's why they sent me to boarding school. The station is a really big one with a homestead and a veranda. We have a dog called Flossie and there are kangaroos and cockatoos. And budgies, of course.'

'What's it like exactly?'

'I've kind of described it already. It's very big and we have cows – er, beef cattle and all that.'

'No, the school. What's it like in the dormitories?' The youth moved from side to side, rocking on his heels. His hands were agitated inside his pockets. 'Do the boys doss in together?'

'No.' I was now sure he wasn't a librarian. 'We have separate beds. Kapok mattresses on wire-wove springs. Lumps as big as duck eggs.'

'I've heard some stories about those dormitories.'

'What kind of stories?'

'About the prefects. How they . . . you know.'

'No.'

'How they creep into the dormitories at night and rape boys in the bottom.' He was talking rapidly in a hoarse whisper. Moisture had collected on the fine stubble above his lip. 'I'm sure you know better than me.'

'I don't know what you mean.'

I knew exactly what he meant. My father had warned me about his kind often enough. I was not supposed to take rides in his Hillman Hunter or accept boiled sweets or chocolate. I was supposed to be afraid of him. I wasn't. The teenager probably didn't have a car or anything other than his hands in his pockets. He wouldn't have belonged to a club or had a boyfriend. He was lonely, even pitiful. I felt sorry for him.

'You know, in the bottom.' He tapped the diagram of the penis then twisted around to point at his bottom.

'Oh, that? Yeah, that happened to Ralph Waters.' I said this quietly for effect.

'This Ralph character was a party to this business?'

I lowered my voice even further. 'He asked for it.'

'In the bottom?' The youth was moving his hands about in his pockets, shifting from foot to foot.

'It happened in the showers.'

'You boys shower together?'

'The prefects make us share the nozzle.'

This was too much information for the youth. He groaned and moved off rapidly without saying goodbye.

Back at the club, I relayed the information about ejaculation to the others. We'd now all mastered the climax except for David Perk. I was sure he was giving himself hell at home but he was a painfully slow developer. Even his ginger pubic hair was sparse. David was shy and always sat in the darkest area of the club after removing his clothes.

Pubic hair was an obsession for me. It was like panache. You either had it or you didn't. I watched mine develop with impatience and monitored the hair growth of all the boys at school. Most of my research was carried out on Saturdays with Jimmy Budge at the Ulverston Municipal Baths. There were no partitions in the pool's changing room, which made it difficult for boys to undress in a modest manner. Jimmy and I had a name for the room: the Pubic Hair Hall of Fame. The one boy I desperately wanted to see naked was Peter Grubb. He was a footballer with a deep voice and hairy legs, one of the most well-developed boys in our year. Peter Grubb had glamour.

'Grubbsie's climbing on to the diving board.' I pointed to the deep end of the pool.

Jimmy and I were in the middle of the pool where we'd been practising back flips. I still couldn't spin backward without getting water up my nose and a chlorine-perfumed sinus headache. Jimmy could do two flips in a row without coming up for air. He was sure to achieve the punishing triple backward flick-roll by the end of summer.

'So what?' Jimmy was treading water yet somehow managed to shrug his shoulders. He reached out underwater and playfully pinched my bum. I pushed his hand away and pointed to Peter Grubb.

'Look at his hairs.'

'Others have got hairs.'

'Yeah, but Grubbsie's got real ones. The hairs frill out from underneath his bathers.'

'Mine do that, too, if I pull my bathers up.'

'I'd like to see him without his bathers. I bet he's huge.'

'A huge wanker.'

'I'm going over to the diving board.'

'But you can't even dive.'

I dog-paddled to the deep end and clung to the side for a moment. With one hand under the water, I tugged the front of my bathers down. As I climbed up the ladder, they sagged below my abdomen to expose a moustache of pubic hair. I walked casually up to the diving board and stood to the side, watching the boys run and dive off. Jimmy had followed me to the deep end and was in the water near the diving board, close enough for his voice to ring out like the Sunday service bark of Father McMahon.

'Look at Corkle trying to show off his new pubes!'

All the boys waiting by the diving board turned and laughed. Grubbsie hesitated. He looked down at me and smiled before diving off the end of the board and slipping into the water with a perfect *plop*. I ran to the side of the pool and jumped in, hugging my legs to create a pocket of air under my knees. My bomb sent a wall of water over Jimmy's face. I loved Jimmy Budge but sometimes he was just too much. He was like my mother. He knew me too well.

11

Singing was part of the Catholic way. You had to do it in church and religion class but it wasn't meant to be enjoyable. There was nothing original about the hymns we had to sing, no glamour and no entertainment value. Mum called church singing 'a foundation' and liked to remind me that Frank Sinatra was a Catholic. But Ol' Blue Eyes had lost some of his gold dust for me since I'd discovered David Bowie. Bowie was my new god, a passion I shared with Jimmy Budge. We'd both bought turntables with paper-round money and both owned all his albums. I played *Hunky Dory* at least thirty times a day. I sang his songs out loud on my bike in the mornings and performed them for the boys at the club in the afternoons.

St Kevin's had a choir but it wasn't something a sensible person would join. Thomas Owen had actually auditioned for it and been rejected. The choir was led by the most sadistic of all the Christian Brothers, Brother Dooley.

I was surprised to bump into Thomas coming out of the music room with the red cheeks of a chorus girl. He was such an earnest loser.

'Hi, Thomas. I thought you didn't get into the choir.'

'Brother Dooley said I could still participate.'

'You sing?'

'Brother Dooley says I'm tone deaf. I'm allowed to follow the words with my lips as long as no sound comes out.'

'Dooley's a bastard.'

'I don't think you should use that word.'

'I think Dooley is that word.'

'What word would that be, Corker?'

It was Brother Dooley. He'd sneaked out of the music room and was standing behind me with a smug expression. Dooley loved catching criminals in the act. He crept around the school corridors collecting swearers and chewers and then marched them off to his special cloakroom for a hiding. In the real world, Dooley would've been a laughing stock. His shoulders were almost non-existent and his pelvis jutted out like a dinghy's bow, a body shape that earned him the nickname of the Human Question Mark. Despite these obvious shortcomings, Dooley enjoyed the status of God in the Catholic school environment where he could pick and choose among hundreds of boys to beat and humiliate.

'That word would be impresario, sir, but Thomas doesn't think I should use foreign words to describe you.'

'Is that right, Thomas?' Dooley's left eye blinked like a camera shutter.

Thomas looked at me, then at Brother Dooley, then back to me. He silently opened and shut his mouth in choir-practice style, and then nodded. The brother lingered, looking at me through narrowed eyes, before moving off to the toilet block. He didn't like me and the feeling was mutual. I hated his weekly hour of religion. The hymns were old-fashioned songs that had been written by madmen.

The next time I crossed Brother Dooley was in religion class. I should've known he had it in for me and simply mouthed words like Thomas. But I was too much a showman to do something sensible and Dooley happened to choose the Prayer of St Francis: 'Make me a channel of your peace; where there is hatred let me bring your love.' I'd created my own version of the prayer and performed it whenever I had an audience: 'Make me a flannel for your penis; where there is mayhem let me bring your rub.'

Jimmy elbowed me but I could tell he was proud. All the boys around us were laughing. I had them eating out of my hand.

'Corker, get to the back of the class.' Brother Dooley's left eye blinked dangerously. He couldn't hear what I was singing but he knew by the boys' reaction that I was up to something.

I moved near the back but was too fired up by the boys' response to stop. Even Ralph Waters was sniggering. I sang louder. 'Make me a flannel of your penis . . .'

Boys turned, snickering. Jimmy looked back at me and shook his head. Brother Dooley called out again.

'Corker, get outside.'

From the doorway I sang even louder, driving the boys into a frenzy. I was laughing so hard I didn't see Brother Dooley until he was standing in front of me blinking and twitching. He grabbed the back of my shirt and, half lifting, half pushing, hurled me into the cloakroom where he kept his strap.

The walloping I received should've put me off singing forever but I was too deeply involved with David Bowie to let a killjoy like Dooley silence the Songbird of the South. I'd pinned a life-size poster of Ziggy Stardust in a leotard to the ceiling of my bedroom. Every night, I removed this leotard in my mind's eye and ran my hands over his pale, hairless body. I knew Jimmy did the same thing every time he climbed into bed. He had the same poster pinned to his ceiling. David Bowie was our official mascot, ten out of ten on the panache scale. We used him as a yardstick to measure the value of anything male.

Carmel had no idea of my close relationship with Bowie but she did share my enthusiasm for his music. The one thing we still did together was listen to Port Sounds every Friday when the radio station ran a pop quiz. I was grilling two pieces of cheese on toast when the DJ asked listeners for the birth names of Elton John and David Bowie. I ran to the phone.

'Grooving Port Sounds radio. Your name is . . . ?'

'Julian Corkle.'

'Mr Corker. If you can tell me the names correctly, you'll receive two tickets to the big concert in Ulverston.'

My chest felt as if it was going to burst. David Bowie and Elton John were coming to Ulverston!

'It's Corkle.'

'Sorry, that's not correct.'

'No, that's my name. I'm Julian Corkle. Their names are Reginald Kenneth Dwight and David Robert Hayward-Jones.' I hoped every kid at St Kevin's was tuned into Port Sounds.

'Mr Corker, you've just won yourself two tickets to the Ulverston Town Hall this Saturday.'

Carmel looked over at me as she removed the smoking cheese toasties from the grill. There was new respect in her eyes.

Jimmy Budge agreed that the Port Sounds studio was the Paramount Studios of Ulverston as we pushed through the main doors. It was the perfect place for someone with my kind of panache, he said. I put on a swagger and approached the plump blonde receptionist. She was looking at herself in a pocket mirror and didn't acknowledge our presence.

'My name's Julian Corkle and I've come to pick up my tickets to the big concert.' I turned to wink at Jimmy. 'I won them.'

The young woman stopped applying lipstick with a sigh and vaguely consulted a list on her desk.

'No tickets here for Corkle.' She looked back to the mirror and resumed her make-up business.

'But they told me they'd be at reception.' My voice went high at the end.

'They're not.' She said this without looking our way.

'I have to get my tickets.' Panic was making it hard to breathe.

The woman began applying blue eye shadow with a small fluffy stick.

'Try looking under Corker.' Jimmy Budge's adolescent voice started as a growl and ended high. He moved to the side of the desk and glared at her.

The woman gave a squawk of surprise and raked her make-up into a pile with her fingertips.

Jimmy didn't move. 'I said look under Corker.'

Her eyes darted from Jimmy to the list. They widened. She removed an envelope from a box and threw it in my direction. It fluttered to the floor in front of me. 'Why didn't you say Corker in the first place?'

'Why don't you learn some manners, you stupid mare.' Jimmy snatched up the envelope and pulled me out of the studio.

I ripped it open and held up the two tickets, dancing around him and waving my fists in the air.

'Hang on, Julian, I thought you said it was an Elton John and David Bowie concert.' He'd taken the tickets and was examining them.

'I had to give their names.'

'It's a Rolf Harris concert.' Jimmy glanced back at the glass doors with a frown.

There it was in black and white: 'Rolf's Big Aussie Sunset Spectacular'. I wanted to cry. A Rolf Harris concert was not something for boys our age. Rolf was too friendly, too much like family-approved fun. Jimmy put his arm around my shoulders as we walked away from the station. He didn't say anything until we reached the bus stop.

'It's a funny thing but Peter Grubb will probably be at that damned concert.' Jimmy turned to read the bus timetable.

'Peter Grubb the footballer?'

'He's a big Harris fan. You wouldn't expect it from such a hairy bastard.' Jimmy said this without looking at me. He was running a finger down the timetable. 'You could probably give the tickets to Perkie or Humdinger.'

I hesitated.

'They'd love a freebie.'

'Nah, they wouldn't appreciate it. We should probably go ourselves. I won those tickets fair and square.'

Mr Budge dropped us off at Jubilee Park in his Ford Cortina. Jimmy had dressed up for the event in a pair of baby-blue Grouse cords and a clingy turquoise stretch shirt. He looked very French with his perfect hair slicked back and a hanky in his pocket. The woman in the ticket window raised her eyebrows as she clipped the tickets. I could tell she was impressed.

Jimmy smiled as we sat down in the front row. 'It's just like a real concert.'

The lights dimmed and a hum began. Rolf emerged in front of a faint orange glow and started singing 'Sun arise, she bring in the morning . . .'

I gripped Jimmy's hand as a spotlight fell on Rolf.

Jimmy squeezed back and moved closer in his seat.

The concert was magic, better than colour TV. We were so close we could see the zips and buttons on the outfits of the musicians. One of these was a trumpeter who moved his hips as he tooted. He had the lithe body of a dancer and a beautiful face with large soft lips. These he licked between blasts on his instrument. Rolf Harris didn't have the trumpeter's panache but he was an excellent showman. Near the end of the concert, he looked directly at Jimmy and me and announced: 'Listen to the music in your blood. Your heart has rhythm.'

We came away from the concert buzzing, pushing through the crowd until we hit the park grass and then started running. I was ahead of Jimmy with my chest out and arms pumping when he ankle-tapped me, sending me tumbling forward into a bed of municipal begonias. Jimmy fell on top of me with a thud. He pulled his face up from the fresh soil laughing. He had dirt up his nose and in his eyebrows. He looked stupid and adorable. I was sandwiched beneath him bucking with laughter when I heard three sharp blasts of a horn. Our new second-hand Holden Torana was parked on the other side of the flowerbed. Dad rolled down his window and called out.

'What the bloody hell do you think you're doing? Get in this bloody car at once!'

I went to see Mr Turtle after school on Monday. He taught the school band and wore plastic-soled suede shoes that squeaked on the parquet floor of the school hall. He was the father of the school's only accomplished musicians, Neville and Kelvin. The Turtle brothers were gangly and awkward like Thomas Owen but got away with it by playing the cornet like demons.

'Mr Turtle, I'd like to learn an instrument and join the band.' I arranged my hands and played a little air guitar for his benefit.

'How old are you, Julian?'

'Fourteen.'

'That's quite late to pick up an instrument.'

'There's music in my blood. I can feel it. My heart has rhythm.'

'Were you at the Rolf Harris concert?'

'What Rolf Harris concert?'

'Playing an instrument requires dedication. It's not as easy as it looks.'

'Dedication is my middle name.'

'Your middle name's Sidney.' It was Neville Turtle. He'd been lurking behind us, listening. I gave him a sharp look and turned back to the teacher.

'You've done a fine job with your sons, Mr Turtle. You can make something great out of me.'

He nodded and smiled modestly. We headed to the instrument room, squeaking our way across the school hall.

'For your first instrument, I suggest something not too ambitious.'

I pointed to the enormous bass tuba leaning against the wall. It was constructed like a factory smokestack. If I was going to play in a band, I wanted an instrument that said *player*.

'You think you can manage it, Julian? It's quite an ambitious choice.'

The instrument hadn't been used for a very long time and smelled of oxidised metal and pee. To get it home, I had to curl it over my shoulder and push my bike with one hand. Once there, I laid it in the bath and used toilet cleaner and John's Jethro Tull T-shirt to give the brass a shine. When I put the mouthpiece to my lips again, I tasted oxidised metal and toilet cleaner.

Mr Turtle shrugged indulgently and let me swap the tuba for a cornet. It was smaller than a trumpet but to an audience seated in front of a stage it would have the same sex appeal. I screeched away on it for two band sessions until Neville and Kelvin threatened to quit. Mr Turtle took me to the storeroom one last time, warning me that it was the last exchange. 'I'm not running a pawn shop here, young man.'

As soon as my eyes fell on the fancy cloth case, I knew I

wouldn't be swapping again. I'd found my Golden Microphone instrument: a spanking new trombone made of shiny musical brass. The instrument had never been used. Mr Turtle had led a vigorous fund-raising campaign to buy it and was very proud. He handed it to me with a tight smile.

The band practised in the school hall two evenings a week. For a month, I attended faithfully, riding my bike to the practice with the trombone balanced across my handlebars. I could've put the instrument in my newspaper saddlebags but no one would've seen it. The whole point of playing an instrument was to be a showman.

One evening I was running late and took a treacherous shortcut across the sun-baked lawn of the cricket pitch. I'd been at the club with Jimmy and Grant when I realised the time. We'd been talking about the defection of David Perk, who'd surprised us all by getting a girlfriend. She wasn't just any girl either but a stocky member of Carmel's hockey team.

I'd made it midway across the cricket pitch when I hit a wicket hole and the trombone slipped out of my grasp. It twirled around on the handlebars and fell forward. The bike came to an abrupt halt as it caught in the spokes and I was hurled forward at great speed like a slingshot missile.

When I got up, my knees and elbows were already starting to bleed. My bottom lip was numb and rapidly swelling into something enormous. The front wheel of my bike was bent away from the forks. The trombone lay in a clump of grass a couple of metres away. I walked over with fear banging inside my chest. The cloth case was bent like an old turned-up shoe. I didn't need to unzip it to know that its beautiful brass arm was bent at a forty-five-degree angle.

It was difficult enough to walk with my injuries let alone with a bent trombone and bike whose front wheel didn't turn.

I had to carry the trombone under my one good elbow and drag the bike behind me.

The band stopped midway through its third practice number when I opened the door of the hall. Neville Turtle pulled his cornet away from his mouth and pointed in my direction. Mr Turtle turned and took two squeaky steps toward me.

'Mr Turtle, I've had an accident.' My swollen lip muffled the words.

'The trombone . . . It's . . .' Mr Turtle's voice was shaky.

'Buggered!' The comment came from somewhere in the band.

'It was an accident, honest.' I was fighting back tears.

'Julian, I'm very disa . . .' Mr Turtle couldn't finish his sentence.

'Pissed off.'

The voice belonged to Ralph Waters. He had not been a member of the band for very long and been put in charge of the triangle and xylophone. Ralph wasn't band material but the Christian Brothers thought music therapy might do him some good. Mr Turtle had tried his best but when that failed, he removed all but five bars from the xylophone. Ralph's job was to hit the remaining bars on time and ding the triangle every now and then. He smirked at me and made a cutting motion across his neck with a finger.

I had blood streaming down both legs and elbows dripping red on the parquet. I ran my tongue over my huge, swollen bottom lip. Some dry blades of grass fell from the side of my face. Mr Turtle squeaked the remaining steps over to me and took the trombone from my one good hand, cradling it like a baby. 'I'm afraid your musical career is finished, young man. I'm very, very disappointed.'

A tear escaped. I loved the band, with its shiny brass horns and pretty wooden string instruments. I thought of Tania from

Geelong and turned away to hide my tears. She'd won the Golden Microphone award for her trombone medley of Herb Alpert and the Tijuana Brass tunes.

Mum was going to be disappointed. So was Jimmy.

12

The club was falling apart and I'd lost the trombone but at least I still had Jimmy Budge. Jimmy and I liked the same TV programmes and read the same magazines. We shared the same taste in music, fashion and celebrities. What I liked, Jimmy liked. Our latest obsession was Maria Callas, who was basically Elizabeth Taylor with the voice of an angel. She was not only beautiful and talented but she was also tragic and formerly plump. Her heart-breaking affair with Aristotle Onassis fascinated me. So did her wealth and glamour. It was Maria Callas who inspired me to get to work on my vocal cords. Jimmy said the Songbird of the South would be good to go in six months. I just needed to master the warble.

It was Sunday night and I was in the kitchen warbling to my mother while she fried sausages when Dad came in and announced we were moving. He'd landed the sports editor's job at the *Hobart Star*. Trevor Bland had recently transferred to the paper and put a word in.

'It'll do the family the world of good.' Dad had the confident grin of at least four Tickworth lagers.

'But Carmel and Julian will have to change schools.' Mum turned the hotplate off and placed a hand on my forearm. 'All their friends are here.'

'Hobart's the state capital. They'll make new friends.' Dad didn't care that he made no sense. 'It's a step up the ladder. I'll be making more money.'

'I don't know, Jim. It's all so sudden.'

'Too late now. The deal's done.' He gave Mum a hard look. It was like an accusation. 'I thought you'd be pleased. We'll be closer to John.'

John was already living in Hobart where he was a first-year student at Wattle University. He had a room in the university dormitories.

'But you've got two other children.'

'You don't think I've thought of that?' Dad smiled triumphantly. 'Hobart's got a brilliant women's cricket team.'

That was it. The family was moving. We had two weeks to say our goodbyes and prepare for a new life on the other side of the island. Dad put our house on the market and went on ahead to start the job and find us somewhere new to live.

Everything I knew about Hobart had come from school lessons and TV. It had Tasmania's state government and Mount Wellington. It also had a floral clock and a harbour big enough for a luxury liner and fleet of fishing trawlers. The Abracadabra television studio was based in Hobart along with at least five radio stations. It was home to the state's politicians and celebrities. Dick Dingle lived in a big fancy mansion in Battery Point.

I couldn't imagine leaving Ulverston, or, more to the point, I couldn't imagine life without Jimmy Budge. My mind had flashed to him when Dad made his announcement. I would've immediately dashed over to the Budge house but Jimmy wasn't there. His father had taken him to Devonport for the sheep trials. The next time I'd see him would be Tuesday morning for the paper round.

Monday was almost unbearable. I trudged around the

grounds at St Kevin's on my own feeling numb. The school didn't have the smart brick buildings of Pendergast or the swimming pool of a state school but I knew every student and teacher by name. I was passing the old half-buried white tyres when Ralph Waters called out, 'Hey, Four-Eyes!' It was a friendly enough greeting and I smiled. I'd started school with Ralph and watched him grow from delinquent into full-fledged thug. Ralph had never thumped me despite his flair for violence. Our early discussion about the Stromboli mound had established a code of honour between us. I watched him rap his knuckles on the back of Thomas Owen's head and realised I'd miss him. I'd miss Thomas, too. He'd joined the band and taken up the trombone after I'd been given my marching orders. The repaired instrument bore two small dents on the metal arm but Thomas didn't seem to mind.

By Tuesday morning, I was a bag of nerves. I looked over at Jimmy rolling papers and felt the weight of something hard and heavy in my chest.

'Jimmy, we're going to Hobart.' I kept my face down and shoved rolled papers into my saddlebag.

'Uh-huh.' Jimmy kept rolling.

'I mean we're leaving Ulverston.' I looked at him.

'For good, like?' Jimmy stopped rolling. He looked at me, sitting very still.

I felt a trickle of sweat under one of my armpits. It was hot in the office. My jaw stiffened and my mouth flooded with saliva. I felt like being sick. 'Dad's got a new job.'

'In Hobart?'

'He says Hobart's good for his career, and what's good for his career is good for the family. It's a career move. He'll make more money.'

'What about your mum? She's got a good job at Tassie Textiles.'

'She says Dad's having a mid-life crisis, and what's a crisis for him is a crisis for the family.'

'But your father could find another job in Ulverston. There's always the Wool Board. Dad says they get paid a whack at the Wool Board. It's criminal how much they make off the sheep's back.'

'Dad's already gone to Hobart to sort out a new house.'

'When are you leaving?'

'In thirteen days.' My voice was a whisper. 'You going to the club after school?'

Jimmy looked down at the papers. He took a long time to answer. 'Nah, can't today. I'm helping Dad with the pigeons.'

I realised then that he was very upset. Jimmy never said no.

Something rearranged itself inside my chest. It felt like a heavy stone tied to a piece of string. It swung painfully against my ribs.

13

Hobart

I knew we were in trouble at Waratah High School as soon as Dad drove off in his old dinged-up Chrysler Valiant. At least he hadn't tooted the horn. The kack-coloured car was a source of shame for Carmel and me. We'd named it Rusty after one of Dad's big kack-coloured sisters and tried to avoid all contact with the car. My father had bought it second-hand before leaving Ulverston and was proud of its horsepower. He said there was nothing wrong with a Valiant; we should be so lucky. When he was a kid, he'd walked everywhere in bare feet. On our last day at St Kevin's, he'd stopped at the main entrance and given the horn a couple of toots to make sure all the kids were looking. My father could be difficult sometimes.

As we crossed the courtyard to report to the main office, Carmel and I became aware that we were the only ones wearing school uniforms. Waratah High was a state school. It had a swimming pool but no uniform.

'Hey, it's the Girl Guides!' A big blond boy was standing in a shaded corner of the courtyard between two girls. 'Rub a couple of sticks together. Earn yourselves some badges. Ha, ha.'

Carmel stopped walking and held out her arm to prevent me from going further.

'We've got plenty of badges already. IQ tests.' She gave him her squinty-eyed cricket bowler's stare. 'But that sort of thing's probably over your head.'

The boy jerked his head and snorted.

'You deserve a badge for that pig snort.' Carmel sniggered.

'Lesbian!' The boy's voice was high and angry. One of the girls had laughed at Carmel's comment.

'I'd rather be a lez than a porker.'

I was stunned by my sister's recklessness. Girls weren't supposed to admit to the possibility of lesbianism. It was like admitting you had a black-and-white TV. Her response left the boy with nothing to say.

Waratah High was a rough inner suburban school populated by tough boys who did wheel stands on bicycles and girls who wore short skirts and fiercely plucked their eyebrows. The most dangerous of these inhabitants hung out under the gum trees at the edge of the cricket pitch.

The first week of school was dreadful, especially lunchtimes when my lack of friends was most obvious. I used the hour to observe the other students, trying to understand their hierarchy and social rules. I was also looking for the familiar but found no one like Jimmy or me. There was no colour or panache at Waratah. The boys were all dressed alike. Despite the free clothing code, nearly everyone wore Levi jeans and T-shirts. As soon as the lunch bell went, they scattered to take their places on the school grounds. The athletic kids charged off to the sports field while the Thomas Owen types drifted to the benches near the office. A handful of Gary Jings unfortunates sat on the fringe of this group or went to the library to read books. The sight of these loners made me carsick.

By the end of the week, I'd moved up benches from under

the office window to one near the playing fields. From here I watched the group at the edge of the cricket pitch.

I'd just eaten a Vegemite and lettuce sandwich and had closed my eyes to deal with its digestion. I hated Vegemite and lettuce but Mum had made my lunch and this was her idea of something healthy. I'd felt so depressed on the bench that I'd eaten it along with the apple she'd supplied.

'Poof!'

My eyes flicked open. Two thugs were standing in front of the bench. I was suddenly very aware of my magenta shirt and lime-green corduroys. At least I wasn't wearing Nana Mouskouris any more. Mum had agreed to new John Lennon frames before leaving Ulverston.

'We want a word with you.'

'I didn't do anything.' The voice of the boy beside me was high and fearful. His eyes darted wildly from the boys to the office and then to me. He'd never make the office and I was clearly no Carmel Corkle.

'What are you looking at, Pink Boy?' The taller of the thugs, a boy with sandy hair and spotty cheeks, had swung his attention to me.

'Nothing.' Blood pumped inside my ears. I looked down at the sandwich wrapper and prayed they'd leave me alone.

I stayed frozen to the bench as they grabbed the boy. There was a scuffle and his T-shirt ripped. I heard him protest then a slap. The boy cried out but I kept my eyes on the wrapper. When I finally looked up, he was being frog-marched across the cricket pitch. He glanced back at me and flashed a desperate look before they disappeared behind the gum trees.

For the next two days, the scene played over and over in my head. I'd never felt so frightened or alone in my life. I spent the weekend in my bedroom on the safety of my bed. The boy's parting look haunted me. The fear and shame it provoked in me overrode the loss I felt for Jimmy and Ulverston. It was as if a heavy woollen blanket had been thrown over me. The weight made it hard to breathe or move. The blanket reduced everything to the grey of an overcast day.

On Sunday evening, after *The Dick Dingle Hour*, Mum cornered me. 'What's up, honey? Missing Jimmy Budge?'

'No.' I couldn't tell her about the boy. I was too ashamed. I'd watched him walk to his doom without lifting a finger.

'Change is difficult. Just give it time.'

I was holding back tears and didn't say anything.

'You need some new friends. Just make a little effort. Take a few risks. You've got to show them how special you are.' She reached out and ruffled my hair. 'Twinkle, twinkle.'

On Monday morning I dressed in a pair of Levi jeans and one of John's old Rolling Stones T-shirts. Mum's pep talk about risks had prompted me to make a decision. I couldn't risk staying on the benches. They were far too dangerous. There was only one safe place at Waratah High.

When the lunch bell went, I threw my sandwiches into the bin and with a thumping heart crossed the playing field to the edge of the cricket pitch. Smoke was rising from the boys sitting along the fence under the gum trees. They looked at me as I pulled out a packet of Gauloises and lit a cigarette.

'The Girl Guide!' It was the big blond boy from the courtyard.

The boys next to him laughed on cue.

'Ha, ha.' I made a show of laughing at myself then took a very French drag on the cigarette. It was now or never. 'I've never been a member of any organisation apart from the Gun Club of Ulverston.'

'You belong to a gun club?' The boy stopped smiling.

'Belonged. My father was president and sharpshooter. I was an auxiliary member.'

'What's that?' The boy moved his bum on the fence, sending ripples along the wire under the other bums.

'I handled the bullets.'

'What are you smoking?'

'Just a French brand. Want one?'

He examined the cigarette for a filter then gave up and shoved an unfiltered end in his mouth. I struck a match and leaned over to light the cigarette. The air flew out of my lungs as he shoved me backward with brute force.

'What are you, a pooftah or something?'

The other boys stopped jiggling on the fence. My body froze.

'I was just lighting your smoke.' I could feel my heartbeat in the back of my throat. 'It's the French Way.'

He snatched the matches and lit the cigarette, inhaling deeply and holding the rough unfiltered smoke in his lungs. His eyes watered and his cheeks bulged. I could tell he was bursting to cough but he gritted his teeth and managed to resist. 'What's your name?'

'Julian Corkle.'

He spluttered. It was the cough he'd suppressed plus a nasty laugh that bubbled up his throat. The fence squeaked as the other boys joined in.

'His name's Wayne Hopper. I'm Christine Kandy. This is Cherie.'

I recognised the girls. They'd been in the courtyard with Wayne. It was Christine who'd laughed at the porker comment. She was a well-developed girl with a pretty face.

'Should be Christine Chastity Belt. That's what she needs.'

With a snort, Wayne leaned forward from the fence. He lifted

102

Christine's skirt to expose a pair of pastel pink underpants. She slapped his hand away, a playful slap without menace.

Wayne Hopper had magnetic animal confidence. His body was solid and muscular and his chin bore the stubble of a precocious shaver. He went everywhere with his two thuggish lieutenants, Ross Gibb and Paul Lamb, but was often surrounded by four or five boys. His appeal wasn't based on brains or charm. It was all about power.

Wayne was the man but it was his followers I had to watch. They were eager teenage boys competing for his approval. I knew they would go to any lengths to prove their loyalty. The dumbest yet most dangerous of the group was Paul Lamb. He was the thug who'd called me Pink Boy and it was he who watched me the closest, waiting for a mistake. Waratah was no place to be a Gary Jings. Neither was it safe to have panache. I had to forget about Ulverston and everything I'd left behind.

I willed myself to stop thinking about Jimmy Budge. Thoughts of Jimmy opened something vulnerable in me and I couldn't have that. When memories arose, I crushed them before my imagination could seize on them and add colour. I did the same with feelings about other boys. When something stirred, I squeezed my eyes shut and thought of Carmel in cricket shorts.

I focused my attention on David Bowie and made free with my mother's Dew Drops lotion. This relieved the urgent feelings of desperation but it didn't dull the ache in my chest. Not even David Bowie did that.

14

Life would not have been worth living if Dad had chosen an ordinary house but through some miracle he'd bought the best thing on Echidna Avenue. The house had started life as a simple Housing Commission home and undergone several flashy alterations. The backyard featured a pebbled barbecue area while the lounge was decked out with a fancy cocktail bar and fluffy stools. My father was particularly keen on the bar. It had black vinyl panels and a wood-grain Aussiemica top. The house was carpeted throughout with speckled Merino Dream shag pile and decorated with embossed wallpaper. There was even a Brady Bunch style rumpus room in the basement. To access this converted garage, a hole had been cut in the lounge floor and a spiral staircase had been installed.

For the first month in Echidna Avenue, Mum and Dad seemed almost happy. The move had shaken things up and made room for hope in their relationship. Their new bedroom helped. It had its own bathroom with mirrored shower doors and a row of mirrors over the basin. It was called The Ensuite and was the most beautiful thing we'd ever owned after the Royal Albert. Its mirrored shower was also excellent for masturbation purposes.

Not long after we moved in, Dad's older sister Dolly paid us a visit. Dolly had lived in Hobart for years and was the closest thing we had to family in the city. She was older than Mum and had Dad's bulbous nose, small mouth and tiny teeth.

Mum had put out the Royal Albert and I'd done her hair in a flick-back Farrah Fawcett for the occasion. I trailed after her as she showed Dolly around the house.

'It's a very big house but comfortable for a family.' Mum was using her *Celebrity Glitter* voice. It was gushy and nasal.

'Housing Commission, wasn't it?' Dolly ran a hand over the bar and examined her fingertips.

'It's been a private home for some years. The previous owner was a wool buyer. A very successful man.'

'And?'

'He chose a quality carpet and made very tasteful alterations. We've now got two lounge rooms, that's one up here and the rumpus room below. Quite handy for entertaining.' Mum was standing at the top of the spiral staircase and tapped the rail with a fingernail. We never entertained but that wasn't the point.

'These staircases catch the hip. I won't descend.' Dolly pulled in her chins for emphasis.

'The spiral can be difficult if you're *big*.' Mum pulled in her chin for emphasis.

Dolly was certainly a substantial woman. Mum said she was trying to eat her way out of an unhappy marriage.

'Let me show you the kids' bedrooms.' Mum moved her hand backward in a graceful follow-me manner.

'Oh my God! This must be Liberace's room. Look at those curtains!' Dolly was standing in the doorway of my beautiful new bedroom pointing at my dragon brocade.

I stared at the floral synthetic of her frock and felt anger surge through me. The fabric was stretched to capacity across the large rectangle of her unhappy arse. From behind, she looked like a gift-wrapped Land-Rover.

'Those were hand-picked by Des at the Blue Gum Plaza.' Mum had stopped using her restaurant voice. Her tone was unfriendly.

'That old Ulverston queen. No wonder the place looks so gaudy.' Dolly chortled. 'Do the boy a favour and run up some proper drapes. Something with a pop group or spaceships.'

'Des is a happily married man and Julian likes these curtains just as they are.' Mum had her hands on her hips. 'They suit his artistic temperament.'

'Is that what you call it? Best to nip that sort of thing in the bud. James told me all about your brother.' Dolly put her hands on her hips, blocking all movement in the hall in the direction of the bedrooms. 'And that Des never had children. There's something queer going on there.'

'Des is a fabric expert and you know *nothing* about my brother. Norman runs a thriving hair-care business in Melbourne. He does the permanents of very prominent people.'

Mum fully extended her elbows, blocking all hall flow toward the kitchen. Dolly was effectively cornered in the bedroom section. She pursed her lips and gave Mum a sour look.

'And we've got no worries about Julian, Dolly. Mark my words, this boy will go far.'

Dolly turned to examine me. I knew what she was thinking: I was a Norman tint and permanent away from Elizabeth Taylor.

Mum didn't wait for Dolly to contradict her. 'I hope Sharon has settled down after all that trouble.'

Dolly sagged a little.

'It was in Cobber's supermarket, wasn't it?'

'It was just a little make-up kit and she said it fell into her pocket by accident.' Dolly turned her head to examine the wallpaper.

'Wasn't there something else?'

'Just a comb.'

Satisfied, Mum pushed past Dolly and led the way to the master bedroom.

'This, Dolly, is The Ensuite. It's very handy in the mornings, let me tell you.' Mum's voice was hushed and reverent again. She opened the door and stood with her arm rigid and outstretched like a game-show host presenting a prize fridge.

'Mirrors are very difficult to keep clean.' Dolly frowned and pushed past Mum. Kneeling down, she ran a thumbnail along the metal trim and then held her thumb up to the light. 'Body grime! A good scrub will get rid of that.'

I don't know what I would've done without The Ensuite. Its mirrored shower gave me a morning dose of glamour before I set off each day for the drudgery of Waratah High. The teachers of Waratah didn't beat students like the Christian Brothers had done but they were just as uninspired and miserable. The one exception was Mr Snell who taught French and wore his shirts ironed, with a silk cravat and cufflinks. His hair rose from his forehead in a tidy wave and his sideburns and eyebrows were neatly trimmed. He was very small for a human being but his devotion to appearance made him seem taller than his actual one metre fifty.

Mr Snell believed in teaching the modern way and had us do role-plays to practise dialogue exchange. Ordering in French at a restaurant came naturally to me. I was paired with Duncan Bacon, an irritating clever boy who wore gold-rimmed glasses with light-sensitive lenses and a digital watch with a fancy flip-up leather cover. Duncan was top in French and intended to stay there.

'Are you the waiter or the customer?' Duncan *click-clicked* the button of his Deskmaster ballpoint pen with impatience.

'I'm the customer.' I held in my stomach and imagined myself in Paris, France.

'*Qu'est-ce que vous voulez manger, monsieur?*'

'*Le boeuf bourguignon.*'

'Mr Snell said it's a fish restaurant. You can't order beef.'

'But there would be something on the menu for people who can't eat fish.'

'But why would such people go to a fish restaurant?'

'They might be on holiday at the seaside.' I didn't like Duncan. He had no imagination.

'But why wouldn't they eat fish?'

'They might be allergic.'

'Can't we just pretend you like fish so we can practise the vocabulary?'

'What's the French word for oysters?'

'You're supposed to be ordering fish.'

'They're both from the ocean.'

'So is a sea sponge, stupid. I doubt you'll be ordering sponge *à la crème.*' Duncan sniggered.

'*À la crème?* Sounds delicious. How's progress?' Mr Snell had been discreetly roving around the class listening to dialogue. His size enabled him to do this without being noticed.

'Mr Snell, I'd like to order oysters but I don't know the French word. Duncan here thinks it's stupid to order oysters in a French fish restaurant.'

'Duncan! The French love oysters.' Mr Snell shook his head and then turned to me with a smile. 'The word is *huître*, Julian.'

Duncan's face darkened. We locked eyes as the teacher patted me on the shoulder.

'*Garcon! Je prends des huîtres, si'il vous plaît.*' I flashed a large *faux* smile at my opponent.

'Bravo, Julian!' Mr Snell pursed his lips like Valéry Giscard d'Estaing and gave Duncan a severe look. 'Monsieur Bacon, do some revision on the dining habits of the French. You'll need to work if you want to stay at the top.'

I was still flushed with victory when I reached the edge of the cricket pitch. It was Friday and I wouldn't see the likes of Duncan Bacon for another three days. The boys were lined up along the fence under the gum trees passing a bottle of wine back and forth. Jackaroo was a supermarket brand and came with a convenient screw top.

'Where's Wayne?'

The boys jostled each other and laughed, bouncing up and down on the fence wire. I waited for them to settle down before repeating the question.

'He's getting a blowie, I reckon.' Paul Lamb's comment set off his friends again.

The boys were still laughing when Wayne appeared from behind the gum trees. He was walking stiffly and winked at them. Behind him was Christine Kandy. She was adjusting her skirt and brushing grit off her knees. Wayne took a swig of the Jackaroo and wiped his mouth with the back of his hand. He handed me the bottle.

'How's the French?'

'*Très bien.*' I tipped the bottle back and filled my mouth. The wine was both sweet and vinegary. Warmth flooded my chest.

'What the hell do you mean?' Wayne was looking at me hard.

'Bonza.' My mouth went dry. '*Très bien* is French for bonza.'

'Tray bee Ann.' Wayne relaxed. 'I'll have to learn some French, ha, ha.'

The boys on the fence started to laugh along with Wayne but stopped when he went silent again. 'Nah, on second thoughts, that fucking French dwarf is a poof.'

I looked at the ground and rummaged in my pockets

for my cigarettes. This was no time to come to Mr Snell's defence.

'Those girl's undies he wears round his neck are a dead give-away.' Wayne bent his wrists and wiggled his bum.

'You're barking up the wrong tree, Hopper.' Christine Kandy's voice was cool and confident. 'Snell's normal.'

'Yeah, fuckin' normal all right.' Wayne put his hands over his bum and grimaced. This provoked another round of laughter.

'He's married, you wanker.' Christine was deadly serious.

'I bet he doesn't have any kids.' Wayne turned away from her and focused on me again. 'I'd watch your fat little arse, Corker. Bums to the wall if you value your hole.'

The boys on the fence bounced up and down. Christine Kandy shrugged and looked over at me. Her face was a hard mask of foundation and heavy mascara but her eyes were soft and intelligent. I liked Christine. She was the only one of the group with anything resembling panache. Underneath all the muck she caked on her face was an uncanny resemblance to Margaux Hemingway. I would've loved to redo her make-up and sort out her hair but this wasn't the time or the place. I hung around until the Jackaroo was finished and then headed for home.

Early evening was a lonely time at Echidna Avenue and I never hurried back to the house. Carmel was always at cricket or hockey practice and my mother didn't get home until seven. Mum had found herself a job at the Boomerang Biscuits factory a month after arriving in Hobart. It was hot, noisy work. She came home every night smelling like sugar and looking frazzled and worn. Dad had settled back into his old routine of going to the pub after work with Trevor Bland. My parents were too preoccupied and miserable to notice that I often had alcohol on my breath.

I leaned on the gatepost as I opened the letterbox and pulled out a handful of letters with windows. An envelope fell out of my hands and landed with a flutter on the path. It was pale blue with a hand-drawn image of a bird under the address. I could feel my heartbeat in my throat as I picked it up and turned it over. It was addressed to me. I ripped it open.

Dear Julian,

How's Hobart? Ulverston is fine. Dad says Hobart is colder than Ulverston. It must be cold then.

The big news here is that Ralph Waters was expelled. He broke into the school at night and was caught by Brother Dooley in the music room. They think he might have been doing it for a while. They didn't tell us anything but I know for a fact that he pissed into that big horn thing you once tried. I think it's called a tuba. Dad heard all about it from Father McMahon. The police came and everything.

How's French? *Parles-tu français encore?*

I'm thinking of leaving school next year. I might try the Wool Board. Dad says they have good jobs. He says you're in the arms of Jesus when you work at the Wool Board. It's the best kind of job to have, especially for a school-leaver. What about you?

Anyway, I have to go now. Will you be visiting Ulverston soon? I hope so. I miss you.

Love,

Jimmy xxx

Jimmy lit up in my mind's eye like a fireworks sparkler. He was smiling, riding his space-blue Pacer bicycle with a clacker in the spokes. The feelings I'd been bottling up for months burst out of me in a painful sob. I began crying uncontrollably as I put the key in the door. Tears were coming out in jerks, making my cheeks hot and slimy. I stumbled into my bedroom and threw myself on to the bed, curling into a tight ball, crying until it was too painful to swallow.

We were never going back to Ulverston and I'd never see Jimmy again. I was stuck in Hobart and it was hell. Nothing worked in Hobart. I was a nobody and had no panache. I had to forget Jimmy or I'd never survive Wayne and the rest of the louts. *No, Jimmy, I'm not going back to Ulverston. I'm not going back anywhere. I can't be that any more.*

My head was thumping and my eyesight was hazy when I walked over to the window. Taking the matches from my pocket, I lit the corner of Jimmy's letter. Flames were licking my fingers as I threw the burning sheet of paper out of the window. I looked down at the garden below. A small, unburned piece of paper lay on the soil. The word 'Love' was still visible.

15

I spent my lunchtimes in the shade of the gum trees at the edge of the cricket pitch and drifted back there after school to smoke cigarettes and drink wine. All my pocket money went on these items but Paul Lamb and the other louts never bothered me when there was a bottle of Jackaroo. These bribes entailed no small sacrifice on my part. I couldn't buy new clothes or LPs and never did anything on the weekends. Waratah had destroyed my panache but at least I'd made it through half a year without any new scars.

Trevor Bland told my father that Cobber's Super Central was looking for schoolboys to stack shelves and pack boxes. Without consulting me, Dad visited the supermarket and put my name down. He'd never done anything like this for John or Carmel. They played sports and in his mind deserved their pocket money. Dad didn't like me being idle. Neither did he like forking out for me every week. He thought he was teaching me a lesson but he did me a wonderful favour. Cobber's was a glamour job. The store was big, bright and colourful. The checkout girls wore make-up and nail polish and the deli counter stocked anchovies and capers from Europe. The supermarket even sold my new brand of cigarettes, John Player Specials.

I wasn't the only Waratah boy at Cobber's. Frank Burger

worked the boxes on the express lane and was renowned for his high-speed packing technique. The checkout girls called him Fast-hand Frankie and gave him packets of broken biscuits to take home. Frank was part of an elite club at Waratah. He was a prefect and wore his prefect's jacket everywhere, even on the express lane. Prefects were elected by the students who naturally went for good-looking athletes. The most beautiful of these was a high-jumper called Terrence Fig. He was not only head prefect but also worked as a DJ on Youth Hour every Friday at Hot Rocking Radio Hobart. When Terrence strolled around the school grounds looking for smokers or kissers, he may as well have been riding in a golden chariot. Students stopped what they were doing to offer him sandwiches and tinned drinks. The bolder ones asked about his radio work. I would've thrown rose petals at his feet but never dared move a muscle in front of Wayne.

Frank didn't have Terrence's panache but he was still handsome in a clean-cut, normal sort of way. These pleasant features plus the jacket made him look older than fifteen which was very helpful for purchasing alcohol. Frank agreed to buy Jackaroo for me as long as I paid him 20 per cent commission. This was steep but Frank had an enterprising nature. The other box boys said he got tips from ladies, something unheard of in Tasmania. After a month of packing boxes together, he invited me to his house. I was delighted.

Frank lived in a brick bungalow on a tidy street with late-model Holdens in the driveways. The family was well off by Waratah standards and had a Holden Monaro in the garage. It was green with a yellow racing stripe down the side. Its steering wheel even had a leather cover with little air holes to absorb racing sweat. Mr Burger was the sort of man my father called flashy. He ran his own accountancy firm, which employed the very flashy-looking Mrs Burger as a receptionist. Dad didn't like accountants. He blamed one for bankrupting his father. He said the accountant had fiddled the books and caused Granddad to lose the pub.

Mrs Burger was cooking something foreign with rice when we walked in. She had blond blow-waved hair and wore a lot of make-up for a mother. Frank led me to the source of the television noise in the lounge. I froze in the doorway. His sister was watching *Pretty Pony Pals* in colour on a glorious twenty-six-incher. Frank came from one of the lucky families. We knew who they were at Waratah. The arrival of a colour TV was announced and discussed. Those who didn't have one kept quiet and prayed for a miracle. Frank hadn't said anything and I'd assumed he was one of us.

'You want to watch some telly, Julian?'

'You've got a colour TV? Didn't even notice.'

'Had it for a while.'

'Yeah, we've had ours a while, too.' I'd never be able to take Frank back to our house now. The Ensuite would have to remain a family secret.

'Infinitely better than a black-and-white set.'

'I try not to watch the box.' I watched television whenever possible and followed weekly programmes like *Pop Stop* with fanatic dedication. I sat through cartoons, soapy serials, family programming, police shows and old movies. I watched *The Dick Dingle Hour* every night and never missed his Sunday *Tales of Tasmania* feature. I sat in front of anything with movement and sound with two exceptions: sports programmes and war movies.

'You got your own room, Frank?'

'Well, yeah, I'd hardly be sharing with my sister, would I?'

Frank's bedroom was a bitter disappointment. Not only did

his curtains have a pop-group pattern, but his bedspread was covered with little spaceships. Above the bed was a larger-than-life poster of Suzi Quatro squatting in leather hot pants. Photos of footballers and car stickers desecrated the other walls. It could've been John's room.

I made an excuse and set off for home, passing Mrs Burger on my way out. She was standing next to the rubbish bin, folding up cardboard packaging. The cardboard had come from a big-ticket item, something with a width of at least twenty-six inches.

I was still thinking about the television when I turned into Echidna Avenue and heard a loud screech of tyres. The screech was followed by a thud and then the revving of a car engine. A moment later, a Tip Top taxi swerved into view, travelling at high speed. As the car flew past, the driver glanced my way and I recognised what Carmel called a 'Tickworth Flush'. The man's cheeks were bright red and his eyes were bloodshot.

Mum and I were in the dinette when Dad came home. He was earlier than usual and didn't smell of beer. His face was serious. He sat down at the table and propped his chin on his fists, clearing his throat before making an announcement.

'There's been a hit and run up the end of our street.' He hesitated and held his bottom lip between the small crumbs of his teeth.

Mum walked over from the sink, drying her hands on a tea towel.

'A boy's in hospital with a broken leg. It's a compound fracture. They say the bone was poking out of his leg.'

'What kind of animal would leave a boy in that condition?' Mum pulled up a chair next to me and squeezed my forearm.

'Probably some drunk idiot.' This was rich coming from Dad.

'He could've hit one of our kids.' This was the most I'd heard

Mum say to Dad in months. She ran a hand through her hair, exposing a nest of grey hairs near the temple. 'What time did this happen?'

'About six or so.' Dad banged his fist on the table Kojak-style and let out a hiss of air between his tiny teeth. He was doing an impression of a concerned father and clearly enjoying his performance.

'Dad!' I'd come home from Frank's place at six. The screech of tyres and thud suddenly made sense. 'I saw who did it.'

My father gave me a look. The hit and run had been his moment of glory. He wasn't about to give it up without a struggle.

'It was six on the dot when I came home. I heard a thud, then a terrible noise, a blood-boiling scream. A Tip Top taxi flew out of our street with blood on its bumper. I'd swear I saw hairs in the blood. I thought he'd hit a Labrador.'

'Julian, this better not be one of your stories.' Dad was frowning.

'The taxi driver was drunk and swerving all over the road like a maniac. He could've hit Carmel coming home from hockey practice. They could've been *her* hairs on the bumper.'

Dad's eyebrows shot up. 'All right, all right. We'd better get you down to the police station.'

Information was currency at the edge of the cricket pitch. I lit a cigarette and made sure the usual suspects were assembled before casually mentioning the accident. Someone had procured a bottle of sweet cooking sherry and the boys were passing it up and down the fence. No one else had eye-witnessed an attempted murder. I had them eating out of my hand.

'The bone of his leg was sticking out like a chopstick. You should've seen the blood. Buckets of it. They had to physically scrape him off the road with a butter knife.'

'A butter knife! Jesus wept!' Wayne's face had a rapt expression. 'Was he an Abo?'

'Who?'

'The perpetrator.'

Wayne wasn't only interrupting a good story but he was also displaying his ignorance. There were virtually no Aboriginal people in Tasmania. The early white settlers had hunted down and murdered nearly all the original inhabitants. Mum called it genocide. She said it made her ashamed to be a white Tasmanian.

'He was white and stupid.' The only non-white person I knew was Mr Patel and he wasn't stupid. People said he'd been a brain surgeon in India before moving to Ulverston.

'Just asking.' Wayne looked surprised, even hurt by my answer. 'You can't trust them black fellas.'

'You've only ever seen them on TV.' Christine Kandy was looking directly at Wayne. 'And your TV's not even colour so you don't know what they really look like.'

'Piss off, Kandy pants.' Wayne hunched his shoulders and stopped bouncing on the fence.

Christine had gone too far with the TV comment. Showing someone up for being a bigot was one thing. What you couldn't do was expose someone without a colour TV. Wayne remained silent for a few minutes before leaving with the other boys trailing after him. Cherie said goodbye and headed for the bus stop. Christine sat down under a gum tree and patted the ground next to her.

'Wayne's just thick, you know.'

She held out the dregs of sherry to me. I took a mouthful and handed it back. I didn't think Wayne was just thick. I'd seen a flash of something else when she'd mentioned the TV.

'Ever kissed a girl?'

'Yeah.'

Of course I hadn't kissed a girl and neither did I want to start. I was thinking of an excuse to leave when Christine suddenly leaped on top of me and planted her lips on mine. Her tongue was in my mouth before I could say Jimmy Budge.

'What did you say?' She pulled away.

'Nothing.'

We kissed hard for five agonising minutes, long enough for it to seem normal, before I pulled away. I told her I had to finish a police report and walked home on hollow, shaky legs. Christine Kandy scared me but I wasn't the only one. I'd seen fear on Wayne's face when she'd confronted him.

I was still shaken up when I arrived home. The back door was unlocked and I could hear cursing coming from the lounge. It didn't sound good. Lifting my heels, I tiptoed through the dinette to the lounge door. My heart leaped.

Dad was on his knees next to a pile of cardboard packaging. Next to this was a big fake mahogany box with a twenty-inch screen. I was looking at a brand-new colour TV and it was beautiful, the most beautiful thing I'd seen since Peter Grubb's frill. I could watch Dick Dingle in colour and invite Frank home. We were one of the lucky families. We had a colour TV *and* The Ensuite. The Corkle family was on the up and up.

'Thanks, Dad. You don't know what this means to me.'

'What?' Dad grunted. He was bent over, tugging at the antenna wire.

'The TV really means a lot to me.'

'I'll tell you what it means to me, fifteen bloody dollars a month. That includes the chair, of course.'

I turned and saw a large brown vinyl reclining chair wedged next to the couch. It had a wooden lever to work the footrest. Fifteen dollars seemed an extremely low repayment for two large purchases.

'It's worth it Dad. Now we can watch everything in colour.'

'That's why I rented it, you idiot.'

'Rented?'

'You don't think I'm stupid enough to buy one, do you?'

I couldn't believe my father. You didn't rent colour TVs. You bought them. You were still unfortunate if you rented. I walked over and took a close look at the set. At the bottom of the dial panel was a small Rentascope badge. It wasn't something you'd notice if you were watching the news or passing through the room to get a cheese sandwich. You'd have to look really hard; squint your eyes and look really, really hard. I heard the back door slam.

'What's all this?' Carmel stood in the doorway of the dinette, removing her muddy hockey boots on the lino.

'It's the colour TV you've all been whining about since Adam was a cowboy.' Dad stood up and wiped his hands on the sides of his corduroys. He was wearing his Carmel smile.

'Ugh, it's from Rentascope!' Carmel hesitated for a moment then stalked off to her bedroom.

The smile disappeared from Dad's lips. He turned back to the TV and pointed to the rusty tools scattered over the carpet.

'I don't want to hear another ungrateful word from you, Julian. Clean up this bloody mess and put these tools away.'

16

Colour reception completely transformed television viewing for me. I couldn't get enough of it. Colour made everyone look better, even the likes of old Val Doonican and Andy Williams. Mum and I were delighted with the new TV. She now rushed home every night to watch *Coronation Street* with me. Len Fairclough had never looked more lively.

Sadly for us, the joy of colour didn't escape the notice of my father who began making an effort to leave the pub earlier. It didn't matter what Mum and I were watching, once he parked his bum on the recliner and took the remote control in hand, the television was tuned to sports. There was certainly plenty of it on television. Sports were a Tasmanian obsession. Even Dick Dingle got in on the act, occasionally reporting on youth athletics and swimming events.

At Waratah High it was impossible to get out of sports. If you didn't do phys. ed. you were a poofter and this was one label I definitely wanted to avoid. The best and worst thing about our weekly hour of violence on the playing field was the dressing room afterward. Showering was compulsory but the showers had no curtains or partitions, a cruel arrangement for boys with sparse pubic hair or small penises. These were no longer pressing issues for me but I'd developed another problem, one a lot more hazardous to my health. I was suffering from the spontaneous erections of youth. I could get a stiffy packing Tiffany biscuits at Cobber's or watching Danny in *The Partridge Family*. More often than not, there was neither rhyme nor reason to them.

When it was my turn for the shower nozzle, I followed Brother Punt's soap and flannel routine. I also kept the water dial turned to cold and fixed Carmel with a hockey stick in my mind's eye. These precautions usually did the trick and I could be in and out of the shower with the best of them. There were days, however, when even the vision of my sister in shorts wasn't enough to prevent nature taking its course.

'Corkle, you queer bastard!' Paul Lamb had watched me scuttle out of the shower sideways like a crab.

I had a towel around my waist but my erection was jutting out like Sir Edmund Hillary's tent pole.

'Corkle's a pooftah, Corkle's a pooftah.'

Paul Lamb circled me, chanting, with his hands balled into fists. Blood surged up my neck and into my face. I fought my damp legs into underpants and jeans with my heart slamming inside my chest and my eyes on the floor.

'Shut the fuck up!' Wayne's command cut through the chant.

Everyone heard it and froze. Paul Lamb dropped his arms and unballed his fists. He moved away and started rifling through his bag. I quickly put on my shirt and left the room, breaking into a run once I got outside. I didn't stop running until I'd left the school grounds. In those few terrifying seconds of torment, I'd seen hatred in Paul Lamb's eyes. He was itching to get his hands on me.

I got home and flopped on my bed with the door closed and the curtains pulled. I had to make a decision. I could go back to the benches and risk being dragged off or I could return to the gum trees and face the possibility of more immediate violence. I filled my lungs and looked at David Bowie. It was dim in the room but I knew the poster so well I could fill in its details. I focused my eyes and tried not to blink. David Bowie's face blurred and then seemed to move. The hint of a smile appeared on his lips; then it vanished. It was a sign.

The boys were the same as usual the next day. No one mentioned the erection, not even Paul Lamb. They were talking about 'stink finger' and paid me no attention as I sat on the grass below the fence and removed a bottle of Jackaroo from under my jumper. Stink finger was something boys did to girls and then discussed with their mates. Christine Kandy's name came up. Wayne turned to me.

'I hear you were pashing up Kandy.'

'Who told you that?'

'You want to watch yourself. She's one of them sexual maniacs.'

The boys laughed and jiggled on the fence.

'Did you cop a feel?' Wayne had raised his eyebrows. The boys went quiet.

It was a Ralph Waters moment. If I said no, I was a chicken or a poofter. If I said yes, I might be asked to describe the lady hole. Wayne was looking at me.

I shrugged.

'Yeah?' He raised his eyebrows.

I shrugged again and handed him the unopened bottle of Jackaroo.

Wayne hesitated and then took the wine with a nod. Ross Gibb put two fingers in his mouth and gave a sharp whistle. I'd seen sheep farmers use the same whistle on TV to control border collies. The boys used it to indicate the presence of undesirables such as teachers and prefects. Christine and Cherie were approaching.

'What are you looking at?' Christine went straight for the weakest link, Paul Lamb.

'Nothing.' His face flushed.

'So we're nothing then?'

The other boys laughed nervously. They were intimidated by Christine Kandy. She didn't need a gaggle of weaker kids to prop her up. Neither did she filter her opinions to please the fence-sitters. The boys said things about her behind her back but never contradicted her in person. She was too fierce.

Christine sat on the grass next to Cherie and took a few swigs of the wine. The boys started talking about Kawasaki motorcycles. Their voices became a soft buzz as I lay back and looked up at the sky through the leaves. I'd hardly slept the previous evening and soon dozed off in the shade of the gum trees.

It was quiet when I felt someone lay down beside me. I opened my eyes and realised with a shock that I was alone with Christine. My chest tightened. Smiling, she took hold of my hand and guided it into her underpants. She kept pressure on the hand until I began to feel around. My fingertips moved but met no resistance. There was nothing inside her underpants apart from pubic hair. Her hand was on top of mine again, forcing it further down into a rubbery moist crevice and then pulling it up again. She moaned. I was rubbing an empty humid strip of flesh but Christine was moaning, pushing and pulling at my hand.

I didn't understand and didn't want to know. As soon as it was politely possible, I stopped moving my fingers and removed my hand.

'Let's go a bit further next time.' Her voice was low and velvety.

'Sure, Christine.' I pushed myself up into a sitting position and discreetly wiped my fingers on the grass behind me. If that was the lady hole, the ladies could keep it. It was tragic. I glanced down at Christine and felt something between guilt and pity. 'There's something you should know.'

'What?' She sat up, defensive.

'You'd look so much prettier without all that foundation and eye make-up. Try a lighter lipstick, peach or pastel pink.'

Christine's eyes widened. Her smile was incredulous. 'Anything else I should know?'

'If you stopped pinning your hair back and let it fall forward naturally, you could look like Margaux Hemingway.'

'Who the hell is Margaux Hemingway?'

'Probably the world's most beautiful model.'

In the end, it wasn't Paul Lamb who put the cricket pitch out of bounds for me. It was Christine Kandy. The threat of having to repeat the crevice experience was more frightening than a Jackaroo bottle over the head and a knee in the testicles. I didn't understand how girls worked down there and didn't want to find out. The horror show I'd encountered inside Christine's underpants terrified me. I started spending my lunchtimes in the library and did extra afternoons at Cobber's. I even invited Frank back to our house.

'You've got a Relaxator Recliner chair. My dad's got one in the same brown leather.'

'Yeah.' I wasn't about to tell Frank it was vinyl.

'Nice colour telly.'

Frank made a move toward the Rentascope but I threw myself in front of him. He frowned and tried to move around me. I moved with him, blocking his path.

'I just want to see the news, Julian. They caught that hit-and-run driver.'

'The mad dog from Tip Top Taxis?'

'That was some crank's fantasy. The driver was an eighteen-year-old. He was joy-riding in his father's Ford Falcon.'

'Oh.' I was glad I'd been avoiding the cricket pitch. 'Then I definitely don't want to watch TV. Those media vultures thrive off people's misfortunes. They love blood and guts.'

'The kid just broke his leg. I doubt there was any blood. Anyway, isn't your father a journalist?'

'Editor.'

'Same difference if you ask me.'

'I didn't, Frank. Let me show you The Ensuite.' I pronounced *ensuite* the French way, lingering over the last syllable. I knew Frank's parents didn't have an ensuite and it made me feel good. I opened the door of the bathroom and immediately tried to close it. One of my mother's bras and a pair of underpants were drip-drying on a coat hanger from the shower nozzle. The door hit Frank's foot.

'Nice foundation garments.' Frank's eyebrows were raised. He smirked.

I looked at the underwear and felt like slapping Frank. The bra itself was passable. It was coral pink with lacy cups and satin straps. Its relative prettiness made the old cotton under-pants look overworked and unhappy. They were vaguely beige, with a hole at the top where the elastic stitching had come undone. Poor Mum. She deserved better.

'Want to see my room?' I grabbed Frank by the arm and spun him around. My face was burning as I opened the door to my bedroom. I propelled him through the doorway with a shove. He stumbled inside and gasped.

'That's jacquard on your bed, isn't it?'

My resentment evaporated.

'I wanted the jacquard but Mum thought Dad would say it was for . . . you know.'

'It's aqua blue.'

'It's wonderful. And your curtains. What are they, jersey silk?'

'Royal-blue brocade. There are little highlights.'

'I can see the dragons from here.'

I could've kissed Frank then and there. He looked adorable, smiling at my fabric. The room was warm from the afternoon sun. Frank's neck was giving off the smell of Bird's Beauty Savon. It was the same brand of soap that Jimmy used. Something stirred.

'You've got a David Bowie poster.'

'Yes.'

'He's such a weirdo with all that make-up. You should listen to Eric Clapton.'

That did it. I pushed Frank out of the room and away from the murky undertow of the past. David Bowie was not a weirdo. He was a sex god and musical genius. Eric Clapton wasn't even good-looking.

'Let's go to the Small Print and get the evening paper.'

'I thought you didn't like the blood and misfortune, Julian.'

'Where did you get that idea?'

'From you, actually. Why can't we just watch Dick Dingle? He'll be on at seven. I'm keen to hear the truth about that accident. There were all sorts of crazy rumours going around at school.'

'I thought I'd made myself clear.'

'Not to me. You've made yourself anything but clear.'

By the time we reached the newsagent, Frank was sulking and said he was going home to catch the news. I walked over to the rack of foreign magazines and opened *House and Patio*. I was looking at a feature on Julie Andrews's kitchen when someone bumped me from behind. It was a sudden yet purposeful bump. An erection grazed my buttocks. I turned

127

and locked eyes with Wayne. My muscles froze in fear. He jerked his head in the direction of the door and walked out of the shop.

I didn't know how long I stood frozen with the magazine in my hands but the next thing I knew, the newsagent was calling out that he was closing the shop. He didn't sound friendly.

'Try the public library next time, mate. I have customers come in here to actually buy things.'

17

The box boys had been asked to work late at the supermarket for stocktaking, which was just fine by me. I didn't have anything else to do and was now saving feverishly for elocution lessons. I'd learned the importance of speaking properly while watching a *Tales of Tasmania* feature on a youth theatre group. Dick Dingle had been giving the young thespians pointers on voice control when he revealed the secret to his signature voice. 'Vocal excellence is sixty per cent inspiration and forty per cent perspiration. I had to train hard to get this golden voice. Young Tasmanians need to shorten their vowels and enunciate their consonants. You won't get on TV sounding like a merino.' I definitely wanted to get on TV and the brush with Wayne had made one thing clear. I had to get out of Waratah. At fifteen, I was now old enough to leave school but I needed parental consent. I knew my mum wouldn't provide that unless I had something up my sleeve.

By the time we finished work, night had fallen and the supermarket was obliged to pay for our taxi fares. When I opened the door to mine, a heavy odour of Tickworth lager rose out of the cab to meet me. I decided to use the seat belt for good measure and was buckling up when the driver took off. He drove extremely fast and didn't say anything until he pulled into our street.

'If I ever catch that effin' squawking cockatoo, I'll wring his effin' neck.'

'Beg pardon?'

'The effin' kid who told the effin' police a Tip Top taxi done that hit and run. He lives in this street somewhere.'

'Uh-huh.'

'The cops treated me like a common criminal.'

'Uh-huh.'

'They had me fingerprinted and everything.' The driver slowed as he approached our house. His hands twitched on the steering wheel. 'The kid was about your age. I'll effin' well kill him if I ever find him.'

'Kill is a very strong word.'

'I have very effin' strong feelings.' The driver glanced at me in the rear-view mirror. His eyes narrowed.

I had the door open even before the taxi came to a complete stop. I threw the fare on to the front seat and then sprinted up the drive to the safety of the porch. When I looked back, the driver was still watching me from his taxi. I gave him the fingers and darted inside the house, locking the door behind me.

Mum had already gone to bed but Dad was sitting in the dinette with Carmel. He was talking to her about an advertisement he'd found in the *Hobart Star*. In his hands was an application form. My ears pricked up at the mention of Abracadabra Television. The station was recruiting teenagers for a series of human-interest features on Hobart. The programme was to be called *Cub Reporter*. Carmel shrugged at Dad's news and continued polishing her hockey boots.

I couldn't believe my sister. This was a Golden Microphone Moment par excellence and all she could do was shrug. My heart felt as if it was going to burst through my ribs as I stepped in to fill her shoes.

'You've already got a good job at Cobber's.' My father wasn't impressed with the idea.

'But, Dad, it's television. Lights, camera, action and all that.' I had to get this job. I just had to.

'Exactly. I don't want a son of mine with a hairpiece doing bath-salt commercials.' Dick Dingle did bath-salt commercials.

'Sorry to disappoint you, Dad, but I'll be seated in the press box behind a microphone. Sports commentator is high on my list of career possibilities.'

'You? Sports?'

'Playing the game and having a genuine interest in great sportspeople are two different things. You of all people should know that, Dad.'

'I've never seen you show any interest in sports.'

'I'm a late starter with untapped potential.' I held a ballpoint pen out to Dad. 'The school's vocational-guidance counsellor has been very encouraging.'

'About sports?'

'Male nursing.'

Dad wrote my application and I got an audition at the Abracadabra studio.

A snowy-blond man and a red-haired woman were seated in the interview room when I arrived. The gingery woman frowned at my tie-dyed T-shirt and waved me into an empty chair. The man smiled. He was wearing an open-necked Firecat shirt and floppy trousers. My fate lay in his hands.

The woman got down to business. 'Corkle's an unusual name.'

'It's Irish.' I thought of Dick Dingle and put effort into my consonants. 'We can trace our family back to the first ship.'

'The first ship of convicts?'

131

'My great-great-great-great-great-great-grandfather was an Irish poet. The English didn't like his poetry.'

'A poet? That's great, really, really, really, really great.' It was Snowy. He was laughing.

Ginger pursed her lips and pushed on. 'Why on earth would the English not like his poetry? It's the home of Wordsworth, Blake, Shakespeare.'

'His poetry was about the potato famine.' We'd just studied the potato famine at school. It was a massive human tragedy that struck a chord in every red-haired Australian. I nodded gravely at Ginger.

'But the famine occurred in the middle of the nineteenth century. The convict ships arrived at the end of the eighteenth.' She tapped her ballpoint pen on the clipboard and wrote something down.

'Did I say famine? Ha, I meant fashion, potato fashion. My great-great-great—'

'Yes.' She looked up from the clipboard.

'He wrote poems about how much the Irish loved potatoes. This upset the English. It was a class thing.'

'That's the most ridiculous story I've ever heard.' She was writing at high speed and didn't bother looking up from her clipboard.

'It wasn't ridiculous for the English. They shipped off my great-great-great—'

'For goodness' sake, I think we've heard enough. Kindly close the door on the way out.'

I made sure to leave the door open a crack then lingered to untie and retie a shoelace.

'What a ridiculous performance! And that pretentious voice!' The woman sounded outraged. 'Julian Corkle is a filthy liar.'

'He does do something funny with his consonants but he's certainly not lost for words. Potato fashion. Ha, ha.'

'That was a bare-faced lie. I don't believe the convict story for a minute. His grandparents probably come from County Cork.'

'Ha, ha. The Corkles from County Cork. It's a great, great, great story.'

'Brendan, that was a great big fat lie.'

'I want him, Leila. He's comical. You said it yourself, ridiculous.'

The day before the shoot, Cherie invited me to eat sponge roll in the home-economics room. She said she wanted to talk about the rumours going around the cricket pitch. Cherie was one of the few people I trusted at Waratah. She was soft-hearted and never said a bad word behind anyone's back. She'd made the sponge roll in class that morning and said it was too good to leave for the teachers' afternoon tea. We'd sneaked into the room at lunchtime and had just started in on the sponge when Christine's head appeared in the door's window. Without thinking, I threw my arms forward and dived like Peter Grubb behind a row of benches. I must've closed my eyes because I didn't see the enamel handle of the Bingo oven that slammed into my forehead. My John Lennon glasses snapped and I landed with a thud on the hard linoleum.

'So this is where you've been!'

'Hello, Christine.'

I pushed myself up on one elbow and realised the two halves of my glasses were dangling from either ear. I felt my head. A large duck egg was forming above my eyebrows. I had half a metre of vision without my glasses. From where I lay, Christine looked like Margaux Hemingway. She was standing next to someone in a dinner jacket. The jacket spoke.

'Hi, Julian.'

'Frank.'

'I was surprised to hear about Abracadabra. I thought you didn't like media.'

'Changed my mind.'

'You'll probably do well. You've got the gift of the gab.'

'Thanks, Frank.'

'I thought you should know.' A blurry smile appeared on Frank's face. 'I don't believe the rumours those thugs have been saying.'

'About the taxi driver?'

Frank said something I didn't catch before disappearing from my field of vision. The white cushion shoes of Mrs Stone appeared in front of me.

'Off my home-economics floor at once! I have hygiene standards.' Mrs Stone dug her shoe into my shoulder. 'And you, Cherie. I'm surprised at you. I had plans for that cake. The male teachers are very partial to an afternoon roll.'

'Julian's had a mishap, Mrs Stone.' Christine's voice was calm and full of authority. 'We dragged the poor thing in here and gave him some sponge roll to revive him. He's got quite a bump on his head. It was those ruffians from the cricket pitch. They've ruined his glasses.'

'I'm all right, Mrs Stone.' I stood up shakily and leaned against the Bingo oven.

'You're not all right if those hoodlums have had their way with you. It was those boys who stole my cooking sherry. They've broken your glasses.' The teacher tut-tutted and gently lifted the two halves off my ears. 'I'll take Julian to the sick bay. The rest of you can wait on the benches until the bell.'

*   *   *

I had no alternative but to use my old Nana Mouskouris for the shoot. It was tragic. My one shot at television and I looked like a horror show. The lump had gone down overnight but there was still something freakish about my forehead. From side-on I looked like a Neanderthal. Mum came into The Ensuite while I was examining it from different angles. She adjusted the glasses under the bulge and smiled encouragingly.

'They have a classic frame. Ronnie Barker wears classic glasses and we all know how big and successful he is.' She was trying to be cheery but I could tell by her voice that she was tired. Dad hadn't come home. 'This is your big moment, Julian. I'm so proud of you.'

'I'm more worried about the lump, Mum.'

'What lump?' She ruffled my hair. 'Twinkle, twinkle.'

Abracadabra had given me a feature on the Free Musketeers, a club of Hobart antique-gun enthusiasts. I was driven to a sheep farm in a TV van along with a sound technician and cameraman. Brendan appeared briefly in a denim leisure suit and handed me a list of questions. I was then pointed toward the shooting range, a wooden maze of old sheep pens with sacks thrown over the barriers, and introduced to Joe, the club's founder. Joe wore his checked woollen shirt out to cover a Tickworth beer belly and tucked his trousers into knee-high gumboots. He worked at Digger's Hardware and managed the musket club in his spare time. He told me this while eyeing Valerie, the sound technician. Valerie wore tight jeans and a lot of make-up. She ignored Joe as she dangled a fluffy thing on a pole over our heads.

I felt a strange calm take hold of me as I took my place in front of the camera. With cool ease, I slipped Brendan's questions into my pocket. Hard-man cub reporter Julian Corkle would ask the questions the public wanted answered. This was my Golden Microphone Moment and no one was going to take it away from me.

The camera was rolling when Joe handed me a musket and gave me instructions on how to use the weapon. I didn't want my side profile on screen, but I could hardly point the gun at the cameraman. Delaying the inevitable, I rested the gun on the barrier cowboy-style. I turned to Joe and gave him a suave Gregory-Peckish look. It was time to probe.

'Could I kill someone with this gun, Joe?'

'Well, yeah, that's what they were designed for really.' He looked at Valerie for confirmation and laughed in the condescending way adults laughed in front of teenagers. 'My advice, young man, is to aim for the target.'

'But what if someone was out for a walk and happened to pass behind the target and I happened to miss the target and hit that certain person in the chest, through the heart, and all that?' The TV audience would love this stuff. Julian Corkle, Abracadabra hitman.

'I'd say you'd have a very good chance of killing that certain person.' Joe gave a patronising snort in my direction and glanced at Valerie again.

'I'll aim for the target then. Ha, ha.' Some humour for the camera.

'They are safety glasses you're wearing, aren't they?' Joe had stopped looking at Valerie and was examining my Nana Mouskouris.

'No, they're just normal glasses. I mean, they're not my normal ones. I usually wear John Lennon glasses with little metal frames and round lenses.'

'I'll be damned. I thought they were safety glasses.' Joe snorted again and winked at Valerie. 'Hang on, come to think of it, they're more like those things that Greek lady singer wears.'

'Well, they're not! They're Yves Saint Laurent signature frames. Your shirt looks like it comes from Cobber's. The supermarket does a nice line of cheap woollens.'

'It's a pity they're not safety glasses because you'll have to put some real ones on before you shoot that gun, son.'

'Can't I just wear these? The lenses are quite thick.' I'd ask Abracadabra to cut this part and the bit about the Greek singer.

'Nope. Them's the rules. Put these on.' Joe was trying to show Valerie who was boss. I removed my Nana Mouskouris and slipped the safety glasses on. The pens and pastures were reduced to blobs and shadows. I placed my elbows on the fence and held the gun in front of me. I aimed for the target and pulled the trigger. The bang nearly dislocated my shoulder and left my fingers tingling.

'What the hell do you think you're doing?'

Joe's voice was loud. He sounded angry, borderline hysterical. I put my Nana Mouskouris back on and looked at the paddock. There was no target, just a sheep running toward a gate. I could hear the *click, click, click* of its dags rattling. The target was in another paddock to my left. I'd been leaning on the wrong sack. Joe wasn't looking at Valerie. I had his full attention. On his face was a nasty self-righteous expression.

'I was trying to hit the target.' My voice was shaky and went high at the end. I was upset and it was all Joe's fault. He'd made me remove my glasses and shoot blind. Now he was trying to humiliate me on Tasmanian television. I pictured Jimmy watching the Budge black-and-white set in Wallaby Place and shuddered. I had to put Joe in his place. 'You said sheep made great moving targets.'

'I said nothing of the sort.' Joe blew air out of his cheeks.

'But you said they're good for practising.'

'Look, son, I don't know what you're implying here.' Joe's voice was a low growl.

'I'm not implying anything. I'm referring to our earlier conversation, about how you practise with sheep.'

'How dare you!'

'I can see this is a sensitive subject for you and the other gun fanatics.'

'We are not fanatics! We're enthusiasts. And, no, it is not a sensitive subject.'

'So it's out in the open then, an open secret and all that?'

'What?'

'The sheep business.'

'There's no sheep business.'

'I don't mean business as in business. I mean funny business. The stuff you and the other fanatics get up to when the TV cameras aren't around.' I winked at the camera. The viewers would lap this up. Jimmy Budge would have a smile on his face.

'For once and for all, we do not get up to funny business, especially not with sheep.'

'I don't mean funny ha-ha. I don't see any sheep laughing. Do you, Joe?' Another wink at the camera.

'I'm not laughing, son.'

'Neither are the sheep, just like I said.'

'You have no right to call our members fanatics and you had no call shooting at an innocent sheep.'

'Who said that sheep was innocent? I mean, how often do you and the other fanatics use these sheep pens for this practising business?'

'I'm going to start counting and if you are not sitting in that Abracadabra van by ten, I'll show you what a musket enthusiast is capable of doing. Now get the hell out of my sight, you little poof, before I pepper your tail end.'

'That's a threat of bodily harm if I ever heard one.' I gave the camera a serious look. 'Journalism, freedom of the press and all that. Not in Hobart.'

'Nine, eight . . .'

'That wraps up our fascinating feature on the gun fanatics of Hobart.'

'Six, five . . .'

I turned and ran as fast as I could, hooting at Joe over my shoulder.

18

Abracadabra told me the shoot would be aired in a week. I couldn't wait. It was going to be the most compelling programme of the *Cub Reporter* series. Mum agreed. Before leaving for Melbourne to spend a week with Norman, she told me I would be the next Dick Dingle. Dad didn't say anything about my television debut. He was disappointed I hadn't covered a real sport like cricket or football.

I didn't know what to feel about my parents. Mum's trip to Melbourne was called a trial separation. They were talking about winding down the marriage and living separately. I felt numb when I thought of Mum and Dad living in separate places. The only strong feelings I had concerned our belongings. I worried about the division of cars and furniture. Knowing Dad, he would take the Valiant, Relaxator Recliner and Rentascope. Mum would get us, the Royal Albert, Torana and The Ensuite. The thought of going back to a black-and-white set made me carsick.

I was relieved when Dad left Hobart with Trevor Bland for a weekend of fishing. Carmel didn't want to talk about our parents, which was just fine with me. She'd never been a cuddly, teary sister. Carmel's way of expressing herself was vigorous physical activity. She'd recently taken to pounding the back fence with a cricket ball. The sheets of corrugated iron had lost most of their corrugations but Carmel said her bowling technique was all the better for it.

It was a special weekend in Hobart. The USS *Enterprise* was anchored off the city and Hot Rocking Radio Hobart was running a friendship campaign for the aircraft carrier. The radio was asking families to invite members of the crew back for a home-cooked meal. Carmel called and gave our address and our mother's name.

We didn't get a lot of Americans in Tasmania but we knew plenty about them from television. They had a lot more money and nicer clothes than Australians. They also had Hollywood and Malibu. Julian Corkle's star was on the rise. Contacts in America were essential.

My heart sank when Carmel opened the front door on Saturday afternoon. The two sailors were dressed in ironed khaki trousers and white shirts and didn't look particularly American or rich. Seen from a neighbour's window, they could've been two dairy-farming cadets from New Zealand. Their hair was razor cut to their pink scalps and their shirts were buttoned to the top. The tallest one did the introductions.

'Hello, ma'm, my name's Conrad and this is Calvin. Your parents home?'

'No, but they gave us strict instructions to be good ambassadors for Hobart. We're just following orders.' Carmel gave a salute before leading them into the lounge and seating them on the couch. 'Would you like a glass of Jackaroo?'

'We are not supposed to drink liquor, ma'm. We are nineteen years old.'

'It isn't liquor. It's Jackaroo. Anyway, you only have to be sixteen to drink in Tasmania.' Carmel was an inspiration.

'That so? What would your ages be?'

'I'm twenty and he's the same age as you. He's short for his age because he smokes cigarillos.'

'Just how old do you have to be to smoke them cigarillos, ma'm?'

'Thirteen.'

'You've got the strangest laws in this state.'

'Sex with animals is also illegal in Tasmania.' Everyone turned at my comment. The sailors seemed startled by the information. They looked at me as if I was a lawbreaker.

'It's just one of the laws and all that.' I shrugged. 'You're also not allowed to steal car radios.'

'Steal?' Conrad's eyes widened. 'We cannot do that back home either.'

The sailors were both looking at me with suspicion.

'I'm a cub reporter.' I needed to assert myself and establish some credibility. 'Got my own TV show.'

'I find that hard to believe.' Conrad's focus shifted to my Nana Mouskouris. He shook his head.

'I just did an exposé on the local gun club. They say I'll win a Tassie Wallaby for it.'

'Gun club?' Conrad smiled for the first time. 'Is that like the National Rifle Association?'

'A lot bigger.' I had no idea what the National Rifle Association was but I wasn't about to let some sailor one-up me.

Carmel returned from the kitchen with four of Mum's party glasses on a tray. She poured the Jackaroo and made a toast. 'To the Starship *Enterprise*!'

Calvin opened his mouth to say something then closed it again and took a sip. While his mouth was open, I'd noticed two rows of huge Marie Osmond teeth.

'You've got very big teeth.' I pulled my lips over mine as I spoke. 'I mean, they're nice, but in a big way.'

'I was five years old when I saw my first orthodontalist.' Calvin smiled. He looked proud.

'But you wouldn't have had your grown-up teeth.'

'They can do a lot with the gums, sir. I had intensive fluoridide treatment and Mom gave me plenty of them supplementations.'

'And that made your teeth big?'

'No, the die-mentions are genetical. Mom says she don't need no reading light when I smile. I just light up the whole wide world.' Calvin laughed. The room brightened.

'You take teeth seriously in America.'

'You're right about that, sir. Our dog wore an orthodontalist brace for a year. He had these long canines. Lordy, did they stick out.'

'Isn't that kind of normal for a dog?'

'Yeah, but it didn't look no good when he smiled.'

The tooth conversation seemed to relax the sailors. Conrad and Calvin sat back on the couch and drank their Jackaroo. They took pride in their teeth and it showed.

I left them with Carmel and went to the kitchen where I removed a frozen chicken from the freezer. I ran hot water over its back and left it to thaw in the sink. When I returned to the lounge, Conrad was explaining how he came from a long line of military men. He'd grown up with a gun cabinet in something called the den and had been given a lifetime membership in the National Rifle Association by his father. He and his brother had used squirrels for target practice when they were kids.

'Pow! Those little critters just pop.' Conrad's face lit up like John's.

I returned to the kitchen feeling queasy and checked the chicken. It was still rock solid inside. I took a knife and tried driving it between the body and a drumstick. The blade pierced

143

the skin and then came to an abrupt halt. I got a rusty screwdriver and hammer out of my father's toolbox. Placing the tip of the screwdriver in the middle of the chicken's back, I brought the hammer down fast. The screwdriver drove into the frozen flesh up to the handle and lodged there like King Arthur's sword. It was stuck fast.

I had one last trick up my sleeve, a trick I'd seen performed on a coconut by Ralph Waters. I went outside where I raised the chicken above my head and threw it as hard as I could against the side of the house. The chicken didn't behave like Ralph's coconut, which had exploded on impact. Instead, it ricocheted off the corrugated iron and hit Rusty, shattering the windscreen into a spider's web of glass cubes. If I hadn't drunk two glasses of wine I might've had a heart attack there and then. The ugly old Valiant was Dad's pride and joy.

I decided to worry about the car later as I got down on my hands and knees to search for the chicken. After bouncing off the windscreen, it had hit the wall again before rolling under the car. I located it sitting under the muffler looking a great deal the worse for wear. Its breast had caved in and the drumsticks were loose. The screwdriver fell out as I retrieved the carcass and dusted it off against my jeans. I took it inside and began rendering the semi-frozen flesh into a cacciatore. While it was cooking, I fried chips and made carrot rounds with parsley, the *Australian Ladies' Companion* way.

Conrad stopped talking about his father's service in Vietnam when I put the food on the table. The Americans were hungry but still insisted on saying grace with their eyes closed before launching into the food. I was taking a second helping of chips when I heard a loud crunch. Calvin coughed and spat out a mouthful of half-chewed food into his hand. He removed a cube of glass and half a tooth and placed them on the tablecloth.

'Lordy, that's my tooth.' His face was white.

'That's just half a tooth.' I nudged the piece of glass aside and pointed to the broken piece of tooth.

'*Just* half a tooth?' Calvin's voice was a whimper. He opened his mouth and fingered the bottom row of his teeth.

'Is it a bicuspid or a molar, Calvin?' Conrad looked serious.

'That ain't no bicuspoid, Conrad. It's a God-damned molar.'

'It couldn't be a wisdom tooth.' I felt compelled to state the obvious.

The sailors ignored me, determined to make the worst of the situation.

'Man, that's a root canal right there and probably some bridge work. Maybe even a crown. That's gonna cost you, buddy. The medical plan don't cover no fancy stuff.' Conrad was doing his bit to calm Calvin down.

'Lordy, lordy.'

'Are you sure that piece of glass wasn't somewhere in your mouth before you started scoffing the cacciatore?' I had to ask. It was a natural enough question.

'Watch it, pal!' Calvin shot me a dangerous look. Blood had collected in the corner of his mouth.

'It's illegal to hit a minor in Tasmania.'

I jumped up from my seat and stood behind Carmel. She'd been observing the turn of events in silence with a fascinated smile.

'You're nineteen years old. I have the legality.'

'You're a minor until you're twenty-five in Tasmania.'

'I'm gonna break the law.' Calvin lunged at me but was restrained by his friend who stood up abruptly, wiping his hand on the tablecloth.

'Man, let's get outta here.'

'You better not steal the car radio on the way out.' I was

holding Carmel in front of me like a shield and pulled her backward as Calvin lunged again.

Conrad bundled his friend out of the door.

From the dinette window, I watched them stop in front of Rusty. Calvin gestured at the shattered windscreen and rubbed his jaw. He let out a yelp as Conrad tugged him away. I ran to the front of the house and opened the lounge window to monitor their progress.

'We lucked out, man. It's a God-damned cab.' Conrad pointed to a Tip Top taxi outside the house. It was a very strange place for a taxi to be parked.

'Did you see that khaki Chrysiller? It was God-damned wind-shield glass in that chicken o'catcheetoray. I'd bet a bicuspoid on it.' Calvin was still rubbing his jaw.

The light went on inside the taxi and I recognised the unhappy driver. He turned and began talking to the sailors as they climbed into the back seat. I saw him nod at Calvin who pointed to his mouth. Carmel's voice suddenly rang out in the night air.

'If you do not leave immediately, I'll call the police, the Starship *Enterprise* and Tip Top Taxis.' She was standing by the letterbox with a cricket bat in her hand. 'I've taken down your number plate, Mr Tip Top. So piss off!'

The inside light went off and the taxi's engine started. As it moved off, I saw Carmel raise her right hand and give them a two-finger salute.

'Dad, I can explain everything.'

'I don't want to hear one of your stories, Julian.' Dad was running his hand over Rusty's windscreen. He bent down and picked up his screwdriver.

'I'll tell the truth, the whole truth and nothing but the truth, so help me God.' I crossed my fingers. 'And Jesus, of course.'

'You watch too much TV.'

'Funny you should say that because I was watching the footy when all this happened. You should've heard the bang. I came outside to find the Valiant's windscreen shattered and a coconut lying on the ground. A car drove off at high speed.'

'Shut up or you'll pay for the new windscreen.'

'It was a Tip Top taxi.'

'Enough!' He held his hand up like a stop sign. 'I'm moving out tomorrow. Trev's got a bachelor flat out the back of his place. It's furnished.'

'Does it have a TV?'

'No, I'll be taking the Rentascope.'

'And the recliner.'

'You're not as stupid as you look.'

Mum called to say she was sorry we couldn't watch the Abracadabra show together. She was staying on at Norman's until Dad moved out. 'It's for the best. Once we get rid of him we can start getting back to normal.'

She talked as if we'd had a normal family life at some point. From what I gathered from television and other Tasmanian families, normal was comfortable and harmonious. Our family life had never been either of these.

I was relieved that Carmel wasn't home for my big Abracadabra night. She would've made things difficult with a running commentary on my performance. Carmel had hockey practice on Tuesday evenings. She usually came home late after a sauna with her team-mates at the YWCA. Mum didn't understand the appeal of the sauna. 'I'd rather have a needle in the eye than sit naked with twenty girls in a steamy sweat box.'

I was prepared to watch the programme alone when I heard the fly screen slap against the back-door frame. My heart sank.

The show was starting as Dad walked into the lounge with a parcel of fish and chips under his arm and a bottle of beer in his hand. He parked his bum on the Relaxator Recliner with a vinyl *whoosh* and opened the packet on his knee.

The screen showed Joe and me walking toward the pens. A narrator's voice was heard over our muffled conversation. 'The musket enthusiasts of Hobart put safety before everything. Their weapons may be antiques, but they're still capable of killing a man.' The camera cut to my side profile.

'Look at that shiner on your forehead. It's glowing like a miner's lamp. No, it looks more like a fluorescent golf ball.' Dad laughed and stuffed a handful of chips into his vicious little mouth.

I could've told him how stupid he looked from the side, even without a bump, but I bit my tongue and concentrated on the television. At least I was watching myself in colour. I prayed that Jimmy Budge was watching me, too.

The camera pulled back to show Joe and me talking. I was holding the gun over the edge of the barrier, very Gregory Peckish. Our voices became audible.

'They are safety glasses you're wearing, aren't they?'

'No, they're just normal glasses.' My voice sounded oily and squeaky at the same time. Valerie had messed up the sound.

'I'll be damned. I thought they were safety glasses. Hang on, come to think of it, they're more like those things that Greek lady singer wears.'

My father started laughing, the sort of laughter that involved rocking on the cheeks of his bum.

'Well, they're not!'

The tone of my voice made Dad laugh harder.

'It's a pity they're not safety glasses because you'll have to put some real ones on before you shoot that gun, son.'

'Can't I just wear these? The lenses are quite thick.'

My father had stopped making noise. The laughter was caught somewhere between his lungs and his cake hole. He was wriggling on the vinyl with his eyes bulging.

The camera zoomed in on my face. I was wearing the safety glasses and leaning over the fence. I squinted and shot the gun. The next scene was a montage of two moving images: a sheep running toward a fence and me running toward the van. My voice sounded more like a howl than a victory hoot. The two scenes were shown again and again. It was intended to be funny. It wasn't. The programme was all wrong. I prayed that Jimmy wasn't watching.

'Look at your arse.' Dad was pointing at my moving image on the screen. 'You and that sheep could be related.' His joke was too much for him and he started the silent rocking again.

The next scene was something I didn't remember. It was of Joe talking earnestly to the camera. He was wearing a pressed business shirt and standing in front of a row of spades and garden rakes.

'A musket is not a toy. This is something we try to drum into the likes of your young cub reporter. I don't blame the boy for running like he did. It's a frightening weapon and not everyone is ready for that kind of power.'

The montage of the sheep and me was shown again as the credits rolled. I hoped the Budge television set had exploded by this point and the electricity to the house had been cut off. The programme was a complete disaster. I would never be able to show my face in public again.

'That's not what happened.' My throat was tight and sore. I felt the pressure of tears behind my eyes. 'I didn't run away because I was scared.'

'No, you were racing that sheep to the shearing shed.' My father was moving about on the chair again. 'Rattling your dags.'

'They cut out all my questions. That Joe's a bastard.'

'That's enough! There'll be no language in this house.' Dad stopped laughing and sat up straight with a self-righteous look.

I hated it when he did that. I was glad he was going and he could take his high horse with him. The phone rang.

'Twinkle, twinkle. You were fabulous. Norman says you're a natural comedian.'

'Mum, they cut out all my questions. They made me look scared.'

'Scared? Don't be ridiculous. You were brilliant. A real star.'

'I wasn't a star. I was a real dag.' I hated myself and wanted to die.

19

Cherie stopped me at the main entrance to Waratah. She said it was a matter of life or death; my life or death. I hadn't been to school since Dad moved out. I couldn't face the cricket pitch or the supermarket. The Abracadabra show was supposed to have been my small-screen triumph, a leg-up to a dazzling career. Instead they'd turned me into a laughing stock. It wasn't fair.

In the chaotic aftermath of the separation I'd been avoiding school and hanging around home but things had definitely not gone back to normal. Mum had quit her job and spent her evenings crying in front of the old black-and-white set. During the day she lay on her bed with the door to The Ensuite open, looking at her bedraggled image in the mirrors. It should've been wonderful to have her to myself but she was too unhappy. Dad was the biggest mistake of her life, she said. She'd wasted her youth on a dud marriage. I did my best to cheer her up but most days I had to work like a drover's dog just to get a single 'Twinkle'.

My one source of real comfort was an *Australian Ladies' Companion* recipe for the twenty-minute sponge cake. In my expert hands, the twenty-minute sponge naturally led to the forty-minute trifle. With practice, I found I could pack quite a few trifles into a hard day at the kitchen sink. Ultimately, the trifles took their toll.

One morning Mum caught me coming out of The Ensuite shower with a towel around my middle. It was a regular bathroom towel but didn't have enough wrap to cover both my lower half and my bottle tops, which peeked over the towel edge like a couple of baby bottle-nosed dolphins. Mum gave the dolphins a hard look and told me to lay off the trifles and get back to school.

Cherie placed a steadying hand on my arm. Her face was serious. 'Paul Lamb and Ross Gibb said they're going to pound you into a rissole.'

'Why?' I scanned the school grounds with a thumping heart.

'They reckon you're a pooftah. There's a story about you trying something on Wayne in a newsagent.'

I swallowed hard. No one was going to listen to me. Lamb and Gibb didn't want the truth. They wanted to pound me into mincemeat and serve me to Wayne. Boys could do what they liked to poofters because no one was stupid enough to defend them. I was doomed. I had no allies and nowhere to hide.

'You'd better keep away from Wayne.'

'How can I keep away from him? I can't stay home. Mum and Dad are getting a divorce and we've lost the colour TV.' A sob flew out of my mouth. I wanted to explain that I was upset about the TV and not the divorce but I couldn't get the words out.

Cherie's hand moved to my elbow. She propelled me across the road to the bus stop.

'You should leave school and get a job. They're taking on school-leavers at the Wool Board. Mum's got a new boyfriend called Bruce who's a fleece-grader. He could put a word in.'

I imagined myself grading daggy fleeces in a windy barn and

shuddered. Wool was not a career option. 'Bruce doesn't know anyone in television?'

Cherie blinked.

'I'd be interested in a position in Sydney or Melbourne.'

'Julian, I can't miss typing. We're doing business letters and apparently they're quite important. Stay here till the bus comes. You'll be safe.'

I looked around after Cherie left. The bus stop was anything but safe. It was directly across from the school entrance and consisted of a dinged metal timetable nailed to the side of a wooden pole. My thigh was thicker than the pole which was covered with swearwords. These had been carved into the wood with pocket knives by the likes of Lamb and Gibb. The next bus was in forty-five minutes, plenty of time to get rissolled.

'*Salut!*'

I lunged for the pole and swung myself behind it, pulling in my head to avoid a punch on the nose.

'We've missed you.' Mr Snell raised his eyebrows and laughed. 'That TV show had us all in stitches.'

'It wasn't supposed to be funny.' I came out from behind the pole, trying to look as casual and French as possible.

'You're just being modest.'

'No I'm not.'

'Why haven't you been at school?'

'I've been sick. The old lungs are playing up.' I thumped my chest with my knuckles. The sound was dull, like a beer bottle falling on carpeted concrete. 'Got too close to the neighbour's pigeons. Fancier's lung.'

'What a comedian.' He laughed again.

Something moved behind Mr Snell, fast and unexpected like an anvil falling from the sky. It was Paul Lamb and he was doing a sitting wheel-stand on his souped-up Fireball

153

bicycle. He'd planted his feet either side of the rear wheel and was leaning back hard against the sissy bar of his banana seat, *Easy Rider* style. Lots of boys had banana seats but only the toughest had sissy bars. The bigger the sissy bar, the bigger the bully.

Mr Snell looked at his watch and turned to leave. I couldn't let him abandon me. This was a matter of life or death.

'They say you end up in an iron lung.'

The teacher smiled good-humouredly and indicated that it was time to go.

'It's a very unattractive machine, sir. Your head sticks out and you look like a rotisserie-cooked chicken.' I glanced across the road. Paul Lamb was now running a finger across his throat. My pulse rate soared. 'The electricity costs a fortune. It's like running a tumble-dryer day in, day out.'

Mr Snell looked up at the sound of the school bell.

'There's not enough room in the house.' My voice was high and desperate. 'They'd probably set me up in the garage and run a power cable over the back lawn.'

'It's a fascinating story, Julian, but I have to go.'

'But my parents are getting divorced!' There it was again. I wasn't worried about the divorce. It was the television. 'Dad's taken the colour TV!'

Mr Snell smiled. 'At least you'll have room for the iron lung then. Ha, ha.'

'I'm serious.'

'You're a riot!' The teacher was still laughing as he crossed the road, shaking his head.

Paul Lamb waited for Mr Snell to enter the grounds, then he shoved two fingers in his mouth like a sheep farmer. His piercing whistle made the hairs stand up on my arms and probably roused every border collie within five kilometres.

Within seconds Ross Gibb and two other thugs had arrived on stripped-down bicycles with long ape-hanger handlebars. None of them had carriers because none of them carried schoolbags. The boys from the cricket pitch didn't waste time on schoolwork. They had more important things to do – like rissolling poofters.

I'd read in the *Companion* that time slowed during a car accident and a traumatised brain absorbed events in fine detail. The boys dropped their bikes and moved towards me in Hollywood slow motion. With the clarity of a trauma victim, I took in their greasy hair and spotty skin, traces of facial fluff and evidence of recent shaving. I'd just bought my first razor and hadn't even taken it out of the packet. I imagined running the blade over cuts and bruises and felt like crying.

I clutched the pole as the boys fanned out around me. Joan of Arc flashed through my mind as I dropped to my knees and put my hands over my face. The one thing I didn't want was scars. I hunched my shoulders and waited for the blows.

'Bully one! Bully two!'

I couldn't believe my ears. I pulled my hands away and saw a miracle. Carmel was standing in front of Paul Lamb with her hockey stick raised. The rest of the hockey team had formed a noose around the boys.

'Carmel!'

My voice started off as a deep croak and ended in a squeak. I didn't care. Carmel was the cavalry, a St Bernard with a barrel of brandy. I was saved.

Paul Lamb sniggered and Carmel made her move. Her hockey stick slashed down, forward, then up, stopping just millimetres from his testicles. He opened his mouth but no sound came out.

'Piss off, the lot of you.' Carmel looked at the boys with a scowl. 'The Girls' A hockey team has more important nuts to crack.'

Paul Lamb squeaked.

Carmel pointed to the school gate with her hockey stick and the cordon opened to let the boys pass. A couple of thugs made a show of swaggering but no one challenged the hockey team. No one ever did. Carmel watched them go before turning back to me.

'Catch another bus.'

I was watching *Dick Dingle's Midday Report* in dreary black and white when Frank knocked on the back door. Afternoon was an odd time for him to call around. He should've been at school. He wasn't even wearing his prefect's jacket. I pushed the fly screen open and invited him into the dinette.

'Hello, Frank.'

'I thought you had a colour telly.' Frank pointed to the flickering television through the open lounge door.

'We do.'

'That looks very black and white to me.'

'Why aren't you at school?'

'Been suspended.' Frank wasn't the type to get into trouble. He was a prefect and the darling of the checkout girls. 'It was a set-up. They said I pocketed money from the cordial stand.'

'Why would they say that?'

'They said ten dollars went missing.'

'Why would they say that?'

'Duncan Bacon saw me put it in my pocket.'

'Did you put it back?'

'I was getting around to it.'

'Oh. How's Cobber's? Still on the express lane?'

'Got laid off. A misunderstanding over a tip.'

'Uh-huh. How's Christine?'

'Bonza. We went to Port Arthur on the bus and stayed in a motel. The room had a fridge with little bottles of drinks. There was even a colour TV.' Frank narrowed his eyes at the flickering television. 'We saw your show. Christine said you were real professional. She thought that Joe was a wanker.'

'They cut out all the good stuff.'

'You were probably set up.' Frank nodded grimly. 'Framed.'

'You're right.' I felt something loosen in my chest. Frank understood. For the first time in over a month, I found myself smiling.

'You've got to bounce back. Don't let them win.'

'I've already had offers of more TV work. I'm considering Melbourne or Sydney.'

'With your mouth, you'll probably be bigger than Dick Dingle one day.'

'You're not the first person to tell me that.'

Frank was right, of course. I had to bounce back. One hiccup didn't ruin a small-screen career. I felt inspired after he left and got out Mum's rose-perfumed writing paper.

Dear Joe,

I was thoroughly impressed with your performance on TV. You're a real professional. You're also very handsome and charming. I love sideburns on a man. I call them mutton chops. Ha, ha. The life of a sound technician is a lonely one. I get quite hungry for male company, if you know what I mean. To be frank, you're my type, a real man. Whiskers and all. Ha, ha.

Please come to the Abracadabra Television studio next Wednesday evening at five. There is no need to call beforehand. Just come dressed for dinner in that lovely Cobber's checked shirt. I have somewhere special to take you.

With a big kiss,
Valerie

I got the address for Digger's Hardware and posted the letter to Joe. There, at least I'd done something constructive. I felt a lot better.

20

I was trying to figure out what Elizabeth Taylor was wearing around her neck at the Academy Awards but the black-and-white television was hampering my research. Monochrome had an uncanny way of removing all pomp and glitter from an international gala. Liz may as well have been a Tasmanian Weight Watcher attending the dog trials. The diamond around her neck could've been a lump of pastry dough.

I'd become quite an expert on pastry since quitting school. The short crust was a particular obsession. Through trial and error I'd discovered that the less flour I used, the faster the pastry dissolved in my mouth. I'd upped the butter and sugar content but a rich pastry made all the difference to a tangy lemon tart.

Leaving school would've been impossible if Dad still lived in the house. Despite their differences, my parents had always formed a united front when it came to school, church and family. These were things you did regardless of whether or not they were worthwhile. Once the marriage collapsed, unnecessary institutions began to fall like dominoes. It was relatively easy to convince Mum that school was a waste of time. I just had to take over the kitchen and vacuum cleaner and make a few key changes to the way the house was run.

My first improvement was the removal of all religious and sports paraphernalia. I then filled the cake tins and made sure the toilet seat was down and stayed down. The built-in bar was uprooted and moved to the rumpus room downstairs, which had now become the exclusive domain of Carmel and anything else related to sports.

The only two real problems were the crap television and my impending financial crisis. Despite cutting down to four cigarettes a day, my savings from Cobber's were rapidly running out. Mum was on drip feed from Dad who'd vowed to pay the legal minimum in family support and nothing more. The little she received, however, was still more than I had. Sacrifices had to be made.

'Mum, can I have two dollars? We need butter.'

'Again? But you bought butter yesterday.'

'According to Graham Kerr, butter is the basis of all fine cuisine.' I was a big fan of Kerr's show, *The Galloping Gourmet*. Nearly everything he cooked had a French name and required butter and cream.

'You watch too much television.'

'Not as much since we lost the colour TV.'

Mum sighed and rummaged in her handbag for her clip purse. She pulled it out and emptied its contents on to the Aussiemica bench top. There were only coins.

'Just buy one block this time.' She sighed again, heavily. 'That's all the money we've got till his nibs coughs up tomorrow.'

Things would've been easier for Mum if she'd had a friend in a similar situation but all her former Boomerang workmates now avoided her. Mum said that separation was a disease married women didn't want to catch. She could now call Norman without Dad's interference but what she really needed was a friend for cinema and tea purposes. On good days she could look like a faded Natalie Wood but on bad days she looked empty, like a collapsed birthday balloon. We'd had a run of bad days.

When I got back from Cobber's Mum was sitting in the dinette with the remains of an afternoon tea in front of her. The Royal Albert had been set for two and my lemon tarts were displayed in the centre. She was dressed in her best skirt and blouse and had brushed her hair. Her cheeks were flushed. She looked ten years younger.

'You look ten years younger, Mum.' I counted the tarts on the plate and took the biggest. 'Are you going out?'

'I'm going for a job. It's time we sorted ourselves out.'

'Uh-huh.' I didn't like the sound of 'we' but Mum hadn't looked so good in weeks. Putting my own needs aside, I placed a tart on the plate at her elbow.

'You can thank that Dolly. She called just after you left to say she was on her way. What a cow.'

'Hereford heifer.' I refilled Mum's teacup and got to work on my tart.

'She told me I'd been neglectful as a wife.' Mum's face hardened. 'Yes, I told her, for nearly twenty years I'd neglected to notice her brother was a bastard.'

I stopped chewing. Mum had never used the word 'bastard' in my hearing, ever. Another domino had fallen. Either she'd suddenly started swearing or she now thought I was old enough to deal with it. I sat up straighter.

'She told me it takes two to tango. She said I wasn't asking myself the difficult questions.' Mum's mouth was a hard line. 'I told her, I should ask myself why I've tolerated her for so long. You should've seen her, frozen to the spot like a bag of Tucker Box peas. Then of course she said something about you. She said you were, you know.'

'No.'

'Like Liberace and all that. I told her at least I'm not a grand-mother yet.'

'Surely not . . .'

'She may as well be the way that Sharon carries on.'

'But isn't Sharon only fourteen?'

'She wears her skirts too short.'

'But Carmel's hockey skirt is short.'

'Carmel's the sporty type.'

'And . . . ?'

'Sharon's not.'

Mum took a bite of her tart and screwed up her face. 'What on earth?'

'I've been perfecting the pastry.'

'It's pure butter and sugar.' She shook her head and stared at my chest. 'This has to stop, Julian. We've got to pull ourselves together.'

My mother woke me at six to ask whether she looked all right. She was wearing her favourite rose-pink dress with dressy maroon sandals. I sat up in bed and rubbed my eyes. Mum's outfit required my full attention. She'd landed a job at the Wool Board as the cafeteria cashier.

'Give us a whirl, Mum.'

She spun around with her arms outstretched.

'Perfect.' Her handbag matched her sandals. 'Just let me give the back of your hair a fluff.'

Mum had come prepared. She handed me a comb and can of hairspray and then sat down on the edge of the bed. I got to work while she did her face in a hand mirror. When I'd finished, she stood and did another twirl.

'Even perfecter.'

'Tell Carmel to go see her father before school. I haven't got time to see the idiot today and we're out of money again.'

By ten o'clock I was convinced that Carmel was not getting up for school. There was no bread or butter in the house and I'd smoked half my quota of John Player Specials for the day. Something had to be done.

To get to the lower half of the house, I had to climb underneath an old velvet curtain that Carmel had rigged up over the spiral staircase. It was pitch dark underneath and the smell of Tickworth lager rose up to meet me as I began my descent. I knew that she'd been celebrating and I feared the violence of a hangover. The previous evening I'd heard Helen Reddy and female laughter coming from the rumpus room.

'*Carmel.*'

I kept my voice low and soft. My sister hadn't punched me for a while but I didn't want to tempt fate. Her arms were like table legs.

I reached the bottom of the stairs and touched down on carpet. I couldn't see a thing.

'*Carmel.*'

The room was filled with the faint *whooshing* of sleep. Raising my arms in front of me like a cartoon sleepwalker, I felt around for the safety of the wall and its light switch. I circled a few times but then lost my bearings. My arms were moving in empty space.

Someone snorted. Glass clinked. With horror, I realised that there was more than one person in the room. Dad could wait.

I spun around frantically, trying to relocate the stairwell. My foot landed on something cylindrical that rolled with me as I tried to regain my footing. I lost my balance and fell forward. The crown of my head hit the cast iron of the stairwell with a loud *gong*. The fluorescent lights flickered to life.

'What the hell are you doing here?'

I was grabbed by the seat of my pants and yanked upward. I kicked the offending lager bottle clear of my feet and moved away from my sister.

'Mum needs the maintenance money. You've got to go see Dad.'

'I'm not going anywhere.' Carmel winked and motioned with a thumb to the sleeping forms on the couch and bed. 'You're looking at two of the finest players on the Hobart team.'

I hadn't spoken to my father since he'd moved out. He hadn't called me and I hadn't called him.

'Hello, Dad.'

'G'day, Sunshine. How's my champ bowler?'

'It's Julian.'

'Oh.'

'I need to talk to you.'

'You've caught me on the hop. We're gunning for the deadline.'

'Mum needs the maintenance. Can you bring it round after work?'

'Tonight's out. I'm going to the track with Trev. You can come and pick it up at the *Star*.'

'You want *me* to come to the office?' John and Carmel had both been to the newspaper office but I'd never set foot in the place.

'On second thoughts, meet me at the Copper Kettle on the corner. It's got a big brass teapot over the door. You can't miss it.'

I'd been waiting for half an hour in the coffee shop when I saw Dad stop in front of the pub across the street. It was strange to see him outside the context of marriage and family. He looked like a normal Tasmanian man, insignificant, even harmless.

The brown and beige of his clothes were typical of the men of his generation. So was his build: small head, big belly and skinny legs. He turned his small head as a Toyota Hiace pulled up, and smiled at the members of a rugby team as they clambered out of the van's sliding door. I knew they were rugby players because they were all wearing blue blazers with a gold rugby ball on the pocket. Most of them had necks as wide as their heads.

My father was still smiling when he entered the Copper Kettle. He didn't bother to say hello.

'You must be proud of your sister making the Hobart team.' Dad threw a very thin-looking *Hobart Star* envelope in front of me and then turned to survey the cakes and sandwiches in the display cabinet. 'That girl's on her way to the Tassie team.'

Now I knew why Carmel had been so pleasant. I slipped the envelope into my pocket and stifled an urge to flee.

'John's another shooting star.' Dad sat down with a cream-filled butterfly cake and toasted cheese sandwich. 'He's already cutting up bodies.'

'That sounds about right.'

'He'll make a fine heart surgeon one day. He reckons he'll do transplants.'

'That could come in handy.'

'What do you mean by that?' Dad gave me one of his looks and tore the corner off the cheese toastie. His small teeth made short work of it.

'Nothing.'

'I should probably tell you.' Dad took another bite of the toastie and talked while chewing. 'A couple of weeks ago I bumped into that blond thing from the TV. He asked after you.'

'Brendan! He's a director of Abracadabra Television.' My stomach fluttered. Brendan had asked after *me*.

'I don't care what he calls himself. He's too much like your uncle for my tastes.' He swallowed his mouthful and jutted his small chin out in a self-righteous way. 'Said he wanted a cub reporter.'

'Me!'

'Too late. I told him you've already buggered everything up by leaving school.' Dad smiled in a satisfied way and shoved the sponge wings of the butterfly cake into his mouth. He still followed the sweets after savouries rule.

'But . . .' I thought of Tania from Geelong and felt my chin tremble.

'You should've thought of all that before, mate. They wanted a school kid.'

It started drizzling while I was waiting for the bus, the sort of drizzle that starts out looking harmless and ends up soaking its victims to the skin. By the time the bus arrived, my *Scary Monsters* T-shirt was stuck to my torso and David Bowie's face was a wrinkle between my bottle tops. The bus driver did a double take as he handed me my change.

'Jesus holy Christ. You should wear a lady's brassiere, mate. They're indecent. Ha, ha.'

I flapped the T-shirt away from my chest and made for the empty bench seat at the back of the bus. The seat was giving off an unpleasant, intimate smell of wet wool and dog pee but I was beyond caring. Rubbing my arm across the window, I took in the passing suburban streets. Kids were coming home from school in raincoats and cars with steamed-up windows were waiting outside fish-and-chip shops. I closed my eyes and thought of Ulverston. Things had gone to hell since we'd come to Hobart and it was all Dad's fault. I would've still been at school and had Jimmy Budge if we hadn't left.

'Get yourself off of the bus.'

I woke with a start.

The bus driver was bellowing from his seat through a cupped hand. He swivelled his body and swung one of his meaty legs into the aisle. It was naked from the sock line to the hem of his micro-shorts. All the working Tasmanian men wore such shorts – electricians, sheep farmers, helicopter pilots – and they nearly all teamed them with indecently thick hairy legs. The bus driver's kelpie-brown shorts were strained to capacity by the pink beef of his thighs. He deserved to be told but I was in no position to do it.

'Where are we?' I walked to the front and squinted through the windscreen.

'You've got eyes in your head. Four of them by the looks. Ha, ha.'

'I can't see anything.' The wipers were off and the windows were steamed up.

'What do you think that is then?' He pointed through the open door to a ticket booth.

'Surely not the bus terminal?' The terminal was a good half-hour's walk from home. It was pelting down outside.

'Well, it's not bloody Fiji, is it, you big twit.'

As I stepped off the bus, my right foot disappeared up to the ankle in a large brown puddle. I leaped to save the other sneaker and managed to get my left foot on dry land. The doors of the bus hissed shut and the driver revved his engine. The bus jerked forward, sending a wave of filthy water over both legs below the knee.

21

It wasn't the black-and-white TV or the lack of money that finally forced me out of the house and on to the job market. It was my father and the way he'd broken the news to me about Abracadabra. His smug expression haunted me. The only way to wipe the smirk off his face was to pick myself up and get myself back on the small screen. I had to do it right this time, but for that, I needed connections.

The one place in Hobart with real gold dust was the Dingo Hotel, a glorious high-rise tower adjoining the state's only casino. People called it the Finger Pointing to God. The former state premier, Bernie Pouch, had certainly benefited from the assistance of higher powers to get the state's gaming laws changed and the casino approved. He'd overcome public opposition by promising a windfall of charity funds. 'The money will be channelled back into the community. There'll be new handicraft schools for the blind and youth centres for idle teenagers. We'll get these lowlifes off the streets and make our neighbourhoods safer for women.' Tasmanians were proud of Pouch. They said he was a man of vision.

Hobart's only VIP suite was located at the summit of the tower on the ninth floor. The place for Julian Corkle to start making connections was at the top. I silently thanked my mother for buying big as I squeezed into my First Communion shirt. This I teamed with a blue pinstriped suit from the Catholics Do Care charity shop and one of Dad's old paisley ties. The Julian Corkle in the mirror not only appeared four years older but he also looked damned good. I spent an hour getting my Bryan Ferry sweep-over just right and then caught a bus to the hotel on Hobart's waterfront. The bus stopped in front of the casino, a good three minutes' walk from the hotel entrance. The bus driver told me to get off.

'Don't you go all the way to the hotel?'

'Nah.'

'But the sign said the bus stops at the hotel.'

'Not when there's only one whinger aboard. Then the bus stops here.' The bus drivers of Hobart were in league against me.

'I don't understand.'

'What's there to understand, mate?'

'Why you're not going to the hotel.'

'Because I don't feel like it.'

'How do I get to the hotel?'

'You got legs, mate.'

'Through the casino?'

'Suit yourself.'

I'd never been inside the casino and the reason was printed above the main entrance in large gold lettering: 'Persons Under 18 Not Permitted. No Dogs Either'. I silently congratulated myself on the pinstriped suit as I whirled through the revolving door and into the deafening *bing-bing-bing* of the gaming hall. The enormous room was ringed by banks of colourful slot machines and decorated in the style of an upscale sideshow. In the smoky distance were the tables where the real players gambled away bungalows and automobiles but at the fruit machines near me most of the clients had grey hair and wore cardigans.

'Cherry! Cherry! Give me a damn cherry!' A pensioner stood on the rungs of her stool and thumped the side of the slot machine with a tiny fist. The machine whirred before giving a half-hearted *bing*. She plonked back down deflated. 'Bugger!'

A hand fell on my shoulder. 'You'll have to leave the premises, young man.' The security guard said this without a smile.

'I'm only passing through. I'm a guest at the hotel.'

'You'll have to take the outside path.'

'I'm staying in the VIP suite.'

The guard gripped my shoulder and pulled me close. He didn't need to say another thing. His face had the joy and liveliness of Ned Kelly's death mask. I'd seen this plaster cast first hand when it had travelled around Tasmanian primary schools as part of the 'Australia of Yesteryear' exhibition. When it came to St Kevin's everyone in the class had hurried past the gold mining pans and wooden washboards to get to the important lump of white plaster. We knew the cast had been taken off a famous dead person and wanted to make the most of it. When Brother Punt turned to slap a boy for jostling, Ralph Waters had leaned across to put a finger in one of Ned's ears. His *ring-a-ding-ding* sound effect had been too much for Gary Jings who'd fainted and hit his head on a butter churn.

The reception of the Dingo Hotel reflected the hotel's status as the flagship of Tasmania's Own hotel chain. The lobby was big and shiny and furnished with clusters of orange vinyl armchairs and glass-topped coffee tables. I breathed in the lavender air freshener and imagined myself with a manager's badge gliding through reception to welcome VIPs, asking about their children and refusing twenty-dollar tips. After a hard day of gliding, I'd kick back to drink a coconut cocktail with Dick

Dingle. 'You're wasting your talent,' he'd say. 'Your face is made for the small screen.' I know, Dick, I'd tell him. 'But I insist on having my own show this time.'

I swaggered up to the front desk. It was a long pinewood construction done up in the shape of a cruise ship with porthole display windows for Dingo-theme cigarette lighters, pens and key rings. The young receptionist noticed my suit and put away her nail file. She sat up straight when I asked to see the manager and dialled through my request. I was shown directly into Bevan Bunion's office. My entrée into the world of movers and shakers was going to be easier than I thought.

'What can I do for you?'

Bevan Bunion seemed surprised by my appearance. He stood and stretched out an arm. It was short and thick and went with his short, thick body, which bulged out at the middle like a spinning top. He was dressed in a blue pinstriped suit, white shirt and paisley tie. The only difference between his outfit and mine was the gold and onyx ring on his pinkie. The finger stood out like a rigid antenna.

'I want to apply for a job.'

'Oh.' Bunion slumped back into his chair with his thick legs open. His trousers rustled as he scissored the legs against the vinyl. 'As what?'

'I'm thinking of management.' I didn't bother telling him that my position would be temporary. I'd only be staying long enough to meet the right people.

'How old would you be, Mr . . . ?'

'Corkle, Julian Corkle. I'm almost nineteen.'

'You look very young for your age.'

'I live a very healthy life. No alcohol, no cigarettes and no flesh. I'm a vegetarian.'

The word 'flesh' seemed to rouse him. He looked at me

more seriously. 'Have you any experience in the hospitality industry?'

'My family ran the Cracker Hotel in Sydney for years. I grew up in the hospitality business and was weaned on Caterers' Choice products.' I moved closer to his desk and bent forward to give him the full force of my managerial charm. 'Mr Bunion, Hospitality is my middle name. Industry would naturally be my other middle name.'

'We might have a position for a person with your background.' Bunion shifted his large bum in the chair. 'The job's a great starting point for an ambitious individual with managerial aspirations. I'm looking for someone who can think on his feet.'

'I'm not short on aspirations or fancy footwork. You could call me a shooting star.'

'You'll be supplied with a uniform, a gold name badge and your own shelf in the service bay near the kitchen.'

'My own shelf?'

'Responsibility has its rewards.' He rocked back in his chair and formed steeples with his stubby fingers, regarding me through the fingerwork.

'Is there anything else?'

'The glasses.' Smiling, he unsteepled his fingers and made twirling motions around his eyes. 'You remind me of that Greek singer.'

'Nana Mouskouri?' This was no time to be a poor loser.

'No, the bigger one.'

'She's about the biggest.'

'Demis Roussos.'

'He doesn't wear glasses.'

'I didn't say he did.'

I quickly decided I didn't like Bevan Bunion. The job he

assigned me was the lowest on the Tasmania's Own food chain. I was hired as a porter, a position that put at least five years between an assistant manager's desk and me. The VIP suite may as well have been in Alice Springs. I soon discovered that most of its occupants were unfriendly businesspeople who never spoke to or even noticed porters. They had rude assistants for that. Worse still, porters weren't allowed near the VIP suite. We had to deposit VIP luggage in the lobby for a duty manager to take up.

My uniform consisted of a Queen Mother pillbox hat and a piddle-coloured suit with a blue stripe running down the trouser leg. It was hotel policy for porters to personally carry all luggage to the rooms below floor nine. Bevan Bunion refused to supply us with wheeled carts or carrying aids. He said we wouldn't be getting motorised golf chariots either. 'Guests lap up the personal hands-on touch.' He thought he was a funny man.

My first hour on the job coincided with the arrival of a Tasmania Razzle Dazzle Tour bus packed with thirty tired and thirsty tourists who wanted immediate access to the clean underwear in their luggage. It was a brutal initiation to portering and left me with a personal hatred for the Little Swag line of baggage.

Little Swags were locally made products with a 'Proud to be Australian' emblem sewn into the stiff, reinforced vinyl. The suitcases were designed in the shape of the Australian mainland and came with a toilet bag in the shape of Tasmania. Not only was the plastic boomerang handle hard to hold, but the Queensland part of the suitcase jutted upward awkwardly. This unsymmetrical design made carrying difficult, particularly when the suitcase was stuffed with thirty kilograms of souvenirs and pastel clothing.

'Makes you proud to be Australian.' A large cattle farmer on holiday was watching me heave his Little Swag through the door of the room. It was my eighth Swag.

'A word of advice, sir, from a professional.' I lowered my voice in a confidential way and put the Swag down in the middle of the room. I pointed to Queensland. 'Be extremely careful with this suitcase. One of our porters lost a testicle on Cape York Peninsula.'

'A test . . .' The sheep farmer didn't want to say a dirty word. 'I think you mean a ball, mate.'

'Tore it clean off poor Geoffrey. He's suing the company. Naturally, they'll have to pay for the rubber implant.'

The farmer drew breath sharply.

'Geoffrey's lawyer is demanding a recall of all suitcases. He's campaigning to get Queensland removed from the Little Swag map.'

'But it wouldn't be Australia without Queensland.'

'Where would you be from, sir?'

'Near Brisbane.'

The one benefit to working as a hotel porter was obvious within a couple of weeks and didn't slip my mother's notice. Mum was an expert at finding the silver lining wherever I was concerned.

'You've lost weight, honey.' She reached out and gently pinched one of my love handles. 'Give us a twirl.'

I held in my stomach and did a new fancy aerobics twirl with my arms at shoulder height. Aerobics had arrived in Tasmania and was taking the island by storm. I didn't know anyone who actually did the exercises but hundreds now wore the fluorescent Lycra outfits. Body-hugging leggings were a particular favourite of the bigger Hobart lady.

'Svelte.' Mum was learning new words at the Wool Board. She was also dressing better and had allowed me to rinse the grey out of her hair.

I let out a lungful of air and sagged back into my trousers. 'Mum, I'm not sure if the Dingo is the right place for me.'

'It's a four-star hotel and you've got at least four stars.' Mum tucked the back of my David Bowie T-shirt into my trousers and patted my bum. 'Twinkle, twinkle.'

'But I haven't met anyone famous yet.'

'Keep smiling, honey. You look much better when you smile.' She flashed lots of teeth to remind me of how it was done. 'This job is just a stepping stone. You're bound for bigger and better things but you've got to start somewhere.'

'But I look so stupid with a biscuit tin strapped to my head.' I was starting to whine. I hated my whine almost as much as Dad did.

'Julian, I'm proud of you. You're the only one with pizzazz.' She lifted my chin and ruffled my hair. 'Just a little patience, honey. We're doing pretty well, the two of us.'

Mum was right, of course. I was her only hope. John might be able to cut up bodies but he would never look good in front of a television camera. And any pizzazz Carmel had was wasted on the sports field.

Mum said she didn't understand her daughter any more. 'She takes no notice of anything I say.'

'And what's with the haircut?' I raised my eyebrows and pursed my lips. The subject of Carmel's hair never failed to get my mother started. Once she got started I was assured of complete support for the Julian Corkle cause.

'What kind of salon does a short back and sides in this day and age?'

'A barber probably. Apparently the clipper cut is very *à la mode* with sheep farmers. You should see the types we get at the hotel.'

'Oh my goodness!' Mum closed her eyes and shook her head. 'It's all your father's fault, insisting on those damned cricket balls. He's ruined that girl with his sport, sport, sport. The man's a fanatic.'

'He certainly never helped me.' I was going for gold. Mum was eating out of my hand. 'It's a good thing I never played ball games.'

'Thank goodness.' Mum smiled. She was proud of me and it felt right.

'At least I listen to you, Mum.' I'd hit gold and was going for platinum.

Mum frowned. Her smile faded. 'Carmel's drinking.'

'Are you sure?' Of course Carmel was drinking. She'd been drinking for years. Lager was her drink of choice and like her father she followed 'the more lager, the merrier' rule.

'I can smell it in the house.'

'Uh-huh.' This was definitely not a line of conversation I wanted to pursue. Since leaving school I'd been working my way through the spirits in the china cabinet. I'd started with the Irish Mist and sherry and, as choices dried up, had moved on to the eggnog and crème de menthe.

'It's hard to believe your birthdays are only a day apart. Surely you should have something in common.'

'It's certainly not dress sense.'

'At least she's stopped wearing those shearer's singlets and started covering her arms. I was at my wits' end with those arms.'

There was a very good reason why Carmel now wore sleeved shirts at home but it wasn't something Mum needed to know. One evening I'd bumped into her on the corner of Echidna

Avenue. She was dressed in a woollen shearer's singlet and cricket trousers. My eyes had been drawn to an ugly blue blot on the upper part of her bowler's arm. The skin around the blue area was angry red.

'What's that on your arm?'

'Tattoo.' Carmel gave a lopsided smile and did a Popeye with her bicep. The dark mark expanded. 'Trudy did it.'

'Trudy from the Hobart team?'

'She's got a home tattoo kit. From America.' Carmel obviously thought that the kit's origins made home tattooing a legitimate activity.

'Why a train?'

'It's a scorpion, dickhead.'

'Looks like a train to me.' There was nothing scorpion about it. 'It's one of those old-fashioned locomotives with smoke stacks.'

'They're claws.' Carmel had decided. There was no changing her mind.

'Why a scorpion?'

'All the other stencils were crap. I didn't want a bloody goat or a fish.'

'Was there a bull?'

Carmel narrowed her eyes and nodded.

'Taurus is a bull. You're a Taurus. They must've been horoscope stencils.'

'Fuck it!'

22

Hotel workers were divided into two groups at the Dingo, indoors and outdoors. Porters were outdoor staff along with gardeners and window cleaners. Indoor staff had it a lot better. They earned more, wore no hats and had no stripes on their trousers. They also got to mingle with the guests at the top of the hotel. I didn't intend to remain on the outside for long and made a point of befriending indoor staff between suitcases.

Anne-Marie Putts was short with the solid, determined build of a shot-putter. Her features were tiny and crowded into the middle of her large, freckled face, which was framed by a bell of wiry ginger hair. Despite these obvious drawbacks, Anne-Marie thought she was better than me because she was a housemaid. Her shelf was positioned a rung above mine in the service bay.

'I hear you have an Italian in the VIP suite.' I'd just discovered that Bruno Bempi was in town for the wool auctions. Bempi was a fashion designer and semi-famous in the international world of menswear. The *Star* said he made tweed jackets for the Duke of Edinburgh. Celebrity clothes designer was on my list of back-up career possibilities.

'Bloody Italians! I must've scooped two handfuls of hair out of the jet bath yesterday. The rim had a fur collar. I had to flush the jets. You'd think the bastard had been washing beavers in there.' Anne-Marie shook her big head in disgust. 'With his money, he could at least get his back dehaired.'

'He's a world-class fashion designer.'

'He's a hairy bastard.'

'He designs for royalty.'

'Big poof.'

I bit my tongue and arranged my belongings into straight lines. My shelf was by far the tidiest in the service bay. The only other that came close belonged to Nigel, the head waiter. Nigel was the one indoor staff member I hadn't tried to befriend. It was common knowledge that he lived with a butcher and kept toy Yorkshire terriers. The kitchen staff called him Tiffany and made his life very difficult. Nigel's mouth was a permanent cat's bum.

'I hear the jet bath is a deluxe.' The best way to get information out of Anne-Marie was to appeal to her sense of self-importance.

'Enormous.' She sighed in a significant way and ran a hand over her stiff triangle of hair.

'I suppose they need it for the really big guests. Elizabeth Taylor would certainly require a deluxe.'

'Why would Elizabeth Taylor use our jet bath?'

'Good question.'

'What?'

'Can I have a look at the VIP suite?'

'Nope.' Anne-Marie held up her hands officiously. They were as wide and flat as Sandy Bay flounders. 'I can't let just anyone inside.'

'But I work at the hotel. I enter guest rooms every day.'

'You're outdoor staff. The VIP suite is restricted access. Bunion would have a fit if he caught you.'

'Discretion is my middle name.'

'He snoops.' She jiggled the keys inside her apron pocket. 'I could lose my job. It's a responsibility.'

'I'll clean the jet bath for you.'

'All right but don't touch anything.'

The VIP suite was huge and had a bed big enough for Elizabeth Taylor and all her husbands. The remnants of chicken in a basket sat on the room-service trolley and clothes were tossed untidily over furniture. I fingered the wool of a pair of black dress trousers and noted the label on a cherry-red shirt. A thrill went through me, Yves Saint Laurent.

I'd seen the VIP bathroom in the hotel brochure but nothing prepared me for its splendour. It was The Ensuite to the power of ten. The room was a classic Roman bathhouse and walled in amber Aussiemica with a marble effect. In the corner glowed the pièce de résistance, a glorious jet bath in brilliant tangerine with matching mini-bar fridge and icemaker. I knew from Anne-Marie that the fridge was stocked with Tasmanian champagne. 'VIPs like to drink it in the bath. It's not called champagne because the French have stolen the name. But Tassie Mist is better than the actual French stuff.' She said our wineries are a lot cleaner.

Anne-Marie was safely vacuuming in the main room when I slipped Bruno Bempi's satin bathrobe over my uniform. It was cool and silky, and fanned out as I did a twirl in front of the enormous picture window. The ocean and grey skies in front of me stretched all the way to Antarctica. I was the Duke of Edinburgh, Freddie Mercury on tour, John D. Rockefeller at a Tasmanian getaway. This was the life. I twirled over to the vanity, removed my Nana Mouskouris and turned on the lights around the mirror.

I leaned forward to view Julian Corkle framed by twenty-watt bulbs and noticed a brown outline over my shoulder.

It was shaped like a rhombus and moving at high speed towards me. I put on my glasses and froze.

'What on earth?' Bevan Bunion's voice was a shriek. He glared at the dressing gown and ground his teeth. His face was purple.

'I'm giving Anne-Marie a hand with the bath.'

'You've no business in here.' Bunion glanced at the bath protectively. 'You're outdoor staff.'

'I was flushing the jets.'

'The jets do not require flushing. The unit was made in California.'

'They're blocked. Beaver hair.'

'That's enough!' Bunion tweaked the satin gown away from my shoulder. His pinky was standing up like an alert soldier. 'Take this off immediately. It does not belong to you.'

'I was just trying to keep my uniform clean.'

'Outside! Now! One more trick like this and you're fired.'

Bevan Bunion was a big fat killjoy. There was only one way to deal with humourless fools like him. On my way out, I stopped at the front desk and leaned in close to the receptionist. 'Be careful around Onion Head.'

'Who?'

'Bunion. He's in a foul mood.'

'Why Onion Head?'

'That's what they call him. It comes from Bunion the Onion.'

'I've never heard that.'

'It's a private joke among the senior staff.'

'Bunion the Onion. I'll have to remember that. Ha, ha.'

There, that put a spring in my step. I knocked off work feeling as if I'd won the chook raffle. The pay packet in my pocket was radiating warmth and joy. Julian Corkle was on the up and up.

*   *   *

Hobart had only one menswear shop worth its trouser rack. New Modern Man was a small, exclusive boutique run by a shiny man with perfect hair and fingernails called Roger Shirley.

Mr Shirley pushed his *Celebrity Glitter* aside and smiled as I entered the shop. The smile expanded as I introduced myself and explained my needs. Only too pleased to help a Dingo trainee manager, he pointed me to the permanent press trousers, tut-tutting when I told him I wanted black.

'Brown.' He nodded for emphasis.

'Black. It's the new brown according to Bruno Bempi. I was just in the VIP suite.'

Mr Shirley tightened his lips and removed a pair of black trousers from the rack.

'Why not go for gussets, sir? The elastic side gussets provide the give and take for an active man of your *stature*.' He stretched the waistband of the trousers to demonstrate its give and take. 'Team these trousers with a thick belt and a designer shirt and no one would be the wiser.'

Mr Shirley held out a cherry-red shirt in a cardboard box. On the pocket were the initials YSL. He waved a hand over the shirt like a magician and then did the same conjuring motions over the top half of my body.

'Heads will spin! It's you, sir. A very rare shirt for a very rare trainee manager.' Mr Shirley tapped the shirt box for emphasis. 'I only have the one and it has your name written all over it, *Cerise de Montagne*.'

'My name's Julian Corkle.'

Mr Shirley gave a hesitant smile and then led me to a booth with curtains that didn't close properly.

Half an hour later, I emerged from the shop with the shirt and trousers to find Debra Fig examining the window display. Debra was the friendliest of all Carmel's friends at Waratah

High. She never hit me and always remembered my name. She also happened to be the sister of prefect god and radio DJ, Terrence Fig.

'Debra!'

'Jerry, I haven't seen you since that rumour at school. What have you been doing?'

'Working with the VIPs at the Dingo Hotel. It's just temporary until they create a new slot for me at Abracadabra.'

Debra raised her eyebrows. 'You're full of it.'

'What are you doing here? It's a menswear shop.'

'I was looking at that bright red shirt in the window. What kind of idiot would buy that?' Debra glanced down at my two New Modern Man bags. 'What did you buy?'

'Trousers and a belt.'

'The belt's got its own box?'

'It's French. They make big belts in France.'

I had one more important purchase to make. Nearly all my money was gone but where I was going that didn't matter. George's Electrical Emporium was a showroom of white goods and appliances that offered same-day delivery and a time plan called 'hire purchase'. George was one of Hobart's self-made men and regularly appeared on Abracadabra promoting his electrical goods. The commercials always began with him pointing to appliances bearing large 'SALE' stickers. His accent was foreign and his message was always the same: 'Bargains, bargains and more bargains. Electricals at rock-bottom prices. Buy today, pay later.' George's message made perfect sense to me.

The showroom seemed a lot smaller and more ordinary than its TV version. Half the lights were off and George wasn't around. I was examining an all-in-one colour television and radio-record player when the lights flickered to life. A pimply youth materialised from behind a fridge-freezer. His name badge said 'ERIC'.

'Walnut.' Eric had a long neck and large Adam's apple. 'Aged in an English swamp.'

'Nice.' I ran my fingers over the wood.

'Probably out of your range.' The youth puckered his lips and blew a jet of air through the puckers. 'I'm not saying you don't have the money or anything.'

'I do have the money.'

'I'm just saying you're better to leave the fancy stuff to those that can afford it. Quality has a price, you understand.'

'I can afford quality.'

'This baby is top of the line.'

'I'm a top-of-the-line sort of guy.'

'No deposit. First month interest free. Payments eased over a generous five-year time plan. You won't even know you're paying it. We'd need a pay slip for verification.'

I patted my pocket and nodded. 'Is it full colour?'

'We don't do half colour.'

Eric got a lot more friendly once I'd signed the agreement. He even gave me a ride home in the delivery van, a white Ford Escort with 'FOR HOUSEHOLD ELECTRICALS JUST ASK GEORGE' painted on the side. He helped me move the black-and-white set down to Carmel's bedroom and rig up the new one in the lounge. It was beautiful.

While the cartoons were playing I prepared a celebratory steak Diane for two. Mum would be surprised. The only things Carmel or John had ever brought home were bad manners and dirty sports clothes.

By seven o'clock the steaks were curled up like old sandals and the chips and garlic bread had wilted. Mum was working late again. It wasn't fair. I'd bought my first big-ticket item and couldn't show it off to anyone. Desperation drove me to the phone.

My father answered on the twelfth ring. 'Hang on a minute, Greg Norman's taking a putt.'

I waited for what seemed like half a day and willed myself not to feel carsick. I heard polite television golf applause and then Dad came back on the line.

'The man's a genius. Bob bloody Charles, eat your heart out. Aussie rules!'

'Dad, I've bought a colour TV. It's got a twenty-six-inch screen. Swamp walnut. Beautiful.'

'What? I don't pay good maintenance money to have it wasted on bloody walnut.'

'It's my television. Mum doesn't even know about it yet.'

'What do you mean?'

'I'm a trainee manager. I've been working for over a month.'

'That's a turn-up for the books.' Dad was full of surprises. He did care about my career.

'I probably should've told you earlier.'

'Yeah, I would've cut down the maintenance payments earlier. You can tell your mother that I'll be docking the next lot.'

'I'm working at the Dingo Hotel.'

'Not that gambling monstrosity down at the docks?'

'The waterfront. I work at the hotel. The VIP suite's got a vista. On a good day you can almost see Antarctica.'

'There's a lot of rough trade on those docks.'

'The hotel has four stars.'

'Don't go anywhere near those public toilets near the car park. Notorious.' Dad paused and lowered his voice. 'There are laws against that sort of thing.'

My father wasn't wrong. Tasmania did have laws against that sort of thing and they were the most frightening in Australia.

We'd been told about them during hygiene class at St Kevin's. The information had been relayed in a let-this-be-a-warning sort of way. Under the law, homosexuals were clumped together with people who sexually abused animals. Men caught having sex with each other could be thrown in prison for twenty-five years. Car thieves and murderers got it better.

By the time my mother came home, I'd eaten my dry steak and chips and fallen asleep in front of the TV. Mum's face was flushed. She giggled as she took her plate out of the oven. This was very un-Mum-like behaviour. She didn't even notice the colour of the sheep being herded through pens. I had to point it out.

'They're merinos, Mum. You can tell by the colour and texture.'

'Tasmanian fleeces are going for gold at the auctions.'

'With wool that colour and texture, I wouldn't doubt it.'

'Our Super Fine's fetching record prices.'

Super-fine merino wool was called Our Super Fine by Tasmanians. Grown men sat up straight and looked serious when Our Super Fine was mentioned. The papers called it White Gold when it sold for world-record prices.

'We had a little celebration tonight. The boss bought Chardonnay.' Mum giggled. 'It was very nice.'

'Look at the colour of that border collie, Mum.'

'It's black and white. They're always black and white.'

'Black and white against a *green* background.' I couldn't stand it any longer. 'Mum, I bought a new colour TV. It's swamp nut from England. There's an AM radio and you can play Roger Whittaker on the record player. I thought you'd be pleased.' I humphed and crossed my arms over my chest.

'Oh, honey! Sorry!' Mum leaped off the couch and ran a hand over the walnut. 'What a big screen.'

'A full twenty-six inches. Six more than the Rentascope. It's top of the line and all that. There's even a remote control and once I buy batteries we'll be able to sit on the couch and switch between the two channels just like Americans.'

'Look at the colour of those fleeces. Julian, I'm proud of you.'

'Dick Dingle will be on soon, Mum.'

'The poor man's going through hell with that divorce. They say that society woman is taking him to the cleaners.'

'Let's see how he's taking it. You get a lot more expression in colour.'

23

A tour bus from Mildura had arrived and a herd of pensioners was milling about on the pavement. I had thirty suitcases to move. The persistent drizzle of Hobart didn't make my job any easier.

'Wet enough for you? Ha, ha.'

The elderly man flashed his large false teeth and rocked back on the heels of his white canvas shoes. He was dressed in new beige trousers, a powder-blue shirt and camel-coloured windbreaker. Golfing apparel was very popular with the older holidaymaker set. I hated the clothes almost as much as I hated the sport. Golf made me carsick. The famous players never did anything interesting with their money on or off the greens.

'Sir, you should've been in Hobart yesterday. Not a cloud in the sky.' This was a lie but I was carrying two Little Swags and the retiree was blocking my way. 'The rain's probably settled in for good.'

'No worries, mate. I'm here for the roulette table.' He patted his pocket. 'Just sold the peach orchard. I might give you a tip if you play your cards right. It'll have to be poker. Ha, ha.'

'Shame about the orchard.'

'What do you mean?'

'You've missed the boat, sir. They say stone fruit is going for gold this year. I just saw a documentary. In full colour, of course.'

Bunion gave me a fierce look as I manoeuvred the suitcases around the pensioner. He'd been standing behind the potted Tasmanian man ferns and observed the entire exchange. Bunion seemed to be everywhere these days. I couldn't do anything without him popping out of the foliage. His constant surveillance effectively ruled out the ninth floor for me. My only hope of meeting a VIP was to stick around the porter's station and keep my eyes peeled for a limousine.

The station was not a glorious post but at least it provided some shelter from Hobart's freezing winds. The cramped chest-high booth was furnished with a bench, stool, telephone and two-way radio. It would've been deadly to spend time in this tiny space if it hadn't backed on to the plate-glass windows of the meet-and-greet area. This position had proved particularly helpful during the annual general meeting of the Tasmanian Caledonian Society when the lobby and bar were packed with men in skirts. Virtually none of the kilt-wearers had been taught to sit in a ladylike manner. When they sat on the armchairs, they did it with their legs open. I only needed to tie a shoelace to make the most of the Scottish disregard for underpants. My shoelaces got a lot of attention that day and the experience left me with a greater respect for Presbyterians.

Hobart was not a dream destination but when foreigners did visit, they tended to stay at the Dingo Hotel. The Japanese generally arrived in large groups and followed the flag waved by their tour guide. They didn't speak enough English to make requests. Americans were friendly and generous with tips but wanted too much bang for their buck. They asked for extra towels and complained about the lack of blow from the hotel blow-dryers. Europeans were by far the best dressed but obviously didn't believe in enjoying themselves on holiday. The Germans had two holiday modes, sour or drunk. Australians from the mainland were easy but indoor staff often complained about missing linen and cutlery.

Guests arriving by plane were picked up at the airport by the hotel shuttle. This minibus was driven by a citizen-band radio enthusiast called Kenny who employed the roger-over-and-out style of speaking and codenamed everything. The hotel entrance was Checkpoint Charlie and guests were graded in terms of size: 'Five Jumbo, nine Economy and a German proceeding to Charlie. No Family Size aboard.' Americans were Jumbo, Australians were Family Size and Japanese were Economy. Germans didn't have a code.

Kenny had just called to say that five Germans were on their way when I saw Nigel dart across the lobby and then out of the front door. He headed straight for the porter's station.

'Hide me!'

Without waiting for a response, he squeezed in through the side entrance of the booth and ducked down. The flimsy hardboard construction rocked as he wedged his back against the stool I was sitting on.

'What are you doing?'

'Hiding from Crabb.'

A cold electrical feeling ran up my legs. The last person I wanted to deal with was Raymond Crabb. He was only a kitchen hand but wielded the power of a head chef. Whenever I saw Crabb's shaved head approaching I went the other way. His skin was a road map of souvenirs from the various prisons he'd inhabited: wobbly handmade tattoos of cobwebs, skulls and daggers. His knuckles didn't have the 'LOVE' and 'HATE' of regular thugs. He'd gone for 'DEAD' and 'MEAT', the last words seen by anyone foolish enough to tangle with him.

Fear had already gelled the lower half of my body when Crabb emerged from the lobby. He made a beeline for me.

'Where'd that poof go?' Crabb grabbed the booth with both hands and rocked it back and forth. Nigel's head thumped against the hardboard under the counter and whip-lashed into my lap. The back of his head nestled against my groin. Warmth flooded my thighs. To my horror, I felt the stirrings of an erection.

'Which poof?' My voice was a squeak.

Crabb narrowed his eyes and curled his lip. 'The other one.'

'Beg pardon?'

A wave of heat and humidity radiated outward from my loins. The synthetic of my uniform prickled against my legs. Nigel pressed harder into me and rolled his head against the erection. I tried to wiggle back on the stool but his head moved with me.

'There's you and then there's the other one.'

Crabb lifted his top lip in a sneer. His gums were bright gingivitis pink. What was left of his teeth were small dark stubs. My erection wilted.

'I'm a porter.'

'You're a pooftah. Only a poof would wear those things.' Crabb pointed to my glasses and sneered again. 'Girl's glasses.'

'They're designer fashion frames.' Pride overrode my survival instinct. I'd just forked out an entire pay packet on my new raspberry-red glasses. According to *Celebrity Glitter*, red was the new black.

'They're pooftah headlights and I should punch them out for you.'

Crabb raised his left fist to my face. 'DEAD' was written in wiggly blue-green lettering across the knuckles. I leaned back and felt Nigel's head move with me. My groin stirred again.

I tried to swallow but my throat refused to cooperate and my tongue bucked against the roof of my mouth. The top half of my body was fighting for its life while the lower half wanted to party.

'Germans!' I pointed to the roundabout. I'd never been so happy to see a minibus full of misery.

Crabb lowered his fist. He looked over at the minibus and his lips unfurled into what passed for a smile.

'Duty calls.' I drove my knees into Nigel's back and sidled out of the booth, pulling my jacket down over the top of my trousers.

'You'll keep.' Crabb gave me one last sneer before making for the side entrance of the hotel. As he passed the shuttle, he clicked his work boots together and gave a straight-arm salute. 'Hi Hitler!'

A big blonde woman with Ronnie Corbett glasses was the first to emerge. She stepped on to the kerb shaking her head. 'This Australian humour is not funny!'

I shook my head in sympathy. 'I'm not laughing, madam.'

'This man is not correct.'

'He is very incorrect. The German nation deserves respect.' I stopped shaking my head and gave her a grim smile. 'The Mercedes is a very nice car.'

She blinked.

'Make a formal complaint, madam. The man's name is Crabb, Raymond Crabb, spelled like the crustacean but with a double B.'

The brush with Crabb rekindled the fears I thought I'd left behind on the Waratah cricket pitch. I came home feeling shaky and vulnerable. Mum and I had arranged to watch *The Curse of Camelot: Who's Killing the Kennedys?* together but despite the glorious full-colour of the TV, I found it difficult to concentrate. We'd seen all four episodes and had been looking forward to watching the final together. I felt for Marilyn Monroe and her Kennedy love child but Crabb now seemed a lot more menacing than the FBI. Carmel arrived from cricket practice as Jackie was marrying Aristotle Onassis. The camera zoomed in on Caroline and John looking unhappy in the back of a black car. As it drove away, the narrator wound up the series. 'Do these little ones carry the curse? Only time will tell.' The credits rolled to the sound of a ticking clock.

'What a load of rubbish.' Carmel was unlacing her shoes in the dinette.

'Don't leave your gear in there.' Mum didn't need to look at Carmel to know what she was doing. 'Your chops are in the oven.'

'I'm going out.'

'Where?'

'Debra Fig's. Her brother's having a party.'

My ears pricked up. A dose of Terrence Fig would definitely lift my spirits. Terrence now had his own late-night radio show on Saturday called *Sounds From Underground* and favoured obscure musicians like Lou Reed, Leonard Cohen and Patti Smith. He was one of Hobart's beautiful people.

'Can I come?'

'No.' Carmel's shoe landed with a thud against a table leg.

'Please. You wouldn't even notice I was there.'

'No.' Another shoe hit the floor.

'Carmel, pick those shoes up immediately.' Mum still had her back to her. 'Why can't you take your brother to the party?'

'He'd do something stupid. That's why.'

'No I won't. Promise. Promise and hope to die.' I crossed my fingers. 'Sort of.'

I had to shell out for a six-pack of Tickworth premium lager before Carmel would agree to take me anywhere. She drank it all before leaving home and threw the bottles at the back fence. It took over an hour to walk to the party with her stumbling and repeating 'Fucking hell' all the way.

All the lights were on and the doors were open when we arrived at the Fig house. The Pretenders were playing at full volume. Carmel stopped at the door and held me back with her arm. She screwed up her nose.

'Boring!'

The party was anything but boring but there was no use arguing with my sister. Her idea of a good party was girls' arm-wrestling and a keg of lager. From over her shoulder I took in the make-up and big untidy hairdos of the party-goers. The young men and women were dressed alike in tight jeans and flouncy shirts. No one was smiling. Terrence Fig was dancing in the middle of everyone in a strange minimal way to Chrissie Hynde's 'Tattooed Love Boys'. His eyes had been darkened with kohl and his white-blond hair was teased high into a fluffy wood-pecker. He was hardly moving to the music. His hunched upper half held steady while his feet made small circles on the carpet.

'Bloody unisexuals!' Carmel growled and shook her head. She made a chopper with her arm and cleared a path through the dancers.

I followed her to the kitchen where Debra was drinking tequila over the sink. She was doing it the authentic Mexican way by licking and sucking lemon wedges with salt.

'Old Magic Fingers Corkle. Didn't think you'd make it.' Debra put an arm around Carmel's neck from behind and tightened it until her face turned red. Debra was as drunk as my sister. She fell back against the sink with a *clunk* when Carmel drove an elbow into her ribs.

'Fucking Fig. How many times do I have to tell you? Never choke a Corkle.' Carmel snorted out a laugh and pulled her friend to her feet. They wandered off down the hall with their arms around each other.

Left alone, I drank the rest of the tequila the Corkle way, by tipping my head back and gulping it down. Inspired by Carmel, I threw the empty bottle out of the window and gave my hair a thorough fluffing. I hunched my shoulders and shuffle-danced into the lounge, nudging my way through the crowd and circling my feet as I went. Progress was slow. Minimal dancing was a lot harder than it looked.

I did a circuit and then stopped against a wall to see what kind of impression I'd made. Nobody smiled or even acknowledged me. Hunching lower, I circled harder, cutting diagonally across the room and breaking up knots of dancers. I clipped Terrence with an elbow but he didn't look up or even apologise.

It had to be my hair. It needed more lift.

A pleasant Mexican recklessness had already taken hold of me as I went outside into the cool night air. Near the washing line was a flowerbed. I scooped out a handful of damp soil and worked it into the base of my hair, feeling it stiffen under my fingers. I worked in another handful, mulching it from the scalp to the tips.

'Urghhh.'

I jumped.

The groan had come from under the windowsill. I squinted into the shadows but couldn't see a thing. Whatever it was groaned again. I bolted back inside.

Terrence glanced over as I entered the room and raised his eyebrows. The dirt trick had worked. Hunching my upper body, I started circling towards him. I was a barracuda going for an anchovy, a Tasmanian devil honing in on a rodent. I was halfway across the carpet when a greasy man in a dirty denim outfit stumbled into the room clutching the top of his head. Blood was trickling between his fingers and dripping on the carpet. He was cursing loudly.

'Some fucking arsehole threw a bottle out of the window! I'm going to kill the fucker.' The sleeves of his denim jacket had been ripped off biker-style and his forearms were thick and hairy. 'The fucker's wearing a red shirt. I'm going to find him and when I do, he's going to die.'

I leaped behind a big woman with red frizzy hair and mirrored her movements as the dancers parted for the intruder. We were near the door when she started brushing her shoulders. 'Where did all this dirt come from?'

The biker looked over and locked eyes with me. 'Red fucker!'

He lunged and the woman screamed but I was out of the door and running before he could touch me. I didn't stop running until I reached the waterfront. Gasping for air, I collapsed on to a large metal bollard with my head between my knees.

When my breathing finally slowed, I sat up and realised I was outside the public toilets my father had warned me about. The small building loomed out of the dark and seemed to beckon me. The tequila in my bloodstream responded.

I entered the Gents with my heart thumping against my ribs and made for a darkened cubicle. Next door someone was shuffling. Light was coming through a hole in the partition between us. I knelt down and put my eye to it. The shuffling stopped. I was looking at a wiry man without clothes. I swallowed and blinked the dirt out of my eyes.

The man was seated on the toilet, stroking an enormous erection. He was looking at my eye, rubbing himself furiously. He bent closer, his voice a hoarse whisper.

'Ready to ride the big pony, boy?'

Fumbling for footing, I wrenched open the door and scrambled out of the toilet. By the time I reached Echidna Avenue, I could taste blood in the back of my mouth. I was shaking all over. My heart felt as if it was going to burst.

I flopped against the letterbox and thought of Jimmy Budge. I didn't want a strange man in a public toilet. We should never, ever have left Ulverston.

24

Carmel left school without telling anyone and had been working for several weeks at Hubs Better Deals on Wheels before Mum found out. By that time, Carmel had already passed her driving test and been given a Hubs utility vehicle to use. My sister drove the Holden ute the same way she rode her bicycle: hard and fast. When she pulled up to the house, she skidded into the kerb. If someone got in her way, she tooted and saluted with two fingers. My mother said Carmel was a worry.

'I don't want her getting into trouble.' Mum waved a fly off a plate of muffins and sighed.

Bran muffins were being touted in Tasmania as the new health wonder. They contained the same amount of butter and sugar as cup cakes but experts said the fibre content made all the difference. High-fibre cereal had been around for a while but most people I knew still ate white toast and butter for breakfast. My father liked to tell the story of a miner in Broome who'd found a human finger in a box of bran flakes. 'That finger must've contaminated millions of flakes.' He said he wasn't going to take the risk.

'She does like the accelerator, Mum.' I waved the fly away again. Tasmanian flies were known for their persistence. Tourists often complained that they couldn't eat a sandwich in peace.

'It's not her driving I'm worried about. It's those young mechanics at Hubs. I don't want her getting in the family way and ending up with a deadbeat like your father.'

'You don't need to worry, Mum.' Carmel now wore a chunky silver charm bracelet. There was only one charm attached, a silver cricket ball with DEB engraved on the back.

'I don't know how many times I've tried to discuss the menstrual cycle and facts of life but she won't hear a word of it.'

'Carmel won't get pregnant.' I wanted to make my mother feel better but I could hardly tell her the truth. 'She's not the type.'

'But what are those things on her neck? In my day, they were called love bites.'

'They're not love bites.' I waved a non-existent fly off the muffins and played for time.

'What are they then?'

'Bowler's trophies. When a team wins, the girls beat their bowler around the neck with a wicket.'

'That's outrageous.' Mum smiled despite herself. She wanted to believe the story. In her book, a friendly beating was better than an unwanted pregnancy.

'It only happens to the best. They call Carmel "The Locomotive".'

'Dreadful.'

My mother was still smiling as I followed her into The Ensuite and watched her fill a toiletry bag with cosmetics. She was going to stay in Melbourne for the long weekend. Norman had promised to give her a makeover.

Mum had invited her brother to visit us in Hobart several times but he always refused. I could've understood this refusal if Dad had been around but we'd been irritation-free for six months. Norman hadn't been to Tasmania for years. There was more to the story than Mum was telling. Roving reporter Julian Corkle decided to probe.

'Why doesn't Norman visit us?'

'He doesn't want to come back to Hobart.'

'So it's true what Dad said?' Dad hadn't said anything but he was excellent Mum bait.

'Don't listen to anything that man says about Norman.'

'He seemed pretty convinced.'

'He's as bad as the other bigots. Norman made one mistake. He never deserved what happened to him.'

So Norman *had* done something bad. I imagined him shoplifting sunglasses or giving the police the fingers. I saw him being hauled off to jail. A thrill went through me. My uncle, the jailbird.

'Not according to Dad.'

'Poor Norman.'

'What actually happened?' I knew I'd given the game away as soon as I spoke.

Mum shot me a look and clammed up. She picked up the Dew Drops container and shook it. 'Another empty bottle. Julian, what on earth do you do with this lotion?'

The four stars of the Dingo Hotel should've had enough pull for the likes of Mick Jagger and Rod Stewart but the big celebrities never ventured further south than Melbourne. Since I'd been at the Dingo we'd had a run of wool- and apple-buyers, three national sports teams and a newsreader from New Zealand. Dick Dingle hadn't visited the hotel once.

The biggest thing to walk through its doors had been an American tourist called Cindy. The driver of the Pearl of Aussie Tours coach told me she'd entered the bus sideways and taken up two seats. 'Gland trouble, of course.' He'd called her a brave lady and bought her a drink at the hotel bar. From the porter's station I'd watched her sip the cocktail in a girlie way and then dab her mouth daintily. Anne-Marie told me that Cindy later ordered three plates of chips and a chocolate sundae from room service. She warned me I'd end up like her if I didn't pull my socks up.

'A two-seater?'

'A fat, lonely secret eater. You're obviously stuffing yourself on the sly because I never see you eating the staff meals.' Her eyes fell on my bottle tops. 'That's stupid when they're free.'

'I'm losing weight as we speak. I'm on the Maria Callas diet.'

'You look exactly the same, only bigger.'

'This job's been helpful for gathering material but it's time to relaunch my career. Small screen.'

I wasn't on a diet and there was nothing to relaunch. I was simply avoiding Crabb and Nigel. The Dingo was a dead end. I hadn't made any contacts or sniffed out any inside information. Worst of all, I couldn't afford to leave. I had no savings, a time plan to pay and a list of things I needed. One of these was a new haircut. I badly wanted a Terrence Fig. The idea of a big fluffy woodpecker had taken hold and wouldn't let go.

'You need to up your fibre intake. One of the best sources is cabbage. Look at my new body.' Anne-Marie put her hands on her fat hips and pulled in her stomach. She loved telling me what she was doing right and what I was doing wrong. 'I went down another uniform size on the cabbage diet. My corns have disappeared. Less pressure inside the shoes.'

'I've never had a corn in my life. I'm corn free.' I cleared my throat, TV-anchor style. 'You probably know that I had my own show on Abracadabra.' Enough time had passed to safely mention my cub reporter debut.

'You're headed for corns.'

'I'm in talks with an agent.'

Anne-Marie leaned over the booth and pointed to the packet of Tiffany biscuits I'd stashed behind the two-way radio. 'That's typical. Lonely people compensate.'

'But you're not lonely, Anne-Marie.'

'I'm not fat. And I have plenty of friends, thank you very much.' She snapped her rubber gloves for emphasis and walked off with the cleaning bucket over her arm like a handbag.

I watched her go and tore open the biscuits, stuffing two into my mouth, sandwich-style. Anne-Marie had hit a raw nerve. I didn't have any friends and it was all Dad's fault. He was the one who'd insisted on Hobart and messed up my life. I could've dealt with loneliness if my career was headed somewhere but I was never going to get on TV working as a porter. I needed a miracle or I'd be stuck in a hardboard booth for the rest of my life. The CB radio beeped.

'This here's the Rubber Duck. You got a copy on me?'

'Kenny.'

'We got ourselves a convoy.' Kenny hooted. He was a country music fan as well as a CB radio buff. 'Motorcade heading your way. Sir Bernie's in town.'

'Bernie Pouch?'

'Copy.'

A thrill went through me. The former premier was a celebrity in Tasmania where a politician was condemned as a crook if he got caught and celebrated as a wag if he got away with it. Pouch had definitely got away with it. After the casino was built, he wound up his political career and moved to Melbourne to pursue murky business ventures. The media loved him for it. Pouch was often on TV and regularly featured in 'Sir Bernie at Home'-type magazine articles. In the glossy photos he was just a normal Tassie man sizzling sausages on a family barbecue, only next to his barbecue was a mammoth swimming pool and next to the pool was a luxurious mansion. Pouch was given the run of the VIP suite whenever he came to Hobart.

The shuttle appeared first and led the way around the roundabout, followed by a black Toyota Crown with a small Australian flag on its aerial. Kenny gave the thumbs up and kept going as the Toyota pulled up at the kerb. I was smiling big and reaching for the door when Bevan Bunion suddenly appeared, waving me away like a fly on a muffin.

'Welcome back, sir.' He shook hands with Pouch. 'Always a pleasure.'

'Nice to be home.' Pouch looked over the top of Bunion's head and twitched a miniature version of his politician's smile.

I watched Bunion lead him into the lobby and cursed under my breath.

'Oy, dickhead!' The chauffeur had stuck his head out of the window and was glaring at me. 'You going to get the bloody luggage or just stand there like an eejit?'

As I removed the suitcases from the Toyota's boot, I thought over my options. I could obey ridiculous orders and miss a Golden Microphone Moment or I could do the right and logical thing and make a key personal connection. It was time for a career relaunch. I'd just said so myself.

After depositing the luggage in the lobby, I made straight for the service bay where I knew a complimentary VIP fruit basket would be sitting on the duty manager's desk, awaiting delivery. I had my hand on the wicker handle when the angry voice of Raymond Crabb resonated through the service bay.

'It's on the bastard's desk!' The voice was headed my way.

I grabbed the basket and dived under the desk as Crabb's heavy boots clomped across the floor.

'Where the fuck's it gone? I just put it here.'

I could hear him muttering despite the swirling pressure in my ears. He shuffled, sighed and shuffled again. I pushed my cheek against the floor and with one eye peered under the desk. The toe of his steel-capped boot moved away and then swung back rapidly, hitting the metal with a deafening *clang*. My body jerked. I stifled a cry.

'Fuck, fuck, fuck!' Crabb kicked the metal again and clomped back to the kitchen.

Jumping to my feet, I dashed to the stairs and took them two at a time. By the ninth floor, I was gasping for breath. I sat down on the stairs to rearrange the fruit which had jumbled inside the cellophane wrapper. Working quickly, I restacked the contents into a mound then topped it off with a banana wedged nose-up between two oranges. I then took out the 'COMPLI-MENTS OF THE DINGO HOTEL' card and added 'Personally Delivered by Julian Corkle'. There, Pouch would be impressed.

A plump blonde wearing too much make-up answered the door.

'I was asked to deliver this to Mr Pouch. Personally.' I tried to look into the suite but the woman moved and blocked my view.

'He's already gone to the gala.' She yanked the basket from my hands. 'I'll take that.'

'Gala?'

The door took me by surprise. I didn't see it until it closed in my face. I stood there for a moment, dazed.

I spent the rest of my shift reworking the door scene in my mind. In the initial version, I wedged my foot in the crack and forced my way into the room. The woman came at me with a knife but I fought her off to save Bernie who was tied to a chair. By the time I finished work, I'd shot the woman with a small gun and was being hailed as a hero by the media.

I left the hotel with a new feeling of determination. Things had gone far enough. Julian Corkle deserved respect. He deserved to be stopped on the street and asked for autographs. That was the sort of attention Terrence Fig got and Terrence had a signature haircut.

The Brush Off was the trendiest hair salon in Hobart and catered to both men and women. I'd walked past it hundreds of times but never had the courage to enter. A thin girl with dark eye make-up raised her eyebrows as I pushed open the door and swaggered up to the counter. Her hair was coloured bright blue and styled into the shape of a fluffy bedroom slipper. She didn't say hello.

'I want a hairdo exactly like yours.' Flattery was an excellent door-opener.

The girl rolled her eyes. 'It'll have to be next Friday.'

'I have to wait a week to see the hairdresser?'

'Sty-list. Hairsty-list.' The girl rolled her eyes again. 'Philippe is our top apprentice but he's already very exclusive.'

'Philippe? He's French?'

'More or less.'

'Next week then.'

The telephone was ringing when I opened the door to the house. I ran to get it.

'G'day, sunshine. How's the Locomotive?'

'It's Julian.'

'Oh. Carmel there?'

'No, only me.'

'Damn.' Dad grunted. 'Tell her I'm getting the flash new Holden next week. Electronic windows, cassette player, the works.'

'What colour is it?' I knew what the colour would be.

'Brown. You can't go wrong with brown.'

'It's the colour of dirt.'

'I'll never have to wash it.'

'I made an appointment today.' I knew I shouldn't be telling Dad this but I couldn't help myself.

'It's even got power steering.'

'I'm going to get a flash new haircut.'

'What?' The phone went silent. Dad took a deep breath. 'Not by one of those male hairdressers I hope.'

'They're called hairstylists these days.'

'Jesus bloody Christ. You'd better not be dragging Carmel into this.'

My father had no idea. I never dragged Carmel into anything. She never did things she didn't want to do. For the past couple of weeks I'd been begging her to stop practising cricket bowling against the back fence. She'd developed a habit of throwing empty beer bottles at the corrugated iron from the back steps. The glass exploded and flew everywhere. Mum never went down the back but Mr Neville from next door had complained to me about the shards he'd found in his lettuces. He told me the Japanese killed people with ground glass, that and bamboo shoots. He knew all about it from an uncle who'd been a prisoner of war in Malaya. The man had lost two thumbnails and half a metre of intestine. Mr Neville said the Japanese were swine, even worse than the Germans.

'Carmel doesn't care about hair, Dad. You've never noticed her legs and underarms?'

'Just as bloody well. Keep away from those Norman types and all other rough trade for that matter.'

'Plumbers?'

'You know what I mean.'

The Dick Dingle Hour was just starting when I turned on the TV. Dick was standing on a stage in a large auditorium filled with people dining at round tables. Above him was a hand-painted banner: 'Hobart Youth and Sports Re-education Centre'. Next to Dick Dingle was Bernie Pouch who was holding a large cardboard key. Dick Dingle spoke into the microphone.

'Sir Bernie will now present the symbolic key of the new centre to a representative of Hobart's sporting youth. The young sportswoman was chosen for her spirited contribution to Tassie sports.'

Music played as the spotlight moved to the audience where the sportswoman was winding her way between tables. I blinked and looked again. I knew that old tracksuit. And the short back and sides. I gasped and gripped the edge of the couch.

Carmel waved as she mounted the stage and was greeted with a fatherly pat on the back by Pouch. He took over the microphone.

'I hear they call you the Locomotive?'

'Yeah.' Carmel smiled at the camera. The smile was crooked, a sure sign that she'd been drinking.

'On behalf of the citizens of Hobart, I hereby present this key to the youth of the city.'

The diners clapped politely as Pouch handed over the key. The applause increased as my sister lifted it above her head. Someone whistled. Female voices whooped. Encouraged, Carmel slid the key to her hips and made a show of playing air guitar. Bernie Pouch laughed politely as the audience cheered, then he made a sign for people to settle down. He took the microphone again.

'I'm sure you've got something to say on behalf of the youth of Hobart, young lady.'

She gave Pouch a wild look. 'Is this live TV?'

'It most certainly is.'

Carmel smiled one of her dangerous smiles and moved closer to the microphone. She held up a thumb.

'Hubs, for better deals on wheels!'

25

It was a relief to have my mother home. She knew all the right things to say.

'What a waste of a Golden Microphone Moment. Pouch and Dingle in one hit and all your sister could do was tout used cars.'

'It was broadcast state-wide.'

'You should've been up there on that podium.' Mum shook her head. 'You're the one with small-screenability. Norman still talks about that cub reporter show. He says you were brilliant.'

Norman's makeover had completely transformed my mother. He'd cut and restyled her hair into a fluffy Olivia Newton-John and done a Debbie Harry with her eye make-up. Mum's shoulders had widened while her waist was pulled in tight with a large belt. Her nail polish and lipstick now matched her handbag and shoes. She could've been an air hostess for Air France.

'You look like an air hostess, Mum.' I squeezed the shoulder pads.

'Thank you, honey. Norm's a miracle-worker.'

'He's put ginger in your hair.'

'They're called highlights and the colour is caramel.'

'Very nice.' I examined my own hair in The Ensuite's mirrors. 'Do you think I should get highlights?'

'They're all the rage in Melbourne. Norm says they completely revamp personal image.'

'I'm looking forward to my revamp.' I circled Mum, fluffing the back of her hair with my fingertips. 'You're going to cause a stir at the Wool Board.'

'They were stirred before I left. Sheep have taken a dip. It's the Common Market. Dezzie says the French are driving mutton prices down.'

'I don't see sheep in France.'

'What do you think keeps those Frenchmen warm at night?'

I stopped fluffing.

'Wool, Julian. The French are great wearers of wool. But they've overproduced. They're dumping fleeces and meat. That's what Dezzie says.'

'Is your job safe, Mum?'

'I make Dezzie's tea, love.'

'Good then.'

The receptionist did not look up when I entered the Brush Off. She was too busy painting her nails black to match her hair which was now black and white like a chequerboard.

'You'll have to wait. Philippe is busy with a client.'

The salon was empty and, apart from the faint tang of chemicals, there was no evidence of recent hairstyling activity. I walked over to a cutting chair and ran a hand over the scissors and combs in a utility tray. A thrill went through me. On the wall next to the chair was a photograph of a severe-looking man. I leaned forward and read the embossed metal nameplate: 'Vidal Sassoon'.

Philippe wasn't French despite his impeccable grooming. His eyebrows were two perfect tick marks and his hair was a fantastic construction in navy blue with red streaks. It rose in a column from the top of his head and exploded outwards like a mushroom cloud.

'Love the red highlights, Philippe.' I'd been wrapped in a plastic poncho and seated in front of a mirror. Philippe was standing behind me with scissors, studying my hair critically.

He rolled his eyes. 'They're called glimmers and they're vermilion.'

'Very nice. I think I'll have exactly the same cut and dye.'

'Style and colour.' He sighed impatiently. 'Midnight blue is *not* your colour. As for the style, your hair is far too floppy and your face is too . . .' He stretched his hands like an accordion player.

'Wide?'

'Fat.' He closed one eye and held up a thumb like an artiste.

'Can you fluff it up like yours?'

'I don't fluff! I *jizsch*!' He rolled his eyes again. 'Hair like yours should not go up but out.'

Philippe had a peculiar way of cutting that I put down to artistic genius. He cut in rapid bursts with his eyes closed. After each flurry of scissor work he sighed and surveyed his handiwork. The cutting took less than five minutes.

'*Voilà, voilà!*' He did a flamenco flourish and clicked his scissors above his head like castanets.

'That's it?' My hair looked like a wilted lettuce leaf.

'I haven't coloured or jizsched yet!' He did the thumb trick again. 'I see amber with nougat glimmers.'

'Isn't amber like ginger?'

'Don't be ridiculous!'

My scalp was tingling from the hair dye and my hair was still wet when Philippe placed two adhesive strips over my eyes and assured me that surprise was part of the jizsch experience. My anxiety rose as the blow-dryer whirred to life next to my ear. I didn't like surprises involving blindfolds and it was all Carmel's fault. My one shot at blind man's bluff had ended in disaster. Instead of hiding behind a bush or a chair, Carmel had lured me into Roslyn Scone's garden and called out from behind a large cactus. It took Mum several days to remove all the cactus needles. The incident left me with a profound fear of all desert plants.

'*Voilà encore!*' Philippe removed the eye strips.

I looked at the mirror and blinked. Then blinked again. My hair was bright ginger and streaked with peroxide white. It had been teased into spikes but instead of standing up, the spikes stuck out sideways like two giant sea urchins. Even more disturbing, I could now see a resemblance to my brother John in my face. When I unfocused my eyes, I could've been John wearing the fright wig of a clown. I suppressed a wave of carsickness.

'The amber-nougat is superb!' Philippe narrowed his eyes and leaned back from his bony hips. 'I've followed the natural horizontal plane from the crown of your head.'

I was too stunned to say anything. My hair was too flat on top to be a Terrence Fig and too ginger to be taken seriously. He may as well have called me Art Garfunkel and be done with it. I was holding back tears as I was unwrapped and bustled toward the unfriendly girl at the counter. Her face lit up when she saw me.

'Fabulous! Love the horizontal effect. *Très originale.*'

'Really?' I touched the outer perimeter of the urchins. The hair had been reinforced with something powerful and felt like fibreglass.

'That amber is *très* David Bowie.'

'*Très?*'

'Very *très.*'

I had to admit, Bowie's hair had been ambery on the cover of *Aladdin Sane*. On *Scary Monsters* he'd gone all the way and done bright orange. I examined myself in the mirror over the counter. There was no doubt about it, the colour was *très* David Bowie. And the horizontal plane was *très originale*. I'd never seen anyone in Hobart with hair as horizontal as mine.

I stepped out of the salon feeling *très* revamped and walked briskly to the bus stop, monitoring my image in shop windows along the way. I had agreed to visit Dad's place and was now running late. The visit was Carmel's idea. She'd talked me into meeting her there to see his new car. The hairstyle must've upped my credibility because the bus driver didn't say a thing as I bought my ticket. He just stared hard and raised his eyebrows.

'You've missed them, mate. He's taken Carmel out for a spin.' Trevor Bland glanced at my hair and smiled. Compliments weren't his style. 'Come in and have a drink while you're waiting.'

This was a turn-up for the books. I'd never been offered a drink by an adult before, especially not by a friend of my father. Trevor led me to the kitchen, a Spartan room painted pastel yellow. 'What's your poison, mate?'

'What time is it, Trevor?' I had to be at work at five.

'Beer o'clock, I reckon.' Trevor flashed me an eager smile and consulted the digital Casio on his wrist. 'It's three-thirsty.'

Trevor's fridge contained butter, sausages, a bottle of milk and beer. Three of the four shelves were stacked with Tickworth lager. This arrangement must've pleased my father. 'You can't go wrong with beer' was one of his stock phrases. He believed beer-drinkers never became alcoholics. A drinker only became one of those if he drank the hard stuff. Dad also insisted that beer was an excellent deterrent to drug use.

He liked to warn against drinks that came in large open glasses. 'Drug peddlers slip things into the fancy stuff and get you hooked but they can't get the drugs down the neck of a beer bottle so easily. Stick to beer. You can't go wrong.' Dad thought he knew everything.

'Have you got whiskey, Trevor?'

'So it's whiskey you want.'

Trevor put down the two opened beer bottles and took out a dusty old bottle of Spirit of Cork. I recognised the bottle from our china cabinet. Dad had won it in a Christmas raffle years ago. He didn't drink spirits but out of spite had taken the bottle with him when he left. Trevor filled a regular beer glass with the whiskey and handed it to me.

The whiskey was like nothing I'd ever drunk. It tasted like the smell of perfume and sent a jolt of alarm across my shoulders and down my arms. The inside of my mouth shrivelled. My tongue stiffened and felt like a wooden clothes peg. I swallowed with a shudder and took another. By the fifth mouthful I'd neutralised my nervous system and my eyes had stopped watering. I looked over at Trevor. He'd quietly finished his first bottle of beer and seamlessly moved on to the second. Trevor Bland was a benign, shadowy person to me. I'd known him all my life but had hardly exchanged a word with him. I now noticed he wore glasses. They were dark, old-fashioned frames that gave him the look of Mr Potato Head. He saw me looking and smiled.

'I hear you're working down at the docks.'

'At the waterfront. The hotel.' The whiskey was sending out heat waves. I felt as if I'd swallowed a hot-water bottle and it had lodged in my chest. The second glass was going down easier than the first.

'Lots of nonsense goes on down there.'

'The hotel's got four stars. The place is a magnet for VIPs. It's a career stepping stone.'

'You ever been into those public facilities?'

My hand froze halfway to my mouth. I looked at Trevor and shook my head, downing the rest of the whiskey. The hot-water bottle exploded behind my ribs. I broke into a sweat.

'Just wondering.' Trevor refilled my glass and expertly popped the top off another beer bottle with a knife handle. 'Lot of rough trade, I hear.'

I nodded and continued drinking.

'You ever considered the priesthood?'

'No.' I shook my head. Conversation with Trevor Bland was a minefield. I knew where this was leading and had to put a stop to it. 'I've never wanted to be a male nurse either.'

'I'd never tell your father this, but I almost took up the dog collar once.' Trevor looked into the distance and smiled. 'Imagine, I could've been taking your confession right now.'

'I have nothing to confess.'

'Don't worry, mate, your secrets would be safe with me.'

'What secrets?'

The front door opened and Dad's laughter filled the house. It had been years since I heard that sound. Carmel called out something from the front step as he walked up the hall. Dad entered the kitchen and his laughter stopped like a turned tap.

'What the hell have you done to your bloody hair?' His mouth stayed open at the end of his sentence.

'I've had it amber-nougated.' I wanted him to laugh again. I tried to stand but my legs were rubbery and elusive.

'That's my whiskey!'

'Spirit of Cork for a corky Corkle.'

Dad didn't laugh.

Trevor got up and started doing something at the sink.

Carmel came in and whooped. 'Hey, it's Coco the clown!'

'David Bowie.'

'It's ginger.'

'Amber.' I'd lost the desire to be funny. 'Where've you been?'

'Joy riding. Dad let me drive the Holden. You missed lunch at the Red Rooster.'

The Red Rooster was my father's idea of quality dining. The helpings were large and the prices cheap. It was furnished with plastic seats and tablecloths and its windows were permanently steamed up. The salt and pepper came in old instant coffee jars with holes punched in the top and you ordered your meal through the service hole over the deep fryer. Half a chicken and chips was the same price as a whole chicken and chips. Dad said only stupid people took the half-chicken option, and on this we agreed. The chickens were preboiled and thrown into the deep fryer as ordered.

I felt a wave of carsickness at the thought of deep-fried chicken. My stomach was turbulent and watery. Trevor's kitchen was suddenly very small and hot. There were too many people and too many uncomfortable unspoken things. I had to get out. No, I had to get to work! It was ten to five. I looked at Carmel. 'We've got to go.'

'Keep your hair on, Ginger Nuts.' Carmel winked at Dad. 'Nothing stops the Locomotive.'

I heard Dad's voice as I stumbled down the hall, 'He's as pissed as a newt on *my* whiskey and didn't even look at the car! And what's with that bloody hair? He's as bad as that brother of hers.' I swung out of the house and into the blinding white of an overcast Hobart afternoon. Carmel's hand landed between my shoulder blades and propelled me into the Hub's ute in the driveway. The journey passed in a sickening flash with 'My Sharona' belting out of the cassette player. It was five to five on the ute's clock when we jerked to a stop at the rear of the hotel. Carmel bundled me out and took off with a screech of tyres.

The effect of the whiskey seemed to expand exponentially as I entered the hotel. I followed my usual route to the service bay but found myself directing action from outside my body. I fumbled into my uniform, leaving half the jacket buttons undone. The hat wouldn't sit on my hair so I gave up on it and scurried out.

A Merino Casino tour bus was pulling up as I got to the front of the hotel. I put on a sprint to reach the door and was almost there when my foot caught on a kink in the carpet. I tripped and fell headlong, skidding the last two metres on my stomach like a bobsledder. My chin came to rest on the foot of a large woman. She shrieked and clutched at the buttons of her cardigan.

The driver appeared. 'What the bloody hell?'

'I saw ginger fur.' The woman removed her foot from under my chin. 'I thought it was one of those Tasmanian wombats.'

'Debble.'

I wanted to explain that it was a Tasmanian devil not a wombat but my tongue had hardened and the inside of my mouth had shrunk. I realised I was thirsty, thirstier than I'd ever been in my life. The idea of water cut through the murkiness of the whiskey. I pushed myself up and lost balance, latching on to the driver. We locked arms at the elbow and I swung him around like a square dancer.

'Get the hell offa me, you clown!' He shook me loose at high speed.

Stumbling to stay upright, I crossed the road and mounted the kerb at a gallop. I made for the fountain in the middle of the roundabout, a large cement structure of a naked woman in a clamshell. Throwing the front half of my body over the

217

clam rim, I scooped water with my hands, drinking greedily until the rage of thirst abated and my head cleared. The front of my uniform was saturated but I was beyond caring.

When I turned, I saw thirty people staring at me from the tour bus. Bevan Bunion was standing on the kerb next to the driver. His face was crimson. He pointed to me and despite the distance and haze of whiskey I could see two fingers. His index finger was doing the pointing while his pinky stood out in self-righteous imitation.

'You're fired!'

'Ha?' *Fired?* My mind whirred. I shook my head.

'I'll ha you!'

'And I'll hardi-ha you!'

'Clown!'

Firing me was one thing but calling me names was pure spite. I sat down on the clam and cupped my hands around my mouth like a megaphone.

'And you're a . . .' I tried to think of something that would really hurt, something personal and below the beltline. '. . . an onion head. Bunion the Onion. That's what everyone calls you.'

There, I'd said it.

Satisfied, I rocked back on the edge of the clam and experienced the dread of freefall. I heard a splash. Everything went dark.

26

I came to in a strange bed encircled by curtains. My mouth was dry and my head was dull and painful. I was examining a plastic bracelet on my wrist when a hairy hand pulled back a curtain. It belonged to a thin, unshaven man in his sixties.

'You right, mate?'

'Yeah.'

'Should've heard them whinging when they carried you in. They reckoned you weighed a ton.'

'A ton?' To my groggy mind, a ton seemed faintly possible.

'They're keeping you in for observation. You've probably got a brain tumour. I've got one the size of a duck egg just behind my ear. They're as common as hell.' The man tapped the side of his head. 'Mine's inoperable.'

I fell back into a feverish sleep and dreamed about my brain tumour. It was the size of a Californian orange and sat on top of my brain toward the back of my head. The growth had forced the crown upward into a point and was attracting comments. Anne-Marie had just asked if I was the oldest child in my family when I was shaken awake. The nurse was a large woman with wrists made for arm-wrestling. She frowned at my hair and told me to get dressed.

'What happened to the man who was here earlier?' My voice

was a croak. There was definitely something very wrong with me.

'He died. Inoperable brain tumour.'

I slumped back on the bed. All the power left my limbs. I imagined Mum and Jimmy Budge weeping at my graveside and felt a stab of pain in the crown of my head.

'Doctor's waiting.'

'Can I have a wheelchair?'

The nurse wheeled me in to see Dr Rhonda Dickey, a big-boned woman with the colourless, no-nonsense face of an accountant. I probed the top of my head with shaky fingers as she read through my notes with a 'Hmm, hmm, hmm.' The crown was definitely higher than the rest of the skull. I braced myself.

'How big is it, doctor?' I tapped my head the way the dead man had done.

'Bigger than normal.' She frowned. 'But the size of your head has nothing to do with your condition.'

'The tumour?'

'You don't have a tumour.'

I felt warm tingling in my hands and toes. My vision cleared. Dr Dickey had to be one of the most beautiful women I'd ever seen. In fact, the entire room was beautiful. The linoleum tiles on the floor were a perfect shade of beige. The curtains were pastel blue. The walls were a soothing mint green. What a symphony of colour.

'You drank too much, fell over and bumped your head. End of story.' She sighed and shut the file. 'I think you should get out of that wheelchair. You look ridiculous.'

'Aren't you going to bandage me or something?'

'We don't bandage hangovers and I doubt we'd have enough gauze to go round that hair of yours.'

Despite the drenching, my hair had kept its basic horizontal structure. The urchins were still intact but the points had lost their sharpness. I stopped in the Gents on my way out and tried to tease some life back into them.

Mum was waiting in the foyer with tears in her eyes. She examined my face and head for damage. 'Thank goodness. I nearly had a heart attack when that buffoon called.'

'Bunion?'

'I told him I had a good mind to sue the hotel.'

'That clam's left a lump on the back of my head. It's a public danger.'

'He said you'd tried to bite a guest's foot.' Mum led me to the car park with an arm around my shoulder. 'I told him to stop right there, that you've never bitten another human being in your entire life. That's slander, I warned.'

'I make one silly mistake and I get fired.'

'The Dingo was never right for you.' She opened the passenger door of the Torana like a chauffeur. 'That porter's hat looked like a biscuit tin.'

'It didn't go with the new hair.'

'What a shame I didn't see it before the accident. It's gone all flat on top.' She shook her head and started the car. 'What on earth was your father thinking giving you whiskey?'

'It didn't cost him anything. It was the bottle he'd won in the Christmas raffle.'

'And that Trevor should've known better.' Mum shook her head again.

I didn't reply to this. It wasn't Trevor's fault. He was only trying to be kind.

'I almost forgot to tell you, Julian. You'll never guess who's featured in the *Wool Board Monthly*.' She paused for dramatic effect as she parked the car. 'Jimmy Budge! Your old friend from Ulverston.'

Jimmy. The sound of his name hit me like a head-butt. My chest felt as if it was caving in on itself. I pretended to cough into my jumper.

'You need to lie down and take it easy.'

My mother made up the couch as a bed and put Tiffany biscuits and a bottle of lemonade on a tray. She turned on the TV with the sound down and placed the *Wool Board Monthly* on the pillow next to the remote control. I was to read, watch TV and put it all behind me. She assured me that something better was sure to come my way soon. 'You've got star quality. Twinkle, twinkle.'

Mum went out of the room and came back lipsticked and dressed to go out. She had an appointment with the doctor for women's business. I knew this sort of business involved a gynaecologist and didn't ask for details. Gynaecology had about as much appeal to me as fire-fighting or speedboat racing. I couldn't understand how any man would willingly sign up for such a job.

I waited until the door clicked shut then prepared myself with lemonade and biscuits. When I'd finished the lot, I lay back with the *Monthly*. It was easy to find Jimmy. His photo was on page one, a head and shoulders shot with the caption: 'Ulverston's rising star of wool and whatnot, management cadet James Budge.' His mouth was closed and he was trying to look serious but I could see the old Jimmy. His hair still had the adorable cow's lick and his perfect nose made a perfect line in the middle of his perfect face. He was more beautiful than ever and, according to the article, he was doing very well at the Wool Board.

I laid the magazine over my chest and closed my eyes. I thought of the Jimmy I knew on his bike, in the pool, in the club. He could run faster and bike faster than me. He was better at French and at smoking filterless cigarettes. Jimmy was perfect. I'd never find anyone like him ever again. I began to cry and didn't try to hold it back. Tears were running around my ears and soaking into the pillow when I fell asleep.

I was looking for Jimmy behind the school hall when the doorbell rang. I tried to stay in the dream and track him down but the bell rang again. The *ding-dong* was loud and insistent. The caller was pressing the button with force.

I should've noted the size of the silhouette behind the frosted glass before turning the lock. The last person I wanted to see was Aunt Dolly. She shoved forward as I opened the door and swept into the house like a tidal wave. I followed her into the lounge.

'What's this, an Irish day off? If you were stupid enough to leave school then you should be working.' Her small bull-terrier eyes took in the bedding, lemonade bottle and empty plate. She was looking for faults, evidence of failure. Her eyes fell on the damp spots on the pillow. Her mouth hardened.

'I've had an accident.' I was feeling miserable. The dream had gone and I'd never reconnect with Jimmy.

Dolly swung her critical searchlights on me, scanning my body from head to foot. Her eyes narrowed. She was going to say something and it was going to be unkind.

'The only thing wrong with you, boy, is that hair. It looks like a fumigation bomb has exploded on your head.' She ho-ho-ho'd at her stupid joke. 'You should be at work.'

I had nothing to gain from taking the bait. It was better to take the moral high ground, hold my tongue and keep the peace. Then again, Dolly deserved a response.

'I didn't know you had a job, Dolly.'

'I'm a housewife. That's work enough.'

'Dad never thought so. Mum had to work and be a house-wife.'

223

'Some women are never satisfied. They trap a man into marriage and expect a flash home and fancy appliances. With that kind of woman, it's always spend, spend, spend.' Dolly ran a finger over the TV and examined it for dust. 'Your father has different priorities.'

'The pub and the races.'

'Jim is a leading expert on sports.'

'He certainly watches enough of it.'

Someone knocked on the back door. Dolly spun on her heel and raced me to get there first. It was Frank and he was dressed in a tight-fitting blue suit with gold buttons. He could've been a Mormon except for his new sideburns.

'Just in the area, thought I'd call in.' Frank entered without being asked and didn't bother saying hello. 'Who's the lovely lady?'

'Dolly. I'm his father's sister.' Dolly elbowed me to the side to shake Frank's hand. With her other hand, she touched her hair. 'Just popped in for a visit. Family duty.'

'Always good to keep up with family.' Frank placed a brief-case on the dinette table. 'I might have something that interests you, Mrs Dolly. You're obviously very family-spirited.'

'I do what I can. Always thinking of others.'

'Ever wondered what would happen to your loved ones if you died?'

'No.' Dolly's voice wavered. Her hand fell on her chest between the curtains of her open cardigan.

'It's probably time you did. You never know when you might pop your clogs.' Frank pulled out several brochures for Sunshine Life Insurance and spread them on the table. 'It could be a bus. It could be a bad chicken leg. Then, of course, it could be *cancer*. Our motto at Sunshine is: "Hope for the best, prepare for the worst, and leave behind a legacy." The keyword is legacy. May I ask if you have life insurance, Mrs Dolly?'

Dolly was shaking her head as the front door bell *ding-dong*ed yet again. A man in white overalls was waiting on the step. I recognised Eric from the electrical appliance shop. He didn't smile. 'I've come to repossess the television.'

'But I've never missed a payment.'

'You didn't tell us you'd lost your job. You need a job for the time plan. It's in the contract. Written in black and white.'

'I only lost it yesterday. How on earth did you find out?'

'I don't write the rules. I just enforce them.' Eric nudged me aside and started down the hall. He met Dolly and Frank coming the other way. 'You must be his mother.'

'I most certainly am not!' Dolly shook her head vigorously and pointed to the lounge. 'It's in there for the taking.'

I watched in numb horror as Eric unplugged the TV and rolled the wires into neat bundles. Not only was I losing the best thing in my life after my mother but I was also losing it in front of the worst possible audience.

'Don't lift that by yourself, my friend.' Frank went over and took one side of the TV. 'You'll give yourself a hernia and end up in a wheelchair.'

'Occupational hazard, mate.' Eric led the way, backing out of the door. 'The fridge-freezers are the worst.'

'You're a candidate for supplementary health insurance. Always good to be prepared. I've got some brochures that might interest you.'

I followed them out of the house and watched them slide the swamp-walnut box into the back of the van. It was like watching a coffin being put into a hearse. I was overwhelmed by grief and loss. Eric waited for Frank to get the brochures before driving off with a toot. My mother swerved to miss him as she pulled into our driveway. She mounted the steps shaking her head.

'What was all that about?'

'The TV's been repossessed. Dolly's out the back with Frank. They saw everything.' My chin was trembling.

'Has that woman been saying things to you?'

'She said my hair needs fumigating.'

'Right! Wait here!'

Mum straightened her shoulder pads and marched down the hall in a determined way. I heard raised voices and a shriek. The fly screen slapped against the back of the house; then I heard someone walking very fast down the path. Dolly appeared and crossed the lawn at a clip. Her head was down and she was holding the two sides of her cardigan together over her chest like a shield. She turned when she reached the footpath and pointed a saveloy finger at me. Her face was blotchy with anger.

'Sharon's a Little Aussie Rising Star finalist!' She nodded her two chins for emphasis. 'Put that in your pipe and smoke it you, you popinjay, you!'

Popinjay? I was considering what this could mean when Frank coughed behind me.

'That's a shame. I almost had a new client.' He frowned as Dolly drove off with a screech. 'Want to come for a spin in my new Ford Escort, have a chat about your future?'

'I don't have a future.'

'Everyone has a future. The trick is to be prepared.'

'I'll have to check on Mum first.'

My mother was sitting in the dinette examining Frank's brochures. 'I see your friend's left school. He's just tried to sell me life insurance.'

'I'm not sure he's a friend. Are you all right, Mum?'

'Fantastic. I gave Dolly an earful. It's done me the world of good.'

Before I got near the yellow Escort, Frank warned me to

keep my hands off the chrome. He was taking Christine out later and didn't want smears. He used his indicator as he pulled away from the kerb and drove slowly, stopping at 'GIVE WAY' signs and using his handbrake on slopes.

'I heard about a job that's going. One of Dad's clients is looking for a manservant.'

'I'm not a servant, Frank.' The lemonade I'd consumed had now descended to my bladder. I gritted my teeth and hoped there was a toilet where we were going.

'Just trying to help. The lady's got more money than sense. She's divorcing that dick from TV.'

'Dick Dingle?' My chest tightened. I forgot about my bladder. 'Not the society woman?'

'Prudence Jipper-Dingle. I wouldn't mind showing my policies to that lady. We're talking top-of-the-line life insurance.'

'A manservant? I think you mean butler. A society woman would want a butler.' I knew all about butlers from *Family Affair*. Being a butler was the next best thing to being a personal assistant and Prudence Jipper-Dingle was the next best thing to Dick Dingle. My hands tingled. Things were looking up.

Frank stopped outside a milk bar and bought me an ice cream on a stick. I would've preferred a cone but he hadn't asked and I could hardly look a gift horse in the mouth. He made me stand away from the car while I ate it. He hadn't bought one for himself.

'You might want to think about making preparations for your death.'

'I'm only fifteen.'

'You're never too young to start a policy. The earlier you start, the bigger the legacy you leave behind.'

'No one deserves a legacy except Mum and chances are I'll outlive her.'

'So you're basically not interested.'

'No.'

'I'd better get going then.' Frank shut the passenger door with his backside and made for the driver's seat.

'You're not giving me a ride back?'

'Sorry, mate. I'm meeting Christine in Rosetta. Can't keep the little lady waiting.'

Frank didn't say goodbye and drove off with his indicator flashing. I licked the stick clean and looked around me. I was on an unfamiliar suburban street in the middle of nowhere with a bladder full of lemonade. I had to find a public toilet, fast.

Walking as quickly and lightly as possible, I retraced our route to the main road where I found a sign for the botanical gardens. Half an hour and an aching abdomen later I was inside the garden's toilets. The feeling of relief was sensational. Urinating had to be one of the most pleasurable activities known to man. I closed my eyes and enjoyed the release of pressure.

When I opened them again I realised that I was standing in front of graffiti. 'Sean Doyle for pleasure' and a phone number had been scratched into the grimy plaster above the urinal. I zipped up feeling a post-urination high and took the house key from my pocket. The message I carved into the wall was twice the size of Sean's and ran along the top of the urinal like a banner: 'BEVAN BUNION SUCKS'. I was scratching in the number of the hotel when someone wolf whistled from inside a cubicle.

Brother Duffy had told us that the wild pig was the fastest animal off the mark, even faster than a cheetah. Julian Corkle was definitely more wild pig than cheetah. I was off the mark and out of the toilets in record time. I didn't stop running until I reached the main road. My hands were on my knees and I was gasping for breath when someone tapped me on the shoulder. I spun around and experienced the sort of fear a victim must feel in front of a firing squad. Wayne Hopper was standing less than an arm's length from me.

'Ahhh!' I stepped back to avoid a blow.

'Thought that was you running out of the Gents.' Wayne smiled. 'Hardly recognised you with the ginger hair.'

I didn't correct Wayne about the colour. He was even bigger and more manlike than his school version. His shoulders had expanded and his shaving stubble was serious.

'Just signed up for the army. Start training in a week.'

'Congratulations.' I couldn't understand how any sane person could voluntarily sign up for the army. It was like signing up for prison and the chain gang.

'It's a great wicket. They give you everything free: meals, clothes, a bed. Don't forget the gun. There aren't many jobs where you get a gun.'

'There's rabbit killing.'

'You even get to travel overseas when there's a war.'

'Bonus.'

'You know what the best thing is?' Wayne winked.

'No.'

'There are no bloody women!'

'Right.'

'Too bloody right.'

'I should get going, Wayne.'

'Take my advice, mate. Stay the way you are.'

'Uh-huh.'

'Keep away from the sheilas. A barge pole, mate.'

27

The idea of being Prudence Jipper-Dingle's butler thrilled me. I was going to be Sebastian Cabot, only younger and a lot better looking. I'd watched Sebastian in every episode of *Family Affair* at least twice and could even remember some of his dialogue. I'd had plenty of opportunity. Abracadabra liked to rerun popular TV shows at least three or four times. Dad said the TV station got a lot of mileage out of each show.

Family Affair had taught me some important facts. Only the filthy rich or foreigners had butlers. The butler wore a dress suit and was called the family retainer. He not only announced dinner and opened doors for VIPs but also solved problems and held the family together in times of crisis. Prudence Jipper-Dingle was going through a celebrity divorce crisis. I'd be there retaining in her hour of need and happily opening doors for VIPs along the way.

I called ahead and arranged an interview at the Battery Point mansion. Following Sebastian's example, I dressed in my old pinstriped suit. I then gave my hair a lift with Mum's Cobber's hairspray.

A distinguished man in a subdued blue blazer met me at the door. He glanced at my hair and nodded solemnly.

'You must be Julian. My name's Ritz.' He had a posh English accent and a cultivated emotionless air. There was no trace of welcome on his face.

'Just like the hotel! Lucky you got a five-star name. You could've been called Tasmania's Own.'

'Yes, I suppose so.' His nod was serious, as if I'd just said something profound.

'Then again, if you got a job at the Ritz, you'd be Ritz at the Ritz.'

Ritz didn't laugh. He led me to a lounge room called the parlour and settled me on a couch called the sofa. It was a pale French-style room with ornaments, curly furniture and tasselled cushions.

When Prudence Jipper-Dingle burst through the twin mirrored doors half an hour later, I'd already turned over every porcelain object and verified makers' names. I was standing next to the marble fireplace with a dirty terracotta thing in my hand.

'Just admiring your knick-knacks.'

'You're holding a figurine from the Tang Dynasty. It's priceless.'

'Dang Tynasty, just what I thought.'

Prudence Jipper-Dingle swooped on me and swiftly took the object from my hands. She placed it back on its pedestal with a gasp of relief.

'Your table's a stunner.' I pointed to the sheet of glass sitting on a lumpy piece of rock. Like the figurine, it looked obscene in a room furnished with real antiques.

She sniffed with obvious pride. 'That is the base of a Greek column.' She spoke with the same English accent as Ritz.

'Wasn't sure whether it was Greek or Roman.' I injected a little Prince Charles into my voice. 'Ritz let me in. Shame to lose a genuine English butler like him.'

'Ritz is not a butler and he's not English. He's a German and a friend, a gentleman caller if you like. You passed his house on the hill.'

'The one with the tennis court?'

'Yes.'

'And the pool?'

'The very one.'

Prudence Jipper-Dingle pointed to the sofa and motioned for me to sit down. She settled herself on one of the curly chairs, moving her bony white legs to one side with an authoritative rustle of pantyhose. She was a freeze-dried woman in her late forties with a pinched expression and a permanently down-turned mouth. *Celebrity Glitter* would've described her hairstyle as Buckingham Palatial. It was a stiff helmet with two Elizabeth Windsor puffs near the ears. She was dressed in a rose-pink skirt and jacket with matching shoes and fingernails.

Inhaling through her nose and exhaling through her mouth, Prudence gave me an overview of the domestic situation. Assuming a low, confidential tone, she explained that her present life was a trial. She was divorcing a *certain person* and this *certain person* was making her life very difficult. He'd taken the manservant and certain personal items and was now trying to take *her* house. She looked into the distance and sniffed. 'Pure greed.'

'You're talking about Dick Dingle?'

Prudence Jipper-Dingle tightened her lips. When she replied it was in the plural. 'Naturally, we expect discretion on the part of a manservant. Privacy is cherished in the Jipper household. We're looking for someone we can trust. There's the media.'

I smiled sympathetically and reminded her of my close

personal friendship with her accountant. 'Family friend and all that.'

'My last manservant catered to my every need. I require the personal touch of a professional. Have you experience?'

'I've just finished a stint at the Dingo and I can tell you, the manager was *very* sorry to lose me. I was his right hand, old Right Hand Corkle.'

'Dingo, the hotel?'

'All four stars of it. I was never out of that VIP suite, especially when Sir Pouch came through. High-profile people thrive on the personal touch.'

'Bernard was in town? The naughty man didn't even call me.'

'He had to attend some ridiculous sports gala. I had my work cut out for me.'

'You can start on Monday.'

'Monday it is, Mrs Prudence Jipper-Dingle.'

'Please, just Jipper.'

'Jipper it is then.'

'Mrs.'

'Mrs.'

'Someone of your calibre, Julian, I'm assuming you cook.'

'I do a fabulous muffin.'

'Thank you, *mais non*. There'll be no call for anything foreign or fatty. They're the two forbidden Fs in the Jipper kitchen. Delicate constitutions run in the family.'

'They're full of fibre.'

'*Non.*'

Prudence Jipper didn't look as if she ate much of anything. Her translucent skin was pulled tight over the inner workings of her body, exposing blue veins and white protrusions of bone around her wrists and ankles. She made a clicking noise when she folded her joints.

'You will be required to prepare a simple yet nourishing daily meal for Solange.'

'Solange?' Dick Dingle had a child? This was news to me.

'You'll meet her shortly.'

Prudence led me through the dining room, past a long marble table encircled by twelve curly chairs. I imagined Dick Dingle reading *National Geographic* magazine and eating toast at the table. He was wearing a bathrobe with a towel around his head.

With a majestic twist of the hand, Prudence turned the light dial and brought the crystal chandelier to life. The matching candlesticks on the marble mantelpiece sparkled in response. She waved her arm, saying she'd had a few things sent over from the Continent.

'You have a lovely house, Mrs Jipper. I bet your bathroom's a beauty.'

'You will not be seeing the bathroom. Out of bounds. My personal chambers are private.' Prudence sniffed. 'There's a servants' *salle de bains* off the back vestibule. Naturally, you'll be responsible for its cleanliness.'

I wanted to be upset about the bathroom but couldn't maintain disappointment for long. The kitchen was a marvel of stainless-steel and glass and had large French windows that gave on to a landscaped garden. The floor was tiled with shiny marble and the stainless-steel fridge looked like a silver rocket ship. I imagined Dick Dingle boiling eggs in the kitchen. He was still wearing his bathrobe but had now removed the towel from around his head.

I tapped a large black screen set into the wall of stainless-steel cupboards. The kitchen even had a colour television.

'That, Julian, is a Miele. It is the oven you will be using to grill Solange's lean meats.'

'Does it microwave?'

Prudence sniffed and ran a finger along the marble bench top as she led me out of the back door to the lawn. She pointed to a pine shed done up like a Swiss chalet. 'That's where Solange spends her days.'

'In a shed?'

'It's a chalet with its own amenities.' Prudence obviously thought she was a good provider. 'Solange! I want you to meet someone!'

Blond hair flashed past one of the chalet windows. I heard an excited yelp and then the tiny door creaked and opened outward like a flap. Something large and hairy poked its head out. Its eyes fixed on me and narrowed.

'Solange is a dog?'

'A pedigree Afghan hound. Best in show, countless times.' She beckoned the dog. 'Solange, come to Mumsy.'

The flap creaked and the dog shot out with its teeth bared. It was enormous, the size of a Welsh miner's pony. I ducked behind Prudence as it lunged for my thigh.

'Don't be silly. Solange is only playing.' Prudence held the dog by a sparkly pink collar and rubbed its hairy ears. 'Babykins lubs a wubba dubba dubba.'

I took an immediate dislike to the Afghan. There was something unnatural about its small head and oversized body. Its long blond hair gave it an uncanny resemblance to Rick Wakeman. My brother John loved Rick Wakeman.

'So I only have to prepare lean meats for Solange?'

The dog was still glaring at me.

'That and grooming. Solange is a champion on the dog circuit.'

'She doesn't seem to like me.'

'She doesn't like many people. It's her star's temperament. Take no notice.'

'Star?' Here was my cue. 'I'm something of a star myself. I did a stint on TV a while back. Perhaps your husb—'

Prudence cut me off with a wave of the hand and addressed herself to the dog. 'We have only one star in this household. Thanks to a certain person I've had quite my fill of TV stars.'

'Mr Dingle?'

'We do not use the D name in this house.'

'We're outside the house.'

Prudence frowned.

I was going to have to work hard to make the Dick Dingle connection but at least I was standing on his lawn and would soon be cleaning his pool-filtration system. Prudence informed me that I'd be doing quite a lot of cleaning. I was also to dust and polish daily, buy groceries and cater to Solange's every need. What I wasn't allowed to do was answer the door or the phone. I wasn't even going to wear a dinner suit. My uniform was to be blue bib-and-brace overalls and I had to buy them myself.

'Given the current financial circumstances, a little belt-tightening is in order.' Prudence glanced at my waist and frowned. 'Naturally your salary will fall below the recommended minimum.'

'Isn't the minimum wage set by the law?'

'Don't quibble. I'll pay what I can but you must understand my situation.'

I understood it all right. I was to receive very little money from a very rich woman. It was daylight robbery, the sort of thing the Queen of England did to her staff at Buckingham Palace.

I looked around the grounds. It was definitely one of the nicer houses in Hobart and Prudence was still legally married to Tasmania's one and only mega-star. I thought about the kitchen and the curly furniture. At least I didn't have to pay to work there.

I stopped at George's Electrical Emporium on the way home to reclaim the swamp walnut. Eric was unimpressed with my new job.

'That's your wage?' He pointed to the sum I'd just written down on the new hire-purchase form. 'Pitiful! By rights I shouldn't let you take the TV.'

'I'm working for Dick Dingle's wife.'

'She must be as tight as a duck's arse.'

'She's going through a divorce, belt-tightening and all that. The press are all over her. I'll be fighting off cameramen. You'll probably see me on TV.' I raised an eyebrow. 'It won't be the first time. I used to have my own show on Abracadabra.'

'Take my advice and get yourself a decent job, mate. Something in sales. Start putting money away. One day you'll want a wife and family.'

'No I won't.'

'You should get into life insurance like your mate. There's a job with a future. Excellent sales potential in the sick and dying. It's all about psychology.' Eric tapped his temple. 'If you convince people they're going to get cancer, they'll sign anything. Earn yourself a commission and buy yourself a tidy little Ford Escort.'

'I don't drive.'

Eric looked at me as if I was insane and shook his head. 'You can't help those who won't help themselves.'

He removed the 'GOOD AS NEW' sign and ran a sleeve over the swamp walnut. I didn't offer to help as he carried it out to the delivery van. He could help himself if he knew so much.

Eric deposited the TV on the front step of our house and

237

left without saying goodbye. I struggled with it into the lounge and was setting it up when I realised the batteries had been removed from the remote control. I was still cursing when Mum came in all dressed up. She was going to a wine bar with people from work. This was news to me. Mum never went to wine bars and she never forgot to do up the top button of her blouse.

I followed her into The Ensuite. 'Your button's undone, Mum.'

'I know.'

I studied her face in the mirror but saw no trace of shame. She was boldly putting on silvery eye shadow with a fluffy stick.

'I got the job, Mum. I start tomorrow.'

'That's wonderful, Julian.' Mum's mirror reflection smiled at me and continued applying the make-up. 'I've got good news, too.'

'The pay's a bit low. That's the only thing.'

'How low?' Mum stopped applying the eye shadow.

'Lower than the minimum.'

'That's illegal, Julian.'

'But she's Dick Dingle's wife.' My voice was a whine. I wanted Mum to be happy for me. I had enough doubts of my own, especially about the dog. 'I'll probably never get another chance like this.'

'Of course you will. You're a star, Julian. That woman must be loaded. It's not right.' Mum meant business. She didn't turn around or smile at me in the mirror. I hated it when she did that.

'Mum, what are those pills in your nightstand?'

'You have no business going through my things.' Her reflection gave me a hard look. 'What were you doing in there?'

'Looking for aspirin. I had a very sore head after the clam

incident.' I didn't need a headache to poke around in my mother's things. I was always going through them. 'It's not *the Pill*?'

'Since you ask, yes it is.'

'You're on *the Pill*?' My voice was shrill.

'To regulate my hormones. You know very well that I went to a doctor for women's business.'

'That's all right then.'

I didn't understand female hormones and didn't need to know. The important thing was that Mum wasn't on the Pill for the wrong reasons. The oral contraceptive got a lot of bad press in Tasmania, especially within the Catholic community where it was talked about in the same breath as heroin. According to good Catholics like Dolly, the Pill made randy girls even randier and set them loose on married men. Girls on the Pill had irresponsible sex for pleasure because they never had to worry about the consequences. Dolly had firm opinions about these girls. 'Disease never stopped a loose woman. They need the threat of pregnancy to rein them in.'

'Let me give your hair a fluff.' I ran my fingers through her hair and gave it a squirt with Cobber's hairspray. 'You said you had good news.'

'I've been promoted to manageress of the Board's cluster refreshment facilities.' Mum slipped on her high heels and looked at her legs in the mirror.

'Congratulations.'

'Thanks, honey. Dezzie's taking us out to celebrate.' A horn tooted. 'That'll be him.'

I went to the bedroom window and pulled back a curtain. An old Ford Cortina was parked in the driveway. It was too dark to see details but I could tell there was only one person in the car. 'But you're going out in a group?'

'That's right.'

'It's a Ford Cortina.'

'Yes.'

'Surely a Wool Board executive should own a tidy little Escort.'

'Don't wait up for me.'

28

Prudence had a way of getting what she wanted and her method had a lot to do with a sense of entitlement and brute force. She never questioned what she did and no one was allowed to doubt her judgement. She knew best and when she didn't, she quoted an expert.

'As Wallis Simpson says, "A woman can't be too rich or too thin."' Prudence pointed a bony finger at the steak I was preparing for Solange's dinner, a mixed grill of fillet steak, veal cutlet and chicken breast with carrots julienne. She'd shelled out more on the dog's dinner than I'd earn in two days.

'Remove all the fat before grilling.'

'My mother says you need a little fat for flavour.'

'Where do you people get these ideas?'

'From my mother, like I said.'

'That's why people like you are *fat*.' She whispered the last word as if it were an obscenity.

I pulled in my stomach.

Prudence drew air in through her nose slowly and released it sharply through her mouth.

'It is my observation that the further one ventures away from Battery Point and out into the suburbs, the larger the human being. The less money people have, the more recklessly they spend on food. If they simply controlled themselves at the supermarket, they'd have money for shoes and handbags and look a lot better for it. As Coco Chanel said, "Elegance is refusal."'

Refusing Prudence was not an option. She stood over me as I cut every particle of fat off the fillet steak. She'd done a lot of standing over me since I began working for her. Everything had to be done a certain way and the cheaper it was done, the better. Vacuum cleaner bags were emptied and reused. The windows were washed with vinegar and newspaper and Cobber's bags were recycled as rubbish bags. Prudence never entered supermarkets but she knew they gave away bags to pack groceries. I was instructed to load up when I did the shopping.

Prudence was like no one I'd ever met. She wasn't just authoritarian and stingy. She was completely unselfconscious about it. Nor did she care that her bullying and penny-pinching made life difficult for me. She was above all that. Her selfishness both upset and thrilled me. I'd never encountered anyone so profoundly self-centred. Each day she upped the ante. Her imperialism had no bounds.

'Julian, I expect you to wear a *clean* uniform every day.'

'You mean overalls, Mrs Jipper?'

'Uniform.'

'Overalls.'

The overalls were a sore point with me. I could only afford one pair and these I had to secretly wash and iron dry every evening before Mum got home. I did this to avoid confrontation. Mum referred to Prudence as a shameless profiteer and told me she hadn't raised a brilliant son to clean other people's homes for peanuts. I couldn't fault her logic, but then again, I was desperate to hitch my wagon to something and Prudence was as close as I'd ever come to a celebrity. She was married to the biggest star in Tasmania and rubbed shoulders with movers and shakers. I just had to be patient and keep my eye on the ball. A Golden Microphone Moment was bound to come my way.

In the meantime I had to juggle to survive. The miserable salary barely covered the TV payments and left virtually nothing for necessities like cigarettes and chocolate. I badly needed a haircut but I could hardly ask Mum for money. Every morning I carefully restyled my hair with Cobber's hairspray but it was impossible to hide the dark band of regrowth which now gave my head the multicolour effect of desert camouflage.

Prudence ran a critical eye over my hair and overalls. Her eyes settled on the grimy overall bib. 'Surely you people have a washing machine.'

'I just cleaned out your fireplace. It's fire dirt.'

'I hope you polished the brass. There's nothing quite as disagreeable as a dull firedog.'

I could think of two more disagreeable things, Prudence and Solange, but I wasn't employed to point out the obvious. My job was to kowtow and, while I was down there, kindly wash the floor. Prudence was selfish and disagreeable but Solange had the bigger teeth. The dog made me paranoid. It watched me constantly and had a nasty habit of leaping out of hiding places, teeth bared.

'Where's Solange?'

'I shut her outside. She tried to bite me again.'

'Piffle.'

'She chased me.'

'Rubbish. Let her in. It's time for her coiffure.'

Dog grooming was one aspect of the job I truly despised. Before every dog show, Solange was washed and conditioned, dried with a hairdryer, trimmed and brushed into a pavlova of fluffy blond fur. The grooming took hours. My only consolation was that Prudence handled the end of the dog with teeth.

I was on my knees, trimming the fur around the dog's bum with a pair of nail scissors, when the doorbell rang. Prudence dropped the muzzle and, without a care for my well-being, flounced out of the kitchen. Solange immediately turned and glared at me. She growled. My trimming hand froze. I was alone and on my knees before the evil empire.

The only dog-handling trick I knew had come from a TV programme on training guard dogs. The show had started with a warning that it contained violence unsuitable for children under twelve. An instructor in a padded trainer's outfit had explained in a slow, educational manner that dogs naturally went for the open, vulnerable parts of the human body. He then approached a dog enclosure and encouraged viewers to watch closely as he threw a shop-window mannequin to an untrained German shepherd. The hard plastic body had barely left his hands before the dog latched on to its crotch and began eating its way to the collarbone. At this point the instructor had performed a manoeuvre called the 'jaw release'. Using a broom handle with a tea towel tied to its end, he gave the dog's bum hole a poke. The German shepherd's jaws opened like magic and released the mutilated mannequin. The camera moved off the dog as it began to throw up bits of pink plastic. The jaw release was a handy trick to know but I needed a broom handle and more distance from Solange. Nail scissors didn't cut it.

The dog growled again.

I clamped my thighs together and gripped the scissors.

'Now where were we?' Prudence sailed back into the room smiling. Her cheeks bore two small pink dots.

'You were holding the dog by its head.'

'Her name is Solange and she's a blue ribbon champion!

She's going to win best in show today.' Prudence patted her chest. 'Stand up for Mumsy if you want a treat.'

The Afghan leaped up and threw its forepaws on to her chest. I jumped to my feet and backed away. Raised on its hind legs, the dog was taller than an American basketball player.

From her pocket, Prudence produced a rabbit soft toy. She waved it in front of the dog's nose. Solange took it gently in her mouth before resuming the four-legged position and tail-wagging like a normal dog. This good-doggy routine didn't fool me. I'd discovered a graveyard of soft toys behind the azaleas. They'd all been gutted and ripped to pieces.

'That was Harrison at the door. We're leaving in fifteen minutes.' With a practised flick of her fingers, Prudence tied a ribbon around the dog's chignon. 'I hope you've done a decent job of the tail feathers. Solange's rear always gets a lot of attention.'

'Another gentleman caller?' Flattery was an excellent way to handle Prudence.

'I'm afraid so.' She glanced at her reflection in the door of the Miele. 'A certain person didn't know how lucky he was.'

'Your husband?'

'We do not use the H word in this house.'

'A certain television star then.'

'Hardly a star. The man's a failure.' She drew air in through her nose. 'Ours was a childless marriage.'

'But he's won the Tassie Wallaby, many times over!' I felt compelled to come to Dick Dingle's defence. Prudence may have been his wife but I was definitely his biggest fan. I'd watched Dick Dingle go from the black and white of my child-hood to the dazzling colour of the swamp walnut. His hair had thinned out over the years and then thickened up again. I knew Dick Dingle's face better than the face of my own brother. He was a Tasmanian icon, a living legend.

'He's on the award committee.' She sniffed triumphantly and then stood back to admire the dog. 'It's remarkable really. You haven't done a bad job with Solange.'

'Uh-huh.' I was surprised at the compliment but she was right. The dog's fur had lost its Rick Wakeman droop and gained a Dusty Springfield bounce.

'Have you ever considered coiffuring?'

My chest swelled. 'I'd consider a career as a celebrity coiffeur but I'd need introductions from someone with industry connections.'

'I don't mean human hair.' Prudence gave her own helmet of hair a protective pat and then did something unexpected and completely out of character. She removed a tiny box of chocolates from her handbag and held them out to me. The chocolates were like the soft toy, a reward for good behaviour.

I selected the biggest in the box but it melted in my mouth before I had the satisfaction of chewing.

'That beats Shelby's any day, Mrs Jipper.' I ran my tongue over my teeth and prayed that another was coming my way.

'You people do not savour your food.' The box was snapped shut and put back in her bag. 'It's a waste.'

'I do savour. I just do it quickly.'

High-speed savouring was a skill I'd learned in the Corkle household where dinnertime had always been an every-man-for-himself affair. The quicker I ate, the more steak, chips and desserts I got. The one person I could never beat for speed was my father. Friday nights had been hell when I'd done battle with him and Carmel over an open parcel of fish and chips.

'One should never hurry a Belgian praline. It should be held on the tongue until it melts.'

'I have a very hot tongue. Mine melted very fast.'

Prudence sniffed and led the dog outside as a silver Mercedes

246

made its way around the circular driveway. Harrison looked like all the other men who patronised Prudence: buttoned-up and wealthy. I didn't understand her attraction but neither did women. Prudence had no female friends apart from Solange.

I waited until they'd left the premises and then dialled my father's number. We hadn't spoken since the whiskey afternoon and it was about time he heard about my Dick Dingle connection. Trevor answered the phone.

'G'day, mate.'

'Hello, Trevor, how are you?'

'Bonza. We've just set up a swimming pool, one of those aluminium and plastic jobs.'

'I thought Dad didn't like pools.' He'd always said that a pool was a waste of money, that we could stop whining because we were never going to get one, ever.

'He reckons it's the best thing he's ever bought. You'll have to come around for a dip.'

'I've moved up in the world, Trevor. I'm working for Dick Dingle's wife in Battery Point.'

'Come around after work then. Don't worry about bathing togs. It's all boys in together here.'

'I can't tonight.' Skinny-dipping with Trevor Bland didn't seem right. He was Dad's friend and, as far as I knew, Dad never did anything nude. 'Is Dad there?'

'He's gone to the track. The pool's here if you change your mind.'

I found a Sunshine Insurance pamphlet in the letterbox when I got home. On the cover was a photo of Frank wearing a dark maroon jacket with wide shoulders. Underneath was a caption:

Frank Burger for all your insurance needs. Talk frank with Frank. You'll find the sun shines out of his arsenal of insurance policies.

There was also an official-looking letter for Miss Colleen Nolan, the maiden name Mum had used on all the divorce papers. The letter had a heavy, ominous feel. I put it on the mantelpiece in the dinette and stood looking at it. My mother and Prudence had very different ways of going about a divorce. For Mum, marriage had been the biggest mistake of her life. When it stopped working, all she wanted to do was shut up shop and move on. Prudence made a lot of noise but showed none of Mum's haste. She liked to call her divorce 'the Cause' and talked about it as if it were a business deal. According to Prudence, nice girls finished last. I hoped, for Mum's sake, she wasn't right.

The house was empty and very quiet. Since her promotion, Mum often worked late and Carmel never came home before eight. I wandered into The Ensuite and surveyed the cosmetics lined up on the Aussiemica vanity. Their number had doubled since the separation. Mum's taste in underwear had improved. Drying on a coat hanger over the shower were a new lacy maroon bra and matching underpants. I examined the labels and was pleased to note that they weren't from Cobber's.

I went back to the dinette. It was Friday night and I didn't feel like watching television on my own. I should've been out partying with the likes of Philippe and Terrence Fig. I wandered into the kitchen and opened the fridge. Mum's Chardonnay clinked inside the door holder. She definitely wouldn't miss a couple of fingers.

The wine was surprisingly tasty, nothing like the sweet

vinegar of Jackaroo. I helped myself to another glass and lit a cigarette, Hollywood style. Being alone wasn't so bad if you had Chardonnay on tap. All the tragic stars drank alone. I thought of Judy Garland and took another glass.

The *Hobart Star* was sitting on the table next to the fruit bowl. I slid it over and unfolded it, bracing myself for the inevitable front-page sports photo.

I sat up straight and swallowed my mouthful of wine.

At the bottom of the page was a small photo with the title: 'Groomed for the Stage'. Sharon was done up like a circus performer in a ruffled dress and tiara. In her hands were the kazoo and tambourine she'd used to win the Hobart Little Aussie Rising Star trophy. Sharon was going to compete in the Tasmanian finals.

Tears pricked my eyes. Something hard and urgent pressed the inside of my chest behind the sternum. I belched and thought of Dolly. It should've been me in the *Star*. What had Mum been doing? I couldn't remember the last time she'd got me to sing and she never mentioned the Golden Microphone any more. I put the Chardonnay bottle to my lips and chugged back the rest of the wine.

Frank Sinatra's Greatest Hits LP was looking the worse for wear but the sound of his voice sent a thrill through me, especially with the volume dial on ten. I started off singing big to 'Strangers in the Night' and sang even bigger to 'Something Stupid'. Julian Corkle hadn't lost the old magic. I was still the Songbird of the South, Tasmania's very own young Ol' Blue Eyes.

I was working my way through the LP a second time when a loud noise disturbed me. I turned off the music and recognised the sound of large fists pummelling pinewood. On the back step was a tall, stocky woman in a tight police uniform.

She had her hands on her hips. Her thick arms were straining her shirt at the armpits.

'There's been a complaint about the noise.' She slapped the truncheon attached to the belt of her trousers. 'You're upsetting the neighbours with your caterwauling.'

'I was practising my routine.' The only way to deal with authority was to pull rank. 'They call me the Songbird of the South. I'm a blue ribbon champion, best in show and all that.'

The policewoman narrowed her eyes. 'Is that alcohol on your breath?'

'No.' I wasn't going to fall for her tricks. 'I just cleaned my teeth with methylated spirits.'

'How old are you?'

'Eighteen . . . more or less.'

'Are you trying to be funny?'

'Ha-ha or peculiar?'

The situation called for humour. I smiled at the policewoman. Her face hardened into a scowl.

'I'm going to report you.' She pulled out a flip notepad from her shirt pocket. 'Name?'

'The Songbird of the South, like I said.' I fluttered my eyelashes. A little charm went a long way.

'Right, you're coming with me!' Slapping her truncheon, she barged into the room like a battering ram.

I jumped back, screeching out my name. The policewoman stopped and looked at me with surprise.

'Corkle? You're not Carmel's brother?'

'Yeah.'

'The Locomotive?'

'Yeah.'

'Why didn't you say?' She smiled and took her hand off the truncheon. 'She's not home by any chance?'

'No, she'll be with the cricket team somewhere.'

The policewoman looked disappointed. 'Tell your sister Big Trish was asking after her. I haven't seen her at the YWCA since she quit hockey.'

29

'There, Julian! More filth!' Prudence tapped the window with a fuchsia fingernail.

I was crouched under her arm following her fingernail taps on the glass slider with a plastic scraper. This behaviour bothered me. Brian Keith never made Sebastian Cabot get down on all fours.

'No, no, no. Over here! Use your eyes! You people just don't see fly droppings, do you?'

'One of those jeweller's loupes might come in handy.'

'Are you being brazen?'

I was most definitely being brazen but it wasn't a very clever thing to do. It gave the advantage. The best way to deal with Prudence was to appeal to her sense of self-importance.

'After your divorce, should I address you as madam or lady?'

Prudence fanned her nostrils and drew breath before answering. 'I've given the subject considerable thought and decided on miss, *comme la jeune fille.*'

'Miss it is then.'

'Jipper.'

'Jipper.'

'Miss Jipper.'

It was thoroughly enjoyable to annoy Prudence but I had

to be careful. It was day five of her diet and her mood swings were ferocious. She'd started on the diet with no fat to lose and was now running on empty. Prudence hadn't chosen a normal method of losing weight like the cabbage diet. She was on the fresh pineapple diet, an exotic choice for Tasmania where pineapple was bought in tins and used for decorating ham steak and cheesecakes. Fresh pineapple was for foreigners and luxury hotels in places like Copacabana Beach. When I discovered that Prudence had bulk-ordered her fruit from Queensland, I decided to join her. I'd discreetly eat my way to weight loss and it wouldn't cost me a thing. The garage was stacked with crates.

Day one was thoroughly enjoyable. I managed eight pineapples and never felt a twinge of hunger. The next day, my mouth felt as if I'd eaten a packet of razor blades but I still tucked away six. By day five my trousers had loosened but my nerves were shot and my digestive system wouldn't stop bubbling.

'Is that you making that infernal noise?' Prudence took her eyes off the linen skirt I was ironing and screwed up her nose at me.

'It's my musical intestines.'

'Control them.'

'I can't. They're like my kidneys. They've got a mind of their own.'

'Of course you can control them! You people just don't try.'

With an aggressive sniff, she removed the skirt from the ironing board and left the room.

Prudence had an appointment with the bishop at the Anglican cathedral. Officially it was a private interview about the divorce but earlier that morning I'd overheard her talking to someone about a press photographer. I pitied Dick Dingle but I still wished I was going to the cathedral with her to fight off the press.

My parents' marriage had been dismantled without any such fanfare. The divorce was now official. Mum and I had celebrated with a roast chicken and chocolate log but it was a confusing anti-climax for me. After years of belonging to something called a family, I was suddenly a free agent. I couldn't think about this freedom too much because it made me feel empty, the sort of emptiness I felt when I tried to understand a car engine or outer space.

Prudence came back downstairs looking like a model churchgoer. She'd teamed the skirt with a beige twin set and pearls and was wearing a beige hat shaped like a sausage roll. My mouth watered. I loved sausage rolls almost as much as I loved chips. My intestines gurgled. Prudence screwed up her nose.

'I'll wait for Percy on the terrace. You will kindly lock up when you leave.'

'I don't have a key.'

'Of course you don't have a key. I cannot hand out keys to just anyone. I have valuables, a *private* life.' Prudence sniffed. 'People without a net worth or reputation simply do not understand the importance of security. You people have nothing to lose.'

'How do I lock up?'

'I've set the lock on the kitchen door. Simply pull it closed behind you.'

'And Solange?'

'She will be fine in her chalet.'

I watched the white Bentley disappear out of the driveway before making my move. I breached the second floor feeling like Vasco da Gama and headed straight for the fancy double doors of the master bedroom. I'd imagined the room a thousand times:

the four-poster hung with gauze curtains, the pink satin comforter and tasselled throw cushions. With a smile, I pushed open the doors. The smile died on my lips.

The bedroom was a wasteland of clothes, shoes, handbags and discarded packaging, more like the Ulverston Municipal Dump than the girly room of Barbara Cartland. My eyes picked out the gay purple wrapper of Tiffany biscuits and the gold foil of Shelby's fruit and nut among empty ice-cream cartons, sweet wrappers, soft-drink cans and cigarette butts. I let out a cry of outrage and joy and made for the bathroom.

The door was open and giving off the humid smell of fridge fungus. I poked my head in and did a double take. The marble vanity top was strewn with potions and pills and defiled by dirty tissues, cotton pads and ear buds. The brass fittings were crusty with tarnish and the porcelain sink was dull brown and clogged with hair. Even the shower curtain over the bath was black with mould. I stepped over the carnage of clothes and wrappers to pull it back.

The pain that seized my chest was the sort that accompanies a cardiac arrest. Solange was crouched in the bath looking up at me. Her eyes were narrowed. I was already stumbling backward when the dog reared up and hurdled the bath rim like a gymkhana pony. By the time I hit the kitchen floor, its jaws were opening against a buttock. I heard the dog's nails lose traction on the marble as it skidded across the floor behind me. With a yelp Solange thumped into the cupboards under the sink but I was already out of the door. I slammed it shut with a laugh as the dog threw itself against the glass panel. I would've kept on laughing if I hadn't remembered that my jacket and bus fare were inside. So was the key to the garage.

A cramp tore through my abdomen. I hadn't eaten anything since the previous day's pineapples and was starving. My only source of nourishment was under lock and key. Cursing Prudence, I circled the garage, then went back to the house and made a circuit. Everything was closed and locked up tight. When I returned to the front of the house I noticed Solange in the window of the parlour. The Afghan was watching me with narrowed eyes. Its eyes widened as I stooped down to tear off a yellow bloom from a flowerbed. It yelped as I stuffed it in my mouth.

I'd recognised the bed of nasturtiums from one of Brother Punt's field trips. The flowering plant was edible, a trick worth keeping in mind for times of potato famine or religious persecution. The flower tasted like raw cabbage and candle wax but beggars couldn't be choosers. I filled my mouth and swallowed without chewing. I refilled it. Solange could go to hell. So could Prudence with all her dirty secrets. When I set off for home, the flowerbed was a denuded tangle of stalks.

I didn't need to walk past Sidney Merle Memorial Park but I always made a point of doing so whenever I was near the city centre. The park was another place my father had warned me about. I was walking past it slowly, peering into the gloom of the shrubbery, when an elderly man suddenly emerged. His head was down and he was doing up his fly. We collided and the point of his elbow hit my stomach, releasing with a loud *bang* a fart of pineapple gas I'd been holding. The man gave a cry of alarm and backed away as if he'd been shot. I picked up the pace and hurried toward the shopping centre.

Philippe was sitting in one of the cutting chairs examining himself in the mirror when I got to the Brush Off. I tapped on the window and he turned, his eyes automatically flicking to my hair. He blinked as if trying to remember something and then shook his head. With a frown, he looked back at the mirror. My stomach gurgled and I hurried on.

By the time I got to Echidna Avenue, the hunger had returned with a vengeance. I burst into the kitchen like John Wayne entering a saloon. The packaging on a loaf of bread was ripped apart and two slices were shoved in the toaster. Before they had a chance to warm, they were popped up, buttered and shoved in my mouth. The feeling this gave me was fantastic, something between panic and euphoria. I flicked the switch on the deep fryer and plugged in the electric frying pan.

'What's all this then?' Mum surveyed the wreckage of the kitchen and shook her head. She took off an orange jacket I hadn't seen before and laid it over a chair back.

I belched and smiled. I'd just consumed a loaf of bread, packet of sausages, block of cheese, bag of frozen chips and six eggs.

'I take it the pineapples are old news?' She smiled and I noticed she was wearing a different shade of lipstick: silvery tangerine. It made her teeth look whiter and added dazzle to her smile.

'Don't make me move. I'll be sick.'

'Stay where you are. I'll make a cup of tea.'

'I have no intention of moving.'

'Drink this.' Mum handed me a cup and sat down opposite with one for herself. She was a great believer in the healing power of a tea bag. 'I see you haven't washed your overalls yet.'

'You're not supposed to know about that.'

'We need to talk.'

'But she's Dick Dingle's wife, Mum.' My voice was a whine.

'Not about that vulture. I want to tell you about my new friend.'

'Uh-huh.'

'Dezzie.'

'Your boss?' Icy needles scraped across my scalp. The food in my stomach threatened to move north. I belched and tasted cheese and chips. 'You don't mean *boy*friend!'

'He's just a special friend at the moment.'

'But he could become a boyfriend?'

'Let's see what happens. He's a very nice man. You'll like him.'

'I doubt it.' I could just see this Dezzie: hair slicked back, dark sunglasses, white shoes. He'd be hairy and wear his shirts open at the neck with a thick gold chain, the sort of man who addressed women as 'love' and played Julio Iglesias on his car cassette player. Mum deserved better. So did I. 'Why doesn't he have a wife of his own?'

'He did.'

'And?'

'She died.'

'That's suspicious for a start.'

'Julian, don't be mean.' Mum's face softened. 'You'll never guess who I bumped into today at the Wool Board?'

I didn't answer. My ears were buzzing and I felt carsick.

'Jimmy Budge! He's won Wool Cadet of the Year.'

Jimmy's face rose out of the haze of carsickness and floated before me. It was the beautiful face from the magazine.

'He asked after you. He says he wants to transfer to the Board in Hobart.'

'Did you tell him I was working for Dick Dingle's wife?'

'Yes.'

'That's all right then.'

I stayed in the dinette and thought about Jimmy as Mum cleared the table and cleaned the kitchen. The carsickness had been replaced by a more profoundly uncomfortable feeling of doom. Everything was going to the dogs. What could I say to

Jimmy if he came to Hobart? I didn't have a real job or any money and I could hardly give him a guided tour of the city on foot. Knowing Jimmy, he probably drove a tidy little Ford Escort and had the Terrence Fig clothes and hair to go with it. Jimmy Budge was a shooting star.

Mum finished cleaning up and went into the lounge to call Norman. I knew she was talking about me because she shut the sliding doors and turned up the television. I hated it when she did that. It made me feel sidelined, like a kid, or worse, like an adopted kid.

Tyres screeched outside. A car door slammed. Carmel yanked open the fly screen.

'Aloha.' I gave her my old Frank Sinatra smile. 'How's big sis?'

'What?' Carmel threw her cricket cap on the table.

'Just being friendly.'

'Don't bother.' She opened the fridge and surveyed the contents with a scowl. 'The fridge has been gutted! Where the hell are the sausages?'

'How was cricket practice?'

'And the eggs?' She looked in the bread bin. 'There's no bloody bread.'

'Mum's got other things on her mind.'

'What do you mean?'

'She's seeing a fancy man. He wears white shoes and plays Julio Iglesias.'

'I'm going to the chip shop.'

'Don't you care?'

'About what?'

'About the interloper. The man's a danger.'

'Get a life.'

The fly screen slapped shut. I heard an engine start and the

259

screech of tyres. Carmel would have to find out the hard way. Dezzie was trouble. I could feel it in the pit of my stomach, right next to the sausages and cheese. Mum was a fool. We'd worked so hard to get rid of Dad and now she was about to ruin everything by bringing another bastard into our lives. Yes, *bastard*. That's what he was, a bastard. I rolled the word around inside my head and smiled. Dad was another bastard. So was John. Bastard one, bastard two, bastard three. Three *fucking* bastards.

'Lovely.' Mum had come in from the lounge. 'You're smiling.'

'No I'm not.'

'Was that Carmel I just heard?'

'She took off. She obviously wasn't happy about this Dezzie business.'

'Julian, it wasn't your place to tell her.'

'Someone had to do it.'

'What am I going to do with you?'

'Kick me out of the house, probably. I don't work at the Wool Board like all the other shooting stars.'

'Where do you get such silly ideas?' Mum placed a hand on my hair and ruffled it. 'Your roots are showing.'

'No they're not.' Of course my roots were showing. They were over half the length of my hair.

'Norm's been invited to Hobart.' Mum paused for a reaction but didn't get one. 'They're going to put on a big hair show for apprentice hairstylists and want him to be a judge. The theme of the competition is big hair.'

'I thought he didn't like Hobart.'

'He hasn't said yes yet.'

Norman had been a phantom for so long it was hard to imagine seeing him in person. My memory of him was vague: a quiet spotty teenager wearing tight shorts and a terry-towelling beach hat. I hated terry towelling. It was the sort of thing bus drivers wore on holiday. I didn't know Norman and didn't care if I never saw him again. He could go to hell like the rest of the bastards.

30

I was surprised when Dad called. He was friendly.

'Trev tells me you're working for that New Zealand tart.'

'English.'

'Is that what she told you? She arrived at the docks years ago on a Kiwi trawler. The old gold-digger started out gutting fish.' Dad laughed the small heh-heh laugh he used when he knew best.

'You shouldn't believe everything you hear.' I struggled to keep my voice neutral. My mind was whirring. *Prudence gutting fish?*

'I do when the source is reliable.'

I hated it when Dad pulled rank and pretended to be a real journalist with actual news sources. He was the editor of the sports pages and sat on his bum all day typing or watching television. What was newsworthy about sports? I could hear the *tap-tapping* of a typewriter in the background. Typical. Dad believed personal calls were a waste of money unless they were done on work time. He coughed, something he always did before an announcement.

'We've just had some disturbing news come in at the *Star*. It's about your neighbours, the Finch family. The son's in hospital with a broken pelvis. They say he's going to be OK but he's had a nasty shock. I think he's about your age.'

'I don't know him.'

I knew Peter Finch well enough to cross the street whenever I saw him. He'd once thrown a roasting-hot steak pie at me as I walked past his house. It had splattered against my legs and left red marks for three days. Carmel called him You Big Dumb Dag to his face and shook her fist whenever she saw him. He never tried the meat pie trick on her.

'He was knocked down today on Echidna Avenue. A car drove on to the footpath and rammed him from behind. They caught the maniac.'

'Not that joy-rider again?'

'Nah, it was a middle-aged man this time, a driver for Tip Top Taxis. Pissed out of his mind. It must be the maniac that threw the coconut at the Valiant. Incredible.'

'The taxi could've killed someone. Me.'

'Thank God it wasn't Carmel. We can't let anything ruin her chances for the Tassie team. That girl's a shooting star.'

'She takes after you.'

'I've always been a sports enthusiast.'

'You both love beer.'

'Look, what I want to say is . . . I should've believed you.' Dad drew in air. This was obviously difficult for him. 'Carmel told me some cock-and-bull story about two bloody American sailors and a frozen chicken. It seems stupid now.'

My fingers were tingling when I got off the phone. Dad had more or less admitted he was wrong and virtually apologised. I couldn't remember him ever doing anything so reckless. He was always right even when he was wrong. I didn't feel sorry for Peter Finch. He was a violent bully and known in the street for uprooting shrubs and vandalising letterboxes. There were football-boot dents in the galvanised iron of our letterbox.

I sat still for a moment enjoying the tingle. It was nice to have a virtual apology from Dad. It took the edge off my worries about Mum. My biggest worry was about sharing her with another man. I didn't even want to share a roast chicken with another man, let alone my mother. I could imagine sitting down to a dinner with the womaniser. Dezzie would take the head of the table and lord it over the fowl with a carving knife while Mum shot me the Family Hold Back signal. I hated the FHB rule. It gave the advantage to the opponent and went against the principle of fair play. Dezzie wouldn't play by the rules anyway. I imagined him dumping a dry old drumstick on my plate with a sneer and winkling the oysters out of the back of the bird for my mother. He'd then do something showy like go down on a knee and present them to her on the blade of the knife.

I had to get Mum back on my team and the easiest way to do this was by winning her sympathy. I was weighing up hotplate burns against razor-blade cuts when a church flyer arrived in the letterbox. The church was collecting money to support the campaign of Bobby Sands and the other hunger strikers in the lead-up to Easter. The starvation of Bobby Sands had stirred sympathy around the world and consolidated support for the Catholic cause in Northern Ireland. Bobby was too young and good-looking to die. He was an inspiration.

Bypassing the toaster, I made for the sink where I filled a large glass with water. From now on, water was the only thing that would pass my lips. It was Bobby and I against the world. I'd waste away along with him and make sure Mum knew that I was doing my bit for the motherland. When she suggested a doctor, I'd shake my head. 'Don't worry about little old me. You've got Dezzie to think about.'

My hunger strike would've been a major success if I hadn't chosen a seat near the back of the bus I took to work. Across the aisle, a large woman with short mousy hair was eating a scone wrapped in waxed paper. From where I sat, it looked like a cheese and parsley scone, by far the best scone in the *Tucker Box Book of Classic Aussie Recipes*. The woman noticed me looking and swallowed hard.

'Do you *mind*! I'm trying to eat!' She glared at me and wiped her mouth fiercely with a handkerchief. 'Get your own sustenance.'

'Go ahead, enjoy yourself. I'm only thinking of poor old Bobby Sands. He probably weighs less than one of your legs.'

'Claptrap. The man's a murderer. All those IRA terrorists should be lined up and shot.' The woman gave my overalls a sharp, nasty look and nodded her chins for emphasis.

'And you'd pull the trigger, I take it.' I felt the pride of the Irish grip my chest. Bobby smiled at me benignly from his prison hospital bed.

'I'd do my citizen's duty.'

'You're a Protestant, then.'

'I do not discuss religion with yobs on buses, thank you very much.' The woman turned away and brushed scone crumbs off her skirt.

'If I'm a yob then you must be a yob caller.'

'A *what*?'

'Yob caller.'

'Rude! I'm glad I don't have a son like you.'

'And I'm glad I don't have a mother like you. I'd hate to be a bastard.'

The woman blew out her cheeks and gave the bus cord a hard yank. Clenching the scone to her chest like a weapon, she stormed up to the driver to complain about me loudly. When the bus stopped, the driver turned in his seat and pointed a sausage finger at me.

'You, out! I'll have no filthy language on the bus. I have nice ladies on board.'

'But she called me a yob first.'

'Out!'

It wasn't fair. The woman had started it but there was no arguing with the bus drivers of Hobart. I got off outside Cobber's supermarket boiling with rage and frustration. The next bus wouldn't arrive for half an hour. I'd be late for work and Prudence was going to be furious.

I pressed my forehead against the supermarket window and surveyed the display of Easter cheer. My mouth watered. In the centre of the display of marshmallow eggs and chocolate rabbits sat a glorious football-sized chocolate egg wrapped in gold foil. Its packaging promised: 'A delicious jumbo shell of milk chocolate with a novelty and prize token inside! A Fijian holiday could be yours!'

I thought of Bobby and made my move. The Easter egg would be a reward at the end of the hunger strike, a symbol of good like a dashboard statuette of the Virgin Mary. The egg cost everything I had but I felt like a player when I walked out of Cobber's with the football of chocolate under my arm. It was the best I'd felt in a long time.

I set out for Battery Point on foot with the comforting smell of cocoa butter and sugar wafting up from the crook of my arm. My hand strayed to the foil and lifted an edge. I ran a fingernail across the surface and put it in my mouth. It tasted of happiness, of the birthdays and Christmases I'd spent together with my mother. Scratching deeper, I created a hole and shook out a tiny hula doll on a suction cup. I put my hand inside the chocolate shell but found no prize token. Typical.

The feelings of anger and frustration returned. Hunger gnawed at me as I crossed the road to Sidney Merle Memorial

Park and sat down on a park bench. I thought of my mother and Dezzie as I angrily broke off a piece of the football and stuffed it in my mouth. The next hunk was for the woman on the bus. The bus driver, Prudence and Solange took care of the rest. In less than two minutes, I'd demolished the football and was left feeling carsick and miserable. As I squinted into the shrubbery of the park, I decided Bobby Sands could go it alone.

I jumped off the bench and made for the centre of the park. The light was on inside the Ladies but the doorway to the Gents was dim. I soon discovered why. Someone had removed the light bulb. Inside it was pitch dark. My feet squelched on the damp floor as I felt my way along the rough concrete wall. My chest was tight. I reached the hardboard of a cubicle and stopped. The sound of someone breathing became audible. The breather coughed. 'Over here, mate.'

Prudence was waiting for me on the terrace with her arms rigid at her sides. I'd forgotten all about the Operatic Society. The monthly luncheon was a major event for the small elite club of Hobart that Prudence liked to call 'society'. She'd dressed for the occasion in a powder-blue chiffon frock and matching turban.

'*Where* have you been?' Her face was mauve but the knuckles gripping the handle of her handbag were bone-china white. 'I've had to prepare Solange's meal myself.'

'The bus I was on knocked down a lady.' I walked up to Prudence with a new swagger. 'She was probably about your age.'

'That's no reason for you to be late for work!'

'She was stuck under the bus, in agony, screaming.'

'Yours is a responsible position.'

'I had to help the bus driver. Citizen's duty and all that.

267

We tried to lift the wheel off her.' I pointed to the grime on the knees of my overalls. 'Road dirt.'

Prudence screwed up her nose.

'I didn't give the lady the kiss of life but old Lips Corkle was ready.' I puckered my lips.

'I've heard *enough*, thank you.'

'I'm no expert but I reckon she'd broken her pelvis.'

'Enough! There's George now.' Prudence silenced me as a red Jaguar rounded the driveway. 'Give the flowerbeds a good spray. Something has completely devastated the nasturtiums.'

Prudence had to duck her extended head under the Jaguar's doorframe to get into the car. I bent down as I shut the door.

'Mrs Jipper, that hat puts the Taj Mahal to shame. Bravo!'

Prudence nodded sternly as the car moved off. She looked ridiculous sitting next to the very stiff but normal-looking George. The large powder-blue turban made her head look twice the size of his.

The Jaguar had just pulled out of the driveway when I heard something that made the hair on my arms stand to attention. It was a loud trucker's horn, the horn my sister had recently installed on the Hubs ute to startle road hogs. The cheers of raucous girls reached my ears even before the ute nosed into the driveway. Three of them were crowded into the front and another eight were squeezed in the back waving beer bottles. They cheered again as Carmel ran the ute up on to the grass and over the denuded flowerbed.

I watched in horror as they burst out of the cab and leaped off the back. I began walking backward, trying to form a barrier against the human tide advancing on the house.

'Hi, girls. What's up?' I held up my hands in gentle protest.

'We've just won the bloody Tickworth Cup, you dingbat.' Carmel led another cheer. 'We've come to cool off in your pool. Dad and Trevor have drained theirs while they put in a deck.'

'It's not *my* pool.' It was never wise to say 'no' directly to Carmel. 'Isn't it too cold for swimming?'

'Not if you're hot-blooded.' Carmel winked at Debra Fig and tossed a beer bottle into the azaleas.

'There's Prudence to consider.'

'We just saw her leave with a John. She had a blue onion on her head.' Carmel turned to her team-mates and waved them forward. 'Take the plunge, girls. We'll join you after we've had a look round.'

'I don't think . . .' My heart sank as Carmel and Debra gripped me under the arms and propelled me toward the back of the house. 'You can't go inside. There's a violent dog.'

'Can't be as bad as the dogs on the Devonport team.' Carmel winked at Debra again.

'This one's a highly dangerous Afghan.' I pointed to Solange through the glass panel of the back door. 'A killer, trained to go for the vulnerable bits.'

'That's not a dog. That's a pussycat.' Carmel opened the door and grabbed Solange by the collar, giving the dog a rough rub behind the ears.

To my surprise, Solange didn't growl or try to bite. Instead the dog quietly followed my sister into the kitchen and sat docilely as she replaced the water in its bowl with the contents of Debra's Tickworth lager bottle. Solange lapped at the beer greedily.

Debra Fig had stopped in the middle of the room and was gazing at the wall of kitchen cupboards. 'Jeezus, the kitchen's got a telly.'

'That is a Miele oven. I use it to grill lean meats.' I ran a finger along the marble bench top and pointed to the silver fridge.

'Icemaker. Once you get used to crushed, you find the cubes repellent.'

'You would, you pretentious ponce.' Debra snorted. 'I find fly spray repellent.'

I sniffed and followed the girls into the parlour. Debra made for the mantelpiece and started touching things.

'Please, don't touch anything!' I got as close to Debra as I dared. 'They belong to Dick Dingle.'

'That'd be right.' Debra had a naked porcelain cherub in her hand.

Outside the girls were shrieking and splashing about in the pool. I looked to Carmel for help but she'd plonked herself down on the curly sofa next to Solange. She swung her feet on to the table.

'Bloody ugly footstool.'

'It's part of a Greek column, thousands of years old. An authentic, priceless antique from Greece.'

'Greek my bum. Bet it's Bunyip sandstone.' Carmel reached over and gave Solange's belly a tickle. The dog rolled on to its back and opened its hind legs shamelessly.

'*That's priceless!*'

We all turned. The hoarse whisper was hurled from the doorway and aimed at Debra who was holding the Dang figurine to her nose, smelling its bottom. Prudence had appeared from nowhere. Her face was waxy white and her turban was askew.

'I . . . I do not understand.' Prudence looked at me. 'There are naked girls in my swimming pool. Big girls . . . with big arms.'

'It's not what you think, Mrs Jipper.' I took the figurine from Debra's hand and replaced it on its stand.

Debra screwed up her nose. 'That thing smells like dung.'

Carmel snickered from the sofa. Prudence looked her way. Her eyes fell on the dog.

'Solange! How could you!'

The Afghan rolled off the sofa and slunk out of the room with its tail between its legs. My sister watched it go and then stood with her big arm outstretched.

'Prudential, I'm Julian's sister.'

'Prudence.' Prudence sniffed and refused Carmel's hand. 'Jipper to you.'

I moved back. It was never wise to refuse my sister.

Carmel's face hardened. 'Jipper it is then.'

Prudence drew breath sharply. 'I want you all to leave immediately or I'll call the authorities.'

'The port authorities?' Carmel winked at Prudence.

'I *beg* your pardon.'

'Down at the docks.'

'I have *no* idea what you're talking about.'

'The docks, your old trawling ground.' Carmel winked again and gave me a shove toward the door.

'Get out!' Prudence thrust a bony finger in the direction of the back door. The tendons of her neck were standing out like fingers.

'We're leaving anyway. We've got other fish to fry.'

Prudence glared at me as I was pushed past. Her lip curled. 'You're fired!'

'And you're a fish-gutting gold-digger!' I gave her one of Carmel's winks.

Prudence gasped.

'I don't know who's the bigger bitch, you or Solange.'

A cheer went up as we appeared at the front of the house. The girls had climbed in the back of the ute and were drinking beer. I thought of the *Mod Squad* as I got into the cab between Carmel and Debra. I was part of a team, and even if it was only a girls' cricket team, it still felt good. I pulled the novelty hula girl out of my pocket and stuck it to the dashboard.

271

The wheels of the ute spun over the lawn, chewing up turf and spraying garden soil over the parked Jaguar. George sat rigid in his driver's seat with his hands clenching the steering wheel. A thrill went through me as Carmel rolled down her window. The bottle she threw landed expertly at the feet of Prudence who was standing like a marble statue on the lawn in front of the terrace.

31

It didn't take long for the triumph to wear off and reality to sink in. Carmel and Mum left for work each day like normal citizens while I stayed at home, ate and worried about the TV being repossessed. Not only was I jobless and friendless, but I had no money and my mother was being courted by an unknown factor called Dezzie. The more I thought about the philanderer, the more upset I became. Anyone with a name like Dezzie had to be a bastard. Dezzie, Dazza and Bazza were nicknames of a certain type of man. They were the types that hung around the pub watching football and drinking Tickworth lager. These were ridiculous pastimes but that's what passed for normal in Tasmania and normal was supposed to be good. If you weren't normal you were a foreigner or a poofter.

At least my father didn't have a 'za' name. James never got turned into Jazza. It was hardly a consolation but he had very little else going for him. Dad was typical in every other way and thought he was superior because he passed for normal. It didn't make sense.

I'd agreed to spend Easter Monday at his place after a disastrous Sunday morning at home. I should've suspected foul play when I found three large Easter eggs in my mother's wardrobe. Three? Naturally, I thought Mum had bought me two. I was at home more often than Carmel and a lot nicer to have around. I deserved two.

Mum knew that Easter Sunday was important to me. We'd spent nearly sixteen of them together. It should've been the best Easter yet. We didn't have to share chocolate with Dad or put up with the sickening Sunday afternoon hum of sports programming.

When I carried the tray of tea and toast into Mum's bedroom, I was prepared for a perfect Easter. Bygones were bygones. We'd drink tea together like old times and break open some chocolate eggs for Jesus. She sat up in bed smiling and patted the bed beside her.

'Happy Easter, honey.' Mum handed me a single chocolate egg.

'Where's the other one?'

'What other one?'

'There were three in your wardrobe.'

'What were you doing in my wardrobe?' Mum replaced the teacup in its saucer with a clatter. Her face hardened.

'Looking for a Band-Aid. I cut myself preparing your dinner.'

'You were looking for a Band-Aid in my wardrobe?' Mum crossed her arms over her chest. 'You have no place going through my things, Julian. How many times do I have to tell you?'

'You bought it for Dezzie, didn't you?' Two could play at self-righteousness. I stood up and looked down at her with my hands on my hips, Dolly-style.

'Yes I did, as a matter of fact.' Mum's face flushed. 'I'm having lunch with him today.'

'Well, you'd better not spoil your appetite then.'

I snatched the tray off her lap and hurried out of the room with tears pricking my eyes.

* * *

Later that evening I began preparing for Monday by sifting flour into a bowl. Mum had left in a huff before lunch and still hadn't come home. We'd had words when I told her I was going to Dad's for lunch the next day. She'd called me foolish and slammed the door on her way out. I would've been upset about her gallivanting if I wasn't so angry. The thought of Dezzie eating chocolate that rightfully belonged to me made my blood boil.

Hot-cross buns were a Good Friday treat but we'd never eaten them on a Friday at our house. Dad had always insisted on buying them a couple of days later when he got more buns for his buck. The way to my father's heart was definitely through his stomach. Fresh hot-cross buns was a gesture he'd appreciate. It was Corkle family legend that his mother had made them every Easter.

The secret to making a good hot-cross bun was to leave the dough overnight to rise. I was pouring yeast granules into warm water when the fly screen creaked and John poked his miserable head inside the door. He looked at me and sneered.

'Jesus Christ, what happened to your hair?'

I glanced back down at the box of yeast. It was empty. I couldn't remember how full it had been but now wasn't the time to worry about details. My plans for an Easter détente were in jeopardy. John was my father's golden boy. He was supposed to be in Melbourne where he was now a student.

'What are you doing here?'

'It's Easter.' John took in my satin pyjamas and Mum's apron tied around my waist. He sniggered. 'Joan Collins.'

'Don't you have bodies to cut up?'

'Fuck off, Joan.'

John heaved his suitcase through the door and headed for Carmel's old bedroom. I watched him bump his way down the hall and considered my options. The Joan Collins comment was not only vicious but it was also completely wrong. The satin pyjamas and sweep-over fringe were very Bryan Ferry. The Christian and Easter thing to do was turn the other cheek. Then again, John deserved a little heat. I waited until the shower was running and then turned on the cold tap.

Feeling a lot better, I emptied Mum's currant jar into the flour and added cinnamon and sugar. The yeast was bubbling when I added it to the dry ingredients. I rolled the dough into balls, placed them on a tray and blessed them with sugar-water crosses. As I did it, I muttered Ralph Waters' version of the sign of the cross: 'Spectacles, testicles, wallet and watch.'

I could smell the sweet fatty odour of grilled sausages as the Hubs ute pulled into Trevor's drive. Cursing under my breath, I prayed that Dad had had the sense to also buy steak. A barbecue wasn't worth its firelighters without steak. It was like a birthday without a cake. I followed Carmel and John into the kitchen where we found Trevor stirring Tucker Box gravy on the stove.

'Your Dad's on the new deck. He's fired up the barbie for a mixed grill.'

Carmel and John disappeared out of the back door. Trevor removed the pot from the element and shook my hand. 'Hope you like lamb's fry and black pudding. He's got a good pile of sausages, too.'

'I like steak.' What sane person liked animal organs and blood? Sausages were edible but only as a back-up to a good steak, preferably fillet.

'Just like your dad.' Trevor lifted the tea towel covering the beer crate I'd placed on the table. 'What's this?'

'A hot-cross loaf.'

When I'd opened the hot-water cupboard in the morning,

I'd found a lumpy tray of swollen dough. The buns had tripled in size overnight and joined together. Since I didn't have the ingredients or time to remake the dough, I'd put the tray in the oven and hoped for the best. Twenty minutes later I'd removed a monstrous pillow of bread pock-marked with currants and X's. The loaf looked like a three-dimensional game of noughts and crosses.

'It's very artistic. I've never tried the loaf but I'm a big fan of the buns.'

'It's a traditional Irish recipe from County Cork. The loaf came before the bun, a bit like the chicken and egg story.'

'That'll make a lovely dessert. Go out and say hello to your dad. I'll put it on a platter.'

I stifled a wave of carsickness as I walked out on to the new deck. Carmel and John were setting up wickets on the lawn below. Dad was surrounded by smoke, busily tonging sausages on the grill. He was wearing a plastic barbecue apron printed with 'I'm with stupid' and an arrow. I approached him from the blunt side of the arrow.

'It's a very nice deck, Dad.' From experience, I knew the best way to warm up my father was to congratulate him on something.

'Of course it's a nice deck. It cost enough.'

'But worth it.'

'You can say that again.' Dad smiled proudly as if I'd just congratulated him for scaling K2. 'We've put the telly on wheels and sit out here of an evening with a bucket of ice and Tickworths. You can't beat a game of footy and a decent Australian sausage. Why I ever married and had kids, I'll never know.'

Dad picked off several sausages and added them to a mound of barbecued meats. I eyed the stack of rump steak and told myself to keep calm. Everything was going to be all right.

A trestle table had been set up on the deck. As we took our seats, I made sure to sit as far from John as possible. The plate of meat was in front of Dad. I watched him take the biggest steak, a couple of sausages and a kidney. John and Carmel followed suit and passed the tray to Trevor. When the tray was passed to me all the steak was gone. I probed under the sausages and cooked offal and then double-checked everyone's plate. There was no mistaking it. We were definitely one steak short. Dad coughed and held up his glass of beer to John.

'It's great to have you home for Easter, son.' Dad was an expert at making meaningless toasts. 'I never expected this. A lovely surprise.'

I gritted my teeth. We were one steak short because of John's selfishness.

'Thanks, Dad.' John put down his cutlery as if he was about to make a speech. 'I've got some news.'

Dad lowered his glass. 'You're not quitting medical school, I hope.'

'No. I've met a girl from Devonport. I'm driving over there tomorrow to meet her parents.'

'A nice Tassie girl. Now there's a spot of luck. What does she do?'

'She'll be a gynaecologist in a few years.'

'Uh-huh.' Dad frowned. Gynaecology wasn't real science to men like my father. It was something indecent, definitely not the sort of thing to discuss over sausages. 'But she'll be a doctor all the same?'

'A specialist.' John had noticed Dad's reaction and wanted to convince him of the profession. 'They make a lot more money than GPs.'

'Now you're talking.'

'What's her name?' My question was aimed at John but

278

everyone looked at me in surprise as if they'd forgotten my presence.

'Susan.' John shot me a dangerous look.

'John and Susan. Now there's an original combination of unusual names.'

'It's better than Julian and Cecil.' John sniggered into his steak.

'I don't know anyone called Cecil.' It was true. I'd never met a Cecil in my entire life. It was a very unpopular name in Tasmania. 'Cecil sounds like the name of a gynaecologist.'

'Enough of that talk!' Dad glared at me as if I'd just said 'bastard'.

The conversation went back to the cricket World Series and everyone relaxed. Everyone except me. The sausage in my mouth had turned to tasteless rubber. I chewed my way through its gristle and cursed myself for coming.

With a belch, Dad pushed his plate away, a signal that the meal was coming to an end. Trevor stood and took the meat tray to the kitchen and returned with my loaf on a large roasting dish. He placed it in the middle of the table with a 'Ta-dah' and then discreetly took his seat. Carmel and John stared. Dad leaned forward and frowned, prodding it with a finger.

'It's a hot-cross loaf.' I hurried to name it before Dad said something I'd regret. 'Just like Nana used to make.'

'Your grandmother was a lady.' Dad snorted out a laugh. It was his free-and-easy Tickworth laugh. 'She never made anything vulgar.'

He laughed again. John sniggered.

'I put in lots of currants.'

'I can't eat another thing right now. I'm as full as a cattle tick.' Dad pushed his chair back and patted his stomach. 'Right, who's ready to work off their steak?'

John smirked and walked off to the wickets in the garden. I watched Dad take a seat on the step as Carmel picked up the bat and took her place in front of the other set of wickets. It was just like old times. All we needed was the television on wheels screening sports programmes and the nightmare would be complete. John turned the ball in his hands and winked at Dad.

'I'll do an Uncle Norman.' Instead of bowling the regular way, John tossed the ball underarm. It looped up in a weak parabola and fell at Carmel's feet.

Dad laughed and slapped his knee.

'Wanker.' Carmel kicked the ball back to John. She didn't joke around when it came to cricket. 'Throw the bloody thing properly or I'll wrap this bat around your head.'

When I turned back to the table, Trevor was helping himself to a slice of the loaf. The interior of the bread was full of holes and looked like lacework. Trevor smiled and took a bite, chewing slowly.

'Very tasty. Unusual.'

'Trevor, what happened to Norman?'

'Your uncle?'

I nodded.

'It was a long time ago.'

'But something happened.'

Trevor winced.

'Please, Trevor.' My voice was a whine. 'He's my uncle and everyone knows except me.'

'He got into a spot of trouble when he came to Hobart.'

'What sort of trouble?'

'It's old news, mate.'

'Please.'

'There was some nonsense inside a public lavatory.' Trevor glanced over at Dad and lowered his voice. 'Down at the docks.'

'He got caught?'

'With another gent.'

'By the police?'

Trevor nodded. 'They couldn't prove anything in court but once his name got in the paper, he was done for.'

My body felt boneless and electrical. My heart was pumping but my limbs had lost power. All the blood was going to my head, which felt like it was going to shatter. I looked over at my father and John and tried to control the nausea that had stiffened my jaw. They weren't funny or original. They were just normal and normal was dumb and mean-spirited. Mum wasn't normal like them but she'd still betrayed me. She should've told me about Norman. We were a team and team-mates didn't keep secrets. Now I understood why my uncle had fled Tasmania. What kind of life would he have had after such a scandal?

I sat completely still. The electrical feeling had travelled up my spine and spread to the outer edges of my body. I felt as if the membrane separating me from the rest of the world was dissolving. I knew Trevor was going to pat me on the back before I felt his hand. The touch made me feel solid again.

'You've gone awfully pale, mate.'

'I think I'll get going.'

Trevor followed me through the house to the front door. He looked back over his shoulder before speaking. 'I was sorry for Norm. He was a nice young man.'

I nodded. I wanted to thank Trevor but my chin was trembling.

'He did the right thing getting out and starting over again. He would've regretted staying on.' Trevor looked into the distance. 'It's a terrible thing to live with regret.'

I took a roundabout route home to avoid Sidney Merle Memorial Park and ended up near a small row of shops I'd never seen before. Something in a window caught my eye and made me stop. It was a small notice on pink paper: 'URGENT APPRENTICE WANTED'.

I looked up at the shop sign. It was a hairdressing salon called the Curl Up and Dye. A bell tinkled as I pushed open the door. A woman appeared. She could've been fifty or seventy. The busy network of wrinkles on her face were either the normal wear and tear of age or the premature effects of cigarettes and Australian sun. Her hair was a big teased-up ball of tobacco-coloured fluff but her eyes were alive. They glittered like two shiny currants.

'Yes, love, what can I do you for?'

'I saw the notice. I wasn't sure you were open.'

'I opened up special for a lady customer.'

'On a public holiday?'

'Just doing my bit. The lady's in an unhappy marriage.' She held out a small hand. 'I'm Dot, love.'

'Julian.'

'Your name's got religious significance.'

The woman's hand radiated warmth. It flowed up my arm and into my chest. I felt like crying again. My eyes watered.

'There's no need for all that. Sit yourself down. I've just made a pot of tea.'

Dot came back with a tray of tea things and a plate of Easter eggs. 'The customers give them to me but I'll ruin my dentures if I eat them all.' She laughed, a raw smoker's laugh. 'So you might be interested in hairdressing?'

'I don't know. I'm no good at anything else.' I knew it was wrong to tell the truth in a job interview but I was on the verge of tears and felt flippy-floppy. 'I like hair. I mean . . . I love hair. Hair and fashion. And make-up.'

'That's a start. I'd call that passion.'

'I've always done Mum's hair. Not so much lately. Not since she got a fancy man.'

'You've had some experience then.'

'And I've got no job and no money.'

'Motivation.' Dot nudged the chocolate my way.

'My uncle's a hairdresser.'

'So it's in your blood.' She refilled our cups with tea. 'When can you start?'

'You mean I've got the job?' I couldn't believe it. An image of myself doing Elizabeth Taylor's hair flashed through my mind. My eyes filled again.

'It's an apprenticeship, love. You'll be learning a trade, earning yourself a qualification.' Dot refilled my cup. 'The job's yours on one condition.'

I stopped eating and swallowed hard.

'You've got to let me cut that ginger shite off your head. Why on earth did you go ginger when you've got a lovely head of black Irish hair?'

'I got it done at the Brush Off. Philippe's exclusive.'

'Don't believe everything you hear. Smoke and mirrors, love. He's made a right mess of your do.'

32

I finished ironing my candy-striped shirt and headed for The Ensuite. I couldn't wait to tell Mum about the new job. It was time to forgive and forget. I pushed open her door without knocking and stopped in the doorway. Her bed was neatly made and she was nowhere in sight. I backtracked but didn't find her in the kitchen or the lounge. This meant she'd either left extremely early or – *and surely this couldn't be true* – she'd not come home at all.

My ears were swirling with pressure as I returned to her bedroom and slipped a hand between her bedcovers. Cold! I examined the floor and shower of The Ensuite. Dry! There was only one explanation. Mum had spent the night with her fancy man. No, she'd probably spent two nights on the loose. I hadn't seen her since Sunday.

I couldn't believe it. I finally had the career break of my life and my mother was out painting the town red. What on earth was she thinking? Mothers weren't supposed to stay out all night. Their job was to be home in times of need. Mum was being irresponsible. She'd probably start bringing her fancy man home next. My heart skipped a beat at the thought.

I took the jotter out of the kitchen drawer and with trembling hands wrote her a note using a thick red marker pen.

Mum would see it on the table as soon as she walked in the door.

To Whom It May Concern,

    I've got a new job potentially involving celebrity hair and possibly the small screen. I'll be pretty busy from now on. So you might not be seeing a lot of me. I would've told you yesterday but you obviously didn't come home. It's a good thing we didn't have a fire or plumbing emergency.

    Your son

The Curl Up and Dye looked completely different in the bright light of morning: smaller and a lot shabbier. A rubbish tin outside the milk bar next door had overflowed and wrappers were collecting in the salon's doorway. I pushed them away with my foot and stepped inside.

The bell tinkled and I felt a wave of carsickness. It was the pink of the place. The overhead fluorescent tubes gave the rose-coloured walls and furnishings an unnatural fleshy glow. I recognised the dense pastel pink of the vinyl chairs. It was the colour of the fibreglass elephant ride of the Ulverston sideshow. One summer, in a surprising show of generosity, my father had let me ride one of the elephants. I should've known something was up when he helped me saddle up. He'd started laughing as soon as the whirligig got going. His voice had boomed out over the crowd. 'Look at little Princess Infanta on her baby pink elephanta!' It was impossible to get off the moving elephant until the end of the ride and there was no way to avoid the laughter of the small crowd that gathered around my father. I never went near a mechanical animal or coin-operated ride again.

Pink was clearly Dot's signature colour. She'd chosen it in varying shades for the floor, ceiling and cone hair-dryers on swing arms. Even the curlers in the utility trays were the colour of candyfloss. What was I thinking? The Curl Up was no fast track to celebrity hair. It was a suburban hairdressing salon for middle-aged women in floral frocks and cardigans. I was turning to leave when Dot walked through the back door. She was dressed in a simple pink smock with a gold chain around her neck and dangly earrings. Her hair was in curlers and she wasn't wearing any make-up. Her eyes looked tiny without mascara but they still glittered like Easter currants.

'Just having a fag out the back before my ladies arrive.' Dot laid a warm hand between my shoulder blades and gently nudged me into the salon. 'I'll put my face on while we get you started.'

'Dot . . .'

'We'll start you at the trough. Shampooing will give you a feel for the scalp.'

The warmth of her hand was impossible to resist. I was guided to the washing basins and given an introduction to hair-washing. Dot tied a scarf around her head and made herself up in the mirror as she gave directions. My first client was a bleached blonde with grey roots.

'Go easy on the shampoo and heavy on the conditioner.' Dot made massaging gestures with her hands. 'Use your fingertips. The ladies love a good rub.'

Dot showed me how to towel off and then led the woman away to a cutting chair in front of the main window. I was on my own for the next client, a big freckly woman with a bush of springy red hair that filled the basin and required a thorough drenching before it would absorb water.

The morning passed quickly. I was too busy washing hair

and talking to the women to think about my mother or even food. At midday Dot closed the door and led me through the laundry room to the backyard.

'Welcome to the shrubbery.'

She pointed to a plastic chair in a tiny but lush garden decorated with plaster animals and miniature wooden structures. The flowerbeds were planted out in bright annuals and small flowering bushes.

'You're a gardener, Dot.'

'I like somewhere nice to sun myself and smoke my fags.' She expertly tapped the bottom of her Pall Mall menthols. A cigarette popped up and was offered to me. 'You like the job?'

I nodded. The menthol numbed my tongue and made my mouth tingle.

'It's a human vocation. You get to know the ladies very well.' Dot took a long drag on her cigarette. 'Did you notice Mary's scalp?'

'The nobbly one?'

Dot nodded solemnly. 'You learn a lot from a scalp. It's like the palm only more accurate. Old Mary's got something wrong with her bowel. I'd put my money on cancer.'

'Oh.' Apart from a few bumps, Mary had seemed completely healthy. I resisted the urge to feel my own scalp.

'I'd give the poor girl six months, max. You do what you can.' Dot took another long drag and looked into the distance. 'What say you get yourself a quick sandwich and I'll cut that ginger business off your hair?'

I'd seen what Dot had done to her clients' hair and didn't want to look like Princess Anne. I took my time buying an egg sandwich and then attempted to eat it in slow motion. Dot watched me for a few minutes then whisked me over to the cutting chair.

'I know what you're thinking. You think I'll bugger it up.'

'It's just that I have a specific idea in mind.'

'Spit it out, love.'

'Short on one side and longish on the other, with a fluffy bit that sticks up on top and falls forward over one eye.'

'You want the Classic?'

I'd just described a Terrence Fig original. There was nothing classic about it.

'Sit still, love.'

There was no resisting Dot. She ran her hands through my hair and frowned. 'What kind of cut was this? It's shorter on top.'

'It's called a horizontal plane.'

'It's called a hack job.'

'Philippe's an artiste.'

'Load of rubbish.'

Dot took less than five minutes to remove the amber and transform my hair into the cut I'd just described. I was stunned. All this time I'd thought Terrence Fig was an original. Dot was fluffing the top with hairspray when I asked the obvious question.

'Is my bowel normal?'

'Clean as a whistle.'

'That's all right then.'

'Now you can do something for me.' Dot pulled me out of the chair and sat down in my place, removing the curlers from her hair with professional efficiency. 'When you do your mum's hair, what exactly do you do?'

'I kind of fluff it and then I get it to stay in place with hairspray.'

'Is the hair wet or dry?'

'Dry.'

'Just what I thought.' Dot smiled, flashing two rows of very white dentures. Fluffing was clearly a good thing in her books. 'Anyone can learn to cut hair but dry styling is a gift, something you're born with.'

She handed me a comb and a can of hairspray before running a hand over the curled halo of tobacco-coloured hair.

'Double the volume, up and out.' She circled her hands over her head. 'Remember, love, the secret to a good set is air. The volume and lift depend on how much air you can trap between the hairs. A good setter can defy gravity.'

I lifted one of the curls on Dot's head and let it fall. It was typical Irish hair, thin and very fine. I combed a clump away from her head and gave the base a squirt of hairspray. The hair stiffened. Fluffing with my fingertips, I added more spray, working from the bottom up, willing the hair to open and absorb air.

'Higher, Julian. Go higher!' Dot caught my eye in the mirror and winked.

My fingers moved faster, channelling and trapping air into the maze of hair that was taking shape below me. I was building upward, teasing Dot's hair to open outward like a Dutch tulip.

The doorbell tinkled. I looked over at the large woman in the doorway and heard air escape from the side of Dot's hair like a punctured tyre. I grabbed the hairspray.

'Focus! Stay with the hair!'

Dot's words sent a jolt of electricity through me. The outside world blurred and emptied. I heard the door open and close but kept my eyes on her hair. I was an artiste, Michelangelo painting Adam's thighs on the ceiling of the Sistine Chapel. Something powerful was working through me, guiding my hands.

After what seemed like a week of fevered activity, I folded the top of the hair over to form a closed beehive and lifted away my hands. Dot's hair had tripled in size. It was a glorious Tower of Babel, the most beautiful thing I'd ever created in my life.

'Gawd almighty.' A small puckered woman was standing behind us with her hand over her heart as if she was about to recite the national anthem. 'Now that's what I call a *do*. What do you call it?'

With a shock, I realised that a small group of women had gathered in the salon. They were looking at me solemnly, waiting for a response. I had no idea what to call my creation.

'You did good, love.' Dot nodded in the mirror. 'Name it and claim it.'

My mind was blank.

'A big name, love.'

The hairstyle did deserve a name, something powerful and possibly French. It was a creation worthy of Elizabeth Taylor and Maria Callas, the sort of hairstyle that went with diamond earrings and a nice necklace. I opened and closed my mouth. I opened it again and said something unexpected.

'The Hog!'

'All hail to the Hog!'

Dot made a Caesar salute and climbed off the chair. She told me to get back to the trough in a gruff voice but I could tell she was pleased. She was moving in a new, regal way with her head held stiffly.

I kept looking over at the Hog throughout the afternoon, marvelling at its beauty. Despite Dot's constant movements, the hairdo never tilted or sagged. It remained solid and upright like a battlefield monument. I was towelling off the last client of the day when the doorbell tinkled. My hands froze and the towel fell forward over the face of the woman. She pushed it away with a muffled yelp.

There was no mistaking the floral frock and cardigan. Dolly

was standing in the doorway with her hands on her hips glaring at me. When she spoke, her voice echoed across the salon and sent tremors along the arms of the cone dryers. She pushed the door shut with her bum and marched up to where I was standing behind the tub.

'What in God's name do you think you are doing?'

'I'm towelling off a customer.'

'Ridiculous!'

'I'm an apprentice.'

'Load of old cobblers.'

'It's a trade.'

'Hair care is not a trade for a man.'

'Vidal Sassoon's a man.'

'Foreigners don't count.' Dolly huffed in a self-righteous way and adjusted the cardigan over her bosom. 'I suppose your mother's put you up to this.'

'She's happy I've got a job.' I'd deal with Mum later. The present crisis called for a united front.

'That'd be right.'

'How's Uncle Ted's job?' I'd never dared mention Dolly's husband and employment in the same breath before. Mum said he was the dole office's best customer.

'Ted's affairs are no concern of yours.'

'And my affairs are no concern of Ted's . . . or yours for that matter.'

I flicked the towel like a matador's cape and placed it over the shoulders of my client. The small grey-haired woman stood and addressed Dolly.

'This young man's doing a wonderful job. He gives a lovely scalp massage. I feel like the Aga Khan.'

'Dolly!' Dot grasped my aunt's elbow and swung her away from the basin. 'Wash and set?'

'Just a set this time, thank you.' Dolly shot me a frosty look over her shoulder. 'I trust no one except you with my hair.'

'Of course, love. We'll get you gussied up in no time.'

Dot pointed to the basket of wet towels and told me to clean the tools and put the washing on out the back. 'Take your time, love, while I finish up here.'

I was putting towels into the dryer when she appeared with a packet of cigarettes and led me out to the garden.

'There's nothing like a good smoke after a day's hard yakka.'

I had to agree. I was developing quite a taste for menthol.

'Poor old Dolly.' Dot inhaled deeply and held the smoke in her lungs, letting it out slowly in a satisfied way. 'There's a worry spot the size of a Tickworth beer coaster on the crown of her head. It's so bald I could see myself in the reflection.'

I didn't feel sorry for Dolly. She deserved a bald spot the size of County Cork.

'She's had a lot of disappointment with that daughter of hers.'

'Sharon?'

'Expelled from school. Got a bit too big for her boots after that competition.' Dot stubbed out her cigarette. 'Of course, Ted's always been a ladies' man.'

Ted, a ladies' man? My uncle had a small head, big ears, bulbous nose and small lipless mouth. After my father, he was probably the most unattractive man in Tasmania.

'Hairdressing's a bit like social work, love. The ladies come in here worse for wear and our job is to make them feel beautiful. When we make a lady feel good about herself, she goes out and makes other people happy.' Dot patted the side of the Hog. 'I know what I'm talking about.'

The house was empty and the note was still on the table when I got home. I thought of Dot and tore it up, stuffing the pieces into the bottom of the rubbish bin. Julian Corkle was a bigger, better person. Feelings of charity and forgiveness bloomed inside me as I bypassed the cake tin to take an apple from the fruit bowl. I took it into the lounge where I resisted the urge to change the channel when a documentary about India came on the screen. A small raisin-like nun was walking through a slum talking about poverty. The camera followed her into an orphanage where she described the misery of abandoned children. The orphans ran up to her, calling her mother. I was wiping tears out of my eyes when the fly screen creaked.

'Twinkle, Twinkle. How's my little star?' Mum ruffled my hair. 'Love the new do.'

'Thanks, Mum.' She'd just ruined my hairstyle but I couldn't complain. At least I had a mother.

'I've got something for you.'

Mum slid a glossy coffee table book across my knee. It was called *Hair Through the Ages: An Encyclopaedia of Hairstyles from Australopithecus to David Bowie*. The cover design featured a montage of various hair celebrities. I immediately recognised David Cassidy, Marilyn Monroe and Telly Savalas. Inside were lots of colour photos and hardly any text. Perfect.

'It's perfect, Mum. How did you know?'

'I could hardly miss the note you left on the table this morning.'

'Uh-huh.' I suppressed an urge to ask her where she'd been for the past two nights. It felt too good to be on talking terms.

'I'm so proud of you, Julian. Hair care is a real career.'

'With celebrity potential.'

'And small-screen possibilities.' Mum laughed. 'I've got some other good news. Jimmy Budge has moved to Hobart. He's our new trainee manager.'

My mouth went dry.

'He gave me his number and said you were to call him.'

I tried to swallow but met resistance in the back of my throat. *Jimmy was in Hobart.* I imagined him downtown drinking a milkshake, trying on trousers, buying fish and chips, driving an Escort. It was the Jimmy from the Wool Board photo, taller and more handsome than the Ulverston version. He was a trainee manager, a shooting star.

The joy I'd been feeling about the Hog evaporated. I saw Jimmy sitting on a pink vinyl seat inside the salon and shuddered. I couldn't call him. Not yet. I had to get my panache back first. An apprenticeship was three years. By that time I would've convinced Dot to repaint the salon.

33

Over the next few months, Mum and I came to an unspoken agreement. I didn't say anything about her absences and she didn't mention Dezzie. I still monitored her movements but as long as she kept her outings to twice a week, I wasn't going to rock the boat. I had a career to consider.

Things were moving along nicely at the Curl Up and Dye. I had graduated from the trough and was now doing all the hair sets at the salon. I still had to wash hair but only the hair of my clients. Dot had taught me the curlers and cone dryer, and once I'd mastered the tint and perm, I was going to start scissor work. I was not only learning a trade but I was also thoroughly enjoying myself. I could wear what I liked and talk to women all day. Without making an effort, I'd lost weight. I still had my bottle tops but if I stuck to ironed shirts or wore jerkins over my T-shirts, no one was the wiser.

Friday was Hair Day for many Hobart ladies. With careful management, a hair set done on the Friday would last the weekend. It was the day I liked to get to the salon early.

I'd turned on the shower and removed my pyjamas when it dawned on me that something was wrong in The Ensuite. I blinked at the bottle of Max Cougar aftershave. Mum didn't use aftershave. Neither did she own a tartan toilet bag. A shriek escaped from me. My inner sanctum had been breached! I showered quickly and fought my way into my clothes. There had to be a reasonable explanation.

From the kitchen, I could hear someone whistling a Roger Whittaker tune. It was a jaunty whistle, the sort of thing aimed out of car windows at women in high heels. I found the whistler with his back to me working the lever of the toaster. He was shorter and a lot balder than I expected but there was defiance in the way he stood with his legs apart. His clothes were a touch too tucked in for my tastes.

'Morning!' I shouted my greeting loud enough for the neighbours to hear.

'Oh goodness!' Dezzie spun around and banged his head on the cupboard door. 'You must be Julian.'

Rubbing his head, he extended his other hand. I let the groper's hand hang in the air for a second before giving him a powerful squeeze. Dezzie squeaked in surprise.

'You're a firm gripper.'

'I know, Desmond.' I looked him in the eye without smiling.

'Call me Dezzie.'

'Where's Mum?'

'She popped out for more butter. I was getting breakfast on before she gets back. Some toast? I do very good buttery toast. It's my specialty.' Dezzie raised his eyebrows and smiled.

I stared and gave no response. His old buttery toast routine had no effect on me. 'You're not from around here.'

'Not Echidna Avenue, if that's what you mean.'

'I think you know what I mean.'

Dezzie blinked. 'I'm originally from Devonport.'

'Sure you are.'

Dezzie had to be lying. Devonport was a stone's throw from Ulverston. It was too much of a coincidence to be true.

'You're a widower.'

'Yes, sadly. My wife passed away five years ago.'

'You don't let the grass grow under your feet.'

'Sorry?'

'What did your wife die of, may I ask?'

Dezzie jumped as if he'd been slapped. '*Cancer.*' His voice was a hollow whisper.

The fly screen flew open. Mum was standing on the back step. 'I see you two have met.'

'Dezzie and I were just talking about his wife.'

'I heard.' Mum glared at me.

'I'd better be off. Some of us have work to do.' I grabbed a piece of Dezzie's toast and made a move toward the door. I didn't like the look on Mum's face or the way Dezzie had managed to turn her against me. He was more cunning than I imagined. I gave him one last hard look.

'It was a pleasure to meet you.' Dezzie smiled hesitantly. 'You must be excited about your uncle.'

'Uh-uh.' I had no idea what he was talking about but I wasn't going to play his silly game of one-upmanship. I shrugged and looked at Mum.

'Norm's agreed to be a judge for the hair show.' Mum still wasn't smiling.

'Uh-huh.'

'I thought you'd be pleased.'

'I hardly know Norman.'

How could I think about Norman with a home-wrecker in the kitchen? I left the house in a whirl without saying goodbye and started the day on the wrong foot. At the salon, nothing seemed to go right. Hair wouldn't lift or curl. I dropped things and upset clients. Late in the afternoon, Dot pulled me outside for a smoke.

'You're having a bad hair day. What's on your mind, love?'

'Mum's got a boyfriend.' It sounded stupid. Dezzie was no boy or friend as far as I was concerned. He was a middle-aged conman, a moustache and sideburns away from selling used Holdens. 'He's got a tartan toilet bag.'

'Is he Scotch?'

'He's ruining everything.'

'He must make your Mum feel good. I'm fond of the Bay City Rollers myself.'

'How can he make her feel good?'

'She's come out of an unhappy marriage. This Scotsman probably makes her feel attractive.'

'But that's my job.'

'I'm sure it is, love. Just give it some time.' Dot's lips puckered past the filter of her Pall Mall. The tip of the cigarette flared as she sucked in a lungful of mentholated smoke. 'Let's get back inside and make a start on the cleaning. I have to nip out for a minute.'

We returned to the salon to find my sister standing next to the cutting chair, tapping her foot impatiently. It had been a while since I'd seen Carmel outside the family setting. I was stunned by her size. She had the arms of Sylvester Stallone and legs like blue-fin tunas.

Carmel said she needed a haircut and needed it fast. A cricket scout for the Tassie team was in town. 'I've got to get this hair out of my eyes.'

Her fringe was shorter than mine and came nowhere near her eyes. Dot sat her down and put a plastic poncho around her neck.

'Now, love, let's pretty you up for this scout.'

'Just a short back and sides, thanks.' Carmel gave Dot a no-nonsense look.

'I can do something a lot prettier than that.'

'Have you got clippers?'

'If you insist.' Dot pursed her lips and opened the drawer of men's hairdressing tools. 'You can lead a horse to water.'

I pulled up a stool next to Carmel as Dot got to work. 'I met Dezzie today. Slippery as an eel.'

'You can give the top a buzz as well.' Carmel winked at Dot and made a slicing motion over her head. 'Think American Marine.'

'As I was saying, this Dezzie's trouble. He whistles at women.'

'Shorter, above the ears.'

'You won't believe where I found his toilet bag this morning.'

Carmel frowned and shook her head. Her gaze shifted from the mirror to the front window. She turned as the door opened. She smiled. 'G'day, Budgie. Long time no see.'

Cold needles pricked my hairline. I stiffened as they scraped backward along my scalp and down my neck.

The clippers were still buzzing in Dot's hands when Carmel stood, ripped off the poncho and strode over to the door. 'Good to see you, mate. I'm just on my way out.'

I swivelled around on my stool and stood on hollow legs as Carmel paid Dot and left the salon.

Dot said something I didn't hear and then waved a hand in front of my face. 'I said I'll be back in half an hour.'

The door closed and I found myself alone with Jimmy Budge. It was the real flesh-and-blood Jimmy and he was standing an arm's length away. I held in my stomach and tried to calm myself. At least I'd had the sense to choose a big shirt and was wearing my new silver-blue glasses. Jimmy looked like a French sailor on leave. He was dressed in tight jeans and a white-and-blue striped shirt. The shirt had a large collar and capped sleeves. The outfit was smart-casual and looked completely out of place in the tatty pink of the salon.

'Great little place, Corky.' Jimmy smiled. 'I knew you'd do well for yourself.'

'It's temporary.'

'It's a trade.'

'A *métier*.'

'Just like Vidal Sassoon.'

'A hair-care celebrity.'

'You always had panache.'

'It's something you're born with.'

'That and star quality.' Jimmy shook his head. 'I bet you're brilliant at your job.'

'I'm getting a reputation. High profile and all that.'

'I love your haircut.' Jimmy tilted his head and regarded my hair appreciatively. 'Mine needs a cut.'

'No it doesn't.' My pulse rate soared. I didn't like where this was heading. I'd never cut human hair in my life.

'Come on. There's no one here.'

I tried to protest but Jimmy wouldn't listen. He threw Carmel's poncho around his shoulders and plopped down in the chair.

'Don't hold back, Corky.'

Like a condemned man, I took my place behind him and looked at his reflection in the mirror. Just being close to Jimmy made me feel as if I'd grabbed an electric fence. Goose pimples were running riot over my forearms.

'I think I should just give it a fluff, style it high and bring it forward.'

'Cut it like yours.'

I couldn't say yes but neither could I admit that the only hair I'd cut was on a dog's backside.

'Come on, Corky. I've waited a long time for this.'

I'd waited a long time, too, but not for this. This was

all wrong. My hands were shaking violently as I picked up Dot's comb and scissors. I ran the comb up the back of his hair. Jimmy's neck came into view and I was struck by its beauty. Before I could control myself my scissor hand had snipped. A finger of hair fell away leaving a hollow in the back of his hair. It looked unnatural, like a crop circle in a perfect field of wheat.

Jimmy smiled. He had no idea that I'd just butchered the back of his head. I tried to repair the damage but didn't know what I was doing. The circle widened and deepened like the pit of an open-face mine. I was blinking sweat out of my eyes and trying to make sense of it all when I felt Dot gently take the scissors from my hand. I hadn't heard her enter the salon.

'Let me do the honours.' She nudged me aside. 'I like to do the young men myself.'

I sat down and tried to calm myself. I was shaking all over.

'Has Julian told you about the Hog?' Dot had to drive the scissors in close to Jimmy's scalp to even things up. 'He can build a skyscraper from a head of hair. He's a genius.'

Jimmy smiled. My heart beat faster.

'I've just put his name down for the hair show.' Dot winked at me.

'As a competitor?' I looked at the exposed pink skin on the back of Jimmy's head and shuddered.

'It's perfect for you. There's no cutting or perming. It's a hairstyle show called the Big and High. They're saying it's the Tasmanian Olympics of big hair. Apprentice hair-fluffers from all over the state will be there. So will Dick Dingle and his television cameras. It's going to be televised live.'

'Dick Dingle?' I was stunned.

'Sounds like a GM Moment, Corky.' Jimmy had swivelled around in his seat and was smiling at me. 'I knew you'd end up in Dick Dingle's lens.'

His confidence in me was alarming. My eyes flicked back to Dot. 'I don't know, Dot.'

'I've put you down for the Hog.' She shook her head in a friendly way. 'You'll do us proud.'

Dot unwrapped the poncho and brushed Jimmy down. His neck was bright pink. He'd been shorn like a merino.

'Well.' Jimmy ran his hand over the stubble. 'I suppose I'm a good ambassador for the Wool Board.'

Jimmy didn't drive a tidy Ford Escort. His car was an old Mazda with a roo bar in the front. We didn't talk on the way home. I hadn't seen him for two years and now he was too close for comfort. I could've reached out and touched him.

My heart sank as we turned into the driveway. Dezzie's Cortina was parked in the middle as if it belonged there. I steeled myself. I couldn't let anyone get the better of me in front of Jimmy, especially not a cocky intruder.

We found Dezzie sitting with Mum in the dinette drinking Chardonnay and eating cubes of cheddar on toothpicks. He jumped to his feet like a host when he saw Jimmy and gave his hand a vigorous shake. To me, he smiled warily without extending his hand. He turned back to Jimmy.

'Young Budge. I was just telling Colleen about you. You're making an impression at the Board, our very own rising star of wool and whatnot.' Dezzie placed glasses in front of us and filled them with Chardonnay. I controlled an urge to scream as he slid the cheese cubes across the table. He was acting as if he owned the place.

'I'm not the star here.' Jimmy shrugged and turned to me. 'Julian's taking the Hog to the Tasmanian hair Olympics.'

'Really! You're entering the Big and High? Norman will be thrilled.' Mum made a small 'hooray' gesture with her fists. 'Imagine, the two men of my life in the same show!'

I felt something expand in my chest. Mum had said the *two* men in her life. This was Dezzie's cue to pack up his toilet bag and leave the premises.

'Big and High, fancy that.' Dezzie shook his head in mild disbelief and whistled through his teeth. 'The Hog doesn't have anything to do with livestock?'

'Of course not.' My voice was high and defensive. Dezzie was ruining a perfectly good moment of triumph. 'It's the name of a hairstyle, a very big and high hairstyle.'

'Shaped like a pig?'

'It's a signature name!' What was the man's problem? 'There's nothing pig about it.'

'Fascinating.'

'What do you mean?'

'The world of hair is a mystery to me.' Dezzie looked taken aback. 'Wool's my game.'

'You can't compare human hair with merino super fine.'

'I wouldn't for a moment.'

'Hair is a *métier*.'

'You must be a very talented young man.'

'Well, yes.' Something unpleasant was dawning on me. I couldn't work out what exactly but there was discomfort in the pit of my stomach.

'Your mum's very proud of you.'

There it was. My face flushed with the prickly heat of embarrassment. Dezzie was simply being nice. He was probably always nice.

I turned away to hide my confusion and found myself staring at Jimmy's perfect neck. My face grew hotter. Jimmy was looking at me in a funny way. He stood up, saying he had to go.

It took all my strength to walk him to the car. My legs felt like slabs of petrified wood. My body was aching with affection but my mind was busy thinking over how stupid I'd been. Jimmy probably wanted nothing more to do with me.

'Well.' Jimmy flapped his arms against his sides awkwardly.

I could tell he was disappointed. After all these years of waiting, I'd blown it. I'd humiliated myself at the salon and made an even bigger fool of myself with his boss. I had to get the farewell over and done with quickly or I'd explode.

'See you then.' I took a step backward.

Jimmy was still looking at me strangely. He didn't smile.

'Thanks for the ride home and all that.'

He took a breath as if he was going to say something. I waited for the blow. It wasn't going to be pleasant.

'Let's get together again, Corky.'

'*Really?*' My body felt liquid and insubstantial.

'I'm going to Ulverston this weekend to see Dad but I could pick you up after work on Monday.'

'Yeah?'

'Yeah.'

Before I could react, Jimmy spun away from me and got into his car. I stood still, suspended in the moment, as his car pulled away and the tail-lights disappeared around the corner of Echidna Avenue.

34

I woke up on Monday morning feeling as if I'd won the chook raffle. Jimmy Budge was back in my life and he was bigger and better than ever.

I walked past Mum's bedroom door with a smile. Who needed The Ensuite when there was a perfectly good family bathroom down the hall? I'd washed and was working the toaster when someone coughed politely behind me.

'Top o' the morning, Dez.' I turned to face him, smiling big. I could afford to be generous. Julian Corkle was a winner. Smiling was also an excellent skill for Dick Dingle's television camera. 'Buttery toast and a cup of tea?'

'That would be very nice, yes.' Dezzie smiled hesitantly and kept his distance. 'You're up early.'

'The early bird gets the worm, Dez.'

'That's what I tell my cadets.'

'You must be like a father to them.'

'I wouldn't go that far.' Dezzie shrugged modestly. 'I just try to give them a solid grounding in the wool trade.'

'Wool, now that's a fascinating subject.'

'Yes.' Dezzie seemed to relax. He was warming to the subject. 'Did you know that mankind has been wearing wool for thousands of years? They say the first knitted sock dates back to before the birth of Christ.'

'Fancy that. That's probably where the Germans get it.'

'What would that be?'

'Socks and sandals. Jesus was probably a role model.'

'I'm not saying Jesus himself wore socks with his sandals.'

'I suppose Jerusalem must've been hot even then.'

'I'm not sure where the first knitted sock was worn. It may have been in Siberia. I was just saying that it appears to have been worn before or possibly around the time of Jesus.'

'Jesus never went to Siberia.'

'No.'

Dezzie and I were getting on like a house on fire. He was a lot more intelligent than he looked, certainly an improvement on my father, whose only areas of expertise were ball games and beer. Dad also liked the sound of his own voice too much to engage in rewarding two-way conversation.

I watched appreciatively as Dezzie cut the crusts off Mum's toast and took a cup of tea to the bedroom. Breakfast in bed was not a service my father ever provided. He'd hardly provided enough money for food and clothing. Mum certainly dressed a lot better since Dezzie had arrived on the scene. These days, her bra and underpants always matched. It was a comfort to know she looked good under her clothes.

I left the house feeling fantastic and whistling 'Old Durham Town'. As I turned the corner of Echidna Avenue, I stopped whistling. My footsteps slowed. An ominous brown Holden station wagon was parked under an acacia tree on the side of the road. Dad tooted his horn and wound down the driver's window.

'I hoped I'd catch you.' He patted the passenger seat. 'Jump in.'

I didn't want to enter an enclosed space with my father, especially not an enclosed space belonging to him. I hadn't seen or heard from him for months, not since his Easter barbecue. He hadn't called and I certainly hadn't wanted to talk to him. I bent down to get a good look at his face. He was smiling. Reluctantly, I climbed into the passenger seat.

'So how's life treating you?' His mouth was stretched tight. It wasn't his Carmel smile. This one looked like hard work.

'Fine.'

'I heard about this job of yours.' Dad's face loosened into a more natural hard-done-by expression. 'You could've told me. I had to hear it from a third party.'

'I didn't think you cared.' I knew who the third party was. Dolly wasn't so much a third party as a party of three crammed into one big nasty busybody.

'Of course I care.'

Dad cared? Something loosened inside me. 'It's an apprenticeship. I'm learning a trade.'

'That's what I'm worried about.' Dad took a deep breath and pressed his lips together. 'I don't think you know what you're getting yourself into.'

'There's nothing to worry about.'

'You're my son. A father worries.'

Despite myself, I felt a warm tingle in my chest. Dad had just admitted I was his son. He'd never said anything so intimate before. It was almost like saying 'I love you'.

'Didn't I give you a Meccano set?'

'Yeah.'

'And a cricket ball.'

'That too.'

'And we practised your bowling out the back under the plum tree.' The smile disappeared. Dad's face clouded. 'Until we found out your eyes were buggered.'

'But I got fashion frames.' I tapped my new glasses.

My father blinked. His eyes watered. 'Where did I go wrong?'

Dad's reaction took me by surprise. His normal modus operandi was to attack and disable. He'd never blamed himself for anything in front of me before. It was confusing. I could deal with his anger but was defenceless against his disappointment. I found myself feeling guilty and wanting to cheer him up.

'I'll be meeting Dick Dingle, Dad.'

'Uh-huh.'

Dad had taken a tatty handkerchief from his pocket and was wiping his eyes. My own eyes felt moist. It was like a touching father-and-son scene from television.

'The hair show's going to be televised live.' Norman had told Mum that Abracadabra was doing a special *Tales of Tasmania* programme. 'I'll be back on the box.'

'What?'

'It's a state-wide competition with a trophy and everything. The apprentice with the best big hair wins.'

'Oh my God.' Dad's eyes had dried. He gave me a fierce look.

'The trophy's called the Crowning Glory.' I was trying to impress Dad but rapidly losing ground. 'I'll have to make the hair really big and high. Fluffing and all that.'

'Fluff . . .' Dad's voice trailed off into a gurgle. He steadied himself against the steering wheel. His knuckles were white.

'Hairstyling, that's the technical name.'

'Do you realise your sister's just been chosen for the Tassie team?'

This was news to me but I nodded anyway. I didn't like the colour of Dad's face. It had gone from vague pink to mauve.

'That girl's worked very hard for this. We all have.'

I nodded again. A dangerous crimson flush was spreading upward from his shirt collar.

'We can't let anything get in the way of this.'

A bomb exploded in my chest. Heat surged through my bloodstream. I suddenly felt like smashing the brown Holden to bits and battering my father to death. I'd been duped. Dad didn't care about my career or even my happiness. He just wanted me to give up hairdressing. The idea that my job jeopardised Carmel's cricketing prospects was insane. It wasn't about Carmel. It was about Dad. He didn't want a hairdresser for a son. He was ashamed of me.

I didn't look at his face because I knew what I'd find. His I-know-best look, the one he always used to get his way. I willed myself to calm down. When I found my voice it was a low Peter Grubb growl.

'I'm pleased for Carmel.'

'So you should be. That girl's done us proud.'

'She's done you proud.'

'You can say that again.'

The red of my anger scaled down to amber. My pulse rate slowed. I looked over at my father. He'd taken his hands off the steering wheel and was fidgeting with the car keys, eager to be done with this talk and get going. He wasn't even looking at me. He'd said his piece and expected me to accept it.

'Dad, Carmel doesn't give a toss what I do.'

'She's got more important things on her mind. It's the state team. She'll be representing Tasmania.'

'I'm not quitting my job.'

Dad's body jerked as if he'd been jolted with a cattle prod.

'I'm a hairdresser.'

'You can't be serious.' His head twitched in my direction. I had his full attention.

'I like hair. I've always liked it. I love running my fingers through it and making it fluff up.' I made flouncy movements with my hands. 'I hate ball games.'

'That's not natural.'

'And another thing, I don't like girls. It's boys I like.'

Dad made a strange choking sound in the back of his throat.

'Uncle Norman's coming back to Tasmania for the show and I can't wait to meet him. He's an inspiration.' I turned the door handle and swung a leg out of the Holden. 'You can watch us on TV. Dick Dingle. State-wide. We'll do you proud.'

I must've taken the bus to the salon but I completely blanked out the journey. When I came to, Dot was lighting a menthol for me in the garden. It was the warmth of her hand on my arm. I was suddenly crying and choking on the cigarette as I told her about Dad. She listened, shaking her head and tut-tutting in all the right places. Her warmth had spread to my fingers and toes by the time I finished.

'You can choose your friends but you can't choose your family.' She nodded sagely and lit another menthol. 'It cuts both ways, love. Your dad's lumped with you, too.'

I imagined my father sitting in front of the Rentascope watching Norman and me at the hair show. Dad's hands were gripping the vinyl armrests and his face was grim. Next thing I knew, I was laughing. It was a high, violent laugh, more like a spasm than a sound. Dot patted me on the back until it passed. I had to sit still for a moment to collect myself but the outburst had a strange effect on me. My body felt lighter, as if a brown station wagon had been lifted from my shoulders.

The lightness stayed with me and the day passed without the niggling self-doubt that usually accompanied a confront-ation with Dad. My mind was free to focus on the more pressing problem of how I looked. I now realised that my white shirt made me look enormous and my stone-washed jeans were too short. The jeans rode up when I bent my knees, exposing my orange socks. Only golfers and fools showed their socks.

Why had I worn an orange pair? Even my hair wouldn't sweep over properly.

'Are you vain or is that a tic in your neck?' The elderly woman huffed as she got off the chair. She pointed to the mirror. 'You keep craning.'

'It's a tic.'

'Get an injection for that, boy. You don't want it turning into the palsy.'

'What's the palsy?'

'It's like rigor mortis, only once you've got the rigor you wish you were dead.' The woman narrowed her eyes and shook her head at the front window. 'Get a load of that bloody outfit! He must've galloped in from the Melbourne Cup.'

My body temperature soared. Jimmy was standing in front of the salon dressed in straight-leg bottle-green trousers and an oversized stone-washed denim jacket. He had a red bandana tied around his neck and an American baseball cap on his head. The cap's peak was turned to the side, rock-star style. Jimmy lifted his hand and waved. The woman's eyes widened.

'What the hell's that jockey waving at?'

'Me.' I beckoned him inside. 'He's my friend.'

I wanted to tell Jimmy how good he looked but couldn't risk drawing attention to my own clothes.

My heart sank when we got to the movie theatre. Jimmy had already bought the tickets and I didn't have the heart to tell him I hated war movies. They were Dad's second-favourite TV programme after sports. Hollywood gunfire made me carsick.

I was wedged down in the cinema seat, ready to close my eyes at any blood, when Mark Lee appeared on screen. I sat up straight. Mark Lee was a beautiful young man, almost as beautiful as his co-star, Mel Gibson. I sat up straighter and started paying attention. But of course! *Gallipoli* wasn't a war film at all. It was a love story of two gorgeous young men. By the final scene, I was crying openly. Mark had gone over the top of the trench to certain death, unaware that Mel was sprinting through enemy lines to save him. Mel's thighs were pumping and I was on the edge of my seat praying for his life when I felt Jimmy's thigh push against mine. I pushed back and felt my body relax.

I left the theatre feeling as if I'd just lived a lifetime. Jimmy must've felt the same way because he kept bumping against me as we walked.

The Queen's Head had recently converted its lounge bar into a cocktail lounge. I'd never been inside a bar but I'd seen how it was done plenty of times on television. Cocktail lounges were more upmarket and safer than pubs. They were quiet places where women wore short skirts and drank fancy stuff out of straws. I led Jimmy up to the bar and signalled the barman, a large pink-nosed man with receding hair and big rubbery ears.

'Two piña coladas.' I pronounced the pubic hair over the *n*, Spanish style, and winked at Jimmy.

'You what?' The barman shook his head.

'It's a cocktail with coconut milk.' Julian Corkle knew his cocktail onions. 'You have to shake it.'

'You see any bloody coconuts here?'

'What kind of cocktail bar is this?'

'A bloody normal one.' The barman narrowed his eyes. 'How old are you anyway?'

'Almost twenty.'

'Twenty my bum. Show us your licence.'

'I don't drive.'

'Well, you can take a walk then.'

'Let's go.' Jimmy tugged my arm. 'I've got wine at my place.'

The barman turned to Jimmy, taking in the baseball cap,

bandana and fancy denim jacket. He sniggered. 'The stupid poof's probably got a lovely bunch of coconuts, too. Ha, ha.'

'He's not a stupid poof!' My voice was high and very loud. Heads turned. Mark Lee had gone over the top. Mel was sprinting to save him. 'He's a very clever one!'

Jimmy yanked my arm and pulled me out of the bar. Suddenly we were running, legs pumping and laughing hysterically, just like old times. People were looking but it didn't matter. I was with Jimmy and he was fantastic.

35

The Hemi Pacer screeched into our driveway, setting lace curtains twitching all over Echidna Avenue. Mum hadn't told me that Norman had a Hemi Pacer, especially not a red-hot one with tinted windows and racing stripes down the sides. I should've been excited about this development but when I'd woken that morning an icy hand had reached inside my chest and gripped my heart. It was the day of the hair show and the icy hand was fear.

I had good reason to be scared. I was going to compete against fancy apprentices from real hairstyling salons and make a fool of myself in front of Dick Dingle and the entire state of Tasmania. I thought of Philippe and felt like crying. I wanted to pack my bags and run away to Phoenix, Arizona. Only I couldn't go anywhere. Jimmy was counting on me. So was Dot. Mum and Dezzie were going early to claim seats in the front row.

I watched my uncle get out of the Hemi Pacer and run a hand over his large thatch of blond hair. He seemed a lot smaller than the teenager I remembered in terry towelling. I opened the front door with a smile, reminding myself that good things came in small packages.

'Julian?'

'Mum's just popped out to get some butter.'

Norman looked good considering he'd just spent a night on the Melbourne car ferry. His hair was a perfect oval of blond fluff that rose high from his head and tilted forward over a polished nut-brown face. His fitted leather trousers were cinched in by a studded belt but the best part of his outfit was his shirt. It was made of a soft white fabric and had a huge floppy collar with ruffles down the middle.

'Love the shirt. Very Three Musketeers.'

'New Romantic.'

'That's what I meant.' I'd vaguely heard of New Romanticism but it had yet to arrive in Hobart, where the platforms and mullet cuts of Glam Rock were still favoured in certain quarters.

'I'd better wake the diva.'

'Diva?' An image of Joan Sutherland flashed through my mind.

'Norm. I let him sleep to rest up.'

A thrill went through me as my tall handsome uncle emerged from the car. He was dressed in virtually the same clothes as the first man only his ruffles were bigger and his belt had larger studs. Norman strode toward me, running a hand over his huge cushion of black Irish hair.

'Julian. I see you've met Sandy.' Norman grabbed me by the shoulders and cheek-kissed me, French-style. 'Thank goodness you took after our side. You're the spitting image of your mother.'

'So are you.' I felt my face redden. 'I mean . . . you look very New Romantic.'

'It's a bit old hat but I love ruffles.'

So did I. I also loved the matching red suitcases on wheels. Even the Americans at the Dingo didn't have wheeled suitcases. I helped Sandy unload the car and led him to Mum's bedroom, which had been prepared for Norman's arrival. Mum had moved to Carmel's old room.

I watched Sandy put two toilet bags in The Ensuite and didn't know what to say. He obviously thought he was sharing the bedroom with Norman. I didn't know what Mum was going to think. Neither did I have the heart to tell him about the laws in Tasmania. I left him unpacking.

Mum had returned from the shop and was laughing when I entered the dinette. The Royal Albert was out and she was pouring tea for Norman.

'Here's my little star.' She ruffled my hair. 'Twinkle, twinkle.'

'For God's sake, Colleen, get your hands off his hair! You'll flatten it.' Norman gave me a conspiratorial look. 'Ready for the show?'

'Uh-huh.' Of course I wasn't ready. I'd never be ready. The thought of Dick Dingle made me carsick. The Hog wasn't good enough and would never be.

'I'm looking forward to seeing this hog of yours.'

'It's nothing special.'

'What product do you use?

'Hairspray.' I didn't bother adding that I used the cheapest supermarket brand available.

'A purist.' Norman swivelled and bellowed down the hall. 'Sandy! The Kit!'

Sandy materialised like a magician's assistant with a large leather carrying case. The interior was crammed with bottles and jars. None had labels.

'Your products don't have labels.'

'Professional secrets.' Norman winked and sat Mum down on a kitchen chair. Within minutes he'd whipped her hair into something massive and ornamental.

'That's very *big* big hair.' My voice was a whisper. Norman was an inspiration.

'Volume is essential.' He stepped back holding a can of

hairspray and a comb above Mum's head. 'But it's the finishing touch *qui fait la différence.*'

With a flourish, he twisted the top of Mum's hair into a dramatic spiral and tugged it expertly over her face. There was power and majesty in his movements. My skin erupted with goose pimples. I was looking at an artiste.

I'd never been inside anything like a Hemi Pacer. It was a fast and flashy Australian Chrysler, the sort of car driven by men who revved the engine outside milk bars and screeched the tyres when the lights turned green. Sandy stopped in front of Jimmy's flat with a screech and tooted the horn. When the door didn't open, he tooted again. I began to worry. It wasn't like Jimmy to be late or inconvenient. When I knocked on the door and he didn't answer, my worry gave way to panic. Jimmy was one of the reasons I was doing the show in the first place and now he wasn't even coming with me. Sandy tooted impatiently and I got back in the car. As we pulled away, I felt the icy hand squeeze my heart.

The Wool Board Convention Centre had been done up for the hair show by a charity called Little Tasmanian Masters. According to a sign on a collection box by the door, it was a Dick Dingle-approved scheme to support young Tasmanians with flair. The foyer was decorated with a huge calico banner painted in bright colours: 'Big and High, Celebrating Tasmanian Hair'. Along the walls were sculptures made from old junk bearing stickers with fantasy prices. An ugly construction of used drink cans and old toilet-roll dowels was priced at fifty dollars. I looked up and noticed a boy watching me with suspicion. He was one of several boys who had been posted around the room. They were all wearing name badges with 'ART MONITOR' printed on them.

Norman flashed his VIP pass at a monitor called Neil who shooed other boys away officiously as he guided us through the centre. There were more sculptures in the event hall where a television crew was setting up lights and cables. My heart leaped as I stepped over an Abracadabra box with 'DICK' stamped on its side. 'The Prick' had been scrawled underneath but then crossed out with a marker pen.

At the backstage door, Norman gave my shoulder a friendly squeeze and ran a professional hand over my hair.

'You'll do us proud.'

I swallowed hard and tried not to cry as Neil led Sandy and him away to the VIP dressing room.

Where was Jimmy?

I was not only very alone but I was also very hot. The Fair Isle jerkin I'd bought for my television appearance now seemed like a very bad idea. The super-fine wool was doing an excellent job of trapping the nervous heat I was generating. My sweat glands were spurting like shower nozzles but removing the jerkin and baring my T-shirt wasn't an option. I couldn't give my father the satisfaction of viewing my bottle tops on television. My hand was damp on the backstage door as I pushed it open. My heart sank.

The room was bustling with gorgeous young people sporting very big hair. I'd never seen so much fashion or hair gathered in one place. The apprentices were all dressed in tight trousers and shirts with big collars, even the young women. There were no New Romantics but they still looked a thousand times better than stupid Fair Isle Corkle. They were also thinner, busier and more professional than me. All of the competitors had kits like Norman's and none of the products seemed to have labels. I put my Cobber's supermarket bag behind my back and kept walking.

I was desperately searching for a place to hide when someone familiar caught my eye. Relief flooded me. Philippe was standing to one side, talking to a very short man in a very shiny silver suit. The man's hair was honey blond and sparkled in an unnatural way under the lights. Philippe frowned as I approached and continued talking as if I wasn't there.

'I don't style hair, I *jizsch* it.' He waved his hands about in an elegant manner. 'I suppose you'd call it hair topiary. I create living *objets* with human hair.'

'Can you create a mallard duck?' I did a little laugh to round off the joke.

Philippe glared at me and turned back to the man. 'As I was saying, the bigger and more complex, the better.'

'Like a nativity scene.' I was being even funnier. 'The Father, the Son and the Holy Ghost and all that.'

'For goodness' sake!' Philippe didn't bother to look at me. His focus was on the man. 'Tasmania is ready for the Big and High. It's been ready for a long, long time.'

'You could add the Three Kings with underarm hair, ha ha.'

'Shut up! Can't you see that I'm trying to talk to Dick!'

The honey-blond man turned to me and I felt the icy hand tighten around my heart. It was Dick Dingle, only thirty per cent shorter and twenty years older than his television version. His watery eyes moved over my body, taking in my T-shirt and woollen jerkin, stonewashed jeans and oxblood Doc Marten boots. He turned away with a look of disinterest and patted Philippe on the shoulder in a fatherly manner.

'I must mingle.' He winked. 'Can't have them accusing me of favouritism.'

Sweating fiercely, I stumbled away and found a dark corner to the side of the stage. I sat down on a Tasmanian apple box and tried to make myself as small as possible. For years I'd dreamed of meeting Dick Dingle and now I'd ruined every-thing. It didn't matter that he was in his twilight years and had suspicious hair. He was still Tasmania's favourite son. I closed my eyes and willed Jimmy to arrive. I couldn't do the show without him.

The hall filled but I stayed hidden. I could hear people taking their seats and activity on the stage. A microphone screeched and the hall became quiet. The curtains opened and lights fell on ten very professional-looking contestants standing behind ten seated volunteers. Across the stage, I could see Norman and the three other judges. No one could see me in the shadows but I could see everything except the audience. I thought of Jimmy and wondered if he was out there somewhere. Dick Dingle was standing centre stage and opened his arms in welcome. Someone cheered. He said something, people laughed and he walked off. A gong sounded and the stylists got to work.

Nothing at the Curl Up and Dye had prepared me for the show. The apprentices moved with the precision and grace of real experts. They used products I didn't recognise and did things with hair I'd never imagined. The gong sounded and the contestants lifted their hands away. I saw Dick Dingle come back on stage but my ears were buzzing and I didn't hear what he said. The curtains closed and then opened again. The gong sounded and the process was repeated. I stayed seated in the sauna of my jerkin and tried not to breathe. I couldn't compete. Why had I listened to Dot and Jimmy Budge? The Hog was a pig of an idea.

'So this is where you got to.' Dot laid a warm hand on my shoulder. 'I've been looking for you for half an hour. It's the third round. You're up next.'

'I can't go through with it, Dot.'

'Of course you can, love. It's just stage nerves.' She lit a Pall

Mall menthol and slipped it between my fingers. 'Have a fag. It'll do you the world of good.'

'I'll let you down. I'll let everyone down.'

'You can't let me down, love.' She lit another cigarette for herself.

'But all the other apprentices are so . . .' I was about to say thin but changed my mind. '. . . professional.'

'Smoke and mirrors, love. Most of them wouldn't know a kiss curl from a dingo's tail.' Dot closed her eyes and took a meaningful drag on her cigarette. 'To be a real dry stylist, you've got to have a feel for hair. You've got to have heart. And you've got plenty of that, love.'

'But everyone's so good.'

'Like I said, smoke and mirrors.' Dot's hand slipped under my armpit. With a powerful yank, she pulled me to my feet. 'Stay with the hair, love. *Stay with the hair*. I'll be watching you.'

Once I'd taken my place behind the volunteer, there was no turning back. If only my body would cool down and my hands would stop shaking. When the curtains opened I realised that I couldn't see the faces of the audience for the stage lights. What I could see was the Abracadabra cameraman. He was sitting on a high swivel chair in front of the stage with the lens focused on us.

Dick Dingle came and left. The gong sounded and the competitors got to work, busily swishing and rustling all around me. I could hear them opening containers and spraying hair with water but my arms stayed frozen at my sides. A blow-dryer whirred to life beside me. I knew I shouldn't look but my head turned in spite of myself. My heart sank. Philippe had been positioned two metres from me. He appeared to have his own spotlight and was working furiously on his volunteer.

She noticed me staring and rolled her eyes. It was the girl from the Brush Off.

'What are you waiting for?' My volunteer had twisted in her seat and was frowning up at me. Her name badge said 'DONNA'. She swirled her hand impatiently like a movie director and turned back to face the audience. 'The cameras are rolling.'

Cameras. I forced my arms away from my sides then stopped with my hands in mid-air. Donna's dull sandy hair was so thin I could see the freckles on her scalp. I took a comb from my pocket and ran it through, meeting no resistance.

'What's your problem?' Donna clicked her fingers.

All around us, hair was progressing, up and out. Philippe's volunteer already had the makings of a Mary Antoinette. Squinting, I looked out over the audience. My eye caught a familiar tower of hair. Dot was sitting in the front row. *Stay with the hair.*

I gripped the can of Cobber's and gave the base of Donna's hair a blast, simultaneously sweeping it up with the comb. Donna shuddered. Her hair wobbled and sagged. I gave it another jet and repeated the process, willing the hair to absorb air and take flight. It wavered as if unsure, then it dropped back like a cowboy dying in slow motion. Slipping the comb into my pocket, I lifted the hair with my free hand, bombarding the shafts with hair spray and fluffing rapidly with my fingertips. The hair resisted, rose, and then resisted again. It wavered, stopped, then it began to stiffen. Lift off!

Working feverishly with the spray can, I glued the foundations solid and began building higher, layering individual hair upon hair and pumping air into the structure with whisking motions. I finished one can of hairspray and took another from the economy six-pack. I was working in a cloud of spray, sweating like a draught horse. I'd never used so much hairspray in my life but Donna's hair was like a mirage. I could hardly see it let alone feel any texture between my fingers. I went through a third can and then a fourth.

'Two minutes!'

Sweat pumped from my armpits. My hands were a blur as I flicked my fingers upward. Instead of closing the hair into a classic Hog, I sculpted it into tongues, teasing them away from the main body of hair like lotus petals. My back was to the audience and I was facing Donna when she moaned.

'I feel funny.' She coughed weakly. 'It's the spray.'

I caught her by the chin as her head flopped forward. Her pupils were dilated and her mouth hung open. She moaned again and closed her eyes. I had one trick up my sleeve, a hockey player's trick I'd learned from Carmel. My fingers grasped a wedge of Donna's upper arm fat. I pinched hard.

'Fuck!' Donna sat up and blinked.

I had no time to lose. I attacked the top of her hair with rapid staccato movements, tweaking the ends into ever finer points to create the illusion of flames.

The gong sounded and I removed my hands, standing back for the first time to view the hairstyle in its entirety. Donna's hair was magnificent, a huge transparent construction that rose from her scalp to burst open like a gingery bonfire. I was still gazing at it in wonder when Dick Dingle made his way over from the judging panel.

The microphone screeched. As he opened his mouth to speak, someone sneezed violently. I turned to see Philippe's volunteer with a hand over her nose and mouth. Her hair, a big bulbous construction, was shaking violently. Philippe gasped as a large strand peeled off and fell away. Another fell away, then another. The hairdo was deconstructing before his eyes. Within seconds, the girl's head looked like the denuded top of a palm tree.

The microphone screeched. I looked back to Dick Dingle.

'Winner of round three, Julian Corker.'

My knees felt as if they were going to fold from under me. I vaguely heard the audience break into applause and someone whistle. My heart suddenly felt too big for my chest. I smiled nervously as the television camera swivelled in my direction.

The microphone screeched again.

'As host of the show and patron of Little Tasmanian Masters, I'm obliged to make an executive decision.' Dick Dingle paused to give his announcement more authority. 'In light of the unforeseen *force majeure*, Philippe Singer will be permitted to go forward to the finals.'

'That's *Singeur*.' Philippe's shriek rang out over the hall.

Someone shouted from the judging panel. A child started crying. The audience became restless. Dick Dingle motioned for calm.

'We'll now take a break for refreshments. All proceeds from the beverages and cakes will go toward the Little Tasmanian Masters fund. Don't let those kids down, people! See you all back here in thirty minutes for the finals.'

I walked off the stage feeling as if I was wearing cushion platforms. My jerkin was so wet my armpits squelched but I didn't care what I looked like any more. I'd won the semi-finals! The victory would've been even sweeter if Jimmy were with me.

Philippe was lathering his hands in one of the sinks when I entered the washroom. I looked around for some soap. My hands were sticky from hairspray and sweat.

'Well, surprise, surprise.' Philippe nodded in a complimentary way.

'Thanks, Phil.'

I was still looking for soap when Philippe removed a plastic soap dispenser from his kit and placed it on the sink ledge. It was a gesture of fellowship like the passing of a peace pipe. I nodded and helped myself, rubbing the liquid into froth in my hands. Philippe put the dispenser back in his kit and left the washroom without saying anything.

I put my hands under the tap and immediately felt my skin begin to tingle.

36

Something was very wrong. The tingle had become an itch and the skin of my hands was coming out in pink blotches.

'I shouldn't have favourites but I know star quality when I see it!'

My chest swelled at the sound of that golden voice I knew so well. I forgot about the state of my hands and glanced up at the mirror, expecting to see the face of Tasmanian television staring back at me. Instead I found myself looking at its back. Dick Dingle was standing outside the door with an arm around Philippe's shoulders.

'You're only human, Dick.'

'And a human gets lonely at the top.'

'You're an influential Tasmanian. Whatever you say, goes.'

'And I say you look very good in those trousers.'

'I look even better out of them.'

Dick Dingle let out his signature television chortle. His hand slipped down Philippe's back and gave his bum a squeeze. Philippe squealed in a girly way. As they moved off, Dick Dingle gave a low oily laugh.

I looked back down at my hands. They were an unnatural pink and starting to swell. I blew on them to cool the hot prickliness and hurried out of the washroom in the opposite direction to Dick

Dingle and Philippe. The route took me through the curtains and brought me back out on stage. I arrived at the edge of the stage but couldn't find any steps. The only way on to the floor of the hall was to jump. I came down sideways, hitting a pile of coconut shells with my elbow. It collapsed with a loud clatter. A child cried out.

'A hairdresser just vandalised my coconut sculpture!'

I heard busy footsteps and the excited voices of children but I was stuck on my elbows and knees and couldn't get up. A hand snaked under my armpit and pulled.

'What's wrong with your hands?'

The sound of Jimmy's voice made me feel like crying. All I wanted to do was fall into his arms. Instead I drew back from him.

'What do you care?'

'A lot probably.'

Jimmy grabbed me by the forearms and frowned at my swollen hands. They were corn-beef pink and had the appearance of inflated rubber gloves. Blisters were forming around the nails.

'Where have you been?'

'Ulverston. Dad's in hospital. It's fancier's lung.' Jimmy's eyes misted. 'I tried to call but you'd already left.'

'Oh, Jimmy.'

'Dad knew the odds.'

'But he's not going to die?' Mr Budge had always been nice to me. Jimmy would be an orphan without him.

'They've put him in an iron lung.'

'That's a very unattractive machine.'

'It's keeping him alive.' Jimmy shook his head. 'Let's get these hands sorted. We can talk about Dad later.'

Jimmy guided me out of the hall and through a door marked

327

'PRIVATE WOOL BOARD PERSONNEL', down a corridor and out a side door to the car park. He led me to a rock garden and broke off part of a desert plant that looked suspiciously like a cactus. I took a step back. My cactus days were over.

He shot me a severe look. 'Hold your hands out and keep still.'

I obeyed as he tore at the plant and squeezed. A thick slimy liquid emerged and pooled in my hands. It was surprisingly cool and soothing. Jimmy gently rubbed it into my skin.

'What is it?'

'Aloe. Dad uses it on his pigeons when they get inflamed. How did this happen?'

I described Philippe's soap and the conversation with Dick Dingle.

'Sabotage.' Jimmy shook his head. 'Can you compete in the finals?'

'How do you know I'm in the finals?'

'I bumped into that friend of your father's in the foyer. He was talking to your uncle.' Jimmy hesitated and smiled for the first time. 'He said you were magnificent.'

'Trevor?' The thought of Trevor was almost too much to bear. He'd taken an enormous risk coming to the show.

Back inside, Jimmy found Dot and led us to a small room off the hall. Within minutes he was back with Norman and Sandy. My uncle had changed into a billowy jumpsuit. It was pure white and gave him the invincible look of an archangel. His hair had narrowed and gone even higher, like the tuft of a sulphur-crested cockatoo. He filled the room with light.

Norman examined my hands, shaking his head. The aloe had stopped the inflammation spreading but the fingers were still swollen. I had blisters on every fingertip.

'Can you move your hands, hold a comb?'

'I'm not sure.' I looked at the rubbery mess on the ends of my arms and tried to move my fingers. They felt enormous and stiff.

Norman put a comb in my hand. It slipped through the fingers and fell on to the floor. The tears I'd been holding back began to flow.

'I can't do it. It's not fair.'

'But you can't prove this Philip did anything.' Dot put a warm hand on my shoulder. 'The only way to beat him is to prove yourself.'

'It's still not fair.'

'All's not fair in love and hairstyling, love. If he did this to you it's because you're good.'

'But . . .' I took a ladies' handkerchief from Dot and dabbed my eyes.

'It's never fair but we can't let them get to us.' Norman was standing erect, staring out of the window. His eyes were blazing. 'Dick Dingle is a law unto himself. He had no authority to overrule the judges.'

I looked at my hands. The two alien pink things didn't seem to belong to me.

'You've got the Hog.' Jimmy's voice was low and reassuring. 'Don't let anyone take it away from you.'

Outside in the hall, people were taking their seats. Norman caught my eye and held my gaze. 'That's your public out there.'

I thought of Mum and Dezzie in the front row. Trevor would be taking his seat, too. I imagined him making his way past seats marked with cardigans to a place at the back near the fire exit. I looked up. Everyone was staring at me, waiting for my decision. I looked down at my hands.

'I'll do it.'

'That's the spirit!' Norman took a clear plastic tube from his jumpsuit pocket and placed it in my swollen palms. 'I think you're ready for this.'

The tube was unlabelled and just big enough for my hands to hold. I unscrewed the top and squeezed. A translucent gel appeared on the nozzle.

'You hold the future of hair in your hands.' Norman's voice was hushed and reverent. He fluttered his fingertips against the side of his hair like a piano player. The sound was hollow like fingers tapping cardboard. 'Hair gel. It holds like concrete.'

Jimmy went to fetch my Cobber's bag and I was left alone to prepare myself. Only I didn't feel alone any more. Neither did I feel powerless. I wedged the tube of gel into the waistband of my jeans and thought of Clint Eastwood, armed and dangerous.

A minute later, Jimmy was back. Taking a key from his pocket, he locked the door and then helped me peel off the jerkin and T-shirt. He removed the white blouse from the Cobber's bag with a nod of approval. I'd taken it from Mum's wardrobe before leaving the house.

'I love the ruffles.'

'It's New Romantic.'

Jimmy did up the buttons then looked me up and down.

'I like the New Romantic you.'

He leaned over the ruffles and kissed me hard.

The other finalists were already on stage when I arrived and took my place behind a big girl called Noeline. Her face was large and covered in red spots but her hair was plentiful, a huge mass of dark curls. She turned and smiled up at me.

I looked around at the other competitors and caught Philippe studying my shirt. He glanced down at my hands and smiled. The smile became a snigger when he noticed the new six-pack of Cobber's hairspray next to Noeline's chair. I drew the gel from my waistband, Dirty Harry-style, and the sniggering ceased.

Dick Dingle walked across the stage. The microphone screeched. 'Now, ladies and gentlemen, what you've all been waiting for—'

'The chook raffle!'

The shout came from somewhere in the audience and made people roar with laughter. A thrill went through me. The cavalry had arrived. Carmel was here.

'Ha, ha, ha.' Dick Dingle made a show of appreciating the joke before waving his hand for the audience to quieten down. 'Ladies and gentlemen, Tasmanian hair has never been bigger! May the best apprentice win!'

The gong sounded and I squeezed a dollop of gel on to my palm. It stung my skin and made my eyes water. My palms started to burn as I smeared it around the base of Noeline's hair, sweeping upward with my fingertips. I took my hands away to refuel with gel and the hair remained upright. It hardened as I worked my way up the sides and around the back, encircling the mass of curls with a rigid fortress.

When I paused to let the gel set, I realised the audience had stopped moving and talking. The only sound was coming from the blow-dryers of the competitors around me. I waved my hands and blew on them. My palms were on fire and I was losing feeling in my fingertips. They were swelling again. Some of the blisters had burst.

Gritting my teeth, I applied more gel, reinforcing the fortress with firm upward strokes. Noeline's hair was standing up like an exploded Christmas cracker. The base and sides were secured but the ends were refusing to go higher. My fingers were too swollen and ragged to penetrate the bushy interior mass of her hair. I flapped my hands and blew on my fingers again.

'Go the Whole Hog, honey! You're on TV!'

I narrowed my eyes and could vaguely make out my mother's silhouette in the front row. She was standing with her hands cupped around her mouth.

'The Hog, honey. The Hog!'

People started murmuring and moving in their seats. A voice I didn't recognise called out: 'The Hog!'

Then another: 'The Hog!'

People began to clap their hands. They were chanting.

'Hog, Hog, Hog . . .'

I squinted at the audience and realised the entire front row was on its feet. I recognised Dot's hair.

The microphone screeched.

'Settle down, people.' Dick Dingle had returned to centre stage and was waving a hand.

Someone whistled. A cheer went up. The chanting continued.

The sensation in my hands had gone beyond burning. They were numb and disobedient as I picked up a can of hairspray. I pointed the nozzle into Noeline's hair and sprayed, flicking upward with the pink bladder-like object that had replaced my hand. Before the hair could resist, I blasted again and teased it upward. I sprayed again and stretched.

The mass of Noeline's curls stiffened. The hair within the fortress expanded. I whisked in air and teased upward, taking the hair beyond Bee Gees volume and higher. It surpassed Dolly Parton and kept going, higher and higher. My hands had lost all feeling but I didn't stop. The hair was standing impossibly high when I began running my fingers over the outside. I eased the construction forward and down, opening it out like a gramophone trumpet.

Dick Dingle's countdown began. 'Ten, nine, eight . . .'

Reaching into the trumpet, I rapidly teased its interior out into points.

'Five, four, three . . .'

The hair opened at my touch like an enormous cornucopia, spilling its riches out over the top of Noeline's head.

'Two, one!'

The gong sounded and the blow-dryers stopped dead around me. The hairspray fell from my hands with a loud *clang*. The numbness had spread to my elbows. My hands were a ragged pink mess. I waved them in the air but couldn't feel a thing.

I heard a whimper and turned to find Philippe staring at Noeline. I glanced down at his volunteer. Philippe had taken her hair high but his construction was lifeless and uninspired. It was a clumsy asparagus spear that dwarfed the girl's head and made her look foolish.

I looked at the other two hairstyles. Neither of them went anywhere near mine. The Hog was a good 20 per cent higher and 50 per cent more alive than anything on the stage. Noeline turned in her seat and smiled up at me.

'Everyone's looking at me.' There were tears in her eyes. 'I must look beautiful.'

She did look beautiful. The hair worked like an optical illusion, obscuring the size of her face and drawing attention away from the acne.

In the quiet of the hall I could feel the eyes of the audience on me. I didn't dare look at the cameraman. No one moved or made a sound as Dick Dingle crossed the stage from the judging panel. He moved slowly, his suit trousers whistling as he walked. In his hands were the trophy and a white envelope. He stopped centre stage and waved the envelope at the cameraman before opening it with the slow motion of a showman. The microphone screeched.

'And the winner of the Crowning Glory, Tasmania's young champion of Big and High is . . .' He looked down at the card and frowned. He shook his head. 'It appears to be . . . Julian Corker.'

My eardrums felt as if they were going to burst. I swallowed several times before they popped. I felt the thudding of the applause against my chest before I heard it. The audience was going wild, foot-stamping and clapping. My ears popped again. Julian Corkle was a winner! I raised my swollen hands like a boxing champion.

My arms were still in the air when Dick Dingle abruptly left the microphone and returned to the judging panel. I brought them down. The clapping slowed. It stopped. Silence fell over the hall. All attention had turned to Dick Dingle who was talking to Norman in a harsh whisper, waving his arms about.

'Nonsense!' Norman's loud baritone sent a tremor through the audience. People murmured and shifted in their seats. The air was electric. What happened next was totally unexpected.

Dick Dingle's hand darted across the judges' table and slapped Norman on the face. The gesture was fast and underhanded like a fox-terrier nip to a postman's leg.

A woman cried out. People gasped.

Within a split second Norman had leaped to his feet, throwing his chair back with a clatter. His attacker stepped away but not fast enough for my uncle who lunged across the table and gripped the top of his head, pinning him to the spot.

Dick Dingle flailed his arms and tried to break free. He hit out at Norman but failed to make contact, flapping his arms furiously and grunting with the effort. The audience groaned with every swipe, growing more silent as Dick Dingle slowed and finally stopped. His shoulders sagged. He was panting. The hall was quiet. Norman held him for a moment longer, then released him.

'You are a nasty, petty little man.' Norman shook his head in a disgusted way.

Dick Dingle sniffed and raised a hand to his head to adjust his hair. The toupee had twisted on its axis but held fast. With his eyes fixed on Norman, he took a step back and then spun on his heel, scuttling across the stage to the safety of the microphone. It screeched.

'Ladies and gentlemen . . .' Dick Dingle's voice had lost its gold. It was high and shaky. He took a silk handkerchief from his pocket and patted his forehead.

People shuffled in their seats. Someone coughed.

'. . . I regret to announce a revision to the earlier announcement.'

'No!' The cry came from the audience and set off a chain reaction of shouting.

Noeline twisted in her chair and gave me a puzzled look.

Dick Dingle waved his hand for calm. When the noise didn't die down, he simply shouted into the microphone.

'In light of his relationship with the visiting judge from Melbourne, Julian Corker has been disqualified. The award instead will go to Philippe Singer.'

'That's *Singeur*!' Philippe's voice was a vicious cry of triumph.

I swayed and gripped the back of Noeline's chair for support. I felt as if I was going to faint. My chin trembled dangerously.

'That's not fair.' Noeline's voice was a whisper.

I heard Philippe whinny and was overcome by emotion. With my head down, I made for the side of the stage and the safety of the curtain.

The microphone screeched but Dick Dingle's voice was lost in the roar of the crowd. My ears were swirling and it took a moment for me to realise that the audience wasn't cheering. The old defrosted chicken in my chest stirred. People were booing.

I poked my head around the curtain and blinked at the lights. Philippe was standing side-on to the microphone with the Crowning Glory in his hands and a frozen smile on his face. Dick Dingle was waving his arms like someone trying to flag down a train. Noeline had turned in her seat and was looking at me. She raised her eyebrows.

Something heavy and familiar hit me between the shoulder blades and propelled me forward on to the stage. The booing quieted. Someone whistled. Female voices cheered. I stumbled and was greeted by applause. Carmel removed her hand as we drew level with Dick Dingle and Philippe. They turned to us with the stunned look of freshly shorn merinos.

Carmel didn't need an amplifier. Her voice rolled over Philippe and out over the convention hall.

'Bugger off.' She gave him the look.

Philippe blinked and swayed on his feet. His head swivelled from side to side. Carmel took a step toward him. Philippe retreated. Clutching the trophy to his chest, he turned and scurried off the stage.

The audience cheered. Carmel waved.

The microphone screeched.

'Kindly leave, young lady.' Dick Dingle's face showed alarm but his pointing finger stabbed the air with self-importance. 'This is semi-national television. You're on Dick Dingle's *Tales of Tasmania*.'

Carmel shrugged comically and looked at the audience. 'Dick by name, dick by nature.' The people roared with laughter.

'Who on earth do you think you are?'

'I know exactly who I am. And the name's Corkle not Corker.' Carmel had stopped smiling. She squared her shoulders and gave Dick Dingle her bowler's stare. 'I don't like you.'

'You can't talk to me like that. I'm Dick Dingle.'

'But I am talking to you, Dick.' Carmel moved toward him, pointing. 'And I'm telling you, back off, chump. Exit, stage right.'

Dick Dingle squawked and let go of the microphone stand. Sliding backward, he made a cutting motion across his throat. The cameraman either failed to notice or decided to take the law into his own hands. The camera followed Carmel as she advanced on Dick Dingle, shooing him off the stage with the wave of a hand.

People were drumming their feet on the floorboards and cheering as she returned to yank Noeline out of her seat. Grabbing my forearm with her other hand, she pulled us forward into a theatrical bow. As I stood up, I could feel the clapping bouncing off my chest. Carmel pulled me down again for another bow. Then another.

I didn't remember leaving the stage or know how I got to the foyer. My chest was still vibrating long after the applause had stopped. When I became aware of my surroundings, I was sitting next to Jimmy who was gently massaging aloe into my hands.

I looked up and noticed Trevor Bland standing in the shadows near a sculpture made from coat hangers. He was looking at me with a smile. I smiled back. He nodded and turned away. A moment later, Norman walked into the foyer with Sandy at his heels.

'That was quite a show.' Norman smiled. 'Old Dick must glue that rag to his head with Japanese technology.'

'He's a fake.' I felt a thrill go through me. Criticising Dick Dingle was like saying that God didn't exist.

'I suspect his days on semi-national TV are numbered.' Norman laughed and ran a hand over his hair. 'In the end it's not about winning. It's about looking good.'

'He didn't look good.'

'I just had a talk with the crew. Abracadabra wants to do a follow-up feature on the boy wonder.'

I blinked at Norman.

'You.'

'My own feature?' A thrill went through me. Jimmy squeezed my forearm.

'You bet.' Norman turned to survey the foyer.

'Are you looking for Trevor?'

He nodded. 'He was very kind to me once.'

'He just left.' I pointed to the doorway.

'I'll try to catch him. Be back in a minute.' Norman left with Sandy.

I turned to Jimmy. 'Any news about your father?'

'They've taken him out of the lung. He's in an oxygen tent but stable.'

'Thanks for everything, Jimmy. I couldn't have done this without you.'

I was about to tell him that I loved him but a crowd of women suddenly burst through the swing doors. They were laughing and talking in high voices. Dot led them over to where we were sitting. I recognised clients from the salon as they fanned out around us, gushing and congratulating me. Dot hung back, her eyes full of pride.

The crowd parted for Mum and Dezzie. My mother slipped into the seat beside me and put an arm around my shoulders. She whispered in my ear, 'Isn't that my blouse you're wearing?'

'It's New Romantic, Mum.'
'So you're a New Romantic now.'
'I love the ruffles.'
She laughed and straightened my collar.
'You're a star, Julian. Twinkle, twinkle.'